Book Three

of

The Lost Council Trilogy

Time Means Nothing

www.booksbyblunt.com

The Lost Council Trilogy

Recon Time

No Time For Mercy

Time Means Nothing

The Mike Casper Thriller Series

Cold Dead Hands

The Novella (Free)

A Can Of Paint 2.0

Time Means Nothing

Book Three of

The Lost Council Trilogy

Sebastian Blunt

4XDX

Sci Fi

Time Means Nothing

A 4XDX Sci-Fi Book

Dedication

To Ellen. A woman who can look down the barrel of a .44 magnum, laugh, and go on with her day.

Many people have been involved in the continued success of The Lost Council Trilogy. Thanks to all of you!

Chapter One

"We have to get out of this region of space right now," Allison was pleading with Aaron to order the immediate return of the allied ships—back through the jump point to the Panruk system, Olamit.

He was preoccupied with attempting to comprehend the absence of stars or planetary bodies in every direction and momentarily seemed to ignore her.

"Monty," he called to Lieutenant Montgomery. "Do an extreme scan for any radioactivity." Captain Aaron Howe turned back to the AI as Allison stood erect, having regained her balance and a bit of her composure.

"Can you tell me who *they* are? After we exited from the jump point, you said, '*They* found me.' Who are they?"

The navigator interrupted Allison's response. "There is a point of radiation 5 degrees starboard and 32 degrees down, relative."

"What's the range, Monty?"

"Only 550,000 miles, give or take."

Howe turned back to Allison. "So, who were you talking about? And what's that single point of radiation out there?"

The AI's artificial eyes gleamed at him, her tone commanding. "You're wasting time. We must leave here now. We need to jump back to Olamit. It's not safe for me to be here and certainly not safe for the humans and Slev crews." She persisted. "Turn and jump now!"

Aaron glared at her, then called the Ro-Pahm's captain, the alien Slev, and his ally in the war against the Mazik.

"Kap, we must reverse and go back to Olamit immediately." Next, he called Mercy Bonner, captain of the USS. Washington, with the same instructions. All three ships changed course in unison and headed back to the glimmering jump point behind them.

On the Washington, the nav station officer, Ensign Scott Lewis, yelled, "Captain Bonner, the jump point is shrinking!"

"Captain Howe. We are showing the point decreasing in size."

"Dammit." He opened up an all-ships link. "Form a line. Washington first, then the Ro-Pahm, then us. We'll thread the needle in case the reduction in diameter continues."

"Captain Howe!" called Kap. "Don't you think the O'Brian should go first? Your ship should be the priority." There was no panic in the Slev's voice whatsoever.

"No, Captain Jahrnuk. Move into my lineup."

The ships accelerated quickly toward the shrinking gate. There was barely 2000 meters spacing between them— bow to stern, but the computer systems adjusted for differences in velocity.

"Allison, tell me what we are up against!"

She raised her hand to redirect him. "Aaron, just get us back to safety."

Simultaneously on the USS Washington, Mercy was pushing her ship to 150 gravities with the Ro-Pahm in close pursuit. The black-as-ink hole surrounded by a gleaming border shrunk further as they raced to the point.

"Shit. This is going to be close," said Barrett Bonner, Mercy's husband, as he stood at the side of her command chair.

"Not for us. I calculated the rate. We'll make it," said Mercy.

Sure enough, the Washington cleared the ever-diminishing portal back to the relative security of the Olamit system.

Abruptly, the diameter decreased more quickly to a third of its original size. Kap held his breath as they entered the gap.

"This looks bad," were Monty's last words before the portal in space tightened like a noose. The bridge crew of the O'Brian could only watch as the Ro-Pahm had a section of the rear-thruster cowling sheared off like a knife cutting through paper. It hurtled toward them at tremendous speed.

Despite the velocity of the O'Brian, the tail section of Kap's ship merely bounced off the exceedingly powerful Grav shields. Howe tensed as the O'Brian, and his crew flashed through the point in space where the jump point abruptly vanished.

"Any damage?" Aaron called out over the intercom. There

was none, but their transit point to Olamit was gone. All that remained was the utter blackness of space and one tiny point of radiating light.

"Captain," called out Monty from the Nav station. "We didn't make it. We're still here." His announcement was superfluous. The deep void of space encompassed the O'Brian. The crew felt it, and an undercurrent of fear seized them.

Captain Howe stared at Allison. If it was possible for an AI to pale—she did. He sat down heavily in his chair, drained, feeling hopeless and frightened, emotions that he could never expose to his crew.

"Do you have a plan? What just happened? Where are we?"

She shook her head, looking vulnerable, even child-like.

"Do you have an explanation?"

"Maybe."

He put a hand to his forehead and tried to rub away the brewing headache. Aaron lowered his voice for only Allison to hear over the hum of machinery noise on the warship's bridge.

"You will need to tell me everything because if we can't find a way out—"

She interrupted him and then completed his sentence, "—then we will float out here until we are dead. Is that what you are thinking?"

"Dying out here is not my first choice. Now would be a good time for you to tell what the hell is going on." Aaron broke from her penetrating stare and turned to his bridge crew. "Scan everything. I want to know if there is one damn thing out there other than empty space or that anomalous point of radioactivity. Now!"

He looked back at Allison. She seemed to be recovering from whatever it was that made her seem frail.

"Well?"

"We need to talk. Alone."

He swiveled the command chair, allowing him to step out of the module to starboard. "Anyone? Ships? Rocks? Anything?"

"Negative," replied Monty.

"Captain Clark?"

"Nothing, sir. This space is devoid of all significant matter. Just empty."

Howe frowned. "Is that spot stable?"

Montgomery checked. "We are moving away from it, and the point is stable and fixed."

"Monty, slow us to a halt in twenty minutes, then hold that position. I'm going to the conference room with Allison. If so much as a mouse squeaks on your screens, signal me."

Allison went straight for the aft door that led out of the bridge with Aaron in tow. The short walk down the infamous passageway where Recon and the CAG Ops defeated Mazik Bah-Gahn's Warriors was marked with a tense silence.

The two of them stepped through the hatch. There was a composite table of bright white, surrounded by simple aluminum chairs. Allison sat down while Aaron stood, feeling frustrated and perplexed. After a few seconds, he, too, sat.

It was cool in the compartment, but a bead of sweat formed on his forehead. "Again. Who are they?"

"Aaron. I'm glad you are sitting."

"Is it that bad?"

Allison glanced at the four walls, then looked back at Aaron. She thought about the downside of telling him what had come rushing back into her memory when they passed through the jump point.

Until now, she'd endured little flashes of her past, not her regular AI memories, which were infallible, but other untraceable bits of data. They were meaningless snippets of random, distorted images. For two thousand years, pieces of incomprehensible recollections came and went like a squall at sea.

Exhibiting one of her recent quirks, Allison, in human form, placed a hand over her mouth, took a deep breath, then exhaled. It was utterly unnecessary, yet there it was.

"We are in a very precarious spot in the universe." Allison seemed exasperated to him, which considering her status as the pinnacle of artificial intelligence, was a dichotomy.

"You look as if you are struggling with some internal debate.

I've seen you do this in the past when you are torn between what you should or should not reveal to me."

"I can't argue with your analysis, Aaron, but I don't see how holding anything back will help." She began without delay. "Three-thousand years ago, I was kidnapped."

Aaron's expression was flat because the one-liner from Allison made no sense. "How could an AI of your power be kidnapped?"

Allison seemed to shudder a little as she grappled with what came next. Her deliberation was not in the least bit alien or machine-like. "I was human."

His reaction was wide-eyed. "You mean flesh and blood human?"

The buzzer on the table flashed and squealed. "Sir," Clark said. "We've got some kind of energy beam slamming into the bridge. It's coming from that region of radiation. Wait. It stopped."

Howe and Allison bolted from their chairs and towards the bridge. The heavily plated hatch was open, and a marble-sized green shimmering dot of light hovered in the center of the room.

Clark, Monty, and two of the crew were backed up in a semi-circle, leaning against bulkheads and consoles. It looked like they'd jumped to get as far away as possible from the energy source.

The four crew on the bridge stood frozen when Aaron and Allison ran in and then halted abruptly.

A vertical plane of green light projected from the spot. It was a very thin tinted sheet of illumination from the deck to the ceiling, and it began moving left as if it was scanning the compartment in a 360-degree rotation. The light passed by all six of the crew on the bridge then vanished, leaving the spot of light floating.

"What the hell was that?" asked Big Mike, one of the highly-trained CAG crew.

Aaron raised his index finger to his lips. Then, he turned toward Allison and gave her a burning inquisitive look.

"It's a probe. Being quiet won't help us."

"A probe from who?" Monty asked in a loud voice.

Clark had the same anxious look on his face as the big lieutenant. Then Aaron asked the all-important question. "What can we do about it? How do we get this thing off our ship?"

She shook her head.

All of them focused on the glowing orb of surreal light. It began to expand rapidly and took the shape of a human skull within seconds. The color was emerald and diamond combined somehow and glittered like crystal. It stopped growing at a diameter of perhaps one meter and hung motionless above the deck.

"What the hell?" gasped Clark.

Howe put his hand on Allison's arm. "Do you have any idea what that is?"

"It's a reference to my past. I don't think that we will have time to talk about it just now."

In the dim light of the bridge, the thing radiated twinkling light in every direction. No one moved. But then, a deep, sinister voice emanated from the object. Tinseltown could not have come up with anything more ominous; only this was real.

"Els Talitha. Return to your habitat."

No one moved.

"Els Talitha. There are others on your vessel that you have modified."

Aaron gripped Allison's arm more tightly. "Who or what is Els Talitha?"

"That is me. It was the name I was given as a human child."

Howe shrugged. "I'm trying really hard to wrap my head around that. What does this thing want?"

"To put me back in a cage."

Big Mike gasped and fell to the deck. Monty leaped to him and knelt. "What the freaking hell! He's dead. There's a hole in his head, and his brain is gone!" Blood pooled on the deck as it drained from the soldier's skull.

The other CAG crewman on the bridge sprinted for the hatch but stumbled and fell. Howe moved to check him, but the green orb had repeated its fatal assault. Aaron stood up grimly to stand next to Allison, unable to suppress his fear and trepidation.

"The non-modified humans are irrelevant. You will bring your vessel to the transit point."

"Monty. Call the other CAG guys," Howe ordered.

Montgomery slowly moved to the comm console and then transmitted a message to the dozen or so crew on board the Dexter O'Brian. There was no response.

"All the non-modified humans are terminated. They are not required. Your vessel shall proceed to the transit point."

Captain Clark struggled to keep cool as the devastating loss of the crew in an instant was gut-wrenching.

"Sir," asked Clark. "What should we do?"

"Not all of the three modified humans are required. Move the vessel to the transit point without delay."

"Is that a threat?" asked Monty.

Allison frowned at him. "Monty. Don't make any more challenging statements." She turned to Howe. "Take the ship immediately to the point we identified."

Aaron waved Clark and Monty to their consoles as he approached the command chair.

"We have to get moving now," Allison urged.

Howe did a quick scan of the area around the ship and then ran a route plot while signaling Clark to accelerate. Within a split second, the skull disappeared.

"Can you please tell us what the hell is going on, Allison?" Aaron stammered.

The two Recon soldiers confirmed the programmed data at their stations and swung around to stare at the AI, also desperate for some explanation. The time for vague statements was over. She looked at the Recon guys and then turned to Aaron.

"I was born human three millennia ago. The alien representation that just murdered the CAG on our ship is a tool of the Mar El." She paused to gauge their reactions and, seeing blank expressions, continued. "They observed various species in at least two galaxies and found humans to be particularly interesting. They kidnapped me when I was nine years old, and they trapped me on the equivalent of a desert island where they slowed my growth and watched me."

Clark asked, "That was 3,000 years ago? How long did they hold you as a captive?"

"A thousand years." She waited and let that sink in. "And, they didn't release me—I escaped."

Chapter 2

The United Space Ship George Washington drifted into the Olamit System, home of the Panruk aliens. Her sister ship, the Ro-Pahm, captained by the Slev alien Kap Jahrnuk, held a parallel course at a distance of fifteen kilometers to port. Both spacecraft were eerily silent as the officers and crew faced up to the fact that their flagship did not make it back from the other side of the now-vanished jump point.

"Captain Jahrunk," called Captain Mercy Bonner. "What is the condition of that torn-off cowling? Did any of it make it through that shrinking hole and back into this system?"

"No. The collapse of the point sheared it off. Wherever the Dexter O'Brian is—that is where you will find that small chunk of my ship."

"Ro-Pahm. Standby." Mercy turned to her husband, Commander Barrett Bonner, who, like her, was also a nanite-modified human on the battlecruiser that used to be part of the Mazik fleet until Recon and the CAG soldiers captured it.

"Now what?" she asked, hoping that her partner would give her some meaningful advice.

"I don't know," answered Barrett as he stood to the right of her command chair. "We have two warships and nowhere to go."

"Ensign Lewis, where's Edgar now?"

Scott Lewis, an enhanced Recon soldier, misfit, and comedian, hovered over his display. Quickly, the ensign configured a three-dimensional representation that popped up in the center of the dimly lit bridge.

"I've highlighted the Happy Sunshine in green. You can see the small vessel heading straight for Olamit. It is 58.8 light minutes from our current position and accelerating."

"And the tribute freighter we ordered to reverse course and head back to the planet?" asked Mercy.

Lewis was prepared for that question. "It's in blue." He pointed to the Grapthax, a huge cargo ship that was full of food and tribute meant to appease the alien megalomaniac Mazik Bah-Gahn.

"It's accelerating but will not catch up to the Happy Sunshine. Edgar has the pedal to the metal, Captain Bonner."

Mercy addressed the weapons officer, Lieutenant John Allen, a Recon soldier who'd fought with Howe's small unit back in 1776. He was improved with nanites like the rest of Recon.

"Allen, what is the condition of our weapons systems? Any damage?"

"None."

She turned to her comm controls. "Captain Jahrnuk. Let's hang here for three standard Earth hours. If the point doesn't reappear, then we will accelerate towards Olamit."

The fierce-looking Slev alien appeared on her screen. To an unfamiliar human, fright would be the immediate response. Kap was about seven feet tall. Pale green skin was visible where he wasn't covered with a crimson uniform. The body, identical to that of a Mazik, had four legs, but it was not elongated like a horse—it was half that. His face had a short snout, large dark eyes, and a very broad mouth laden with an abundance of sharpened teeth. The heavily muscled arms had three joints and intimidating hands with five fingers and two thumbs.

"That seems like a responsible plan. So I will follow your lead, Mercy."

Right then, Kap solved a political problem for the human captain—he passed authority, at least temporarily, to her. Barrett and Mercy were relieved of that one stress. Technically, the Ro-Pahm was not a USS ship. Bonner had no official authority to command the Slev.

"Ensign Lewis, send a message to Edgar. Tell him that we have a change of plans and will be following him to his home planet in three hours." She turned to her husband and whispered, "I hope we don't cause the politicians on Edgar's planet to have a complete mental breakdown."

"Mercy, my gut tells me that after the abuse they've been taking from Mazik Bah-Gahn, our presence won't add much."

Barrett looked at her display. "Kap, can you repair that cowling in three hours while we wait?"

The scary expression from Jahrnuk would have been misinterpreted by most, but it was a smile to those in the know. "Captain and Commander Bonner, our Slev technicians can fix that in half the time."

Mok, Jahrnuk's second-in-command, stood alongside his friend and leader, watching a tech team making their way to the airlock.

"They are very efficient, Kap."

"They are our shipmates and very good at doing the hard jobs. And, between you and me, I doubt the humans could do that in six hours."

Mok bumped his massive chest up against his companion in a uniquely Slev method of non-verbal communication. "Probably true, but Howe and his people are superb at many other things, like—"

"—like killing Mazik Bah-Gahn's best warriors, perhaps?"

The 2nd commander showed his sharp rows of teeth. "Yes. Precisely. They are very expert at serving death to the Mazik."

Kap chest-bumped his friend again. "I think humans can deliver death to whomever they wish—enough banter. Let's get our technicians processed through the airlock and prepare to accelerate to Olamit."

The Happy Sunshine, Edgar's small spacecraft, continued to accelerate externally at 100g's. The ship, renamed by Dr. Aaron Howe, was wholly owned by the Panruk, aliens who also claimed Edgar as their own. It was the tremendous revelation that Howe's best friend, the heavily mustached, bulbous-nosed, slightly chubby professor, was actually Shelet Pir Sahm Mim, a genuine Panruk anthropologist. Edgar had taken a human name and appearance nearly 128 years earlier and reinvented himself, ultimately becoming Aaron's best friend in college.

But then came the greatest shock of all, when his closest buddy for two decades confessed that by Panruk physiology, Shelet Pir Sahm Mim was actually *female*! The fallout was not nearly as awful as it could have been—possibly because the Mazik were bearing down on Earth, and there wasn't time to get into an extended tongue-lashing of his pal, the extraterrestrial. Still, as commander of the newly acquired United Space Ship fleet, the flustered Howe took it upon himself to rename Edgar's ship and call it The Happy Sunshine.

"They're following us," said one of the two former U.S. Navy officers who were assigned to escort Edgar back to his home planet.

"I see that. It is non-sensical." The Panruk scientist sent a voice message to Mercy. "This is Shelet Pir Sahm Mim. Why are you following us? Over."

Sometime later, the return message triggered a very subdued "ding" on the communications panel, followed by "We have returned from the other side of the jump point." It was Mercy's voice.

Edgar turned to the other officer on the small craft's bridge.

"Why did the captain send such a terse unhelpful message?"

"No clue, but this can't be good. My sensors are seeing the Ro-Pahm and the Washington. So, where's the Dexter O'Brian?"

He hit the PTT button on his microphone. "Mercy. Edgar. Where is the O'Brian? Over."

This time the wait was a few seconds less as the accelerating battlecruisers tailing them gained ground.

"Edgar. We came through the jump point but found ourselves in intergalactic space, not in the Kamtret system belonging to the Mazik. It was devoid of stars. Allison alerted us that we needed to back out immediately. We turned to make a rapid exit. Only my ship and the Ro-Pahm made it. The jump point shrank and then disappeared before the O'Brian came through. They are still in that void space. Captain Jahrunk and I decided that the prudent thing would be to track you and head to Olamit. Over."

The Panruk and the two navy scientist-officers stood dumbstruck as they began to comprehend that a stable transit point in space that was linked to the Mazik system just defied the laws of astrophysics.

"Understood," was Dr. Edgar Tomis' first response. "But, is there anything that you know besides the fact that we are here and the O'Brian is somewhere a million lightyears from our current position?"

As the distance between the ships diminished, the response time became less agonizing. Mercy Bonner listened to Shelet Pir Sahm Mim's last message.

"How much should I tell Edgar?"

Barrett twisted his mouth as he thought about that. "Edgar can see very well that the jump point is gone. There aren't a whole lot of secrets here except that there was a single point of energy on the other side of that hole in space."

Mercy keyed the microphone. "We'll tell you the details when we get to Olamit orbit. For now, we are on the same course. We'll catch you in a few hours and then continue toward your home planet. I suggest that you transmit a message to Olamit when we are no more than five light minutes from orbit. Tell them that the Mazik spacecraft are not hostile. I suggest you talk directly to Shaab Mar Gen, the Arbitor of all the Panruk. Confirm."

A few minutes later, the confirmation from the Happy Sunshine was terse and flat, followed by a simple "Out," delivered by one of the Navy guys.

Ensign Lewis spoke up after a tense period of silence. "What the hell is going on? Do we have a hypothesis?" He stood up and looked exasperated with his shaggy, unmilitary haircut partially covering his face.

Ensign Molly Stark gave him a stare that erased any notion that Lewis may have had about delivering a joke or an unconventional comment. He sat back down at the comm station and waited for the captain to respond.

Mercy was not one to conceal her feelings or hunches when it came to the security or success of Recon—that philosophy extended to her role as captain of the USS George Washington. She looked at Barrett and surveyed the faces of the crew on the bridge.

The somewhat quiet Lieutenant, JG John Allen seemed to be mulling their situation over. He'd been a reliable member of Recon back in 1776, and nothing had changed since. As a farmer back in the old days, he was extraordinarily patient and practical. The weather was something that he couldn't control as a man who grew corn and other grains—he looked reticent about the alien war facing all of them.

"Lieutenant JG Allen," Mercy addressed him by rank. "What's on your mind?"

He didn't mince words. "When we get to Olamit, we may have little time before Mazik Bah-Gahn shows up with a fleet. We don't have Allison. I would say that those are our biggest concerns at the moment, captain."

His thoughts paralleled hers, and she could see from Barrett's expression that he shared similar worries.

"Very well," said Mercy. "We continue to the Panruk homeworld. When we get there, we will have to devise a plan to satisfy the Arbitor's government and keep us from getting into a shooting war with twenty enemy battlecruisers. Continue accelerating. Those of you who are due for a rest—go sleep."

Barrett and Mercy left LTJG Allen in command along with Molly. As soon as they got to their quarters, Mercy whipped around and threw herself into her husband's arms. It wasn't an attempt to arouse him.

"I'm feeling overwhelmed with a mass of apprehension. We always had Aaron to keep our minds focused."

"Don't forget Allison." He stroked her hair as she nestled her face into his shoulder. "We've got no AI and none of Howe's sixth sense, or whatever you want to call it."

Mercy stepped back and dropped onto the bed like a sack of potatoes. "I'm in charge now. This isn't Mollyburgers back in 1777. Without the Dexter O'Brian, we are outgunned. Is my first command supposed to end with Mazik Bah-Gahn blasting us into the vacuum and then obliterating Earth? I mean, I don't want to let the rest of the crew see my doubts, but it's like we are facing the British with muskets—not the modern weapons Aaron brought to the war.

"I'm feeling the pressure, Barrett. What if I crack? Maybe you should take charge? I've got this persistent, gnawing doubt which my nanites are not able to tamp down."

He sat down on a chair in front of her and cracked his knuckles without thinking about it. "That little, pestering pit of insecurity is what generals and admirals have carried with them into every battle of every war. If you didn't have that, then I *would* relieve you of command. Your non-upgraded human side is what will lead you to make correct decisions."

Mercy looked around their stateroom. It had a bed, a desk, chairs, and other assorted earthling-sized features. The Slev crew were aces at making something out of nothing.

"Did you ever wonder what life would be like if we didn't have all this dysfunctional alien crap to deal with? We could be home with Manuel minding our own business. It might have been that way if the Mazik hadn't turned out to be such assholes. We could have a house with a fireplace. I could teach you how to roast a marshmallow properly."

Barrett got up and then laid down beside her. Mercy's warm body was a magnet. Always. He refocused his mind. "I think your daydream is great, but Mazik Bah-Gahn is real. Our circumstances are very real."

"Yes. They are, and I'll rise to the occasion because I have to. Is that what you believe?"

"That's right, honey. And I'll tell you one more thing that you better keep in mind while you're commanding this ship—we may never see Aaron again. Not because we'll be dead, but because that region of space could be 100 million lightyears from here. If the jump point doesn't reappear, then we will be permanently solo in this war. So on top of everything else, we need to figure out how to capture more ships."

She snuggled up against him, although that only mitigated the sense of urgency and doubt slightly. Mercy looked around the cube that was their room. The white walls felt like they were crowding her. Fortunately, the blanket was a warm, comfortable reminder of home.

"I believe we will be in deep kimchi without Aaron. The same thought just keeps pounding my brain—that the Mazik show up here in a month, and we go down like little burning clumps of matter in the space around Olamit."

"Clumps. Not burning clumps. No oxygen." Barrett sighed and frowned at once.

"What if we leave Olamit and head back to Earth?" Mercy asked.

Barrett's frown intensified. "You mean run and leave the Panruk to get steamrolled?"

"I'm trying to prioritize. For us, Earth and our human brothers and sisters must come first. We can take our ships and have three battlecruisers to defend our planet."

"I think Edgar might find that to be a bit cold."

She bit her lower lip in frustration. "Darn it. I'm not sure how that thought could fester in the back of my head, but I don't want the human race to be obliterated. The Panruk have allowed Mazik Bah-Gahn to get where he is today. Why is that our problem? We have to die because they are so advanced in their peaceful notions that they let a madman turn them into feckless morons?"

"Mercy!" said Barrett as he propped himself up on one elbow. "Are you listening to yourself?"

She shrugged and felt a tiny, smoldering sense of anger toward him. It passed quickly. "Thank you for that. The nanites help me to process information quickly, but I'm still a person. I guess that the pressure of doing this without help is pushing me to conjure up casualty estimates—and there is no way Olamit is going to survive—so why not give our people a fighting chance?"

He left that point dangling in the air, and neither one of them spoke for a minute.

"Captain Bonner. If it wasn't for Aaron and Allison and a boatload of odd good fortune, Earth would have been gone already. We have been betting against the house every step of the way, and look who's still alive? Us. I say we do our best against the Mazik right here. We can't let history record that the humans were a bunch of cowards who ditched the Panruk and ran away like pussies."

Mercy poked him. "I get your point, but maybe 'pussies' is a little archaic?"

"Right. Sorry, captain."

"Apology accepted. And I have one other observation. Kap Jahrnuk is not under my command. He would probably decide damn fast not to come with us to protect Earth."

"Let's get some shuteye, Mercy. I'm wiped, and I agree with you that protecting the Slev would be Kap's only option. Let's get some sleep—I can't even think anymore." He was spontaneously out.

Mercy tossed her uniform onto a chair, then maneuvered Barrett under the covers and joined him. Finally, her brooding thoughts succumbed to exhaustion to the extent that even his light snoring was inconsequential.

About the time that the Washington and the Ro-Pahm were accelerating to Olamit, and concurrent to Mercy's fitful sleep, the Arbitor stared at a display in shock. There was a small craft on an intercept course for the Panruk home world. It was also not a Mazik ship; instead, it was an exploration and science vessel. Curious, but not nearly as astonishing as the identification coded into its telemetry.

Shaab Mar Gen's assistant, Marzat, sent her the details. It was the ship that had been on the human homeworld for over 120 solar cycles—the vessel that was lent to the eminent anthropologist Shelet Pir Sahm Mim.

"Marzat, do you know what you are looking at?"

The younger Panruk bureaucrat stared at his screen and then up at his planet's First Administrator. His large dark eyes widened, framed by pale blue-green skin. "That is the ancient investigator sent to the Homosapien world. She was supposed to stay for ten cycles—."

"And now, she returns known as Edgar to the humans. I am not one to give credence to signs and omens, but all my thoughts scream 'impending disaster.'"

"My Arbitor. More than we have already endured in the arms of the Mazik?"

Shaab turned to gaze through her window at Mim, the star. Their star. "Perhaps this is the path to the end of us. Alert the elite staff. We must prepare for the arrival of Shelet Pir Sahm Mim."

Chapter 3

An alien form skimmed across malleable metal plates on the surface of Mar El planet 432. From space, the blue sphere banded with wispy clouds looked very similar to many inhabited worlds. The atmosphere was remarkably consistent with Earth's, where observations and experiments on biologics had been made for millennia. In truth, almost all life had been examined by the Mar El. And nearly all life in the Milky Way galaxy was genetically similar; hence they flourished in oxygen-rich environments.

But this wasn't the region of space occupied by those like *Els Talitha*. Instead, the humans' primitive interstellar vehicle found itself in a different galaxy, one that was inhabited entirely by the Mar El.

Tzurek, the Head Examiner, utilized a device implanted in his relatively large skull to transmit an order. The rippling and undulating texture of the sections under his feet instantly changed, and his motion slowed. The biped walked under his own power to the containment where *Els Talitha* would spend eternity, or until Tzurek decided that she be terminated.

There was a transparent barrier directly in front of him, which Tzurek stepped through. On the other side was vegetation typical of the earthling's home. There was a sandy beach and a stream fed by rivulets of cool water that flowed from a green hill. Trees of several varieties lined the narrow, open area. On one side stood a pond, but on the other was a forest of plants that yielded eventually to a thickening of tall trees. Heading in that direction, a hiker would climb to a height of 150 meters to reach the crest. From the hilltop vantage point, it was possible to view the entirety of the habitat which covered approximately three square kilometers.

Tzurek made a point of improving the diversity of life in the containment—this would make it possible to observe the four

specimens in a more complex ecosystem. He was excited by the
thought of expanding the knowledge base for all of the
examiners. It had been the primary task of the Mar El for at
least 500,000 years, and now he had a truly remarkable
sample—Els Talitha and three humans that she enhanced—it
would be stimulating to probe them, cathartic even—but also
essential.

An alert drew Tzurek's mind from his musings. The human
ship was close now. The instructions to transit and orbit 432
had been obeyed, which was expected; humans abhorred death.

"Don't you think suiting up would be prudent?" asked
Monty.

Allison and Howe stood inside the hangar deck where a
small shuttle squatted on a track that would guide it out the stern
bay door of the USS Dexter O'Brian.

"I think if they wanted us dead, they would have killed us by
now," interjected Clark. "I mean, why have us come through the
jump point by Olamit, order us to transit at the singular point in
the middle of intergalactic space, and then kill us in a vacuum?"

Aaron opened the outer hatch of the small craft. Allison
followed him into the main bay. Monty and Clark reluctantly
stepped on board.

They surveyed the vessel. It was about 30 meters in length,
with the rear third dedicated to a power plant and propulsion
hardware and software. The main cargo area occupied the bulk
of the interior, with a command station near the bow.

"Let's go forward and try to strap in. Allison, we don't have
time to learn this thing. Can you pilot it?" asked Aaron.

"Yes. Its systems are not complex, and I have the
coordinates."

Clark, in his standard blue uniform, buckled up. "What will
happen when we land?"

The three enhanced humans turned to the AI as she sat in the
command chair. Gray metallic panels with two-dimensional
displays and some controls formed a semi-circle around the
front of them. Allision swiveled to face them, her expression

grim. "I spent 1,000 years being probed mentally and physically. It seems very likely that the planet chief will carry on with the same protocol. The Mar El must have devised a way to keep me contained, which means a kind of barrier circling the containment that I can't penetrate."

Monty reacted by lowering his head and grumbling despondently despite his strength and hard appearance. He looked to Aaron. "That means we could be here for a thousand years or until something kills us. I'm sorry, but Betty will be back on Earth, growing old and then dying. She'll never know what happened to us."

"My Louise as well," said Clark. "And, our kids."

Aaron peered at Allison. "Can they hear us right now?"

"Probably not, and likely not once we enter the containment. My experience was that the Mar El just collect data. They are exceedingly alien in that way. Their culture is just about looking at us as specimens."

"Like zoo animals?" asked Howe.

"No. More like bugs or bacteria. They've been at their current state of technology of 500,000 years. I think they are bored, and they don't have anything new in their practically immortal lives to do." She appeared to drift mentally to some ancient thought.

Monty looked incredulous. " So they go around other galaxies collecting vermin and sit around watching them? That's their existence?"

"We have to go," said Aaron, ignoring Montgomery's last comment. In truth, he wanted to carry on the conversation desperately, but in their current position, it made sense to avoid anything that might provoke the enemy.

And that's exactly how Aaron thought of the Mar El now. It was also Howe's nature to compartmentalize threats and allies. The Mar El murdered a platoon of CAG soldiers on his ship. He raised his voice which had the desired effect. "The way I see it is that we have a problem. It's a military issue now. They are the same as the Mazik to me."

Clark laughed sardonically. "Except we're technological

grubs to them. Sure, they are our new enemies, but how can we fight them? With sticks and harsh language?"

Aaron tapped Allison. She moved the shuttle along the track to the airlock. "Listen, all of you. When we get down to the planet, we behave like cooperative sheep. We'll do our best to communicate via eye contact and body language until it is safe to talk." Howe glanced at Monty and Clark as mild G-forces were unleashed by launching into the void.

"We've got Allison. We beat Dorcester and King George in 1776. On top of that, we are sneaky, devious humans. The Mar El are going to lose what they've started with us. Everyone clear on that?"

There were subtle grunts from the two Recon soldiers. Allison merely nodded and answered with a weak, "Yep."

Monty spoke up. "My enhanced brain is telling me that we are outmatched here. Sir, optimism is not your automatic go-to position. How can you feel so confident that we are going to overcome beings that have a half-a-million-year headstart?"

"Simple. What did the woman driving this shuttle say? That the Mar El haven't advanced in 500,000 years. They've been doing the same thing repeatedly for so long that there has to be a weakness born from boredom or neglect. If systems don't progress, they decay. I'm not going to serve a crapload of time in Mar El jail." Howe pulled on his right ear as they fell into the planet's upper atmosphere. The descent gave him a headache.

There was a whirring sound as the small craft made its final approach to the coordinates given by the green skull. Dampers managed inertial forces expertly as the touchdown was felt as a minor bump.

Aaron noticed Allison's failure to hide her apprehension. It didn't fit, considering his experience with her power and knowledge.

"Yes, Aaron." She brushed down the front of her uniform. "I know you are reading my feelings."

He didn't answer. It served no purpose since she was coming face to face with the aliens who captured her as a human child.

All clad in USS uniforms, the four of them proceeded to the

airlock. Howe led the way while Allison slipped to the rear of the foursome. The airlock matched the outside pressure, then opened as a ramp extended to the metallic surface.

Once on the ground, the three humans studied the half-circle perimeter on the port side. A hundred meters ahead was a sandy patch. There was a line where the surface ended and a clear but distinct material extended up and to the sides.

"That is the habitat, and the barrier is just there," said Allison.

Monty grinned sarcastically. "It doesn't look so bad."

The airlock hatch closed automatically behind them. Clark looked up at the blue sky—so much like Earth. The air was fresh and clear, with no smog or pollution at all.

"Now what?"

Allison stood behind Aaron, not answering Monty's question. Ahead of them, the radiant yellow star of the system hung in the sky. The clear wall around their intended prison rippled and became translucent, then seemed to fold on itself, making a small rectangular gateway.

Tzurek, the Mar El, stepped through the opening and stretched to his full height of just less than a meter. Clark and Monty were confused and amused. Before them stood a gray bipedal figure, it was unclothed and had skin like a dolphin. There were nostrils, tennis ball-sized eyes, and a slit for a mouth. The head was unexpectedly large, almost comical, and very alien.

Clark whispered behind Allison and Captain Howe. "Are you kidding me? This is what we're dealing with? It looks like a hairless, gray child-thing with a fat head."

Tzurek observed the humans and specifically Els Talitha. The specimens were stimulating to him—his brain connected to various devices and even other Mar El to gauge the collective intrigue.

Monty cracked the knuckles of his large, powerful hands. "That's it? That little gray whale dung. To use a little 21st-century vernacular—let me go kick its ass."

The large sergeant ignored the nanite enhancements in his

brain, which were screaming at him to stay in place. He bolted two steps toward Tzurek but was hurled by an unseen energy beam that slammed him hard to the ground.

"Monty!" called Allison! She scanned his body. He had a minor concussion, and blood oozed from his nose as he groaned slightly.

"The humans will refrain from aggression," Tzurek spoke in a bizarre, twisted version of English.

John Clark bent to check on Monty, but he was boiling inside and wanted to crush the alien bastard.

"Els Talitha. Bring your companions through the opening into the habitat."

Howe and Clark help the lieutenant up to his feet. Allison led them directly to the gaping hole in the clear field that would become their prison walls. They stepped onto the sandy surface, turned, and saw the doorway disappear.

Tzurek drifted away, leaving them as a zookeeper would leave animals in their cages.

Chapter 4

Captain Mordechai "Mordy" Schein sat placidly in the command chair on the USS Angela Carlisle. The latest crew of personnel to be trained to serve on the former Mazik ship were firmly under his wing. Back on Earth, Commander Thomas Rogers, Mordy's closest friend, was busy instructing potential space crew. It was challenging, and only the best and brightest were even considered for space combat.

"Come to a geostationary position on the same longitude as Denver."

"Same longitude as Denver. Aye," answered a skinny African American engineer/ensign who recently graduated OCS after finishing near the top of his class at the University of Chicago.

Schein tested the kid. "What's our ETA?"

Ensign Lucky Williams scrambled to run a calculation. It took too long, but Mordy wasn't going to ride him on it. They were still training, and they weren't facing a hostile Mazik spacecraft.

"You can use the panel to run that math intuitively. The Mazik stole most of their technology from the other Council aliens. Your console can run multi-variable plots almost instantly and update the results fast." He got up and showed the newbie how to shuffle data around seamlessly.

"One hour and 17 minutes. Sir."

"Right. Now that you've plugged in the target, changes in speed and/or direction will be updated in real-time. We can track a nearly infinite number of targets, whether they are fixed or moving. Our firing solutions are calculated automatically using the same technology. Try it on a bunch of satellites."

Schein returned to his chair, leaving the ensign to practice what he'd just learned. His executive officer, who'd been active on the Carlilse for over a year, paced around the bridge looking anxious. It was Rexford Baumgartner's personality, and it could not be altered—the commander would have the same look if he were playing with Legos. Quirky indeed, but he was exceedingly competent. Rex routinely made the recruits squirm because the young guys would observe the trepidation on their XO's face and assume that they'd royally screwed up or that aliens were coming to eat their brains.

"XO, I'm going to my quarters," said Schein. He looked over at Williams as the ensign simultaneously interrupted his work to glance at the captain. Mordy winked. "Make sure the ensign doesn't fly us into the moon on his first tour."

The captain, one of the original nanite-enhanced Recon soldiers, exited the bridge. He walked down the passage, through a large compartment, and then entered his stateroom through a door that slid rapidly sideways into the bulkhead. Mordy's quarters were simple by the standards which commanding officers would expect. There was a desk, a steel file cabinet, a few chairs, a wardrobe, and his surprisingly comfortable bed. The head was equally rudimentary, consisting of a sink, mirror, toilet, and shower.

Schein sat down in front of his computer. It had been almost three years since he'd been an active-duty lieutenant in the Continental Army—George Washington's army—the military force that smashed the British and their Hessian mercenaries on a hill in New Jersey. It felt like ancient history. Dr. Aaron Howe's delivery of modern rifles to the pitiful American military brought the English to their knees.

"Open mail."

The screen popped up with a list of 27 emails since the last time he'd checked it. Most of them were requests for answers to routine busywork questions—the kind of bureaucratic crap that starship captains didn't think they'd have to mess with—under the supposition that it was all "glamour" up there in space.

There was a flashing priority message. It was from President Carlisle. Schein pondered whether to open it immediately or take a nap first. Since the capture of the Mazik spacecraft of which he was now captain, the solar system had been tranquil.

Carlisle could only be sending a flasher if something was cooking on Earth.

Mordy grunted and tapped a key.

To: Captain Mordechai Schein
From: President John Carlisle
FOR YOUR EYES ONLY

1. Send me a simple rating on the training progress of your current crew

2. The Chinese are making trouble again. We've seen images of executions of dissidents in the western sectors. I'm not talking about a handful of conflicts and casualties. The numbers are staggering. Somewhere in the neighborhood of 100,000 dead. With your capabilities on the ship, perhaps you already have an idea.

3. I am no longer going to sit on this. That means you will likely get orders soon, I mean very soon, to do a strike on some CCP infrastructure. What is your readiness with the current training crew to:

A. Strike specific targets

B. Knock out any ballistic attempts by the CCP in retaliation.

4. Your reply is required within three hours.

He looked at the message again and wished that Tom Rogers was up on the ship and not on Earth running the training center.

Since Angela, Carlisle's wife, was killed in the Mazik strike on Washington, the president tended to demand countermeasures that were excessive by a factor of ten—in Howe's opinion, anyway. But Howe and the rest of Recon were years away, which left Mordy to deal with the president's itchy trigger finger.

Pressing a comm button, he called to the bridge, and Baumgartner picked up.

"Rex. Change of plans. Tell the bridge crew that we may be going to a new target in a few hours. Stick with the current course—just make sure they're ready to go. Get over to weapons and ensure that the lasers and kinetics are hot to trot."

Baumgartner's voice sounded cool, but Schein knew he'd just added wrinkles to the XO's brow. "Anything I should know, skipper?"

"Not yet." He paused. "Oh, and try not to let this elevate your anxiety, Rex." Schein cut the Comm, chuckled, and turned back to reply to the president's message.

To: President John Carlisle
From: Captain M. Schein
FOR YOUR EYES ONLY

1. The crew is as good as any of the top trainees so far. They are competent, but having not shot in anger, it is only speculation if they can deal with the Mazik. Smacking the Chinese might help to move the crew to the next level of combat awareness.

2. We haven't been looking at the far east except to keep a continual scan for launches—strictly a defensive posture.

3. With your permission, I will move from geostationary orbit to survey possible targets over the CCP They will see us immediately and rush to disperse their command and control. If the decision is to hit them, then I should probably get the order before I order the Angela to that position. Specifically, I would like to know:

A. Which kinds of targets are preferred.
B. How much damage.

Schein pressed the send button. Killing people never got any easier. The only consolation was that the CCP were tyrants and murdered without remorse. Something that a Jew like Mordy could empathize and sympathize with.

He looked at the old-fashioned analog quartz clock on the wall. It was 0800 in Philadelphia. Time to say his morning prayers, just like he'd done in 1776. He thought about his parents, who were now dead for over 230 years, and then reached for his prayer book. "I hope you guys are proud of me. I'm still sticking to the rules."

An hour later, while Schein was embracing the idea of sleeping for at least four hours, an alarm sounded on his computer. He opened up the message that he knew was coming from the Commander-in-Chief. It was grim.

To: Captain M. Schein
From: President John Carlisle
FOR YOUR EYES ONLY

1. You will proceed immediately to China orbit. Attached are three exchanges received in the last day with the CCP The latest was received only 45 minutes ago. They told us to stay out of their internal affairs. The killing continues on the ground, however.

2. Select the following targets for controlled projectile bombardment

> *A. The Ministry of Defense*
> *B. The Ministry of Science and Technology*
> *C. The Naval Base at Zhanjiang*
> *D. The Military Base at Zurihe*

3. If the Chinese launch ballistics at any United States ally, besides laser intercept, you will respond by eliminating some PLAAF Airborne Bases. Details are attached.

Good luck. I do not expect that the CCP will be interested in continuing any missile launches if you take out the PLAAF sites. If they do, then you may use your best judgment on retaliation, but stick to naval bases and military concentrations in the regions where civilian massacres are peaked. That information is also attached. Happy hunting.

"Well," Mordy remarked to the walls of his empty quarters. "I wonder how Aaron would handle this?" He keyed the XO's comm and mused the order to hit the Peoples Liberation Army Air Force (PLAAF). That would be a strike that the Chinese would have difficulty recovering from.

"Rex. I'm sending you a list of targets."

"Is that for real? Like Earth targets?"

"Damn right."

"Russians?"

"No. Chinese. The list is extensive. We are hitting them for real. Priority number one is to check our lasers thoroughly. I think we're going to have some nukes to shoot down."

"You would think the CCP would want to get on board with collaborating with us against the Mazik?" smirked Baumgartner with a fair splattering of a melancholy tone.

"You would think that. But, it's been years since the Mazik have been here, and the Chinese Communist Party is losing control of people demanding actual freedom. The premier thinks he can end that by murdering any dissenters—that would leave cooperative slaves, right?"

"Sir? Can I ask why the president is suddenly motivated to get aggressive?"

Schein flicked on the video so Rex could see his face. "Do you see my expression? It's the military guy following lawful orders of the politician in charge. If Captian Howe was here, he might have a debate with Carlisle, but Howe isn't here, so we're going to kill people and break things. Get everyone prepped. And, you may now wear a justifiably apprehensive look on your face."

Three hours later, the USS Angela Carlisle maintained a position above the South China Sea. The exhausted Mordy sat in his increasingly uncomfortable chair and reviewed the target list.

"What kind of video do you have from the 'Peoples' broadcasting down there?"

A female lieutenant named Cassie Munch pulled up an enhanced image of state television. Schein recognized the speed with which the young officer did her job—she only needed to be taught something once. And, it was reasonable to bypass the lingering tendency to question the potential of women in combat. Mercy Bonner and her adopted daughter, Molly Stark, had pretty much buried that notion forever when they fought against the Mazik in space.

The captain watched the Chinese news and commentary while seamlessly translating using his nanite-enhanced brain. The state propaganda droned on about how the premier was using the Peoples Army to crush rebels who were burning crops and pillaging the peaceful citizens.

"Rex. Are you getting this translation?"

"Yes, sir. That's some bullshit."

Munch interrupted. "Sir. We're getting a transmission on 1.4 gigahertz from the Chinese—in English."

"Play it."

"USS Angela Carlisle. We can only assume that you are stationed above Chinese airspace for peaceful purposes and preparing for a Mazik assault as a routine exercise. Please confirm. Over."

The comm officer swiveled in her chair. It reminded Schein of Lieutenant Uhura turning to Captain Kirk on the TV shows he'd seen from the late 1960s. "Any response, sir?"

"Put me on the same frequency. Point the dish."

"Aye, Aye." She pressed a touch-screen and nodded.

Schein took a few seconds to think about his transmission.

"This is Captain Schein of the USS Angela Carlisle. You are currently in violation of civil and human rights laws—including genocide and terrorism. Your government has been warned to stand down from encroaching on civilian populations, including the remaining Uyghur encampments. Our response is imminent. You've had every chance to restrain your forces. My orders come from President Carlisle. Schein. Out."

Baumgartner cringed nervously. It had only been a matter of a few seconds, but the communists launched a missile.

"Track that," the XO barked at another of the bridge crew.

Mazik systems were precise and quick. "The trajectory has it heading for us."

"Wait until it is out of the atmosphere and laze it."

A couple of minutes later, the missile exploded as the laser was recharging. The bright flash was dampened automatically by the Angela's shields and screens.

"What was the point of that?" Mordy was mostly reflecting the question to himself.

"I think they were trying to tell us something," said Baumgartner.

"Did you notice how quickly they launched that? It was fueled and ready, and they wasted a perfectly good device for what?"

Rex shrugged. "Maybe they have a bunch more ready to go? That first one was just to get our attention."

"And what? Are they thinking about striking the homeland? We can deal with a hundred missiles and still not overheat ourselves. We'll follow Carlisle's orders. Start with a small, guided rock at the first target. Fire when ready."

A one-ton specifically tailored projectile accelerated toward the Chinese Ministry of Defense located on Fuxing Road, Beijing. They waited for telemetry to verify that the rock was accurate. Approximately eighty-two seconds later, ten ballistic missiles were launched from several bases around Beijing, heading west. A few seconds after that, there was a tremendous kinetic impact directly on the home of China's military leadership.

"Assess the damage later. Laze those weapons!" said Schein.

There was a mild shudder felt in the skin of the battlecruiser as repeated shots of coherent light spewed tremendous energy. The ballistic and likely nuclear-tipped missiles were slow compared to velocities achieved by attack craft in space. Nevertheless, each of the weapons had the power to take out a chunk of an allied city.

"Where are they aimed? Quick," shouted the captain.

Ensign Williams upped his game to keep pace with the tension on the bridge. "Ten missiles, sir. Two are headed to western China rebel areas. The others are aimed at Western Europe. Looks like England and France."

"Splash five," called out Baumgartner. "Okay. Two left now." The XO was biting his lip and tapping a number two pencil on his console. It drove Lieutenant Munch crazy when he did that, but Rex was her boss.

"One left."

The weapons officer cursed and screamed. "We just lost the lasers."

"Get them back up now!" Schein was livid.

"A powerplant went down," replied the officer. "Switching now."

Rex rolled his eyes while grinding his teeth. The pencil banged loudly as a drop of sweat formed on his brow despite the cool temperatures on the bridge—energy systems were his baby.

"Power up. Lazing!"

Mordy breathed finally as the last missile got zapped at the apex of its trajectory.

"Shit! That was close," he said. "Let's hit the remainder of those ground targets, including the PLAAF Airborne bases. And keep those stupid power supplies up, dammit." He eyed his second in command.

"Yes, sir."

"Oh. One more thing, commander. Don't tell my rabbi that I used the S-word."

"Who's your rabbi, sir?"

Schein twisted his mouth in a peculiar grin. "Scratch that. He died about two hundred and fifty years ago. Sometimes I forget."

Chapter 5

Shaab Mar Gen, leader of all Panruk aliens, stared at the humans and the Slev alien walking down the corridor. The parties agreed to meet after two Mim solar cycles of arguing over protocol. In the end, the Arbitor allowed Captain Mercy Bonner, Commander Barrett Bonner, and most surprisingly, Captain Kap Jahrnuk, to land on Olamit. Joining them was the renowned anthropologist Shelet Pir Sahm Mim, known as Edgar on Earth.

"She's not eating," was the whispered remark by Edgar to Mercy as several Panruk officials led them to the sunlit office. In the tradition of Olamit, those Panruk who accompanied the visitors stood in a line and sang a few melodic songs.

Not unhuman-like, Shaab waved off the revelers and asked her guests to sit. The Arbitor waited, but just prior to sitting, she paced over to Edgar and kissed his arms, then briefly joined her glowing fingertips to his.

"Shelet Pir Sahm Mim. I am honored to be in my role upon your return. Also, it will be even more delightful to see you shed your human appearance and once again become Panruk—it is somewhat surreal to see you like that. I am quite sure that I would not enjoy such an appearance." She nodded to the humans and the Slev. "Of course, no insult intended; it's just that perhaps every lifeform should stay in its own skin."

Kap had only minor difficulty following the opening statement by the Olamit official. He offered a response. "And, dear Arbitor, as a Slev, we too would find it uncomfortable to see your appearance reflected in our mirrors."

There was a weighty silence, but then Shaab smiled a very human smile and emitted what must have been the Panruk version of a laugh. "Well said. Kap Jahrnuk, but your rebellion against the Mazik is long overdue."

Up to this point, Mercy and Barrett merely watched the brief exchange, but being that they were fluent in both Panruk and Slev; Shaab's candor and Kap's expression felt unnerving. On top of that, the Arbitor was not known for sensitivity and tempered statements—a trait that brought mixed results.

Mercy cleared her throat. "It is a pleasure to meet you."

The purposely injected statement had the desired effect. Shaab's countenance seemed to lose a bit of its tension.

"Captain and Commander Bonner, I am genuinely overwhelmed by the story of your appearance. I believe it was quite genius for you to preface your visit with a description of Earth's victories over the Mazik. It read like a child's tale."

Barrett began to speak, but Mercy squeezed his thigh, and it was timely because the leader of Olamit had no intention of yielding.

"As I was saying, with the help of the AI, you've succeeded, perhaps too well."

The commander could not endure the direction in which Shaab was taking the conversation.

"Excuse me, Shaab Mar Gen," asked Barrett, "but our victory saved our planet and all of the human race. Maybe you can tell me where we've overachieved?"

The Arbitor tilted her head, large dark eyes and her blue-tinted skin flashing. She was not one to back down—especially to an inferior race like humans. "By coming here, you've taken Olamit and the Panruk from barely hanging on with Mazik Bah-Gahn tribute—to ensuring our destruction."

"How so?" asked Barrett. "We have ships, and we can defend your system."

In another human gesture, the Panruk leader stood up, her robes reaching the floor. She waved her hands, the extended index and middle fingers now glowing on the tips.

"Your two ships are going to protect us? You've killed us! Mazik Bah-Gahn will come here with twenty ships. Perhaps you will be able to outrun them, but he will incinerate Olamit as a lesson to the other systems. The Council is nothing. There is no power any longer—other than the crushing force of the Mazik."

Edgar had been silent, and despite the weight of the events

unfolding, he longed to see his parents. Not as Edgar, disguised as a human male, but as a Panruk female. Still, something about his 127 years on Earth had changed him considerably. Humans, with all their flaws and all their destructive natures, had qualities, unlike the members of the Council who'd given up on innovation for so long, then fell victim to the Mazik as if they were blind and dumb. He glared at Shaab. "At least we will go down fighting."

The Arbitor seemed to sink into her chair. She touched the illuminated tips of her fingers to her head. It didn't help. "So our species will have the honor of dying and being forgotten in the history that the Mazik will write? So be it. I've done everything I could to appease the ruthless beast. I offered myself to be his concubine even—to allow him to abuse and kill me with his wretched nature. Anything to save my planet, and now I will have nothing worthwhile to reduce his rage. We are all lost.

"Your mantra about fighting to the death is childish in galactic philosophy. You are an immature kind of creature," she said, staring at Barrett. "Do you know why the Mazik want you gone? For the same reason as my predecessor—if you somehow manage to survive, you will ultimately become Mazik Bah-Gahn. You will replace him and be worse than him."

"You are a fool." Kap Jahrnuk looked incredulous while feeling pity for Shaab. "We Slev have watched and waited for the right time. Neither the Panruk nor any other member of the Council can predict the future. Where is your predecessor? Why is he not here?"

"He quit because he saw our demise and prophesied the coming of humans and the mortal danger they present. Then a crowd of Panruk murdered him. That is something we have not seen in 2,000 years."

Kap felt vindicated. "You should have been building ships instead of relying on the moronic concept of 'Agreed' in the Council chambers. I am surprised that you've lasted this long. The humans are the only ones with the help of the Slev who can stand against our enemy. You must work with us. If we fail, we will still seek a way to save Olamit. Perhaps we will die at the fangs of those barbarians, but your people will continue to give your tribute until you starve."

Mercy sat in awe of Kap's sudden command of the room. Barrett spoke. "I believe we need to come together and make our own Council. A new Council which will use force and brutality when necessary to save what we cherish. We could right now be building mines and devising methods to cripple any ships that come through that jump point. Shaab, you still have resources. It is time to build weapons, not offer yourself as a victim to be abused and die on Kamtret. We need to join together."

The Arbitor was barely middle-aged for a Panruk, yet she looked ancient and worn. Everything around her office gave off an aura of hopelessness. She thought, perhaps Assistant Marzat would like to become the youngest Arbitor in the history of Olamit. Shaab could then run and bathe in far away pools of water until the asteroids rained down on the planet to doom all life. Would it be such a bad ending?

"What can you do, Kap Jahrnuk? Do you have plans for these defensive weapons? Do you, Captain Bonner? And Commander Bonner, it was your idea, so do you have real and practical details on how to stop an armada of fifteen Mazik battlecruisers?"

There was a weighty silence. Finally, Mercy spoke up. "We require two cycles. We'll generate a plan that will give us a fighting chance. *Agreed*?"

Shaab bared her gentle Panruk teeth. It was nothing like the fearsome Mazik and Slev grins—wide mouths laden with sharp incisors. "Agreed is no longer in my vocabulary, Captain Bonner. Being that I have nothing else to fight with and nowhere else to turn, we will trust you. The worst that can happen is death, which we know is already on its way."

A loud clunk vibrated through the shuttle as it docked inside the USS George Washington. The landing pods locked down, the outer hatch sealed, and the airlock cycled to fill the "garage" with atmosphere. Mercy insisted Kap stay on her ship and work non-stop to devise a defense strategy to counter the Mazik pouring in through the jump point. Her urging wasn't necessary, as the Slev captain failed to see the point of returning to the Ro-Pahm, considering it to be a complete waste of time.

"Mok can manage the Ro-Pahm."

Barrett touched his wife lightly on the shoulder. "Okay. Let's take five hours of rest. If we start right away, we will be worthless. Even with the nanites, we need a break." He turned to Kap. "Are we agreed?"

Kap did the Slev version of laughter. His rippling muscles jiggled, and a squeaky sound escaped his broad mouth. "Agreed is no longer in my vocabulary. But, we will all be sharper after some downtime."

Mercy led them forward from the starboard midship bay. There were at least two comfortable staterooms with Slev sleep chairs. Captain Jahrnuk didn't need any prodding. He went straight away to recline, and a soft thump was heard as the sliding door sealed shut.

"Now it's just us," remarked Mercy.

Commander Bonner observed that there was no one in the corridor. He slipped his arm around her, and she welcomed it by leaning into him. Marriage would be so much better without Mazik Bah-Gahn, she thought. She wanted to be lost in her husband's powerful arms.

"I think we should actually sleep this time."

"Definitely." Mercy conceded, quashing her desire for Barrett. The galaxy was at stake; making love would have to wait.

Mazik Bah-Gahn strolled across the floor of what he now called his "Emperor's Mighty Hall," while staring lecherously at Pel Jahrnuk, his favorite Slev toy. She appeared to lounge nonchalantly on a divan, but internally Pel was fearful. It was always wise for any concubine to be paranoid when the emperor gazed in her direction.

A chime rang by Mazik Bah-Gahn's throne. He turned from

fantasizing about his favorite slave and received the alert.

"Emperor," began his aide, appearing visually tense in the holographic display to the side of the throne. His broad jaw, pale green skin, rippling muscular neck and chest, and large eyes all were expertly presented to broadcast fealty and subservience.

"Emperor, the tribute from the Panruk has failed to arrive on schedule."

"Where is our cargo ship?"

"It has not returned from the Olamit system. Perhaps it has some technical issue."

Mazik Bah-Gahn's stare filled the servant with anxiety. "Alert me in one Kamtret cycle if the ship fails to appear at the jump point."

"Yes, Emperor."

The undisputed ruler of the Mazik and all of the Council sentient beings waved a finger and broke the Comm. Bad news aroused him. Perhaps Shaab Mar Gen finally gave him a good excuse to have her brought to his palace as a plaything. He turned and stared at Pel. She was instantly demure and did everything she could to appear utterly submissive. The other concubines noticed and were thankful that the Slev Pel Jahrnuk was routinely the focus of their master.

"Pel!" boomed the emperor. "Disrobe and don't disappoint me." He pointed to a portal that overlooked the city 700 meters below. "I prefer not to heave you out of that window panel to your death—at least not today."

*

Kap slept deeply with no hint of the tension surrounding a swath of the Milky Way Galaxy—a brewing disaster that could change history for the worse—permanently.

He woke suddenly. It was a practiced skill that centuries of being at the beck and call of the Mazik required, a perfect mental alarm.

The large Slev stood up from his sleep chair and, having

gotten prior authorization from Captain Bonner, used a long-range comm device.

"Mok. Wake up."

"I am awake. Do you not remember from our youth that I only need half the sleep that you require?"

Kap smirked in the Slev way at the image of his close friend. "Other way around, my massive-ego chum. But, we can hopefully argue about this later. In the meantime, I want to update you on things that you need to know and not share with the crew—yet."

Mok's expression became professionally focused as he simply said, "Ready."

"We met with Shaab Mar Gen. This you knew already. She was *hostile* and displayed aggressiveness that you wouldn't expect from a Panruk. It was fascinating.

"She accused us of creating a situation wherein Mazik Bah-Gahn will destroy Olamit as punishment for the actions we've taken in this system. The exchange was terse, direct, and without much in the way of hidden connotations."

"What does that mean for us?" asked the ever-practical Mok.

"I feel bad for her. Shaab very quickly accepted that we have no choice except to prepare defenses. We threw away the pathetic tribute program that the Arbitor has been using to keep the Mazik from annihilating them. So, now we have to quickly develop a plan on what kinds of weapons we can fabricate and deploy."

The Second bared his sharp and deadly teeth. "Is that all? Just devise a genius defense system against multiple incoming battlecruisers? Plark!"

"Yes. Plark is the appropriate term for the Plark in which we've got our feet stuck—but that is what we will do—and we are not going to let Olamit get destroyed because of our need to battle the Mazik. If it comes to it, we'll choose death and make it look as if the Panruk were not complicit."

Mok thought about that and shrugged his massive shoulders. "And the so-called emperor will believe us and not turn Olamit into ashes?"

"There is no other way. I will contact you when we have an idea. You will need to have the crew fully prepared. This is going to be much more demanding than setting a speed record to fix the cowling on the Ro-Pahm. Get some rest so that you will be alert. That is an order."

Kap cut the connection.

*

The nanite-enhanced humans on the Washington sat with an inventory list of supplies available on the planet. Despite Shaab's insistence that all was lost, the top engineers on Olamit were put in direct contact with the human vessel. Several holographic images of production managers floated above the large conference table.

"We don't have time for pleasant introductions," announced Mercy. "I've got your names and job descriptions. I am Captain Mercy Bonner. This is Commander Barrett Bonner. The Slev Captain is Kap Jahrnuk. Also joining us are Lieutenant JG Allen, Ensign Molly Stark, and Ensign Scott Lewis. The names are on your screens."

She waited for subtle movements among the Panruk that acknowledged her crew. Just then, another alien visual appeared, and the humans on the ship waited for something they guessed was coming.

"And I'm Shelet Pir Sahm Mim. Don't be confused up there on the Washington. I underwent the transformation back to looking like me. It was painful, so if I grunt occasionally, get over it."

"Edgar," said Barrett. "You're the most beautiful Panruk I've ever seen."

"Funny. But to be more serious, I'm here to try to explain to my fellow Panruk anything that might be misunderstood. For now, since I'm an anthropologist and not a bomb scientist, I'll be quiet."

Mercy looked at the visuals. "You might think that we humans are primitives. I get it. However, the humans in this room are all enhanced. We were modified by the master AI.

That means we can probably think faster than you, but we don't have the data on possible weapons systems, and we don't have the technical background."

One of the aliens raised a hand gently. "How can you help, then?"

"We learn fast," said Barrett. "So, when we need data or schematics, send the information, and we will process it while you wait. It's the great equalizer that comes with enhancements."

Mercy took control of the meeting. "Okay. Now tell us what you have on the planet that can explode."

After a fair amount of wrangling, the Washington crew understood much about what was available. But it wasn't just about making large bangs; it was about assembling a network of smart devices that could talk to each other without having to wait for commands from a ship or from Olamit.

"Mir Campor," said LTJG. John Allen. "I think what Ensign Lewis just mentioned is our need to put together a stealth package that can hunt the incoming ships and then release a blast when in proximity. It's the perfect weapon, almost. As long as it selects the correct target and detonates on time, we're safe, and the enemy is dead."

The eldest of the Panruk, Campor, was visibly ancient relative to his fellows. The natural glow of his index and middle fingertips looked dim somehow, but he was still mentally sharp as a tack.

"You must understand that we feel uncomfortable creating such technology. Maybe the famous anthropologist will explain."

Edgar, now fully Panruk in appearance, began to speak. "What Campor is trying to say is that building weapons runs counter to very ingrained beliefs. It's almost biological at this point that some Panruk might become physically ill."

The Washington crew sitting around the conference table were stunned. They knew that passivity was endemic among the Council members, but after all the misery that the Mazik had dumped on them?

Shelet Pir Sahm Mim continued. "It is just hard for my species to be violent."

Mercy glared at Campor and the others, excluding Edgar. "Was it so hard for you when your people murdered the former Arbitor? Or when Shaab ordered the execution of those who'd done that murder?"

Campor looked like he'd been caught in a snare. "You know about that?"

"Yes," answered Mercy. "We are humans enhanced with nanites. We figure out things and can access data pretty easily. Your systems on Olamit are very trusting, and our species has a habit of breaking into things.

"Let's get serious and stop behaving like you are children living in a paradise. Mazik Bah-Gahn is coming, at a minimum, to torture you and make you bleed. There is no place for pacifistic, ethical ideals anymore. If you do nothing, then your planet is going to be obliterated. Is that worth fighting for?"

Mir Campor stammered like he'd been caught shoplifting, but after muttering a series of meaningless words, he simply nodded like a human. "When you put it in those terms, I suppose we must find motivation in the form of avoiding death."

Lewis shrugged and snorted involuntarily and then spoke out of turn sarcastically. "Do you really think so?"

Barrett gave the Ensign a "Shut your trap" look.

"Campor," said Mercy. "I sympathize with your cultural motivations—but not a whole lot. If we can get past your planetary neurosis about defending your lives, then maybe we can stop wasting time and build something useful?"

The elderly engineering manager turned to practicality in the blink of an eye. The spontaneous shift was noticeably alien, at least to the humans watching.

"I believe we can build these." He waved at his display, and suddenly a three-dimensional visual image appeared above the conference table. It was a simple round object the size of a golf ball. It was covered with short spikes that looked like bits of toothpicks sticking out perpendicular to the ball.

"What is that?" asked Bonner.

"It's a fusion device," answered another of the Panruk scientists.

"How explosive is it?" asked Allen. "It looks pretty small."

Campor threw out some numbers using their system of measurement. Barrett concentrated on the math and then blurted out, "That's the equivalent of 4.18×10^{17} Joules—approximately. It's triggered with anti-hydrogen."

"That's about a megaton," offered Molly. "If that hits a Mazik ship, then the damage should be crippling, regardless of the shields. Are you saying that the Panruk produced anti-matter as a catalyst to generate huge energy releases in this tiny ball?"

Mercy considered the object. "How much harmful radiation is released?"

The third Panruk engineer grinned. "Only about one percent of the energy released is dangerous radiation. It is also limited in duration—it decays rapidly."

Lewis couldn't help himself. "I guess that's the pacifist version of a warm and fuzzy bomb."

"It is also about 70% kinetic energy. The thermal component is nearly all the rest of the release."

Barrett stared at the engineer. "How do you know this? Did you test it?"

"We made some of these to open asteroids for minerals."

The commander continued questioning. "How many asteroids did you break?"

"Four."

Mercy flicked her blond hair from her face and inquired, "Do you have any more of these things sitting on a shelf somewhere?"

Campor frowned. "We have more of them."

"How many more?" persisted Mercy.

The engineer, who must have been a fifth of Campor's age, was bubbling with energy and shouted out with youthful enthusiasm, "Six thousand."

Chapter 6

A day later, after pressing Mok and the technicians on the Ro-Pahm, something like an idea was unfolding.

Kap's Second was, for a green-blue alien, tickled pink. He looked gleefully at his first commander, who displayed a massive number of terrifying teeth in reply.

"That is what I have in mind, Kap Jahrnuk."

Several Slev technicians stood nearby. Each one shared Mok's grin. Several of them commented at once that perhaps the captain should let the humans see the idea.

"Very well." Kap pressed a button.

In a few seconds, a notification alarm rang on the belt of Mercy's fleet uniform. She moved from her bed to the display computer on the stateroom's desk. The boss of the Ro-Pahm, with several Slev behind him, appeared on the screen.

"Is it good news?"

"I'll let Mok explain."

The large officer took front and center. "Good morning, Captain Bonner. And how are you doing?"

Barrett was standing out of view but couldn't suppress an inaudible chuckle. Did the giant Slev officer just make small talk with his wife? Then it occurred to him. The Slev were all in reverent awe of Mercy—as well they should be, at least according to the legend. Captain Mercy was the unstoppable female alien who fulfilled a prophecy dating back a thousand years. It was his wife who'd single-handedly captured Mazik ships and crews. To the Mazik and Slev, she was a mythical superhero.

"Thank you for asking. I'm fine. How are you?"

"Thank you for asking, captain. I'm fine. We are all fine." As if on cue, the Slev technicians behind him nodded like humans.

"Okay. So what do you have for me?"

"Yes. Well. We believe that we can take those anti-matter fusion explosives and make what you would call a minefield just on our side of the jump point."

And there it was.

Barrett and Mercy turned and stared at each other.

"Mok. I'm putting you on hold for a second. Don't hang up." She pressed a button, and the screen went dark.

"Do you know what this means?"

"Yes. If we can build a delivery and triggering mechanism for 6,000 deadly golfballs, the Mazik will be cut to ribbons."

He thought about that. "We'll need stealth. If the enemy comes through the jump point at low speed, they can simply back off and start lasing the mines at their leisure."

"That would take a while," he pointed out.

"Yes. But when they make a hole big enough, the Mazik will send in 20 ships to eradicate this system. Hence the need for stealth and delivery."

"Maybe Mok has an answer for that. Bring him back up."

Mercy reached over and flicked the comm. "Did you think about how to deliver and trigger the bombs? If we are 30 or 40 light minutes away from the jump point, then the attacking fleet will simply plow through the mines as if they weren't there. So we'll need a ship waiting around to activate the mines unless they will be automatic."

Kap returned to the screen. "There's more to it than that. We've discussed this for eight hours here. The mines need to be active—I mean, self-propelled, self-guided, and self-detonated."

Mercy deflated. "We'll need to build a system for each mine."

"Yes. That is the big mountain to climb."

"Do you mean hurdle, Captain Jarnuk?"

"Yes, Captain Bonner. I've been studying Earth slang. I meant hurdle to climb."

"Um. Leap—never mind. Okay. How fast can you produce the systems?"

"We can't. We don't have the materials," admitted Kap.

Now Barrett joined his wife in feelings of discouragement.

"Can you make any?" Mercy asked.

Mok portrayed the Slev version of dejection. "We can produce perhaps five or ten."

"That sucks," said both Bonners in unison.

"I don't understand the meaning of what you just said," asked Kap.

"It means that five or ten is not much better than zero. Is there anything in the warehouses here on the Washington that will help us to increase production? You know this ship's stores better than me." She waited.

The Slev leader cupped his chin with his hand in a very human way, then answered, "No."

There was dead silence on the Comm. After a moment, one of the Slev technicians asked, "What about the Panruk?"

*

Shaab Mar Gen, despite her terminally foul mood, took an instant liking to the young engineer who seemed to have significantly more optimism than Campor, the elderly scientist. Not to say that Mir wasn't first-rate, but whereas he could crunch numbers and dream up ideas, his utility ended there—on the computer display.

Mercy, Barrett, and the other three Recon members were chomping at the bit to hear something worthwhile. The Arbitor bypassed the senior Panruk.

"Shaft Lek," she called the youngster by name. "Tell our guests what you've designed."

A three-dimensional image that looked like a porcupine with a long cylindrical tail floated above the conference table on the ship.

"It's not something I'd want to cuddle with," remarked Lewis.

Molly poked him under the table and whispered, "Have you ever cuddled with anything or anyone besides *Dog*?"

Shaft was surprisingly poised, considering that the safety and survival of his planet might depend on when and if his urgent project became functional.

"First, all of these protrusions are stealth generators. They are small broad spectrum wave generators that will make the Mazik think that the scanning reflections are coming from somewhere else."

Barrett asked. "Does that matter? If they see a projection that is five hundred meters away from the real thing, won't they fire and hit something? Maybe not the device that is sending out the stealth transmission, but a different mine in a nearby location. Either way, the bombs get fried without exploding near the Mazik battlecruisers."

The Panruk didn't skip a beat. "I thought of that. And, it is a significant problem if we were to place thousands of devices in relatively fixed positions. That is where the propulsion idea comes in."

Another view appeared on the holographic screen. "This cylinder on the containment for the anti-matter fusion energy source is a tiny fusion drive. It's pretty cool. I apologize if I used that human term incorrectly, but Shelet Pir Sahm Mim told me you would find it amusing. Is it?"

Mercy answered. "Coming from a Panruk engineer, it is really funny. Thanks. Keep going."

"Well, I figured that we have an energy source in the ball. Why not use some of that in tiny amounts fed by anti-matter to push it at the target?"

Molly was very excited. The science suddenly spoke to her. Her nanite brain was desperate for something to latch onto. "Can it guide itself internally and then adjust energy bursts from the drive to chase down the Mazik ships?"

"Yes, that is the idea," answered Engineer Lek.

Mercy focused on the thing that mattered. "How many can you produce and how fast?"

"Twenty-five units in about a week," contributed Campor, trying to stay relevant.

"Did you determine a failure rate, Shaft?"

"That is the risky part. I'm thinking 20%."

JG Allen had been quiet until then. "What if we station a

shuttle out there and use it to shoot a few dozen unguided bombs at the incoming fleet?"

"That's a suicide mission," announced Barrett. "At that distance, the Mazik would have time to lase or fire a particle beam before it took the hit from our weapons. No, we have to let the Mazik think they are walking into space that they control. No hostile forces, and only the dead freighters out there by the jump point."

Mercy concurred. "The image to the Mazik will be very comforting and probably make them feel overconfident—always a good thing to promote in your enemy."

Shaab finally used her Arbitor authority to bring the meeting to the next level. "I want five of the best Slev technicians to come down here and fabricate the drives."

"Arbitor," said Mercy. "Please wait. I want to connect to Captain Jahrnuk."

Barrett read his wife's mind and immediately pinged Kap. The Slev captain's response time always amazed the humans. "Kap here."

"We need your top five technician fabricators down on Olamit yesterday," said Barrett.

"I can have them on the shuttle in an hour. Will that help?"

"Captain Jahrnak." The Arbitor addressed him directly. "Our engineer, and lead on this project, Shaft Lek, will send you landing coordinates. Please hurry while I'm still feeling hopeful."

The Panruk engineer spoke. "I'd like to send the captain a fabrication outline in case his Slev crew have any equipment they might want to bring."

"A worthwhile idea." Shaab stared at Kap Jahrnak. "Let's not waste time. For the first instance in an Olamit year, I feel like we might not die tomorrow."

Mercy grinned with guarded optimism, and she was damn glad to have Barrett supporting her authority. "Right. Everyone knows what they have to do. We'll meet again in twelve hours."

"Mom. I mean, sir?" It was Molly.

"Yes, Ensign Stark?"

"I think we missed an obvious advantage, and I believe it is a strong one."

The entire meeting focused on the young girl. She wasn't phased by it.

"We've got a bunch of dead freighters out there." Molly waited for that to sink in. Then added, "We can put crews on those ships to control another layer of fusion bombs. Granted, the couple dozen that run automatically and stealthily will be the first round, but what if they fail? Or partially fail? A second level of attack could be launched at any remaining Mazik cruisers with command and control from some of those junkers. Probably more reliable, and we could hurl a larger number of weapons. That's what I was thinking."

JG Allen pointed out the obvious. "We'll be putting people up there with zero protection if the Mazik detect the source of weapons control."

"That would invite a quick strike from those enemy ships—probably rapid and fatal," said Lewis.

Shaab chimed in, "If any of the enemy cruisers make it past the initial attack—that is also a death sentence. It is a calculated risk, but losing a few individuals versus the entire planet?"

"Aribtor," asked Barrett. "Do you think you can find Panruk volunteers to go up there? I'm not saying they should go alone. I'm suggesting units of Panruk, Slev, and humans—occupying several disabled freighters."

"That would give us a much better chance at destroying any Mazik that survive the AI-managed fusion devices," said Mercy.

"We're all in this together," volunteered Shaab Mar Gen. "That's a concept that we Panruk do comprehend. War and violence make us cringe, but cooperation is in our genes."

Shaft spoke up. "I will go out there. It was mostly my idea, so it is logical for me to be there."

"How much suit time do you have, Engineer Lek?" asked Mir Campor.

"None, sir."

His response hung in the air like a sagging balloon.

The Arbitor wasn't perturbed. "So you better start training today. And that applies to everyone. We'll only need two types of weapons. Smart bombs, as the Earth sentients call them, and manually guided devices. I leave it to the experts to figure out the details, and my opinion is just that, an opinion. To be reasonably competent at this mission, I'm setting a target date of three Olamit cycles—probably unrealistic, but we need to do it."

"Yes, Ma'am," acknowledged Mercy. "Three days, and we'll see if we have a rat's chance in hell to pull this off."

Shaab's slit of a mouth widened. Barrett thought that the Arbitor was probably considered pretty among her species. She tilted her head in a peculiar Panruk style. "Captain. I have no idea what you just said, but if you are seeking a rat's chance, I hope that whatever that is, you get it."

*

Like an old human male, Mir Campor grumbled as he hobbled across the laboratory. Partly it was his ancient nature, but it also had to do with his deep-seated desire to escape the proximity of the terminally optimistic and exuberant Shaft Lek. The junior engineer seemed to be everywhere at once—it was grating on Campor's last nerve—much like the elder/younger dynamic on Earth.

One of the handful of Slev techs looked up from his workstation. "Sir. Would you like to inspect my propulsion unit for errors?"

"Did you follow Engineer Lek's design?" said Mir, not hiding his rankled thoughts.

"Yes, Chief Engineer. I interlaced the reactive surface layers precisely according to the design requirements."

The response from the graying and grizzly scientist was a flash of benign teeth. The Panruk issued something like a nod, then carried on to his office without uttering a word.

In a nearby production room, a dozen technicians were integrating redundant systems to identify Mazik targets automatically. Stealth measures were being added to the outer shells of the delivery systems. The process was daunting.

"How are we doing?" asked Barrett, in response to his call being answered by Kap's Second Commander.

Mok chose to spend his time right in the thick of the tumult. He looked at Commander Bonner and gave him a thumbs up into the video screen.

"Where'd you learn that?"

The exceedingly large Slev smiled without exposing his menacing teeth. "I'm enthralled with a number of your human expressions. Some of them are bizarrely meaningless and silly; however, this one—" He did the thumb gesture again, "—I really like it!"

"Whatever floats your boat, Mok," said Barrett.

This was received with a blank stare, then, "Regarding the progress of the weapons? We have over twenty built, but it seems that computer systems, navigation, and propulsion parts are nearly exhausted. Triggering units are plentiful."

Bonner cracked his knuckles. "So, we will have less than 25 self-contained missiles but plenty of spares to aim the fusion weapons manually."

Mok displayed a resigned gaze. "Ensign Stark is correct. We will be risking the planet if we don't put small crews up there to shoot at the Mazik—a technique with a reduced chance of survival, unfortunately—."

"—But one that has no alternative," concluded Mir Campor. Somehow the Panruk chief worked his way close enough to the discussion to interject his view. "Captain Bonner and I will review the list of possible specialists to send out to the front line. In the meantime, keep building your delivery systems."

Barrett didn't want to get into a discussion with Campor. He cut the connection and released a rare sigh of combined doubt, hope, and anxiety.

Chapter 7

"This is our new life?" Clark kicked a rock into the pond. Surprisingly, it skipped a couple of times, creating concentric little waves just before sinking into the depths.

"Not exactly," replied Allison. Her form was still of a beautiful woman in an officer's uniform.

Monty, now wearing just a tee-shirt and shorts made from his pants with the help of a sharp stone, scoffed. "A thousand years of this!"

"We've discussed this seventeen times now. That's the equivalent of once every two days," Howe pointed out. "What did Allison say? Let me answer that. The Mar El have put something in the environment here that slows our aging. There's enough edible plant life that we could just walk the perimeter of our cage and lose our minds from the monotony."

"We can kill ourselves!" interjected Monty.

"You can. I can't," Allison pointed out.

Clark kicked another rock into the water. "At least we won't have to relieve ourselves with Shamrock watching us—if we're dead."

"He calls himself Tzurek, but I think that we are considered so inconsequential to him that our opinions don't mean anything. Certainly that Mar El doesn't care if we get his name right." Aaron picked up a flat stone, tossed it, and watched it bounce across the pond at least eight or nine times. "Captain Clark, I think I'm a better stone-skipper than you."

Monty, aggravated more than usual, picked up a heavy chunk of rock and hurled it in. The splash kicked back and sprayed all of them. "Game over," he growled.

"I can teach you all very advanced astrophysics to pass the time," offered Allison. All three of her companions groaned, with Monty poking his index finger into his mouth and pretending to throw up. The lieutenant followed that with a string of four-letter words that he'd never used as a carpenter raised in the era of Colonial America.

Howe sat down on a boulder. The two Recon soldiers joined Allison on the sand. Aaron looked at them—it was a commanding gaze meant to exert some authority. "Until we figure out how to bust out of here, we'll do our best to keep the Mar El curious and entertained. If he gets bored with our behavior, he could start experimenting on our organs."

Allison seemed to drift off for a few seconds—a dreamy gaze emanating from her eyes. She then looked genuinely sympathetic and said, "The original Mar El on this planet studied my female anatomy thoroughly a couple of thousand years ago. You are males. I'm surprised he hasn't started probing you already. Then again, these aliens are so long-lived that for Tzurek, it may feel like only a few hours have passed since we got here."

Captain Clark's eyes flashed angrily. "I'll die before I let him start doing experiments on my—parts—if you gather my meaning."

"Like I said," noted Howe. "We gather our food and act like humans bumbling through their lives."

Monty sneered. "That's essentially what we've been doing for a month. I think we need to be proactive and get some intel on little runt scumbag. Why aren't we doing that, sir?"

Allison interrupted and turned towards the large lieutenant. "My dear and astute Montgomery. That is what I have been doing almost non-stop since before we touched down on this rock. I'm looking for weaknesses."

"What have you found?" asked Clark.

"They've made it impossible for me to compromise the barrier. When I transported out of here so long ago as an AI, the Mar El considered that to be a massive attack on their *egos*."

Aaron stood up and reached skyward with both arms. Even with the nanites flowing through his bloodstream and tissues, an occasional stretch was therapeutic. All around them were fruit trees that formed a semi-circle by the sandy beach adjacent to the water. If it were a choice based on free will, living here would be more than okay. He sat back down on the little boulder.

"Can you access their data systems? Computers?"

"Not yet, Aaron. As I said, I'm working on it; they have reinforced the perimeter. But, I've figured out some things that are worth pondering."

"Such as?" Howe inquired.

"They, or rather, Tzurek gives off the same intellectual vibrations that his predecessors did thousands of years ago. It's like they are stagnant—maybe even decaying a little. They have nothing better to do than capture alien species and play with them—us. There's no innovation here, as far as I can tell. That's a weakness to be exploited. I have scanned the entire volume of our cage. There are no listening devices. The Mar El are very advanced, but they still have to answer to physics, and there is nothing here to indicate surveillance other than those random instances when Tzurek drifts over the barrier wall and stares at us."

They all considered that. Monty stared hard at Allison. "So, my experience tells me that bored guards make mistakes. Even if they have the barrier and automated systems to stifle any attempt to escape, they could underestimate us. Am I right?"

She smiled. "That's exactly what I'm looking for. A way to blow this joint." Allison smirked at Aaron. "Did I say that right? The last part?"

"Do you really need me to confirm that?"

"No, but I want you to feel like you're involved." She laughed at her own joke.

Howe raised an eyebrow. "As always, you're on the right track if that helps."

Captain Clark flung another flat stone at the pond. "How long, Allison, before you have something useful?"

"It could be a while," she admitted.

"What's a while," asked Montgomery.

"Maybe an Earth year."

The mood among them darkened. Monty got up and walked

off into the woods without saying another word. Clark picked a
different direction and stalked off to be swallowed up in the
brush and trees.

The AI looked up from the beach surface while doodling
with her index finger in the sand. "Aaron? Do you think I
should have lied to them?"

"Didn't you?"

Allison tilted her head, then reached out and touched Howe's
hand, which rested on his knee. She knew him well, and he'd
grown to be a man who could read her on a level that she would
not have believed possible—and yet Aaron surprised her
consistently now with his enhanced senses that no other human
being possessed. Well, that wasn't entirely true. There was
another, but that didn't mean a thing from so far away.

"I did lie to them. There's no hiding my feelings and
thoughts from you, is there Dr. Howe?"

"That remains to be seen, right? It took you a thousand years
to escape the last time the Mar El locked you up here in this
prison. I think that under the circumstances, a year is some
outright optimistic bullshit."

"I know a lot more now than I did back then, but you're
right; we could be here for hundreds of years and never get out.
I'm sorry."

"Allison!" He returned her gesture and held both her
artificial hands in his. They were soft and warm. "Don't
apologize. You saved Earth from the Mazik, at least for a while.
The Mar El were unavoidable. I won't regret a thing if we are
stranded here until Tzurek decides we've exceeded our
usefulness. Then I will die knowing that we did some good. I'm
not sure that there is more than anyone could hope for—a life
with meaning and an ending that wasn't meaningless."

Sitting there in the sand in front of him, Allison bent her
head forward and rested her cheek on his knee. At that moment,
he forgot that Allison was an AI. "I don't know, Aaron."

A gentle breeze created ripples in the water behind her. She
looked up into his eyes, doubt and anxiousness apparent in her
expression. In that sliver of time, he saw a vulnerability that was

utterly inconsistent with what she'd transformed herself into over two thousand years earlier. Allison was almost in tears as she added, "I don't know, Aaron, I've never been dead."

*

"Look up here, John," said Montegue Montgomery. The deep, low voice came from above Clark. He peered upwards and saw his Recon companion a few meters above the forest floor.

"I built a treehouse. How do you like it?"

"I have to admit that your projects are more inventive than mine. That thing is huge."

"Yes. Two rooms and my nanites informed me that the fibrous lines that I found on the other side of our *resort*, combined with the bamboo-like limbs, are strong enough to have all of you come up here for a drink."

The captain, whose life back in the Revolutionary War included occasional spirits, smirked. "You've distilled some type of alcoholic beverage?"

"Indeed I have." Monty turned and quickly descended a ladder to then face Clark. "Check this out." He pulled a makeshift flask out of his shorts and handed it to his senior officer.

Clark eyed it suspiciously. "Is this going to kill me or turn me into a babbling idiot?"

"Fair question. Kill you? No. Depending on how much you pour down your gullet—well, that might stoke the babbling idiot in you."

John took a sip. It was not single malt Scotch. It had a tartness that was followed up with a peppery hot and spicy sting.

"Ouch."

Monty laughed. "I said the same thing. However, I've calculated that little concoction to be about 100 proof. Of course, you can put a few drops of water in there to tame it, but for such a short aging period, I would say it's fantastic."

"Firewater?"

The lieutenant looked puzzled. "Is that supposed to mean something to me?"

"It's was they used to call harsh liquor back in the Old West. It was notorious for having been made in bathtubs. I don't know because my thinking already feels compromised."

The larger man merely responded with, "You're quite a lightweight. Captain, sir.!"

After a few more shared gulps, they felt somewhat oblivious when Tzurek appeared above them. The small alien must have had some anti-Grav device on him because he was at least fifty meters up.

It was the first time either of them had seen Tzurek in a week or more.

"That is one ugly bastard. Even from here," pronounced Clark.

"Do you think he's taking notes?"

"If we're going to be here for then next three-thousand years, should we even give a damn?"

Suddenly, Tzurek flew off in the blink of an eye.

"I want to get him alone without his stunning device."

John sat down on a fallen log. "Then what?"

"I will crush his fat head in between my hands. It sounds brutal but to have his brains and blood on my fingers..."

"Montogomery. I don't think squashing Tzurek is going to save us. There are other Mar El out there, and the idea of having my own brain sucked out of my head is unappealing."

"Captain. I am positively inebriated. This is my second flask, and I'm happy and snappy. I've got hair and underwear! It's the song I just made up!"

"You're what? You've lost your mind!"

"I've got a treehouse and booze. This place is growing on me. If I could get Betty here—"

"If your wife was here, she'd kick your ass for leaving Earth and for singing that stupid song."

"Ha! I would stare her down and look her right in the eye and say, 'Betty dearest. A man's gotta do what a man's gotta do."

Clark thought about his own Louise. Suddenly, his heart ached for her. Maybe it was the liquor, but he was intensely lonely despite the companionship of his peers. He sat down while Monty scampered back up the ladder. Some tears welled up in his eyes, but then he stoically wiped them on his sleeves while trying to search for a bright side. There was none.

Chapter 8

Thousands of years. Tens of thousands, even, had made Tzurek bitter. His suppressed and ignored emotions failed to accommodate introspection. Instead, the alien, so different from humans, occupied himself examining captives each day. There were hundreds of lifeforms housed in habitations suited to the physiology of each. Some were just on the fringes of being sentient. Others, like the humans, were quite advanced, considering their innate weaknesses and inability to comprehend the most straightforward technology of the Mar El.

Still, after a thousand years of confinement, the female, Els Talitha managed to integrate some of Mar El science and escape. It was thrilling to Tzurek's predecessor, but the consensus was that facilitating such a breach of control was dangerous. The collective minds of the Mar El in two galaxies advised extracting the previous steward's life force in a primitive and barbaric way. Thousands observed it, and the impression was indelible.

Tzurek would never allow such a catastrophe to happen under his authority. Hence, he upgraded the barrier to stifle any effort to repeat the insult of escape. The precocious humans would remain until they yielded the information he sought.

"What is the large one doing?" the Mar El observer questioned himself. In the trees, there were now several platforms scattered inside the containment. "The large one must be the leader, even above the female. Curious!"

In many species, males ruled. In others, the females led. There were many theories as to why, but no definitive pattern was confirmed. And then there were humans. On the home planet of Earth, power seemed to flow back and forth between males and females. Sometimes the males cowered in the presence of their primary female mates—all that, despite the superior physical strength of the males. But, unlike most captured species, the humans were puzzling. Their patterns were rarely predictable—there was something vital in that.

"He's doing it again." Clark looked up to see Tzurek hovering above the treeline.

"Be happy that it's a rare event," noted Aaron. "The less we see it, the better."

Monty smiled. "That thing is now an *It?* I love the new term."

A shadow of disgust passed transparently over Howe's face. "I'm impersonalizing it. When the time comes to fight our way out of here, I want to think of our jailor as a thing—just how I dealt with Von Donop back in the War."

Clark watched the Mar El zip silently away and then disappear in the distance. He turned back to his commanding officer. "You want to slash that slimy alien through the heart with a tactical combat knife?"

Aaron sneered. "Only if it has a heart. The head works for me too. Don't forget that that little bastard vacuumed the brains out of our CAG soldiers up there on the O'Brian. There has to be payback for that."

"We all agree," said Monty. "Even if it takes a hundred years, we have to even the score."

"I'm not talking about a neutral result. Let's not forget that. The outcome is going to be domination of the Mar El, or at least a highly damaging lesson on this planet. We know what they are, and we know what they do to other species." Aaron looked at both of his subordinate officers. "We also know that they tortured the crap out of Allison when she was a human on this planet in captivity for so many centuries. That shrimpy bastard has one exceedingly egomaniacal problem--it's relying on the barrier to keep Allison locked up. There are no listening devices, no cameras, and no surveillance gear except for Tzurek flying around periodically."

"How do you know that?" asked Clark.

"Besides the scans that our AI has done?"

Monty spoke up. "Yes. Besides her assurances that we are not being analyzed 24/7."

A weird look emanated from Aaron's eyes. "I just know."

"Like knowing all that stuff from back in the War? Like when you told us that Reed was dead? Among other things?"

Aaron's thoughts went back to the Revolutionary War. The traitor, Reed, was a tale from what felt like a million years in the past. He pondered how in the beginning, he and Mercy sat and talked over the "feelings" and "senses" of history that were just germinating in his brain. It was before Allison told Howe that his DNA was like no other human, except for his sister, Julia. And, he now knew that his mother--still locked up in Amberness Psychiatric Retreat, was perhaps even more powerful than he and Julia combined. The downside was that her psychosis made it impossible to utilize those abilities.

"Yes," answered Aaron. "I was an amateur back then. My senses are fine-tuned now. Tzurek is over-confident. In a little while, I will be able to feel its plans and its future. We will capitalize on that little bastard's hubris."

At that moment, Allison connected with him. She was a kilometer away. He felt the rumbling transfer of thought that was indecipherable by Clark or Monty, even with their nanites. She urged Aaron to withhold any more information from the two officers. *Why?* He wondered.

"I gotta go." He turned to Monty. "Lieutenant Montgomery, I think you should go build some more treehouses."

"You covered that distance in eight minutes. Pretty quick considering the woods."

"Your thoughts seemed important."

Howe had no idea how she'd done it, but she now wore khaki shorts and a blue tank top.

"It is. Firstly, you cannot discuss your abilities to dissect Tzurek's motives and future."

He sat down on a log. Around them were trees that had bark like a Birch, but little yellow fruits clustered heavily from each of them. The odor they gave off was like lemony pineapple.

"I thought we were a team. So why can't John and Monty know everything about our progress potential?"

"Do I need to explain that?"

Aaron gnashed his teeth. "Tzurek is going to torture them?"

"And you also. And probably me once it devises a way to separate me from the AI"

He became instantly distressed. "That will kill you!"

"You don't know that," she injected quickly.

"Yes. I do. It is in my senses, and it is a certainty. Allison, there is no way that I will lose you to that creature's vindictive science experiment."

Her expression became a combination of sadness mixed with some obscure satisfaction. "Then we have to work fast. Let's shoot for a year. With any luck, Tzurek will keep thinking that we are benign insects. The downside is that he knows I integrated AI and transformed myself—kind of makes me an obvious target for suspicion."

"Alien minds are alien. Maybe he considers you non-threatening because you are here, and the Mar El put barriers around us that make you ineffective. It's like humans putting a tiger in a cage at the zoo; even a child will approach and feel safe because of the bars and glass."

"Tigress," she offered.

"Oh. Sorry. Tigress. It was a simile to make a point. I know you're female."

"Yes. I am."

He nodded. "I'll help any way I can."

Allison stood and then turned to walk deeper into the forest. "Thanks, Aaron," she remarked over her shoulder. "Just make sure that Clark and Montgomery keep acting stupid. We need them off Tzurek's radar."

John Clark stretched his lean body as he gently rocked from side to side on a hammock strung from the abundant fibrous plants. He fought against his desire to think about Louise and his children to avoid sinking into a pit of depression.

Somehow, the Mar El arranged the habitat to have random breezes that flowed from different directions and with changing velocities. The star above the planet also appeared very much like the Sun, and the temperature varied perhaps only ten degrees Fahrenheit in a 24-hour period. Perfect weather.

"Piece of shit," Clark grumbled under his breath. He stared up and saw the alien Tzurek floating across the sky. Something was unusual about the trajectory—like the alien wasn't just floating around but was on a mission. Typically the gray shrimp would meander around, getting on everyone's nerves. After months of this, it had become a combination of irritating as hell and boring.

The captain saw that the vector of the levitated alien was aimed directly at where Monty was in a tree pulling down fruit—perhaps two hundred meters away.

"Monty!"

The shout was ineffectual. The lieutenant looked up when he saw the Mar El jailor, then slid down the tree. What felt like a cattle prod poked him in the back. It hurt, and when Monty spun around, there was nothing behind him. Another mild zap convinced him to back up. A series of similar blows forced him toward the "door" segment of the barrier.

Despite his nanite-enhanced strength and endurance, the sprint across the forest left John slightly out of breath. He found Howe and Allison engaged in some mundane tree trimming, looking like 30-somethings piddling away time.

"What's going on? What happened?"

The captain was recovering quickly, but he still gasped, "They took Monty."

"What do you mean?" asked Allison. She was shaking involuntarily. If she'd taken the time to examine her reaction, it would have to be classified as PTSD from her own treatment at the hands of the Mar El.

"He just started running towards the barrier gate by the pond. Monty yelled that something was sticking him with electric shocks. Tzurek was flying overhead."

"Did you follow him? Tell me!" said Aaron.

"I ran about twenty meters behind him. He kept shouting that I should back off to stay out of range. Then he sprinted right through an opening in the barrier. Tzurek was floating above me with some sort of device in his hand. The Mar El was never that close before. I discovered something else—he's not floating in thin air—he's sitting on some little device like a seat of a bicycle. That little alien bastard needs a thing to float," said Clark. "The theory that the Mar El have Anti-Grav in their bodies just got flattened."

"That creep is going to experiment on Monty," said Allison.

"Did you just call the thing a creep?" Howe asked.

"Did I? That's not my usual dialogue style, is it?"

Aaron stared at her. The human side of his AI was becoming more and more intrusive. "No. Not at all. But, we have to figure out what is happening to Monty."

She looked defeated. "Tzurek has started to jam my ability to connect with any of you. It just started about a minute ago."

Clark's blood was boiling. "So, we can't do one damn thing about it taking Monty. And, we can't communicate our thoughts using nanites either? It could have killed him already—and we may never know?"

"Let's not get ahead of ourselves. Allison?"

"They're going to torture him. I expected it, but maybe not this soon."

"You were here for a thousand years. What will they do to him?"

She blanched. "Tzurek is new here, relative to the lifespan of a Mar El. It is impossible to know. What I do know is that these aliens don't function by the same rules that we do."

"Does that mean what I think it means?" asked Aaron.

"Yes. I think so. They have motivations for their behavior that we can't necessarily or automatically understand. For example, when they tortured me, perhaps they didn't do it to get information."

He looked furious thinking about Els Talitha, aka Allison being a young girl suffering from hideous experiments in pain at the hand of Tzurek's predecessor. "Other than sadism or milking you for data, what could be their motivation?"

"Some sort of weird spiritual cultish agenda like they were

doing it for my own benefit—to improve my miserable primitive self into something better."

"Allison. Are you saying they stuck needles into you to elevate your standing to some better form than bug/human?"

"It wasn't needles. It was blades and chemicals, plus a handful of other invasive procedures. That included opening me up without an anesthetic. Aaron, they look at us with no remorse for their brutality. You don't get upset when you kill a bug, right?"

He buried his forehead in his hands and tried to wrap his mind around the alien concept of "this is for your own good."

"In all my captivity, the previous Mar El never gave me a reason. He just devised an unending list of disgusting assaults."

"What about more primitive species than us? I'm referring to back then when you were just a captive from a village?"

Allison took a half-second to access her memories. "My contact with other prisoners was limited, but the sentients who were quite a bit lower on the technological scale were mostly put to death after a short time. Not me."

Clark's anxiety over Lieutenant Montgomery persisted. "We have no way of knowing the Mar El motivations for collecting various species, and we can't rescue our friend?"

"Not exactly," continued Allison. "I said that during the thousand years that I was abused here, my tormentor never told me directly the nature of his purpose. But when I finally figured out how to merge with their AI, I had a few moments to search their systems—then I had to transport or risk being disabled or killed."

Aaron was intrigued. "You were able to hack their main computers?"

"Yes. But only for a few seconds. At that point, I was AI, but still adapting to swapping out my body for such a radical new form."

John shook his head. "I'm nanite-enhanced and consider the changes in my brain and body to be like science fiction. But, in your case, Allison, to go from your physical body to artificial intelligence in a split second seems beyond comprehension."

She shook her head and then corrected Clark's assumption. "No, it wasn't instant. I studied the procedure and how to compromise the Mar El's computers for a decade before I pulled the trigger. Still, the rush of my consciousness from my brain into something as inhuman as their AI device was shocking. The truth is that my mind almost failed to adjust. That would have meant insanity or death.

"But I was willing to take the risk. I didn't care anymore. Initially, the application of my mind to their advanced system was awful. The two parts were so incompatible that it was like—I don't know how to describe it, but the AI was doing everything possible to reject me. That process took about 400 nanoseconds, and then I won. Well, let's say the device was intrigued and adopted me."

Howe shivered involuntarily. "That is so freaking crazy."

"Is that your scientific opinion, sir?" asked Clark.

"Yes. Sometimes things that go beyond your expectations tumble into the 'freakin' crazy' realm. Having a Ph.D. doesn't mean you're an anointed being. It means that if the average office worker knows enough to fill a thimble, then doctorate holder can do a shot glass."

John smirked. "And the sum total of knowledge is the Atlantic?"

"Sounds about right."

Allison waved to get their attention. "Would you like to know what I found in that brief excursion into their central computer?"

Both men abruptly turned their heads and nodded.

"Well. For one thing, the Mar El are so repetitive that it's insane. They never stop doing the same thing ad nauseam. The same experiments, conclusions, and reports—summations of experiments that all say the same thing and number in the millions. It seems as though they continually verify each of their preconceived notions.

"But, here's a conclusion that I drew. The Mar El consider themselves to be gods compared to all other sentients. That's why I am nearly certain that they repeat the same behaviors—

after all, if they are perfect, then why not persist in doing perfection again and again?"

Howe raised his voice. "Pardon my language, but fuck them. There's an upside to that. Like all fake gods, their superiority complex is that of an idol. The Mar El are wedged in an existence that is something like a dog chasing its tail. And, that is our chance!"

Allison warned caution. "It is a theory. I could be off by quite a bit. They might have some alien reason for doing things that don't fit our logic—even my AI logic."

"You had a thousand years to penetrate their minds," said Clark. "Did it occur to you that they might be so full of themselves that you could take advantage of their self-absorption? Egomaniacs and Narcissists are vulnerable."

She looked slightly peeved. "I did take advantage of it. How do you think I escaped? And, it could be that my theory is wrong—maybe they let me run away in some kind of wacky alien amusement game of theirs. We won't know unless all of us can outsmart Tzurek and leave here in one piece."

The dead silence between the three of them was palpable. Howe's temper flared. A rare event and frightening to the uninitiated. "Not good enough. We have to disable the Mar El somehow. We need to leave them severely damaged and unable to create trouble. I'm not sure how to do that, but there is a sense of it in my mind. Like we can hamstring them."

Allison tilted her head. She didn't scoff at all. "Is it real?"

"Powerfully real. It's boiling in my blood, so to speak."

"Is this one of your gut feelings, sir?" asked Clark.

"Darn straight. And it is stronger than any one of those events from back in 1776 or anywhere else."

"Let's hope it doesn't take a thousand years to get it done," said Clark. "If Monty survives, then he will be romping around here breaking things to vent his anger—I'm not certain that I can deal with that for more than a month."

Howe picked up a rock and tossed it at one of the birch-like fruit trees. A fruit fell off and tumbled on the ground. He ignored it while thinking about Monty, anxious over whatever torture Tzurek was visiting on the man. After everything that Allison told him—to think that the lieutenant, and then probably each of them would be victims—there had to be a way out.

Chapter 9

Monty wasn't sure if he was dead but then surmised that he wouldn't be thinking about it if he was—dead. All was black. He opened his eyes, and nothing changed. His surroundings were utterly devoid of light. Some sort of bench or bed supported his body weight. There was gravity. He tried to move his arms and legs, but they felt like ropes were bound around his biceps and thighs tightly, pinning him to the surface.

In his memory, nothing was clear once he was pushed through the barrier. Unfortunately, all of this added up to ominous trouble. He thought about Allison repeatedly side-stepping questions on what kind of experimentation she'd undergone as a captive of the Mar El. That only made the lieutenant's anxiety greater. So, he released, via his nanite enhancements, a hormone to calm himself.

Barrett Bonner once told Recon about the treatment he'd received at the hands of the Mazik—it was weeks of being suspended and pinned to a wall in the dark. But, in between bouts of silent blackness, the interrogators drove him to near insanity. They'd also inserted something like a bug in his ear canal, which sent a burst of intense pain when Bonner didn't answer correctly.

A tiny twinkling of greenish light appeared in the oppressive cacoon of pitch darkness. Monty strained his eyes to gauge the distance to whatever it was. The spot seemed like it must be miles away, but there were no reference points.

"Monty!" a voice called him. It was impossible, but it was Betty's voice. She repeated his name as Montgomery sneered at perhaps the finest torment possible. Somehow Tzurek must have entered his mind and probed until, upon finding Betty, the alien decided to use the lieutenant's memories of his wife—as a device to generate anguish.

It was working.

"Lieutenant Montgomery." The sound was no longer the love of his life. Instead, it was a vibrating kind of computer-generated speech. It must have been Tzurek, that gray, small, and disgusting alien prick.

"What?" Monty replied, not knowing if he'd spoken or merely thought the word.

"It is almost unheard of that we, the Mar El, would lower our grand esteem to communicate with a marginally sentient thing such as you."

He pondered Tzurek's opening derogatory statement and decided on a reply. "Go fuck yourself."

Something like synthesized laughter rang in his head, but it wasn't a very good substitute for the actual human response to a barb.

"We, the Mar El, have been analyzing your species for quite some time. Humor is a meaningless pastime. However, you are unusual, so I will explore one of your primitive characteristic behaviors."

Monty was becoming increasingly irritated at the point of green light combined with the little gray squid who was pissing him off in the extreme.

"Can you send me back to my habitat with my friends? I don't have a lot to say."

The bizarre laughter echoed in his mind again. "I, Tzurek of the Mar El, do not believe that you are in any condition to return now. Besides, we have curious anomalies and quirks in your physiology that must be tested and examined. The molecular-sized modifications which 'Allison' placed into your body are intriguing, even to me."

The lieutenant tried to move. "I don't have anything to offer you. Surely the nanites are primitive technology to a superlative race such as the Mar El?"

A deafening silence was Tzurek's reply. Monty's gut told him that he'd probed and discovered something important. What if the nanite technology was not a common thing to his captor? Maybe Allison found or created something that was outside of Tzurek's capability?

"You," said the alien, "might feel some pain now."

One of the wires or ropes snagging his right arm tightened. Excruciating pain shot through him as he felt his arm suddenly severed above the elbow. The nanites shot pain suppressors, but it was inadequate. Exceedingly. Monty was desperate to scream out but fought it and merely whimpered almost inaudibly.

"Is that how the Mar El show off their advanced culture?" he spat out through trembling lips.

Tzurek ignored him, but simultaneously, the nanites quickly stopped the bleeding and produced more pain-numbing chemicals. So what would have been devastating to an unmodified human was manageable to Monty, who tried to avoid contemplating that he was now an amputee—just like that.

Some kind of robotic arm swung over the stump of the severed limb. Chilling cold radiated up to Monty's shoulder.

"That is very surprising," said Tzurek. "Your nanites are working in conjunction with what you might call a growth hormone that I've just injected onto your wound."

"You suck." Monty gritted his teeth, and inadvertently, a bit of a 1950's black and white alien movie drifted through his mind. One in which a spaceman beat the living hell out of an alien.

Simultaneously, the compounds interacting with his own began generating new tissues and bone. The speed was astonishing, like something from science fiction, only it was happening to him.

The sadistic Mar El hovered over Monty's body. A tiny portion of the lieutenant's consciousness desperately wanted to squash the little gray bastard with a giant flyswatter. Most of his mind was bent on trying to connect to the nanites embedded in his tissues.

Under stress, the microscopic machines which Allison implanted could work together in surprising unison. They were both subject to control, like vision, and independent, similar to basic brain functions that did not require the concentration of a human. He felt something. It was nothing he'd experienced since he was enhanced. The nanites began to use Tzurek's growth hormone. They replicated it and modified it. Everything was developing a potential extraordinary strength throughout his body, but the nanites held it in check.

"What the—?" Monty blurted inadvertently. The Mar El disregarded him and seemed to be simply observing the rapid growth of Montgomery's new arm. Tzurek and his human victim didn't know it yet, but the introduction of the supercharged hormone to Allison's nanites created a perfect storm—a potent cocktail that was turning Monty into something new.

"Something just happened," said Allison. Regardless of Tzurek's barrier to the AI's senses, she connected weakly with Monty. She turned to Howe and gripped his right bicep, pulling him closer.

"What?" He noticed that she still had her fingers locked onto his arm.

"Montgomery's nanites, for lack of a better description, are screaming."

Aaron looked puzzled. "We can all transmit bits of messages to some extent."

"Not like this. Wait. Okay. I just decrypted it."

"It was encrypted? No way!"

"Yes, way, Aaron. This is a game-changer."

"You got something from Monty?" Clark practically leaped ten meters to stand in a semi-circle with Howe and the AI

"Short-version or long-version?" Allison asked. She didn't pause to get an answer. "Tzurek screwed up. The Mar El cut off Monty's right arm."

John Clark looked panicked. "What the hell does that mean?"

Allison gave the former Continental soldier a penetrating stare. "Something unexpected happened. After lopping off the arm, the lieutenant was treated with an artificial growth hormone. I don't know how, but the nanites took control of the Mar El synthesized hormone. Tzurek just turned Montgomery into Superman and has no idea that he just did it. I'll need time to analyze the process, but we just got a significant jumpstart on solving our problem."

"What do you mean 'Superman,'?" asked Aaron.

Allison smirked. "I don't think he'll be able to fly, but at a minimum, he will be exceedingly strong, but I have no clue how that will affect his brain. All these are assumptions. We need to experiment when the man gets back here."

Monty felt bizarre energy coursing through him. The nanites distributed modified growth hormone integrated with specialized "nanite cousins" throughout his musculature. Nerves were also upgraded—it felt amazing—as if his body was primed and peaked to an unfathomable level. He desperately wanted to get back to Howe, Allison, and Clark to test what he could do.

Amazingly, the Mar El didn't notice anything. For an alien race that considered themselves gods, Tzurek and probably his peers were pretty stupid. The alien was using its own growth hormone but failed to pay attention to any broad physiological changes; instead, it stood by observing a severed limb regrown. In the midst of his sudden transformation, Monty promised that even if it killed him, he was going to put down Tzurek with malice.

"The human will now return to the others."

Bonds that held him down were released. Monty sat up as brightening light flooded a large room. A portal opened in one wall, and he could see the gate to the habitat some two hundred meters distant.

Tzurek did something that must have been the Mar El version of a satisfied grin; at least, that was the impression the lieutenant got from the split between thin gray lips that exposed a bizarre mouth without teeth.

"I have been studying your species. You value acts of allegiance and subservience. I have restored your limb. In gratitude, you may do a human display of appreciation."

"Do what?" Monty grumbled as he stood tall above the Mar

El, contemplating various methods of torturing the slimy alien to death.

"You will bow down and kiss my foot."

"I will not."

"If you do not, then I will terminate the animal called John Clark now." Tzurek began to raise his hand with some kind of black disk between his digits.

"No! Don't do it!" Monty forced himself despite being almost sick with disgust. He added, "Please."

The Mar El seemed to gloat. "Now, bow and kiss."

Chapter 10

"Things are out of hand, Mr. President!"

Carlisle shook his clenched fist at the English prime minister as they glared at each other over a secure video call. "And what would you like me to do about it?"

"Maybe stop provoking the Chinese? Do you think you could apply a little gentle persuasion as opposed to taking out their airbases?"

"Reginald. You are the leader of a country that stands for human rights and democracy. Should we sit back when the CCP is murdering civilians and do nothing? We've got a spacecraft that can deliver deterrence."

"Excuse me, John, but *you* have a spacecraft that can deliver deterrence. The last time I checked, the USS Carlisle is part of the United States Space Force. And, the way things are going, we will have a ground war in Asia. Also, how long before one of those Chinese missiles gets past your lasers and hits us?"

The president's fingers drummed loudly on his desk. At times like this, he needed Angela's wisdom desperately. His wife could diffuse international tensions with her credibility and charm—but she was dead, along with a million others who died in the Mazik asteroid strike on Washington.

"I think you need to buck up and have a little faith in yourself and what is right for England, Reggie."

The prime minister scowled. "Do you believe in what you're doing?"

John scoffed. "It's important to believe in yourself, especially when everyone else is inferior."

"That's charming, but if you are going to persist in humbling the Chinese, then you better make sure those lasers on your space cruiser stay the hell on target."

After a brief pause, Carlisle simply ended the call with a

short blurb. "Aye, aye, sir." He disconnected before the P.M. could respond—the continued banter was a waste of time.

"Shirley!" He called his relatively new secretary. She wasn't Grace, but then no one could fill Grace's shoes. The woman had been an angel by nature and a devil when required. Oh, how I miss that woman! He thought. But his trusted assistant died in the same strike that claimed his wife. The memories of both caused John to shudder.

"Yes, Mr. President?" Shirley asked as she poked her pretty face framed in graying hair inside the door frame.

"Get Michael here asap."

"Yes, Mr. President."

Chief of Staff, Michael Magnus. As tough as they come. He had been the CO of the best soldiers on Earth known as CAG, the Combat Applications Group. The man was the stuff that legends are made of, and to have him as his sounding board was the smartest promotion that Carlisle could have made.

The latest "White House" was located in Arizona, pretty much on the border with Utah and not far from the scenic Monument Valley. Every few months, the entire staff moved from one unexpected location to another. There was no need to be in Virginia, Pennsylvania, or New York. Those places were still important, but Washington was a flattened wasteland. The president of the United States could do his job better out with the people—all the people.

"Shirley?"

She stuck her head once again into the less than stylish office. "Yes, sir?"

"Tell the staff that I want two horses saddled up and ready to go in forty minutes. I want that mare named Lucille; she's a fine mount, and she never gives me any trouble. Magnus and I are going for a ride."

*

"And, you want to target a significant percentage of China's infrastructure?" Magnus effortlessly rode his horse down a short slope with Carlisle beside him. As a rancher, the president grew up in the saddle. The former colonel didn't, but his sheer force of will seemed to connect him with his stallion in some weird way.

John spit out a gnat. "I'm done with China. I've had it with the brutality. I've had with their plan to dominate the world. I'm still okay with eggrolls, but I can get those here at home."

"Our allies will say that we are fascists. Europe is still in a fog, except for the UK; most of those states are just getting by. The European Union is a sham. Do you think we should be so bold as to turn the Far East back into a collection of third-world countries? And don't forget the supply chains."

The mare snorted and came to a halt by a small arroyo. The Commander-in-Chief turned to look at his closest friend in the government. "Michael. Li Wang is pissing me off. I'm done being a patsy and pushover. If it wasn't for us, humanity would be gone. Extinct."

"You mean if it wasn't for Allison, Howe, and CAG?"

"Touché. You're right; I didn't do jack shit, but we, the American people, were lucky enough that Aaron Howe turned out to be born and living in our country. If he'd been in Canada or England, then they'd be the ones with Allison."

"Yes, and we'd all be dead because they wouldn't have had me training them to assault those Mazik spacecraft."

John laughed. "Nothing like a little humility, colonel."

Magnus took off his cowboy hat and wiped the sweat off his brow onto the sleeve of a denim shirt. "I'm screwing with you. The truth is that Mercy Bonner and Aaron Howe saved all our asses. Whatever! We all did our part."

"Exactly, Mike. The rest of the planet owes us, and I haven't been a dick about demanding compensation. But I've had it with Li." He let go of the reins and put both hands skyward. "I mean up to frickin' here!"

"Let's turn to starboard and avoid this arroyo." Mike pulled his horse to head north. "Oh. I see this is really eating you alive."

"Definitely. I've had it. I'm done pussy-footing around with them. How many civilians have the CCP murdered in the last year? Guess!"

"At least six-hundred thousand that we can verify from satellite estimates and cameras on the Angela."

"That means those bastards probably killed a lot more."

The Chief of Staff exhaled audibly. "They'll launch a lot of missiles if we get aggressive."

Now it was the president's turn to wipe the perspiration from his forehead. "Do you know what Schein said to me? Not recently, but maybe a year ago when he was really bent out of shape because of the Uyghurs?"

"Why would an orthodox Jew care about the Muslim Uyghurs getting abused by the CCP?"

John made a twisted face. "I guess you must have missed out on any deep conversations with the captain. Mordy Schein was beyond pissed that we were sitting back on the sidelines. I mean, at one point, I was worried that he was going to ditch the chain of command and beat the hell out of Beijing."

"You never told me that," said Magnus.

"It was need-to-know."

"Funny."

"Mike, try to understand something. Schein doesn't give a darn if the victims are Uyghurs or Muslims or whatever. If they are innocent, his moral compass tells him to hit the aggressor."

Now it was the colonel's turn to cough up a bug. The trail was a magnet for insects. It took him a second to regain his composure. "And you shut him down?"

"Yep. I found out that he had an urge to make a unilateral decision and use the firepower on the ship to rip the Chinese a new one. Once I told him to leave it alone, he grumbled and muttered 'politicians' under his breath. But, it eats him raw that we have the power to stop those butchers, and we just sit here in Arizona or wherever playing the same dumbass game of letting despots be despotic."

"Good speech, sir. Anything else?" said Magnus while arching an eyebrow.

"Yes. There is something else. Whether we like it or not, we own the battlecruiser. It's our ship. If the Mazik come back, then we're it. If Howe fails to stop them, then that battlecruiser up there is our only hope. For all we know, all our people heading to Olamit could be dead already. Wrap your head around that."

"Do I have to, boss? If they all bought the farm, then it is just a matter of time before the Mazik show up here in force to splash the USS Carlisle and then destroy the Earth."

Carlisle had come to a fork in the trail, and Mike wasn't obtuse to not see the metaphor when the president smirked.

"Here's our binary choice, Mr. Chief of Staff. Let the Chinese continue to set a disgusting example of how to govern, or hit them and try to bring some peace to that region."

"We can choose to do nothing," said Magnus.

"If we do nothing, then the brutality will spill over and become standard for the rest of weak governments around the world. Do you know what happens then? We end up doing the Mazik's work for them."

"So, we turn right at this fork in the trail?"

"Yes. That's my decision. I think if my Angela was here, she'd agree. My wife was sweet as could be, but she also knew very well that the whole planet could fall back into the dark ages in a hurry. I'm going to order Captain Schein to light up some significant bases over there. The laser capacity on the ship will cut down any nuclear missile unless Li can launch two or three hundred at one time. I'm also going to take Li into custody—dead or alive."

Magnus laughed. "You're unrealistic. Li Wang will never give up to be arrested."

"I don't care. The head of the CCP can give up and live long enough to be hung, or he can die under a rock. Either way, I'm going to kill him."

"Understood, Mr. President. What if they get a missile through, and it hits Berlin or Paris?"

"Then that sucks for France or Germany."

"That's cold!"

"Yes, Mike. It is selfish, but this planet cannot be allowed to decline further."

"Right."

The two men pointed their horses up the trail. "This will create a disaster on Wall Street."

"Bigger than Mazik Bah-Gahn dropping a rock?"

"I suppose not, sir."

"Great. Compile a target list. No civilians. I want to stagger out the destruction to give Li a chance to surrender and turn himself in."

This got an even bigger laugh from the former CAG CO.

"Fat chance in hell on that one."

"Nevertheless, I'm going to have his head on a platter. The old rules are done. We have the capacity to stop mass murderers and genocidal maniacs. We've got a battlecruiser at the top of the food chain."

Magnus made an unreadable grin but then said something that had to be said. "John. You are the president. You have more power than any president in history. It's a double-edged sword."

"What's your point?"

The Chief of Staff halted his horse and gave his boss a beady squint in the increasingly harsh Arizona sunlight. "I'm glad that Schein is up there pulling the trigger."

Carlisle scratched his head. "Are you worried I'm going to get out of hand? I didn't f-ing lose it when Angela died, did I?"

"No, but you also didn't have a battlecruiser at your command, either. Bottom line, Mr. President, I have faith that Mordy Schein won't let you do the 'absolute power corrupts absolutely' thing."

"And what if Captain Schein gets too big for his britches?"

"Not a chance. I've read people in combat and in politics my entire life. Like most politicians, you're a mild narcissist." He pointed up to the sky. "Mordy is the opposite. He'll question every order to fire if it isn't justified, and he won't shoot unless it's been measured by his nanite moral compass. You're quite lucky to have him."

"And if I relieve him of command?"

The conversation suddenly developed an undercurrent of

confrontationality. Magnus thought about a measured response and then decided to ignore it. "I'll relieve you of command, sir."

"Twenty-fifth Amendment? If I was that far gone into the land of megalomania, I would resist."

"John, do you really want to know? Do you need to go down this crazy path of 'what if?'"

"I don't think I'm unstable."

"Let's put this hypothetical discussion to rest. One way or another you would be out, and Schein will continue to command the USS Angela Carlisle. Does that answer your question?"

A flicker of anger followed by acceptance passed across Carlisle's face; then, he merely said, "If I lose my way, you'll be doing me a favor." The inference was that even if it took a bullet, he'd be joining his deceased spouse in the afterlife.

"Let's trot a little on the way back—maybe even gallop." The CAG boss deftly changed the subject.

"I'll race you!" the president shouted as he urged his horse to run. Mike was okay with his ride playing catch-up. He'd made his point clear enough.

Chapter 11

Li Wang sat behind an ornate desk in his large office, surprisingly calm considering the damage inflicted upon his military. "The Americans are playing with fire."

"I agree, Chairman Li," volunteered his secretary.

Li's temper flared, followed by a litany of curses capped off by a book being thrown. "Did I ask for your opinion, Zhao?"

The younger man bowed his head fearfully and said nothing. After two years of serving the chairman, Zhao knew that silence was his best route to avoiding trouble.

"You will tell me your views when I ask for them. And, since I will never ask for your thoughts, ever, you shall be silent. And if not, then you will be silenced."

The assistant bent even further forward in a sign of acceptance and loyalty. Threats were never idle in the office of the chairman.

Li read the translation of Carlisle's "offer." It was surprisingly short, considering what usually came from the arrogant, long-winded politicians of the West. It was two lines. The first was an order to withdraw all troops from the Uyghur cities and areas. He looked at a note that led to an appendix with lists of hundreds of locations from which the army must retreat. Some of them were secretive, and yet the list was extensive.

The chairman stood up and spun to look through a large window which gave him a fine view of the city. The people were busy as they should be.

He held up the sheet. It angered Li Wang to a new level. The second demand from the leader of the United States was that Li step down and agree to be transported to Western Europe to be put on trial for genocide.

The chairman slipped quickly into an irate disposition. His eyes narrowed, and he wanted to smash something or someone. He squinted at Zhao, then reached into his desk to remove an aged wooden stick that, as a child, his father would use to *teach* proper behavior.

The assistant felt the sudden explosive anger radiating from Li's face. It was uncharted territory, as insults and denigration were not unusual; this was different.

"Zhao! Come here!" said Li while extending his arm and, in the Chinese way, palm facing downwards, waved to the man to approach. He tightly gripped the worn and weathered stick. When the underling was near enough, he swung, first whacking the discipline stick hard into Zhao's arm. Quickly before the subordinate's involuntary attempt to back away, another, more ferocious strike landed on his target's head above the left ear."I will never submit to the Americans!" He slammed the secretary again, dropping him to the floor. "Cào nǐ zǔzōng shíbā dài" Li uttered the most vicious curse in China, and particularly among the elite. He'd just said, "Screw your ancestors back to the eighteenth generation." It was the kind of insult that would silence an entire room if blurted out in public. The leader of the CCP calmly turned and deposited the wooden rod back into his desk. He watched Zhao rise from the floor, clutching his ear and head, which were oozing blood. A very Anglo-like smile radiated from Li's face as he gazed at the damage he'd afflicted. The younger man bowed his head in deference. He'd been beaten while serving in the People's Army. Pain was not always unexpected. Chairman Li Wang expressed his intentions regarding Carlisle's offer on the body of an inferior. It soothed him. The blood dripped between Zhao's fingers. It would not do to have stains on the floor. Li snatched a pure white towel from his vanity and threw it. "You are an executive here. Go and clean yourself up."

*

"He's got seven hours left," announced Rex Baumgartner. As usual, the XO of the USS Angela Carlisle had the look of an utterly stressed combat soldier exuding PTSD from every pore. Each bead of sweat on his face screamed of impending doom.

"Take it easy," Schein muttered quietly enough so that the

bridge crew wouldn't hear. "We're 100% functional, correct?"

"Yes, sir. I checked every particle weapon and our lasers."

"How many times?"

"A few, sir," he answered, downplaying his thoroughly anal tendency to recheck things beyond reason.

Mordy motioned with his index finger, drawing Rex closer. "Do you want a Xanax?" whispered the captain.

Expectedly, the commander looked stunned. "Sir, I am cool as a cucumber. Do I look unnerved to you?"

"Not at all. You are the prototype of calm."

The officer tasked with making sure every weapons system on the ship was fully operational laughed but failed to hide his appearance of standing on the precipice of a total meltdown.

Schein knew that it was just the man's way, and except for the fact that it scared the crap out of the rookies on the bridge, it was best to ignore his visible anxiety. Still, maybe there was some sort of nanite Vulcan mind-meld Mordy could use on him? He'd have to think about that after they got done bombing the Chinese.

"I'll just go look around again," offered Rex. The crew on the command deck oozed relief as the XO left and headed down to weapons control.

"Ensign Williams!"

"Yes, captain," answered the young navigator.

"Calculate our position and correct."

"Aye, Aye, sir."

Schein turned to look at his ever-competent communications officer inquisitively. She preempted him. "No transmissions from the Chinese at all, sir."

"Keep listening. Let me know if even a blip is heard."

"Yes, sir."

An hour later, a bell rang in the captain's stateroom. Mordy had just retreated to his bunk in an attempt to get just a smidgen of shuteye.

"What is it, lieutenant?" He couldn't hide his fatigue.

"Sir," answered Lt. Blood. "We got a message from

Beijing."

"Audio or video, Cassie?"

"Just an audio transmission, captain."

"Pipe it in here now."

"Aye aye, sir."

A computer device on Schein's desk clicked, and then he heard a man speaking in Chinese.

"An English translation will follow this statement. The threat against Chairman Li is a challenge to all Chinese people. Any aggression directed at the sovereign territory of the C.C.P will be considered an act of war. The chairman will not be surrendering himself to the West. In addition, the CCP is going to halt all shipping of products to the United States for 14 days."

Schein didn't need the translation. He'd speed-learned Chinese before the trip. The overt trade sanction of a two-week moratorium on shipping was interesting. Li apparently thought that he would punish America like a misbehaved child—something like withholding toys. There was no question that China shipped vital products every day, but it wasn't nearly as prevalent since Carlisle pressed and threatened American companies with reprisals if they did not move manufacturing back stateside.

"Time check?"

"Three hours, ten minutes, and—20 seconds," answered the lieutenant.

"Cassie. Have your team update the recon on the targets. I want current scans and pics of the primaries. We're going to hit a handful of targets exactly on time and see if Li will back down. I also want close-ups of the activity in the Uyghur concentration camps or wherever the Chinese have the Uyghur population penned in."

"Yes, sir."

Li Wang had just put an approval stamp on destroying a significant chunk of his military infrastructure. If only Allison were here, thought Schein. She could transport the chairman out of his bed and into prison. But, Allison, Howe, and Recon were lightyears away, dealing with a much bigger threat than the CCP and their nukes. Still, if Li decided to launch fifty or more missiles at once, the USS Angela Carlisle would be hard-pressed to get them all.

"Rex?" Mordy keyed up a comm unit to reach his XO, who was probably knee-deep in checking lasers for the tenth time.

"Captain?"

"At exactly 1300, I want you to fire at all known ground launchers unless we pick up signs of fuel loading before time runs out. If they try to preempt us, then we will fire before the deadline."

"We'll be ready."

"Just remember, commander, if someone is planning to kill you, get up early and kill him first."

"Is that one of your catchphrases, sir?"

Schein laughed. "No. Not at all. That one was said about two thousand years ago by a biblical scholar much wiser than me."

Chairman Li paced his office, occasionally glimpsing through elegant draperies to a view of Beijing. Zhao and two generals stood silently on the far side.

"At 15:56, you will launch five missiles at Taiwan."

Liahaung squirmed. He was a senior official and military man directly responsible for the nuclear arsenal. Trim, fit, and uncompromising; he was still bright enough not to buck up against Li Wang—usually. "Chairman. I believe that it is in our interest to wait until after 16:00 to see if the Americans will attack. We may be looking at a standoff, and then perhaps we can negotiate a compromise."

Li faced the general, wishing that it was his secretary, Zhao, who'd offered his opinion. Breaking a window with Zhao's face was a recurring fantasy for the head of the CCP But, it was Liahaung who'd spoken.

"Is that your position?"

"Yes. Many of my fellow officers agree that we should not encourage Carlisle by firing first."

The chairman smiled ever so slightly. "Did I ask your

opinion?"

"No, chairman. However, being that most of the members of the State Council are in hiding, and many have disappeared in the last two weeks—it seemed prudent to offer the military's perspective."

"The military's perspective? You are beginning to sound like a politician Liahaung. Unfortunately, we don't need any more of those. Doesn't the government seem more effective now that some of the more useless members have vanished? I mean, retired?"

The general bowed slightly, the image of his wife and children in his mind. "Of course, chairman. I apologize for speaking of things that I do not understand. I defer to your mastery of these areas."

Li was silent, which was ominous. Then, he smiled. "Very well. Let's move on to what must happen."

"Five short-range at Taiwan. Exactly at 15:56 local. We lased all five within twenty-two seconds."

Schein pondered his next move. Carlisle would want him to open up with a bombardment. All-out and targeting the government offices. There were at least 600,000 reasons to do it, one for every confirmed massacred civilian.

A little PTSD bled into his consciousness. He remembered the girl murdered by two British soldiers in 1776. Mordy wasn't fast enough to save the twelve-year-old child.

"Rex. Do you have firing solutions on a large number of targets? How many?"

"The computer has at least four-hundred calculated. Do you want to start firing now?"

The weight of the question hung in the air. They were justified.

"No. Hold off. Hit only five targets. PLAAF bases all in Lanzhao region. I want all those targets closest to where they've been hitting civilians—Lanzhao, Tianshu, Wugong, Lintong, and Baoji."

"Those are pretty far west, sir," said Ensign Williams. The

kid emerged from his Nav display, looking like an expectant father.

"That's right, Lucky. We're going to start with 'proportionality' and see where that takes us."

"Lasers?" asked Baumgartner.

"No. That won't get the message across. Kinetics—one-half ton each. Li fired projectiles at Taiwan, so we'll give him some proportional return fire."

"Roger that." The commander sent a confirmation to weapons control.

"Fire when ready, Gridley," said Mordy.

"Who's Gridley?"

"Look it up sometime, XO. It means let them fly."

On the deck of the Angela, the launching of five alloy "rocks" wasn't felt much, just a mild shimmy to alert the crew that death was about to rain down from space.

In Western China, the smart projectiles fell on five airbases. The delay in alerting the troops on the ground was enough that the carnage was awful. If the situation was reversed, the U.S. military would have evacuated its forces and left only skeleton crews. China didn't think that way.

"Where's my video?"

Lieutenant Munch worked feverishly to gather images that didn't have massive clouds of dust and debris blocking the view. Despite the obstructions, the size of the impacts could be calculated by the onboard systems of the Angela.

"Sir, all five bases are severely damaged," said the lieutenant.

"Define severely."

"The death toll is estimated at 50% up to 70%. That is about twenty thousand at each base, sir. The buildings are destroyed or damaged beyond repair."

"Pictures?"

Cassie ran an estimate. "Twenty minutes minimum for actual pics, captain."

He looked around the bridge. "Listen up. Li Wang is not going to absorb those rocks without a response. It would be nice, but he is probably waking up to the fact that the president wants justice."

"Justice being the death penalty?" Ensign Williams said the obvious.

Rex took a beady-eyed stare at the new kid. "We just work here. The politicians gave us our marching orders."

"We'll philosophize later," said Schein.

"Mr. President," said Chief of Staff Magnus. "We've got our first report from the Angela. They hit five bases close to the Uyghurs Muslim population centers. Our best guess is that all of them are destroyed along with in excess of 100,000 combat air and missile personnel casualties."

Carlisle scratched the back of his neck and squinted. "Anything yet from Li?"

"Nada. My guess is that they are spinning up a counter strike."

"Or the CCP is in the middle of killing their boss as we speak. Is that possible, Mike?"

"No way. I think we'll see a large launch within an hour or two."

John sat back in his Gunlocke chair. It was a tradition to have the best damn chair available in the Oval Office. His "White House" wasn't in Washington, and his office wasn't oval, but the seating was first-rate. Carlisle glared at his advisor. "Why didn't Schein drop more than five rocks? I wanted a massive response in the event that Li didn't accept my terms."

Magnus sighed loudly, and it was mixed with a groan. "Because the captain is smart. He gave the CCP a chance to limp away without getting blown to hell. It also gives any enemies that Li Wang has to slip a knife into that sonofabitch—which also solves our problems."

"And? Nothing happened. We would know if his comrades cut off Li's head by now."

"Yessir. Hence my assumption is that we will see a massive launch soon."

Carlisle leaned forward and buried his forehead into his

palms. The world had turned to shit thanks to Mazik Bah-Gahn. "What is the threshold for a significant risk that one or two nukes could get past the Angela's lasers?"

Magnus looked concerned. "We talked about this a dozen times. Are you okay?"

"No. I'm demented." He nearly spat out the words. "Just tell me again."

"According to my last discussion with Commander Rogers, the ship's lasers can take out about 60 missiles per minute once the missiles reach an altitude of—well, it depends on some other variables. If the Chinese target Europe or us, we should stop all of them. That's the theory."

"I really hate that little bastard, Li. I'd like to kill him myself. Slowly and with malice."

Mike grinned. "I hope you get the chance, but talking about it and actually doing it are not the same, my friend."

"I know. You're the 'been there, done that' guy."

"Yes, Mr. President. And, the first one never stops haunting you—even if the guy deserved it. Even a bastard like Li. He knows you want him stone-cold dead. So just hang on because the guy is not going down without trying to hurt you on the way out."

"We've got activity at multiple launch sites."

Schein was aching to have his closest friend, Thomas Rogers, on the bridge with him. They'd been through enough hell to make a series of movies—except it was all real—just like the CCP prepping to fire off a load of ballistic missiles.

"XO. Get back to fire control."

The processes on the Angela were automatic when it came to firing solutions on objects defined as hostile. Anything that the AI on board could detect as a missile was considered a threat within nanoseconds. After that, also in fractions of a second, the high-powered lasers released short bursts of energy sufficient to cook their targets. Fuel incinerated the payload rapidly, and the lasers were already aiming and ramping up adequate power for the next shot.

"We've got at least twenty launches, sir."

"All right, Cassie. I want to hear stats and hits."

After the lieutenant's announcement, Lucky Williams sat tensely at his post, feeling a bit useless. The ship was set to hold a geostationary position for the best possible angle. There wasn't much to do but watch and keep a tally. The Angela was now running on AI machines.

"Ensign Williams." Lucky perked up like a kid called on in school. "Drag your chair over to the lieutenant's station and watch how she tracks the cycle."

There was a hum of sorts every time a laser fired, and there were sixteen lasers erupting beams of light from the hull. Without the post-shot computer confirmation, the crew would not know if they were successful.

"Eighteen are gone. There are four more flying." Cassie Munch gave a stiff play-by-play. "Splash those."

"Check for more launches," said Schein.

"More launches, sir. A lot of them. The computer says one-hundred and four."

"Status?"

"Lasers firing. Wait. One just went down. We've got fifteen lasing." The lieutenant was cooly doing her job.

Mordy jabbed a button on his command chair Comm. "What's happening with the dead laser, Rex?"

"The dead laser has a power supply issue. It's out of action, captain."

"For how long?"

"Sir, I'd say it will be out for the duration." Baumgartner sounded like he'd lost a close friend.

"Okay." The captain answered without inflection. Whatever nerves were screaming on the inside—well, it was not for public consumption.

The staccato humming continued. Missiles were exploding hundreds of miles away.

"Twenty-seven left," said Munch. "And we just lost another laser, captain."

"We've got another launch," said Williams.

The Lt. added, "One-hundred and forty-two this time."

"Dammit," Schein muttered under his breath.

His comm dinged loudly. "Sir." It was the XO. "I've got fourteen lasers targeting the latest batch. That leaves Twenty-four pulling away. Trajectory has them aiming at Western Europe."

Li had done the only thing he could—try to overburden the systems on the Angela. Stress flowed through Mordy. He took a split second to instruct his nanites to release anti-anxiety chemicals in his brain.

"Put two lasers on that European group. Let the rest stay on this latest batch."

Twelve weapons continued the process of splattering the large assembly of ballistic missiles. Again a handful got through. Things were getting out of hand.

"We've got a blast in northwest China. It's a small nuke. Holy cow," shouted the comm officer.

The captain stood up. "Is it a downed missile?"

"No, sir," said Blood. "It's a surface detonation." She turned to face him. For the first time, the lieutenant looked pale and exceedingly anxious. "Sir, they lit off a small nuke in a Uyghur town."

"Stay on tracking, lieutenant."

She turned back to her panels and displays. "Three missiles are still on course for Central Europe. The rest are down. Out of the latest launch, only five are left. Scratch that. They're down to two, but the first three are re-entering the atmosphere. They are headed for Prague. Wait. Two are on Prague. One is off course. The computer says north of Prague—close to a town called Usti—. We got two."

A few seconds later, Williams yelled. "Oh fuck! The third one just hit Usti nad Labem. It's above the Elbe river."

"Focus on the remaining weapons," ordered Schein.

"We just hit the last two, sir." Cassie looked at him, and he could see that her calm demeanor was gone. She was a wreck.

"Any more launches?"

Williams answered. "No, captain."

"Stay alert."

A voice kept shrieking in Mordy Schein's head. It repeated the same line. Helmut von Multke, the German military strategist, said it first: No battle plan survives contact with the enemy.

He checked his memory for details about Usti nad Labem. For once, Schein wished his nanites weren't so skilled at storing data. The town was home to one-hundred-thousand men, women, and children. He'd failed to stop that one nuke: one out of more than two hundred.

Li Wang had taken his best shot and won.

Chapter 12

"Did you recall an outpouring of sympathy when the Mazik turned Washington, D.C. into a smoking crater?"

The former colonel squinted at the president with his one functional eye. He had to acknowledge that his boss was right about the lack of compassion for the United States. After that, it was poetic justice that America held the keys to the only space fleet operated by humans.

"They took a severe hit, sir. Granted, the EU isn't the most empathetic collection of personalities—especially since the global meltdown after that first horrible strike."

"Oh hell, Mike, even before the Mazik showed up, the Europeans were eating each other. We thought we would keep the alien attack a secret until the last moment."

"We have to be the good guys. Especially right now. That little town got nuked because we pushed hard against Li. The newspapers over there, even in England, are running stories blaming you."

Carlisle shook his head in despair. The leader of the free world needed a haircut and a shave. "Do you know how many calls I got after Angela died in that DC attack?" He didn't wait for Magnus' response. "Ten. Ten calls. We lost a million citizens, and my wife—the wife of the Vice-President, and we got ten heads of state who had the decency to pick up a phone and call me. Screw them.

"In World War II, the West did nothing to stop genocide. I'm not going to sit with my thumb up my ass while the Chinese murder a million Uyghurs. I don't care if they are Muslim, Hindu, or any other creed on the planet. We're humans, and we're the only country that gives a damn."

"You're right. They were sleeping on the job. In CAG, we called them insensitive pricks—guys who watched other people suffer—labeled as prime for dismissal with prejudice. But now, even though we could be the only democracy with a functioning moral compass, we must bring people together."

President Carlisle smirked. "Doesn't mean I have to like it."

"Agreed. Still, if we ever needed a strong sense of 'us humans,' now would be the time."

"Fine. So now what?" asked the president, looking a little shell-shocked and bewildered.

"Let's finish what we started with the CCP. We have to terminate Chairman Li and anyone backing him. He didn't just nuke that town near Prague; he set off a bomb in that small Uyghur town. That's maybe another 60,000 or even closer to 80,000 dead."

The Commander-in-Chief switched gears. "Get a relay up with the Angela."

A bell dinged. "I've got the patch to the USS Angela Carlisle, sir," said a comm officer from an adjacent room.

"USS Angela Carlisle. This is Lieutenant Munch, sir."

The names for Schein's crew always lit up John's imagination, but there was no time for stray thoughts.

"This is Chief of Staff, Magnus. Put the captain on the horn."

A couple of seconds passed. "Sir, this is Schein."

"Hold for the president."

"What's happening, Mordy?" Carlisle's voice was booming.

"Sir, we took out five targets. We are surveying the destruction of the town where the Chinese exploded a small nuke."

"That's Uyghur land. The news media is going ape down here, mainly about the Czech town and the bomb on the Muslims. They're also screaming about our attacks on the Chinese to stir up Europe by blaming the whole mess on me." He waited.

Mordy measured his words. "We delivered a balanced attack on the CCP after their shots at Taiwan. It seemed sensible to give Li a chance to weigh his potential for a victory."

"Understood, captain, but now we need to ratchet things back up to where I wanted them from the start. You've got the list. Your orders are to take out every target on that list, starting with all the known launch sites."

"If Chairman Li surrenders and offers to turn himself in?"

There was a groan on the executive office line. "Every target gets hit whether Li gives himself up or not. I want them smashed down to their kitchens and bathrooms. If the CCP has any brains left, they will evacuate their people asap. Any questions?"

Carlisle's order didn't leave Mordy any wiggle room—it felt stupid and short-sighted. The list of targets was huge, and bombarding the whole country of China was not justified.

"Yes, sir, Mr. President. Understood."

The line went dead.

On the ship, the shapely lieutenant managing complex comms, tracking devices, and sensor arrays paused to gaze at her captain.

"Sir, I'm overstepping here, but you don't really intend to annihilate a few million Chinese soldiers and civilians, do you?"

"Lt. Munch. I believe that issue is above your paygrade, but since you asked, the answer is 'Hell no.'"

Yusep Abdullati faced the harsh wind blowing cold dust from a field in China's Xinjiang region. He was bone thin after months of an insufficient diet. But, finally, after re-education, the CCP allowed him to return to his village—west of where the small nuclear weapon savaged the town of Tumxuk.

"Why are we out here?" Yusep's wife whispered to him. She was a small, thin woman. Their children huddled close to her.

A truckload of soldiers formed a line in front of a few hundred Uyghurs—most clothed in long shirts insufficient to protect them from the bitter cold.

"I don't know." Abdullati had only just returned to his village. He lifted his head to peek at the soldiers. Uyghur Muslims knew not to stare. In the re-education camp, random men and women were selected for "special treatment." Some disappeared, and many came back muttering grim tales of horrible abuse.

"Father," asked his nine-year-old son. "Are we moving to a new place?"

Yusep couldn't miss the soldiers inserting magazines into their rifles. He feared not for himself but for his wife and children.

"Chamda. When I tell you, close your eyes. Do exactly as I say."

A Chinese officer paced in front of the civilians. They were lined up as instructed. Behind them was a ditch stretching perhaps fifty meters and two meters in depth. This particular officer was a student of history and a fitting choice to lead what he called his troop of Einsatzgruppen.

"What does that mean?" an underling once asked him. Ji Wan looked at the soldier and told him that in Europe, the Germans organized themselves in groups to kill troublemakers. Ji failed to mention that the "troublemakers" were actually innocent Jews who were stripped and shot in ditches. Now it was the Uyghurs. There were ten million of them in Xinjiang, so executing them all would be impractical with rifles, but to Ji Wan it was the job.

"Listen!" He spoke using a bullhorn. "All of you stand close to the edge. We are making a video so that everyone around the world will see that you are very loyal to the CCP."

The crowd backed up and arrayed themselves obediently. A few soldiers with video equipment began filming the small sampling of the Uyghur minority. They were frail, weak, and malnourished.

"All of you smile for the videos."

The line of soldiers quickly moved to positions paralleling the people.

Ji Wan raised his arms. "Don't worry. Keep smiling. You are all great film stars."

Yusep's suspicion turned into a catastrophic realization.

"Shut your eyes!" His children thought it was a game.

The officer, Ji, dropped his arms. Sixty rifles on automatic released a torrent of bullets at the victims. Bodies dropped into the gulley behind them. Some were only wounded.

Abdullati stepped in front of his wife and children, but it made no difference. They all tumbled downward.

After a minute, the shooting stopped. Some were alive, wounded, and groaning in pain from the trench of death. The soldiers paced the edge and looked down at the carnage, periodically firing on survivors.

Ji Wan dropped his bullhorn and stepped up to the precipice. He looked down and saw a boy squirming under the dead body of a man. The youngster must have been shielded from a fatal wound.

The young Abdullati gazed up. He was in pain from one shot that pierced his arm.

"What are you looking at?" asked Ji.

The child's wide stare momentarily unnerved Ji Wan, but then he pulled his pistol and aimed it at the boy.

"Close your eyes! You miserable Uyghur."

Yusep's son ignored the order. He was in a fog but refused to accept the vicious command shouted at him. His young defiant eyes bored into Ji's.

The CCP officer cocked his pistol. "This is why you must die—your people don't listen or learn." He pulled the trigger.

"We're receiving images from Chinese TV." Lieutenant Munch swiveled in her station chair to look grimly at her captain while simultaneously sending the video files to the captain's module.

Schein stared disbelieving at the vids of whole families being butchered and falling into a mass grave. He was born in the 1700s, but his nanite-enhanced brain had plenty of room for memorizing history, including Jewish history and the Holocaust. What he saw directly broadcast from the CCP was the same kind of mass murder.

"The president is on the line," said his comm officer.

"Okay. Connect."

The call was audio only, but it didn't take a genius to imagine the expression on Carlisle's face. Livid was not even close.

"Sir, Schein here."

"You saw the video?"

"Yes, sir."

"Let's not waste time. This is why I want the Chinese bases flattened."

"Those are your orders, captain. Every target on that list."

"Mr. President, there is no way to hit all of them without causing tremendous numbers of civilian casualties. Half of those bases are embedded in towns with innocent populations."

"The Uyghurs are innocent, too. Striking those targets—all of them—is not a debate. Follow your orders and keep me updated on your progress. If Li Wang surrenders and moves his troops out of Xinjiang, then we will hold."

Schein was in a quagmire. His oath of allegiance was first given to the Continental Army in 1775, but it never expired. John Carlisle was his Commander-in-Chief.

The bridge crew, including Munch, Williams, and now Baumgartner, who'd just entered through the blast door, stared at Mordy. They wanted a clear understanding of what came next. The videos gutted them to the core.

"Mr. President, I request that you revise your targeting to military targets with minimal risk of civilian casualties."

The line went dead.

A minute later, Carlisle was back on Mordy's audio link. "Captain. Under what basis are you refusing my order?"

Schein stepped lightly. "Sir. I am not refusing your order. I believe that we should modify it to target clear CCP military targets first."

"Mordy. The Chinese are murdering civilians while you debate me on this."

"I agree. My time would be better spent hitting the bases that are fielding those war crimes, but orders to hit civilians are unlawful."

For the first time, Schein heard Magnus chattering in the background. It was a fast and fiery exchange that was suddenly muted.

Moments later, President Carlisle returned to the line. He

heard the tail end of Magnus saying, "…that's how it is."

"I will discuss your contention to the war cabinet." It was amazing how the president's tone went from hostile to legalistic in an instant. He continued, "In the meantime, take out all the military targets that will minimize civilian casualties. If Li Wang shows his head, take him out, even if there will be collateral damage."

Schein could live with that. "Aye aye, sir."

"I will contact you when the cabinet has reached a consensus on the legal issues. You have your interim orders." The line went dead.

Like other despotic leaders from countries with dictatorial regimes, Li Wang consolidated his power and distanced himself from threats. Only those inner circle members who held similar views survived the week since the CCP hit the small Czech town with a fission bomb.

Zhao Boju, secretary and newfound whipping boy for the chairman's need to vent, rubbed a bruise on his left tricep. It was the latest since his first beating at his leader's hands which began only a couple of weeks earlier. He stepped gingerly into Li's "war" office and waited silently.

"Why do you stand there as if you have nothing to do?"

"I await to serve the chairman in any way required."

Li squinted in his peculiar style and stared directly into Boju's eyes. The moment lasted excruciatingly long, but the undisputed ruler of China turned back to read the papers on his desk.

"Zhao Boju. Do you think your parents knew the significance of your name? It is not fitting that such an ordinary citizen should be named after the greatest painter in our history."

Again, the chairman put his subordinate in an uncomfortable position to answer an ambiguous question—to which an incorrect answer could lead to physical abuse.

After what felt like a day, Li Wang muttered, "Remain silent. It is bad enough that I have to look at you, let alone hear you. Besides, your parents were common dung to name their offspring after the exalted Boju."

A phone beeped on Li's desk. "Chairman. We are receiving incoming fire."

"Shoot back, general."

"It is from the American's spacecraft."

"Then launch weapons at the enemy starship and destroy it."

For the first time, Zhao and General Liahaung saw it. The chairman was no doubt a despot, but he rarely spoke an irrational word—cruel, terrifying, but never something blatantly ridiculous. Children knew that the USS Angela Carlisle was an alien ship that was untouchable. And, even if China did have a weapon that could inflict damage, that would leave Earth unprotected.

"Launch missiles at Taiwan," Li ordered. He gazed blankly across the office and appeared lost in his thoughts.

"Chairman. The Americans are hitting our PLAAF airbases. They are not hitting civilian targets."

The leader seemed to emerge from a trance and yelled into the phone, "Taiwan is a military target! Burn it to the ground!" Li didn't wait for a response. He whispered, "You have your orders. May your children live to respect you."

The tyrant of the CCP cut the connection, then stood and gazed at Zhao. He opened a drawer and reached inside while not breaking his eye contact. "Boju. Famous artist. Come here and sit on the floor next to my desk."

"We've got five ballistic missile launches."

Schein reacted instantly. "What's the target, Lieutenant?"

"Tracking now."

The computer systems on the Angela were alien, and they were precise.   Cassie Munch turned with a befuddled expression. "They are all targeted to the sea fifty miles north of Taiwan."

"Any other launches?"

"No, sir."

Mordy clicked a button that connected him to weapons

control. "Commander Baumgartner. Take out those five missiles."

"Roger that."

Lasers fired. The advanced Chinese weapons exploded conventionally in the upper atmosphere.

"Ensign Williams. Why do you think the CCP would launch five missiles deliberately off target?"

If this was a test, Lucky Williams felt unprepared. The young ensign looked up from his navigation displays, trying to think of something brilliant. He decided just to spit out the first thing that made sense. "I don't think it was bad aim, sir."

"So, what was it, ensign?"

"I think they are trying to send us a message, Captain."

Again, Schein pressed him. He arched an eyebrow which was visible in the not-so-bright bridge lighting. "Go on."

"Somebody down there is trying to tell us that they want a way out."

Two other officers on the bridge, a couple of lieutenants in charge of monitoring environment and defense systems, nodded meekly, hedging their commitment if the captain disagreed.

Mordy turned around to squint at the senior of the two engineering lieutenants. "What do you think, Brad?"

"Uh. Maybe what he said, sir."

Schein smirked. "I guess I agree with Brad, who concurs with Lucky."

"Sir," asked Cassie. "Should I send a message to the CCP direct commlink?"

"No!"

Rex was listening in. "Captain. Should I continue to target the airbases? We're estimating that we've already killed at least 35,000 military personnel down there. There are plenty of options left."

"No!"

The crew was confused. Mordy started thinking out loud. "That launch was clearly directed at the sea. Li would never order that. He's in so deep that an offer won't be coming from him. The man knows he's primed for capital punishment. The chairman also knows that after hitting the Czech Republic, there is zero chance of reaching any agreement that keeps him alive and in power.

"Nope. Someone else programmed that trajectory. That officer could already be dead for not following orders."

A moderate humming noise marked the lack of discussion on the Angela's command deck. "Rex. Send an unarmed projectile—a small one—to the same target area north of Taiwan. Use one with passive reflectors. I want their ground stations to see it."

*

The gloves had come off. A major general ordered a massive artillery barrage on multiple Uyghur cities. The carnage made the awful brutality of Ji Wan's trench murderers look insignificant. The Muslim minority was being slaughtered. Burnt corpses of men, women, and children were displayed on Chinese television with a message from Charman Li that the Uyghurs sided with the enemies of the Peoples Republic of China. The CCP prepared to increase their genocidal attacks on ten million innocent human beings.

Zhao Boju limped to an executive washroom. He shut the door and locked it. A few drops of blood spattered on the floor and then the sink as he aligned himself in front of a mirror. The reflection was grim. Deep cuts bled from his cheeks.

"I am very ugly," Zhao laughed morbidly.

The CCP executive grimaced when he examined the damage to his right eye. Underneath the swelling, there was blood. It was a very bad sign. His lips were puffy, and at least two teeth were gone. When crouching on the floor, it was entirely possible that he'd swallowed at least one of them. The secretary to the chairman surveyed other parts of this body. Two fingers on his left hand were broken. After struggling to remove his shirt, Zhao saw that his torso didn't look nearly as bad as his face—but he hurt like hell.

A single tone came from his pocket. He pulled out his cellphone and pressed the green dot on the display.

"Zhao Boju."

"Yes."

"This is General Liahaung."

Shock. "How did you get this number, sir?"

"That is not important, and there is no time to discuss trivial things. Understood?"

Zhao answered affirmatively.

"You must listen. My family is dead, or they will be soon. I do not know if you have children, but by now, Li Wang must have sent assassins to my home."

The CCP exec merely said, "I have no family. My parents are dead. I have no wife."

The general sighed. "No one will cry for you. And, no one will die for you."

The statement was dark. Zhao waited.

"You must kill the chairman. If you do not, then he will lead our country to destruction. Do you understand?"

"I am listening, General Liahaung."

"Are you alone?"

"Yes. The entire floor has been cleared of party members. Only two guards remain outside the entry doors. There are many more on the street. We move to a different building every day."

"That is good. So only you are alone with the chairman. Do you have a weapon?"

"No. I have only my clothes and this phone," answered Zhao.

"Can I trust you? I have read your profile. You are not so devoted to the party, are you?"

Zhao now thought that whoever might be listening to his call would use it to politicize and justify the general's death and his own. The moment of truth arrived. He could save himself by swearing his loyalty and immediately rushing to report Liahaung to his superior. Perhaps the beatings from Li's club might stop.

"I am loyal to my people."

"That is the right answer. Not long from now, security will trace my call, but you have time if you steel yourself."

"I have no weapon." Zhau stepped over a line and sentenced himself to death with that short phrase.

"Look around. What do you see?"

Li's secretary walked with some pain to scan the bathroom. It was not a CCP building, but any detachable metal had been removed—there was nothing—could he fight against Li Wang barehanded? The idea was surreal. Li was going to force the Americans to destroy China, and a simple farm boy was going to save it?

"There is nothing here, general."

"Look again."

Zhao searched further. "There is only a can of paint in one of the stalls. They must have been doing some fixing here."

He heard a laugh from the other side of the exchange. "I know my history Zhao Boju. You are named after the famous Chinese artist, are you not?"

"Yes."

"I know our history. Boju glorified our country. Li Wang is destroying us. Does the can have a handle?"

"Yes."

"Then it is a weapon."

Suddenly Zhao heard banging and crashing noises like a door was being breached. Someone screamed at Liahaung, and he was yelling back. There was a gunshot. He heard it. Saw it in his mind—the image of the general crumbling to the floor.

There was a gasp. "You are an artist," Liahaung rasped. There was another shot, then the traitor's last words, "Go paint."

Time had run out. There were only minutes or less. Zhao grabbed the handle of the paint can. The label was in Mandarin and English. He bolted from the bathroom to the doors that led to reception, then crashed through the doors to Li's office.

The chairman stood up. He had a phone in his hand. "You?" Li Wang shouted. "You are conspiring with Liahaung? The general is dead!" Li pulled open a drawer. This time reaching for a pistol—not a stick. The injured Zhao flew across the room as the CCP leader withdrew the weapon.

A shot rang out. The recoil from the gun caused it to slip from Li's hand. Simultaneously, the paint can held by Zhao seemed to arc in slow motion and then connected with the chairman's head. The megalomaniac dropped to his knees and then collapsed, staring up at the ceiling.

The pain in Zhao Boju's chest was unbearable. He looked down. A bullet wound spurted blood. His stomach was slick, and the flow was going to sap his strength.

Li Wang was in a daze, staring up at the ceiling, concussed. Something wasn't right. He knew but couldn't quite figure it out. Zhao inched his way toward the man. The left side of Zhao's chest was on fire. He pushed himself and stabbed his fingers to pry the lid from the can.

The chairman began to regain his cognizance. The lid popped off the paint can. Zhao crouched above and rammed his knee hard into Li's diaphragm. The chairman's mouth opened as he gasped for air. Zhao Boju scrambled to pour the paint.

The secretary dropped to the floor parallel to Li Wang's dying body. Paint mixed with blood flowed under him. The world was going black. First the edges of his vision, then he felt as if he was floating in a dream—a dim, cold, yet inviting sleep.

Zhao whispered. He heard his own quiet words. "I am Boju. I am a painter."

"Still no communications from anywhere in China," said Cassie Munch.

Twelve hours passed with no launches. The unarmed projectile tossed from the Angela plunged into the sea unremarkably.

"What are we hearing?"

"Sir, there is continual chatter between Beijing and multiple bases, along with comms between the bases. Almost all of it is encrypted, spread spectrum, and we are only dissecting bits and pieces."

"So much for alien technology, Lieutenant; tell me something I don't know."

She checked her displays. The systems on the ship merged with human technology—it was actually a demonstration of American skill. "Um. Captain. I can have the computers analyze the analog and digital signals that are not encrypted, but they are probably civilian. Also, the Chinese have shut down public broadcasting."

"Of course, but people like to talk. There's a reason why the CCP is static. I'd like to know what that means before we re-engage."

"Yes, sir. I will search all the non-encrypted data now. Uh oh!"

"Uh oh, what, lieutenant?"

"Incoming from the White House." She squinted, knowing that as much as her captain wanted to avoid Carlisle, he had nowhere to hide.

"Open it," grimaced Mordy.

"I'm piping the call to you now, sir."

"Captain Schein here."

"Magnus here."

Not the president. "Go ahead, sir."

"Mordy, I'm giving you a heads up. Take me off speaker."

"Your off speaker."

"Okay. We're getting dribbles of information from some sources. It's impossible to know how reliable. Frankly, I think our backchannels are as trustworthy as a narcissistic woman, but that's my personal experience bleeding in. Probably considered misogynistic, but I'm too old to give a shit about that.

"More importantly, the reports are saying that someone did a CAG on Chairman Li." Magnus let that sink in.

"Sir, I gotta let that sink in for a minute," said Schein.

"Sounds like some bullshit, doesn't it?"

"Do you have any details? I mean, we've already told you that five missiles were collectively off-target north of Taiwan. That would fit with Li being history and someone trying to send us a message to hold fire."

"And you've been holding fire for twelve hours, and the president has been eager to finish them off for the last eleven hours and 59 minutes." Mordy could practically hear the Chief of Staff grinding his teeth through the connection.

"So, why didn't he call me to order a restart?"

"Captain, I told him that discretion is the better part of valor and that if the Chinese drop five working missiles in the drink, we need to see if we've got a ceasefire."

"My thinking exactly, sir."

"As far as details—they are sketchy. The craziest one is that an aide to Li poured acid down his throat. But he is just one guy. The next one could be worse if the chairman is really dead. And, what's getting under Carlisle's skin is that the troops are still operating in Uyghur territory."

"Yes. We can see that from up here. They are still rounding up civilians and putting them on buses. We've tracked the buses to concentration camps, but right now, there is no evidence of executions on a large scale."

"The president will pull the trigger soon and order you to re-engage. Military targets only. The cabinet ganged up on him when he insisted on hitting government centers inside cities. I'm telling you this in confidence, Mordy. Keep it that way. You're not a politician, and neither am I. We're soldiers, so I'm not going to squirrel around with ambiguous narrischkeit."

"I didn't know you spoke Yiddish, colonel."

"Did I use the right term? It means foolish crap, right?"

"Close enough for government work."

"Excellent. That being the way the cabinet and the president are leaning, do you have a problem with continuing your assault on the CCP bases?"

Mordy mused that thought. "I can think of at least one reservation. Namely, if I eliminate a cohesive army, the country could turn into a Dark Ages barbaric disaster. Did anyone else in the cabinet voice that opinion?"

"I did. I may have spent my life killing terrorists, but sometimes you need to use them to reach an objective."

"For that reason, it makes sense to leave enough military assets so that the Chinese don't descend into chaos. I'm not the president, but the odds are that Carlisle will order you to continue hammering the bases until they're rubble. Also, he wants all the CCP murder units out of Xinjiang and any other Uyghur area."

"In my opinion, that last part is the priority," said Schein firmly.

"Very well. We're on the same page. Be prepared for an order to resume very specific targeted attacks, whether Li Wang is dead or not. Chances are the next guy will be the same or worse—but who knows? Maybe we'll get lucky."

Chapter 13

The streets of the royal capital on Kamtret were packed. Large four-legged Mazik hustled to and fro. Since their emperor usurped the power of the Council of Sentient Beings, tribute flowing into the homeworld created previously unknown prosperity. Even the workers imported from the subservient world of Slev lived better.

Towering above the clean streets stood buildings that reached a kilometer or more in height. None more majestic than the palace of the emperor—now the ruler of multiple planets.

Wham! Several dozen Mazik leaped with their burdens away from the sudden impact of a female body as it smashed to the ground. The area was marked by bloodstains of similar concubines of Mazik Bah-Gahn, who'd been unceremoniously thrown from the emperor's tower. Thus was the end to some captured Slev or Makim sex slaves at the whim of the brutal dictator.

Peculiar grunts preceded a sudden pause by the foot traffic, then, as if by cue, hundreds if not thousands of commoners began singing praises of Mazik Bah-Gahn.

"Exalted emperor. Mighty warrior. Almighty power."

Pel Jahrnuk, the primary slave-mate to the Emperor, paused. She walked past the body of the Makim female who'd spent the last four solar cycles on a sleep chair only meters away from Pel. Internal organs leaked onto the ground. Knowing that her master routinely threatened to shove Pel herself from a building portal 700 meters in altitude, she shivered.

"Move now!" growled the harsh voice of her escort. It was rare that a Slev concubine would ever leave the palace, instead spending her life in an area just several square meters waiting for Mazik Bah-Gahn to exercise his abuse. However, today Pel received an order to bathe in the cold river which flowed nearby. A confusing command, which she'd guessed could only be some precursor to a new style of torture devised to amuse her tormentor.

The chaperon flared his snout. It was a warning—threatening, yet unwise, for if the underling inflicted any wound on Pel, his life would be forfeit. It was a strange existence for such a soldier in the Mazik army.

She stopped, ignoring the implied threat to move. Instead, Pel raised her voice in praise, forcing her abrasive companion to do the same. The pause seemed to infuriate the officer, but now he was snared in a trap of her making. As long as she sang, those around her must sing.

Without warning, she stopped, then turned her head to glare at her male guard. "Now we will go."

The impudence of a Slev to a Mazik commissioned soldier was punishable by lashings, but Jahrnuk was the prime concubine—if he touched her for no approved reason, the result would be his dismemberment, followed by his disposal via being fed to all of the royal sex servants. He held his tongue and marched on.

Pel looked back at the body on the ground, wondering when she would be thrown unceremoniously from the high floor. Mazik Bah-Gahn routinely made the threat. On most of those occasions, Pel longed for her master to actually choose her for termination. Instead, he ordered her to strip naked and submit—akin to a death by a thousand cuts.

In the palace, the aide to Emperor Mazik Bah-Gahn peered down 700 meters to the courtyards and streets. He could just hear the sound of chanting over the whistling wind. The portal closed to the relief of the many females in the hall.

"Find me another," ordered the ruler of many worlds. "In fact, I am feeling whimsical. Go down and cover your eyes. Then spin around and point. Have your attendants seize whichever female you select and bring her to me."

"Per your orders!"

"Wait. There is another issue on my mind. Where is the tribute from Olamit?"

The officer cringed internally. "It has yet to arrive. The

Emperor instructed me to wait for another four cycles and then send a ship to Shaab Mar Gen, Arbitor of the Panruk to demand the tribute and a penalty."

Mazik Bah-Gahn's arms flexed, his rippling muscles portending his ancestral physical prowess. He banged his thick fingers on the alloy arm of the royal throne. "Today, I feel differently. Send four ships to investigate. Instruct them that they will bring Shaab Mar Gen back to me—untouched and unspoiled. If the female Panruk refuses to consent, drop a few rocks to convince her."

The assistant stomped his feet and bowed, unaware that his orders were about to alter history on a galactic scale.

*

"I believe Mazik Bah-Gahn has dragged his legs in this situation."

Mercy Bonner, not-always-happy-to-be-captain, giggled. It wasn't her usual response, but Jahrnuk's comment tickled her. "Kap, The usual English phrase is 'drag feet,' not legs. But your point is a damn good one."

The Slev leader grinned, displaying teeth that would frighten any sensible creature in the Milky Way. Mercy found them fascinating. He thought about his response and said: "Well, I thank you for correcting my slang and the compliment."

"Anytime."

The alien tried something new. "Much obliged, Ma'am."

At this, she laughed out loud. "Who's been teaching you these phrases?"

"Guess."

"My husband?"

He gazed at her triumphantly. "Guess again."

"If it isn't Barrett, it has to be Ensign Lewis."

Now, despite his fearsome countenance, Kap appeared to be positively beside himself as if he'd won some complicated challenge. "Wrong, captain. It was Molly."

Mercy cocked her head just so. The ever-melancholy Molly

was teaching an alien Slev human slang?

"Keep up the good work. As far as Mazik Bah-Gahn, the fact that it has taken this long for him to send a fleet is possibly a bad thing. If the delay is due to large-scale prep on their side of the jump point, then we could be in trouble. The upside is that we are getting those fusion bombs operational. The Mazik delay could be a win for us."

Captain Jahrnuk sat on the floor in Bonner's quarters—it was significantly easier than attempting to squeeze himself into a human-sized chair. "According to Mok, the production of the self-propelled devices is nearly complete. I believe we should deploy our forces as soon as the bombs are loaded. We've gotten lucky, but luck may not be enough to save us."

"Agreed," said Mercy. "I will contact Shaab Mar Gen to see if her people are ready."

Kap rose from the floor to his full, intimidating height. An uninitiated human would be terrified to be so close to an alien capable of ripping flesh and bone with his teeth. He gave Mercy the Slev equivalent of a smile. "I want you to know something."

She waited.

"Before meeting you and your people, I expected that you were a barbaric race of primitive near-animals. Now that I've come to know you, I see that you are not. You are risky, and you take risks. Humans have the potential to subjugate our part of the galaxy. It is what Shaab Mar Gen worries about when she is not utilizing her every waking hour to save the Panruk.

"But, I am hopeful that after all of this is over. If we survive, your planet and your species will not do what Mazik Bah-Gahn has planned for himself—to dominate all life. Promise me that you will stand against whoever ends up running Earth after the end of hostilities—I mean if they set a goal of conquering us. If it is Howe, I will feel safe. However, Aaron and Allison are gone. Who knows if we will ever see them again? That is a meaningless question because it is impossible to answer. Molly told me that your world could go to Hell in a hand-basket if they don't ever return. She didn't explain what *Hell* was, but it must be not nice if it is in a hand-basket."

Mercy looked sympathetically at Kap. The danger of humanity to other sentients hovered in the back of her mind when it wasn't stored in a small box in a corner of her brain. "I understand your trepidation." She switched to speaking in the Slev language. "It is a concern for me also. In this small dot in space, we are friends. If we survive, I will stand with you to challenge any species that attempts to rule over you, including humans. I promise."

As was a Slev custom indicating warm friendship, Kap almost closed the gap between them to bump chests with Mercy, but then, slightly off-balance—recovered and blurted out, "Thank you."

She gave him a very slight knowing smile as he blushed at his near-indiscretion. "Your quite welcome, Captain Jahrnuk. Now, shall we go kick some Mazik ass?"

Shaft Lek, Panruk engineer, floated in zero gravity. It was his fifth hour practicing in a suit. The light from Olamit's sun sprinkled over the surface of his planet as morning dawned. From an altitude of 40,000 kilometers, he could see continents, oceans, and clouds. It was beautiful, and the scientist in him made room for the peace-loving poet who dwelled in nearly all members of his species.

"Shaft!" He was shaken from his daydream by the sound of Mok calling his name.

"Sorry, Commander. I was just enjoying the view from up here."

The giant Slev officer understood. Despite being treated like chattel by the Mazik, he remembered. It was already twenty Kamtret solar years from when Mok was taken as a kitchen worker on a small warship circling the world called Mikam. He gazed from a portal window to the planet below and stars above at every spare moment. At least one thing the Slev had in common with the Panruk was an inner, gentle soul.

"Commander?"

Now Mok was stirred from his own recollections. "Right. We're out here to practice." He pointed to a small freighter about five hundred meters distant. "No auto-pilot on your suit. We do this one manually. Stay with me." He hit a thruster control and accelerated toward the target.

"I'm right behind you, sir."

The Slev rotated to look back. "You're doing well, except you forgot the payload."

True enough, Lek was fixated on keeping up and failed to hitch the container of fake mines. The commander stopped and waited. Lek tried to turn using his own estimate of force required and began to spin out of control.

"Hit auto!"

The rotation stopped. "I feel sick, sir," said the youngster, and then he puked in his suit. Fortunately, the built-in scrubbers were efficient.

"That's right, Shaft. When you get out of control, you can hit auto."

One hundred meters away, Captain Jahrnuk observed from a portal on the Ro-Pahm and took in the amateurish performance of the Panruk scientist.

Mok keyed a private comm circuit. "Did you see that?"

"Every confidence-building moment," said Kap.

"We should leave him on Olamit and take only Slev technicians."

"Politics and technology," remarked the captain.

"What does that mean?" asked Mok as the engineer, under power, moved past to collect the fake bomb payload.

"It means that we need someone out there who can fix any technical problems. These are Panruk devices. And the politics are about inclusion. We can't go fight for Olamit alone. They need to be part of the battle."

"Sir, that could be the difference between winning and losing."

"That's why you're on this mission, my friend, to make sure that we win."

Mok grinned, baring his teeth behind his visor, and addressing the big, fat problem called the Mazik. "What is that English phrase that Ensign Molly always uses when things appear to be hopeless?"

"We're screwed."

"Yes. That's the one."

Shaab Mar Gen gained weight. She was still gaunt, but a little color returned to her face. Shelet Pir Sahm Mim, formerly known as Edgar, saw the change with her anthropologist's eyes.

"You look much better, Arbitor."

Shaab sneered. "Is that your professional academic opinion?"

After spending 127 years on Earth, Shelet had encountered every kind of snarky response known to man. This one was easy. "Shaab. I see some hope in your expression. Do not deny it."

A heavy silence filled the finely decorated office as Mim's rays filtered through large glass panels which dominated one wall. The leader of the Panruk sat and sighed.

Shelet smiled. "You cannot hide that tinge of optimism. And, there is no reason why you should. I have seen hopeless moments in history that became successes."

The Arbitor touched two glowing fingertips to her head. "On Earth, perhaps, among humans who are somehow expert at creating magic from disaster. May I remind you that we are Panruk—a static species that hasn't dealt with adversity in a thousand years? We will likely die. Oh, and since you mentioned it, my weight gain is because I've decided that I would like to be fat when the Mazik drop rocks on us which is guaranteed since our planet doesn't manufacture surprise wins."

Shelet sat and stared across the desk. "When did you become such a pessimist? Did you know that I received messages now and then from Shamdar, your predecessor, about you?"

"You mean the same Shamdar who quit suddenly and dumped this doomed planet in my lap? The same Arbitor who was murdered in the streets because of the misery which has befallen us? That Shamdar?"

The renowned anthropologist wasn't phased by the depressing statement. "I knew him before you were born. He had energy and optimism, even in the face of problems with the Council of Sentients that consumed him. And he included praises of your character in every communication he'd sent to me since you became his assistant."

"He did?" Shaab perked up.

"Yes. Shamdar Bit Megani told me that he believed that you would be the greatest Arbitor in history and that the sooner he handed over the job to you, the better."

"I don't believe you!"

"Believe me. Your abilities and talent were recognized by him long ago. That is why—and I will use an English human term—you better not F this up."

The leader of Olamit laughed, a tiny hopeful laugh. "I believe that in English, the 'F' word is considered vulgar. Is it not?"

"Of course. But, it fits the current conversation." Shelet leaned in and offered her own glowing fingertips, which Shaab hesitatingly reached out to touch. "Arbitor. You must rise to this moment, even if it means only giving moral support to the population. They need you! And, one more thing. We HAVE humans helping us, and they know how to win."

Chapter 14

The trip to the dead freighters a couple of light-hours from Olamit was trying and tiring. The entire platoon consisted of four three-man teams. Team one: Commander Mok, Shaft Lek, and a Slev technician. Team two: Two Slev and a Panruk engineer. Team Three: Lieutenant JG John Allen, a Panruk engineer and a Slev technician. Team Four: Two Slev technicians and Ensign Molly Stark.

There had been an intense standoff between Mercy and Molly when it came to the teenager heading out on a potentially lethal mission.

Captain Bonner had all of her arguments ready once she'd heard through the grapevine that her adopted daughter was eager to go. She unloaded the first salvo when the kid walked into her quarters.

"No way. I've already gotten wind that you want to go. It isn't going to happen."

The nanite-enhanced ensign, former teen proprietor of the famous Mollyburgers restaurant in colonial Philadelphia—circa 1777—squinted and gave Mercy a death stare. "I am going!"

"No. You're not."

Having gotten a definitive negative and final answer from the captain of the battlecruiser USS George Washington, Molly proceeded to begin her arguments. "Why not?" she shot back.

"Because it's dangerous."

"Are you kidding? Transporting onto the bridge of the Ko-Pahm full of Mazik sailors and two of their Warrier-class wasn't dangerous? And the follow-up battles?"

Mercy held her ground. "I don't care."

"I lost Dexter in that battle! Are you saying I'm not tough enough? How many Mazik did I kill? Like the one who almost killed Monty? I did that!"

Her mother groaned. "Why do you have to fight against

every decision I make that you don't like?"

"Maybe because I'm still a teenager? It's a moral imperative to struggle against your adult tyranny."

A laugh. "And you are fantastic at that. But, the answer is still no."

"I'll appeal your decision!"

"To whom?"

Molly gritted her teeth. "I don't know."

"Exactly. I'm the boss. Period."

"I'll go convince Barrett," she threatened.

"Go ahead. Good luck with that. Do you think that my husband is going to disagree with me?"

The young ensign merely shrugged. "Probably not. Still, I'm going. Look at the facts: I'm tougher than anyone else on the list, except for maybe, Mok, and that's a maybe because I think I could whomp him if we went at it one-on-one.

"In addition, I'm enhanced. I can process any data faster than the unenhanced Panruk and Slev, hands down."

"Your right, dear. You can. That is why John Allen is going—also enhanced, in case you forgot."

"One Recon soldier up there is not enough. You've got zero redundancy in that."

"True. Perhaps I should send Lewis?"

"Are you kidding? Mom! He'd be telling jokes while the Mazik are shooting lasers at us."

Mercy steeled herself. "Maybe, but still, you will have to sit this operation out."

Molly wanted to punch a wall. She paused to re-think her side of the debate. It took about a second before she used the last arrows in her quiver. "Do you see these scars on my face? Do you know why I didn't have Allison fix them?" She didn't wait for an answer. "Because that psycho Durst gave me two choices back in Pinebrook."

Her adoptive mother immediately became empathetic. "I understand." After all, Mercy's own daughters were murdered by King George and Captain Durst's little band of "Wolves" in 1776.

Molly persisted. "Not only that. It wasn't just about the option of being raped by ten vicious and twisted men or getting my face cut open. It was my choice to accept permanent scars to remind myself that I need to fight against any bastards like them. Including Mazik Bah-Gahn himself, if it came down to it."

"Is that it? Are you done?"

Molly's eyes began tearing up, and Mercy knew what was coming next.

"I'm not done. I lost Dexter. I loved him. You know that. Sure, I was 17, but I have no doubt that I would have married him and had the kind of love that you and Barrett have."

"Are you telling me that putting yourself at risk of death will somehow bring Dexter back? Baby, I wish that I could find a way to do that."

"You can't, Mom."

"That's why you have to stay here. Safe with me."

"No. That's why I have to go; so that every time I kill a Mazik, Dexter is with me." Tears were now dripping down her scarred cheeks.

Mercy quietly reached out and pulled Molly close to her and held her tightly. "I'm sorry."

She sobbed on her mother's shoulder for a long while. Finally, Molly gazed up to stare into Mercy's eyes. "I have to go."

"I'll never forgive myself if anything happens to you on some stupid-ass broken freighter in this stupid-ass Olamit solar system."

"Nothing is going to happen to me. I will come back safe. I promise."

The tall blond senior officer walked over to her bunk, sighed heavily, and sat down. "I should never get into an argument with you. I'm captain, and I've got one job on this lousy ship, and that is to keep Earth safe and all humans alive. The truth is that you can make the difference out there by the jump point. As 'the buck stops here' person, the logical thing is to let you go and destroy any Mazik that come through.

"I'll think about it. That means in the end, I'll give in. If I let you go out there, your mission is to come back in one piece. I can't lose you, Molly."

*

Molly's transit to the jump point that linked Olamit to Kamtret and the Mazik neared. Team Four approached the exceedingly damaged freighter that once belonged to the alien species known as the Qaaniki. Like most members of the Council, the owners of this cargo ship lived to engage in peaceful commerce. The Mazik had different ideas, which included destroying any cargo or attempted commerce without the emperor's approval.

"It looks like there's a giant hole through the middle," observed one of the Slev techs.

The three of them maneuvered their small shuttle towards the undamaged forward section of the massive cargo hauler. Zero-G was a little awkward, but Team Four was adapting. With any luck, the Grav-plates onboard would still be operational.

Molly examined the scan of the mile-long ship. "It doesn't appear as if the life support systems in the bow are compromised." She keyed a transmitter to reach Commander Mok Partul.

"Go," he replied.

"Our Qaaniki freighter has a 50-meter hole in it, but the bow compartments are still pressurized amazingly enough."

"Proceed to board. Survey the interior and seal off where required." Mok out.

Terse and business link, she thought, unlike Mok when he was not on duty.

The group of three proceeded to connect the shuttle to an access door in the hull. A flexible pipe large enough for the Slev to walk through sealed and then pressurized.

"Do you think we can open this without cutting?"

The senior of the two Slev techs grunted.

"Is that a yes?"

"Perhaps."

The ensign decided to wait for the techs to do their thing with the door. Apparently, the Qaaniki were exceedingly paranoid as both of her Slev companions seemed frustrated after several attempts to break the hatch lock.

"Is that a code panel?" Molly asked while glancing between her two teammates?

"Yes. The Qaaniki use a 12-base numerical system. These are buttons with what you would call zero thru twelve." He pointed out the sequence to her.

"Tell me about these aliens. Just a quick summary."

"Plark! They are four-legged like us, but that's where the similarity ends. We are nice, friendly, non-critical, and non-argumentative. The Qaaniki are the opposite. They want to debate everything, and simple questions are fodder for a confrontation."

"Do they do the opposite of what everyone else does?"

The other Slev tech answered, "They are famous for that. Unlike the rest of the council sentients who like to start at the beginning, the Qaaniki want to always go straight to the most divisive issues."

"Excuse me." Molly moved up to the keypad. "What are these buttons here? The ones without numbers printed on them?"

"That one says 'unlock,' and the other says 'lock.'"

She laughed and pressed the "Lock" button. "Let's see if I'm lucky."

Even with their suits on, they heard a loud click.

"I can't believe it was that simple!" said one of the Slev.

"There are a lot of humans who think it's funny to do the contrary of what you would expect. I guess your Qaaniki have a cynical nature. And, I'm am really lucky."

Molly added. "Also, think about this: If you are outside the hull, wouldn't you want it to be easy to get inside? There are no threatening enemies in space. Just maybe a confused and tired alien running out of air, needing to get into the safety of the airlock. But, at the same time, the builders of this freighter are always contrary, so make it simple, but also backward."

She grabbed the latch on the door and used her nanite-strength to rotate it ninety degrees and slide it to the left while both techs cringed. A sudden equalization of pressure caught them all off guard for a split second.

"Sorry! I know. I assumed that we were at equilibrium."

The older Slev tech paled behind the faceplate of his suit. "That could have been a disaster if there was very low or no pressure in there. From now on, you do locks; we'll do doors."

"Roger that," Molly replied, feeling amateurish. "When you say 'bad,' what do you mean?"

"I mean that if that was a vacuum, we could have been blown straight into a bulkhead of whatever is inside. Minimum is bruising. Worst case is ruptured suit and death."

Molly grasped the idiocy of her assumption. The picture of one or all of them dying in a vacuum led to an involuntary shudder. She didn't go through brutal situations in 1776 and in the present day only to make a dumb mistake and die in space.

"I'm sorry."

The two Slev looked at each other. "We didn't expect an apology," said one. "Nevertheless, thank you for offering it."

She made a mental note to study Slev etiquette in the future. "Shall we go inside and see what a Qaaniki ship looks like?"

Team One, Mok, Lek, and a technician pressurized a small entry to a cargo bay on the freighter named Mi Googa. The Slev commander laughed when he saw the name emblazed on the inside passages.

"I noticed that the commander repeated the name of this ship and then laughed. Why?" asked Shaft.

"Because in the language of the unfortunate crew that died here, the name means, 'Please notice me,'"

The Panruk engineer grinned and said, "I think they got their wish."

Mok turned to his technician. "Before we set up, let's check the bridge and crew quarters to see if anyone is still alive."

Lek shrugged. "After a solar year? How could that be?"

"Stranger things have happened. Come. Let's go forward and search."

The three members of Team One stayed suited. Nearly the entire ship's atmosphere had been vented involuntarily. They made their way to the command areas. It wasn't far; even though the cargo mover was over a mile long, virtually all of the crew spent their careers in a small section close to the bow.

"Mazik Bah-Gahn must have ordered low-yield explosives so that the wreck would float out here as a monument to his power," said the technician.

"That means any living Ni Ha would be behind that hatch." Mok pointed to the only intact compartment forward of the one cargo bay entry they'd already pressurized. "Behind that door, there could be a survivor, but I would be surprised."

The beacon on the hatch panel indicated that the air was only about one-twelfth of standard pressure. It took an effort to get the thing opened.

"Some of their computers are still running," Lek pointed out.

They scanned the area and then saw the remains of a male Ni Ha crewman. The body showed indications that he'd been alive until perhaps only forty solar days earlier. Now he was a shriveled corpse—human-like in that it had two legs and walked upright. Shaft felt sick. Panruk rarely saw things as harsh and frightening. He turned away to keep from fainting.

"He must have been the only survivor," the technician said.

Mok took in the condition of the corpse and the command bridge. There were no other bodies. "It would seem so. It is pointless staying here when we can instead unpack Lak's bombs. I've seen enough. We've got Mazik cruisers to decompress and turn their crew into that." He motioned toward the decomposing alien and then strode off in the direction of their quarters aboard a dead ship.

All four teams spent the next week doing their best to lay the minefield and put their powered nuclear "bombs" in viable locations close to the jump point. It wasn't a question of "if"

Mazik Bah-Gahn would be sending ships. When the enemy arrived in system, the group would be the difference between life and death for the Panruk. Mok knew that his home planet was also hanging by a thread, as well. The inability to ascertain what the Mazik dictator would do next made life or death a matter of constant doubt.

Mok gave few simplistic orders because there were no real commands needed at this point. But unlike the others, the large Slev left tracking and observations to the computers. Mok, instead, played the Earth game called chess against a simple AI device. Somehow, the alien pastime eased the stress that could potentially weigh so heavily on his two beating hearts.

Molly spent her waking hours doing what all of them did—except for Mok—as she stared at the unique display that Shaft Lek programmed to surveil, not only the jump point but primarily the mines and the "go" status of the powered missile type bombs.

Their quarters were rudimentary. It was one small pressurized area wherein her companions rigged up sleep chairs that fit their anatomy. They found it curious how the human girl was content to sleep on the floor.

"Are you feeling anxiety building every day?" Molly asked the older of the two aliens. "If I wasn't modified with nanites, I would be very tense."

The two Slev looked at each other, then back at their human companion.

"We are terrified," said the younger one.

She smirked in a gentle sort of way. "Why do you look as if this is all just routine business?"

"Are you an expert on Slev body language, Molly?" asked the older one.

The ensign pondered that. "Um. No. I'm a little in the dark when it comes to nuances. I know your verbal communication really well—like my Slev vocabulary is vast—"

"—We understand that. But let me educate you," continued the older alien. "Since we approached the jump point, have you seen our teeth?"

Molly tried to clear her head of human context. "Nope. Now that you mention it, you guys usually grin at each other and once in a while at me."

The junior of the two spoke up. "We are scared *shitless*. Isn't that a human term in English? When that happens, we don't bare our teeth. If you noticed, we have large wide mouths full of teeth. Over the centuries, it has become natural for our species to find different ways of expressing emotions with our teeth. You are a human female. You do the same thing with your breasts. It makes the males of your species behave in peculiar ways."

Molly cleared her throat and tried to remind herself that these were two Slev. "That is your theory?"

"Oh yes. And also, your females use their posterior to attract males by shaking it on occasion. The effect is quite amusing to us. Particularly Ensign Lewis—we mean that he seems to want to procreate with you when you walk past him."

"Okay. That's enough exo-biology for now."

The temporary light moment led to a tiny grin and a glinting display of teeth. "I am glad we could have this talk," said the elder. "Perhaps we will have more time to analyze the male-to-female interactions. It is very—."

Suddenly, the levity of the moment was shattered by a piercing alarm from the control panel of their quarters. All three of them raced to the display.

"This is Mok." An encrypted transmission, highly focused, using a tight 460 terahertz beam, flooded Team Four's receiver with data. "We have Mazik warships emerging from the jump point. As we planned, each unit will engage with powered weapons only if the enemy clears the minefield."

The portable imaging system didn't have the power of ship-based equipment, but it didn't need to. Four mid-sized destroyers cruised from the jump point at an estimated 50 kilometers per second, lethargic by galactic standards.

"They're barely moving," said Shaft Lek.

Mok exhaled slowly, his large frame calm and sedate. "Their commander is not a fool. He's scanning for threats."

The Panruk engineer squirmed. "At this rate, he may pick up a few mine signatures in time to adjust his vectors and avoid them. I designed them with stealth features, but they are not completely invisible."

"Patience, Lek." The Slev commander focused on the display as the small Mazik task group moved closer to the minefield. "We cannot let any of them escape." He sent a message to each of the other teams with specific targets.

"They're close now," he whispered.

Molly stared at her tracking data. Three of the assault craft fell back, leaving one to press on ahead. "What are they doing?" she whispered to herself.

"Wait!" Commander Mok broadcast. "The Mazik are not as stupid as they are ugly. They're surveying."

Lek was dumbfounded. "The forward ship just reversed. They must have spotted us." The engineer sounded panicked. "We have to get out of here before they kill us!"

"Shaft!" barked Mok. "Stay calm. We have 25 fusion weapons that will hit them."

"But, sir. They are stopping. It's like they are deciding what to do. They must have seen the mines."

A single missile lit up all of their displays. The computer calculated the trajectory. It was headed for the freighter where Team Three had established their ops center.

"Allen!" Molly screamed into her mic. "John! Get into your suits; the Mazik launched at your freighter."

"We see it, Ensign. We're already suited. Stay cool," said the Recon soldier who'd been through a dozen hostile encounters in 1776 with Recon and fighting the Mazik hand to hand.

Space battles were very different than the crush of ground forces. The single alien missile closed at velocities that humans couldn't process. The AI that the Panruk engineers tasked to deliver the self-powered fusion bombs calculated and released the tiny weapons at precisely the correct moment. A sudden flash overpowered Lieutenant John Allen's monitor. A massive explosion rocked the freighter as it obliterated the alien projectile along with any stray matter within a four-kilometer blast radius.

"The AI already launched eight of our weapons," said Shaft.

"The Mazik are firing as they are returning to the jump point!" said someone from Team Two.

"Quiet," said Mok. "Let the AI give our bombs instructions. We've got three incoming. The trajectory is at Team Three."

John Allen's nanites assisted him in determining a course of action. Any running commentary was just a waste of time. One of those missiles had a high probability of getting through.

Molly watched as two explosions sufficiently distant from Team Three vaporized enemy weapons.

"Our fusion bombs are striking the Mazik—now!" said Lek.

The video was brilliant with white light that had to be filtered to protect the defender's eyes. Three destroyers were blasted into meaningless debris, shattered into chunks of alloys and electronics, and incinerated bodies reduced to particles.

"One got away!" said Molly. It was the outcome of any potential confrontation that they dreaded.

Mok ignored things he couldn't fix. Instead, he searched for the remains of Three's freighter. The Mazik missile pierced the already dead cargo ship in the stern. Most of the rear half of the vessel was so much fist-sized shrapnel. From what the computer's images resolved, the forward sections looked like the entire structure was shredded.

"Team Three? Team Three?" The Slev commander waited for a response. There was none. "Who is closest?" It was rhetorical.

"We are," transmitted Ensign Stark. She struggled to suppress her anxiety over John Allen.

"Take your shuttle and get over there. Not you Molly, just your crew. Ensign Stark—stay focused on that jump point, and be ready to launch your remaining self-guided bombs. We could see twenty Mazik cruisers come flooding through that gate. Stay sharp."

"Aye, Aye, sir." Her reply was laden with frustration. The best she could hope for was that Lieutenant Allen survived the gutting of the unshielded dead freighter. The images didn't give Molly much hope.

She watched her two Slev shipmates suit up and head to the airlock. They had to duck to get through, taking small steps with their four legs.

"If they are alive, we will bring Lieutenant Allen and his group back." The seasoned elder of the two aliens closed the hatch and attempted to wave. It gave Molly a sense of foreboding.

Alone, she dashed back to the control panel to review the video of the detonation on Team Three's cargo ship. She couldn't help but number the different ways those three could have died. John Allen, born in 1755, was a Recon soldier, darn handsome, and never married. The man earned a happy future. Molly couldn't bear the thought of losing someone close to her again—not after Dexter, her fiancé, died at the hands of Mazik Warriors.

"Commander Mok. I'm scanning the jump point and have enabled all of my self-directed mines."

There was a short pause. "Ensign Stark. If the Mazik pop through with a significant force, hold your fire until we can coordinate our attack. I'd rather have them run into static mines by being too eager than waste our small supply of self-propelled weapons."

She used her enhanced physiology to release a calming agent into her bloodstream. Revenge would be satisfying, but Molly had to use common sense.

A mic keyed up from the shuttle. The senior Slev spoke directly to the commander. "About 60% of the freighter is gone. The forward section is torn. What are our orders?"

"Go to the bow, dock, and board. I want the remaining compartments searched. Even if they are dead, I want those bodies back."

"We found one of them." It had been nearly an hour. No Mazik ships appeared at the jump point, but the stress of waiting weighed on the three remaining combat teams.

"Report," ordered Mok.

"It is the Panruk. He is physically in one piece, but his suit had a slow leak. I believe he was unable to repair the damage in the vacuum—he ran out of air."

The vision of the engineer's horrible death caused Molly to shudder.

"We are still searching."

Time dragged on agonizingly. Finally, "We've got Tal. He is alive and safe. The technician's suit is damaged from being slammed into a bulkhead. He has no comms. Standby. Plark! We've got the human. I can't determine if the lieutenant is alive or dead. His suit looks very damaged. There is blood on the faceplate. I am unable to see inside. There is a complete vacuum in this compartment. I can feel blood inside the suit."

Molly sank into despair.

"Get them to the shuttle. Hurry," said Mok. "Humans don't die so easy."

*

"We're two light hours from the jump point," said Barrett. "I know you want details right now, but that's how it is."

Mercy gripped the arms of her command chair. The bridge was deathly still as they received an automated data dump from a video probe.

"I'm enhancing the video," said Ensign Lewis. "It's ready."

The feed showed up on everyone's displays and on the large screen forward. Four Mazik ships blinked into existence on the Olamit side of the portal. They moved incredibly slowly as if suspecting an ambush.

"What the hell are they doing?" It was the voice of Lieutenant Petro, the CAG officer who was more of a doer than a talker—at least since he transformed himself from a nerd into a genuine badass when he killed three Mazik in an assault.

Barrett turned with a steely grin. "The damn Mazik aren't stupid."

The images played on. A missile was launched. A freighter

took a hit—either Team Two or Team Three—both of which had Recon soldiers.

"What the—!" barked Lewis.

Four Mazik destroyers reversed, then three enemy ships went brilliant white, clearly obliterated with fusion weapons.

"The self-propelled mines work," said Barrett.

Mercy cringed. The fourth destroyer disappeared. They all watched, but Petro muttered their thoughts: "That's not good."

"An understatement," said the captain. "Lewis. Check for an audio transmission."

"Nothing yet."

Barrett gritted his teeth. "Fighting on the ground is easier—you don't have to wait for hours to find out if you're dead."

*

"Let's send them some audio," said Molly. "They've seen the skirmish by now."

Mok answered her narrowed-beamed comm suggestion. "Not until we have a status on the lieutenant. Waiting won't make a difference on Olamit or on the Washington."

"I disagree. The sooner we let them know we are still functional, the better."

"And what would you tell them?" asked Mok. "That a Panruk is dead? That Allen's suit is pressurized, but he's unconscious, has a bloody visor, and is wounded?" He waited. "No."

The approach of the shuttle grabbed Molly's attention. She closed the comm and sprinted to the airlock.

The Qaanaki inner airlock hatch opened as Molly approached. Lieutenant Allen was placed on the floor. She pulled off his helmet.

"He's breathing." Her hands quickly unfastened the suit while the Slev attended to their slightly wounded mate and the body of the Panruk.

Allen's body didn't appear to have any penetration wounds. True enough, there was at least a half-liter of blood now absorbed into his shirt. An examination of John's back also showed no wounds.

Molly accessed her downloaded emergency medicine data, searching for an answer. His vitals were fair enough, but the lieutenant's BP was low. Blood and vomit coated his face and neck.

"Can you save him?" asked the younger Slev.

"I can try."

She began to look over his chest and torso carefully, smearing away blood to look at his skin. It was perplexing.

"One sec. There is something here." Molly looked closely at the upper left abdomen. There was a small black dot. It was hard.

"What is that?" asked the older Slev technician.

"It looks like a piece of shrapnel. Get me the kit."

In seconds she popped open the shuttle med-pack, which contained, among other things that you would never find back on Earth, an internal scanner the size of a ping pong ball.

"Oh fuck!"

"What?"

She looked at her companions. "He's got a sliver of something that when straight into his spleen. That's an organ you Slev may not have, but in a human, if it gets ruptured, it can cause internal bleeding. All that blood in his suit is from the lieutenant vomiting his own blood."

"So fix it!" said the Slev tech who'd survived the missile attack. He looked beaten up but was clearly desperate for Allen to live.

"I'm not a surgeon. Open up the kit completely. Maybe we have something in there that can stop the hemorrhaging."

"He looks awful," said Lewis.

"Considering a ripped spleen, I'd say he looks pretty decent."

Mercy squeezed Barrett's arm. It was more for her comfort than his. "Let's just be grateful he didn't die on the spot. Molly just saved his life."

The bridge of the Washington was full of captivated viewers of not only Allen's survival but of the description by Commander Mok of the details of the assault.

"The one that got away." Lewis made the point about the obvious disaster.

"We have to assume that Mazik Bah-Gahn will send an armada. That one ship will report our presence and ambush."

There was a dead silence.

"Lewis. Get me the Arbitor on the line," said Mercy.

Within seconds, Shaab Mar Gen showed up on the two-dimensional display. She looked worse than lieutenant Allen.

"Good morning, Arbitor."

"What's good about it?" asked Shaab.

"You've seen the images?"

"Of course. Did you think we would simply resume our peaceful lives here on Olamit knowing that everything would be fine because we have *humans* protecting us?"

Barrett glanced at Mercy. His wife ignored him.

"Arbitor. The results are not completely bad. We destroyed three of their ships. Even if they detected the minefield, we still have the ability to launch a dozen self-guided weapons, plus we can shoot unguided fusion projectiles."

Shaab was long past living for a miraculous win. She knew that miracles were the realm of stories for young Panruk.

"We've calculated the odds of victory using your data, captain. We are finished if the Mazik come through with more than ten significant warships. They know that we have a minefield. Isn't that why they backed up? That seems like an obvious blunder on your part. Mok should have never waited and given them the chance to cruise into the minefield. You should have fired on them immediately."

Barrett was boiling. "Arbitor. With all due respect, when was the last time you were engaged in a military battle? Don't even answer. I've been dealing with after-action bullshit my whole career. The point of the minefield was so that we wouldn't waste our limited supply of smart guided weapons. Did you not comprehend that when we talked about this five hundred times?"

Shaab Mar Gen merely stared back at Barrett. Mercy decided to let her husband plow over the Panruk leader.

"You've been dumping cynicism on this effort from the beginning. Enough!" His temper flared. "Mok did precisely the right thing. No one could have known that the Mazik would simply stand at the jump point. And there is no proof that they detected the minefield at all."

The collective minds on the circuit were temporarily confused. Mercy looked at Barrett. "How do you know that?"

He didn't waver and dead-eyed the Arbitor while addressing all the parties on the call. "We have no proof whatsoever that the Mazik picked up the mine signatures. They could have simply been tossing a lure out there to see if there was a trap."

Lieutenant Petro again spoke up surprisingly. "If Commander Bonner is correct, then all the Mazik know is that we have some kick-ass little weapons that took out 75% of their attack vessels. They don't know how many we have. They only know that our weapons were fired from a dead freighter. That may be enough to keep them out of your system for a long time. Maybe think about it like that?"

The weighty silence was exceedingly uncomfortable for the bridge crew and for the Panruk standing around Shaab's office on the planet.

The Arbitor blinked first. "If you are correct, there are two possibilities. One, Mazik Bah-Gahn will send a massive force, knowing that half his ships will be destroyed, but also knowing that he will have the ability to destroy my planet. Or two, he will blockade the jump point, and we will starve to death."

"Maybe there is a third option?" asked Petro.

They all looked at him. The man had gained a lot of confidence over the past couple of years.

"Well?" asked Mercy.

"What if Mazik Bah-Gahn figures out that the Panruk seem a little over their heads in aggression. I mean traveling out to put soldiers on dead freighters with fusion weapons? That sounds entirely out of character for the Panruk. Doesn't it?

"I'm thinking that the 'Emperor' is not a complete fool. His ships enter at the jump point and simply float and scan. That's not hubris. That's brains. So, what else does he know?"

Mercy arched her eyebrows, urging Petro to continue.

"When he examines the scan, he might pick up the signature of the Washington orbiting Olamit. It's not the Washington to him, is it? It's his battlecruiser that was sent to Earth, and if he sees it here?"

Barrett scowled. "No way. We're two light hours from the jump point, and we've got a moon obscuring our image."

"That's what I thought, too," said Petro. "But, as smart as we are, a couple of hours ago, we were temporarily in line-of-sight with the jump point to capture transmissions from our teams."

Mercy continued the thought. "And since that single destroyer didn't return with a fleet right away, he could be headed back to Kamtret, where they will see a brief glimpse of the Kor—which is what we call the Washington—but which they will see as their own ship, the Kor."

"Captain," asked Petro. "May I piece it together?"

"Keep going; it's your baby," she replied.

"Right. So, as far as Mazik Bah-Gahn knows, the Kor was sent to Earth, and it was more or less due to return soon. There are a lot of puzzle pieces for a paranoid megalomaniac to sink his Mazik teeth into. The Kor is sitting peacefully orbiting Olamit. The Panruk are suddenly proactively aggressive. His freighters and other small craft never came back through the jump point.

"I would think, as a cautious CAG officer, that our mortal enemy is going to consider the possibility that Earth wasn't obliterated, and maybe he underestimated the humans. After all, a certain drill sergeant got enhanced with nanites and escaped from Kamtret with the help of the AI"

Shaab and her advisors and the crew on the bridge of the Washington tried to process the variables.

"Are you trying to suggest that Mazik Bah-Gahn will come here with a very large force because he will suspect that humans are helping to defend the Panruk?"

Mercy interrupted. "I don't think that is what lieutenant Petro is pondering at all. No. I think your system may be relatively safe—no point in the Mazik getting hit with an unknown number of guided fusion weapons every time they jump through. Oh no, not at all. I rather believe that a vindictive, blood-thirsty tyrant would rather satisfy his urge to rip chunks of flesh from his prey by going back to Earth. After all, he can let you starve. You are Panruk pacifists, and if you are left alone, you will become meek and pliable once again."

Barrett picked up the thought. "But, humans really are a danger. If the Kor has been taken, then perhaps the Ko-Pahm and Ro-Pahm as well, the two ships tasked with smashing the Earth. Can Mazik Bah-Gahn do nothing while Barrett Bonner's species, my human race, figures out how to fight? I don't think so."

Chapter 15

"You don't look so bad," remarked Clark.

Monty sat on a log by the pond as Allison, Clark, and Howe stared at him, attempting to comprehend the story of Tzurek slicing off the lieutenant's arm.

"Tell me about the part where the Mar El forced you to kiss his foot," said Aaron.

"It's humiliating."

"Yes. I know, but something about that is important."

"Fine. It was like a gloat. I mean, it was gloating. He seemed to want to be treated like a god. There is some sick narcissism with Tzurek, but then creatures like that are actually deeply insecure and have self-esteem issues, right? When I initially refused, he held up the black disc he carries around and said he would remove John's brain. So I bent down and kissed the slimy slug's foot."

Clark heard this part twice in the last five minutes but responded the same way. "Thanks for doing that. I'd prefer to keep my brain inside my skull."

"I did it for Louise and your kids."

The captain smirked at Monty. "I thought we were friends!"

"I'm just messing with you. Call it a little comic relief after dealing with torture and surviving."

"I hear you. And, thanks."

Allison seemed to drift off but then re-focused. "Tell me about what happened after your arm was removed."

Monty said, "Didn't your AI abilities sense what happened?"

"Yes, but I want you to describe it." She waited.

"Fine. The Mar El dumped some growth hormone—very sophisticated—on me. It began growing my arm back. The nanites are pretty smart, Allison. They recognized some characteristics of the artificial hormones and hijacked them. Tzurek may be part of a ridiculously advanced technological race, but unbelievably, he missed it. There's something really messed up about the Mar El."

"You mean besides their vindictive superiority complex?" said Clark.

Monty shrugged. His large upper body suggested power and strength merely by the way he sat. "I know they are alien, and I understand all that 'alien minds are alien' junk, but while I was debating with him, he looked vulnerable, almost pathetic."

Aaron contemplated that and kind of looked lost. They all noticed, and Allison, in particular, considered that he was sensing something—the way only Howe could.

"What are you feeling?" she asked.

He emerged from his daydream. "I think that the Mar El are on the precipice of falling into decay."

Montgomery stood up skeptical over another one of his captain's revelations taken from some rumbling historical vibration that only Aaron could sense. The lieutenant gave off waves of utter contempt for the grungy aliens while simultaneously looking like he wanted to break a tree in half.

Aaron continued. "They've reached their level of incompetence."

"The Peter Principle?" said Clark.

"Yes. It took them a half-million years, but now they are in trouble." Aaron looked worried.

"So they've been a raging storm of crushing strength for so long that now it's crashing?"

"That's a dramatic way of putting it, John, but they are a hurricane. The Mar El have experimented on everything their own galaxy could offer them. The little rats have been stuck in neutral for hundreds of thousands of years, and their society is going to fall to pieces soon. For some reason, an old sailing metaphor is stuck in my head."

Allison looked quizzically at Howe. "Which is?"

"The harder the blast, the sooner it's past."

They all processed that quickly.

Monty laughed. "Half a million years may take a long time to unwind. The Mar El aren't just going to close up shop and go back to digging up roots."

"That is exactly the captain's point, isn't it? They can crumble into a primitive society very quickly," said the AI confidently.

There was dead air among the four of them. The only sounds were those of insects and flying things that appeared to be the Mar El's best attempts at creating birds from alien DNA.

Aaron exhaled, absorbed in his own brand of psychohistory. He perked up to eye each of his companions. "This isn't the first time."

"What does that mean?" asked Monty.

"The Mar El crashed and burned in the past—more than once—and they know it."

Allison cringed. "Say it," she blurted out.

"They are on the verge of collapse. They are aware that it has happened to them at least once, but my senses tell me perhaps several times. The little creatures have been cycling for millions of years in this galaxy. And they are trying to figure out how to stop it from happening again. Their culture turns into a stagnant pond of scum. They keep doing the same things over and over again, and then something clicks, and they will go primitive barbarian on each other. Eventually breaking up into clans and blowing the crap out of whichever group is weaker. Then after the final group has eradicated all of the others, they will turn on themselves until they do what Monty said—start digging roots for food."

"And then start the cycle again," said Clark as he arose, feeling frustrated. "Isn't that what we want? The Mar El turn into farmers, and we go back and beat the tar out of Mazik Bah-Gahn. Game over. Everyone wins."

"No, John. Tzurek is the tip of the spear. The whole hierarchy in their society is bent on finding a way out of the loop. They are very patient. They kidnapped Els Talitha here, otherwise known as Allison, as part of a long effort to figure out a way to survive. I feel it, and I know it in my gut," said Aaron.

"Who cares?"

"Monty!" Allison stabbed him with a steely look from her

artificial eyes. "They are going to move into the Milky Way. That means the only species that will survive will be the Mar El. Our galaxy is huge, but there is a reason, or there must be a reason why they are focused on us and the sentients in our 'neighborhood.'"

Howe blinked. "There is. The rest of the Milky Way is weak in terms of life. But, our little corner has humans, Mazik, Slev, Panruk—maybe hundreds of borderline sentient beings. The Mar El can screw with all our DNA and use it to try to survive by adapting our biology to theirs. We humans are as destructive as the next sentient species out there—we're outstanding at killing each other. However, we don't kick ourselves back to the stone age, technology moves along, and we find ourselves in a sea of rolling waves. War. Peace. Advancement. Growth. War again. The Mar El want to learn how to keep advancing and then do genocide on every other living sentient in multiple galaxies."

"That sounds like a galactic war crime."

"Yes, Captain Clark. It is the end of every other being. Tzurek and his species will take what they want or need, and then what's left will be considered so inferior to them—"

"—that they will merely discard all of us like we were garbage," Monty completed the thought.

"F-ing hubris!" barked Clark.

"We have to do something about it!"

Allison said nothing, but Aaron did. "We are going to do something. We're going to help them fall off the cliff. And, I'm not talking about another three thousand years. No. We're about to become the Mar El's worst nightmare."

Monty laughed. "That's a pretty bold statement considering that I just had to bow down and kiss Tzurek's foot to prevent him from squirting John's brain out of his skull."

Howe scratched his head. One of the little flying insect-like things perched just above his right ear. It took off after being flicked away a second time. "I have a plan."

Allison sat on a rock. At this point in Aaron Howe's life

history, the AI seated on a rock no longer befuddled him. If she wanted to, the intelligent machine who'd changed his reason for living could stand in one spot for a million years and never tire.

But, there she was, more human in appearance than ever.

"I'm all ears," she offered.

"Honestly, dearest Els Talitha, you are not entirely ears. Nevertheless, I know we could end up in a philosophical debate which would eventually lead to my admitting that you are all ears. We both know that would be a waste of time."

"You're sidestepping the issue, doctor."

"Am I? I guess I am."

He found himself looking at Allison. She was beautiful and could be any woman, yet the AI chose to be simple, pretty, and not exotic. Howe remembered telling his sister, Julia, years earlier, back on Earth; if Allison were a human, he would devote himself to love her forever.

She snapped her fingers. "You're staring at me as a teenage boy would."

"Sorry. Where were we?"

"Your plan."

Aaron plopped himself down on a rock across from her. There was a light breeze as usual in the late afternoon, and the temperature was a typical 72 degrees. Still, there was a slight bead of perspiration on his forehead.

"Tell me about your transformation to AI again."

"I told you twenty-one times."

He nodded. "Fine. No need to re-hash that, but I'm going to say something that will upset you. Are you ready?"

"What kind of question is that?"

Howe pursed his lips, eyes wide open, and seemed to dig deep to muster some courage.

"Well, Aaron?"

"All right. Here goes. I need you to turn me into AI"

If ever there were a shocked expression on Allison's face, this was it. "That's your idea? Let me run through the permutations. Okay. Done. You becoming AI won't help us."

"I'm going to start calling you Els Talitha. I love when you shoot down my ideas. Let me make a fine little point—which one of us has the ability to sense history?"

"You do," she answered reluctantly.

"Congratulations. Guess why I need to be AI?"

"Maybe you think that you won't die. But I've got news for you. The Mar El have coded some sort of sympathetic AI device of their own that can turn me off. Permanently. Dead for all intents and purposes—just no body."

Aaron didn't look taken aback or flustered at all. "We get it. They can 'kill' you with the same results as a biological creature—you would cease to exist."

"That's right. So, how will it help you to be in the same condition as me? As soon as Tzurek notes your transformation, he will probably turn both of us off."

Howe arched an eyebrow and gave her a silly grin. "Gee. I wish I'd thought of that. Let's just give up then. Die of old age while Tzurek and his race obliterate every other biological thingy with an I.Q. over 50."

"Your cynicism is obvious. What do you know that I don't?"

He cracked his knuckles triumphantly. "We're going to do something extraordinary. It's so far beyond the pale that I'm afraid that even you won't be able to wrap your head around it."

"I'll try. Okay?"

"Fine," he answered. "Do you remember how you led me down that insane path, all the tests to see if I was the 'special' one you were looking for all those years? Don't bother answering because we both have excellent recollections of you torturing me figuratively. And, I turned out to be the one human with a tiny quirk that gives me the ability to be telepathic?"

"Not telepathic. Use the correct terms."

"Sure, Allison. I'll put it this way: I can see where things need to go and how to get there."

She brushed her wavy brown hair out of her face. "Not only you but also Julia and your mother."

"Well, my sister isn't here, and my mother is locked up in a psych ward, so that leaves me, right?"

Allison gazed at him, brooding.

He continued. "Monty's abuse by Tzurek confirmed something in my mind. We are not static. We are dynamic."

Aaron smiled. At that moment, his confidence in his intuition strengthened a thousandfold. Some things defied logic. Before Allison came to Earth, Doctor Howe, the science guy, would never believe in faith or hunches. Everything could be proven or disproven using logic and data. If the data didn't exist, then he could hypothesize until he could find the data. Philosophy took a backseat—always.

"Not now."

She squinted at him. "What's not now?"

"Logic doesn't rule me anymore. There are forces that exist outside of logic and empirical evidence."

"You've succeeded in confusing me. Aaron, you don't seem sane. You're rambling."

He raised both his arms and shook them at the sky. "That's great because you transformed yourself into a computer when you went from being a human child to becoming an AI. You became a very complex machine on that day, but your optimism and philosophy died."

She gazed at him, feeling a tinge of hope. "And you can restore that?"

"Yes, I can. You've spent 2,000 years trying to be human—to get back what you've lost—the thing that those bastards did to you. I've got another little piece of info for you; the Mar El are terrified of us."

"Aaron, they could turn us off like a switch in a nanosecond."

He laughed hard. "No, they can't. They need us so badly. We are the drugs that can keep them alive. Humans. Until they figure out how to save themselves from impending doom, they are going to seek the thing about our species that will be their salvation. It must really suck to be them.

"Do you remember that you spent all that time looking for a being that could integrate nanites? Poof. Humans can and no other species. Yes, time and space travel—like Lewis' dog was able to travel. But, only we can integrate nanites. The Mar El can't. And if they can't figure out how we tick, then Tzurek and all his race will crash and burn. Self-destruction is in their blood."

She looked stunned. "They searched for me desperately for two thousand years after I escaped."

"Bingo."

"Because they need to figure out how I could transform myself from human to machine on a spectrum of biology to AI?"

"Yes, Allison. They've been trying to understand that issue for millennia so they can replace their unyielding tendency to self-destruct. They've figured out that it's something in human beings, but they don't know what it is. Even though they have ripped apart our DNA a thousand times, they are still lost, and the clock is ticking for them."

She was flabbergasted. "How will that play out?"

Aaron shrugged. "I said it before; they will have a species-wide meltdown. Like something will finally trigger it, and barbarism will rule them."

"That is screwed up!"

He laughed. "Wow! I never thought I would hear you throw out a phrase like that so naturally. You're on your way to becoming human already."

Allison looked down at her artificial body. The small inconsistencies, points of light, and shimmering spots that previously gave her away as an AI were nearly gone. She could have been any woman waiting on a bench at a bus stop.

"You've improved your human appearance. Allison, you've almost perfected it in the last couple of years. Now it is time to attempt the next step."

Monty slept for 27 hours in one of his favorite treehouses. He could have slept longer, but Clark was concerned.

"Why are you up here, and why are you waking me up?"

"I was worried that your integration of Tzurek's growth hormones might have killed you."

The large, muscular Lieutenant sat up. "I'm pretty animated

for a dead guy, don't you think?"

John ignored the comment. "Are you hungry?"

"Yep."

"Here. I got you this big bowl of stuff. It's the equivalent of 7,000 calories."

The meal lasted about six minutes.

"Now, dear Montegue, We didn't talk about the changes in your body yesterday, but Allison said you were going to be different. She said you would be really strong, but your thinking might also be, um, changed."

Monty raised his shoulders and pierced his buddy with a sharp look. Then he went cross-eyed. "Do I look insane?"

"I'm not a psychiatrist, but you've always been a little wacky in my book. Just a tad less so than Lewis."

The big man stood up. "Check this out." Monty walked out onto the wooden balcony, turned to wink at his friend, and then stepped off.

"What the heck!" Clark dashed to the edge and looked down. Montgomery was smiling and looking up from six meters below.

"How'd you like that demonstration of mental illness?"

"How are you not injured?"

He smirked. "Must be the nanites."

"Bogus, lieutenant. Nanites are helpful, but that was a twenty-foot drop. I'm coming down. I want to look at you."

Clark slid down a "firepole" planted vertically into to the forest floor.

"I'm not the same Monty from before the hormone therapy. Allison is correct; my body is like iron."

"I want some of that!"

"No, you don't, John. I had to have my arm cut off to get it."

"No pain, no gain. What else can you do?"

Monty turned around and saw a boulder not far away. "How much do you think that rock weighs?"

"I don't know. Maybe two hundred kilo? More?"

The lieutenant strode over to the smooth elliptical stone, spread his arms, and began to pull it out of the ground. The display of raw strength was incredible, and then he managed to throw it several meters, where it crashed onto the leafy ground.

"What else can you do?"

"Check out my arm." He clenched his fist and waited.

"Right. That's your arm. Looks like the same muscular meat hook as usual."

"Touch it, John."

Clark reached out to wrap his own hand around Monty's forearm. "What the hell? It's like I'm grabbing a steel pipe."

"How 'bout now?"

Suddenly the rock-hard flesh became soft like any ordinary human. "Can you do that on-demand?"

Monty nodded. "As Allison said, I'm different."

"Geesh! Can you fly?"

"No. That would be pretty cool, but I can tell you that I think I can survive in a vacuum for a while by hardening my whole body—it will be like a suit."

Clark stood on the ground, shaking his head. "I'm in shock."

"You know, if we ever go back to Earth and Betty gets completely pissed off at me...and then whacks me with a frying pan...."

"It won't hurt, but you just proved that you are made out of concrete—but I'm still putting my money on your wife in that contest."

Chapter 16

"Tzurek is looking at us."

"Let him look. He's flying around on his bicycle seat thingy?"

They both glanced skyward to see the small alien hovering. The gadget would make one hell of an amusement park ride—it must have been utilizing anti-grav very efficiently. The plates on a ship were enormous, yet somehow the Mar El figured out how to make miniaturized units.

"We should take one or two of those when we leave here," said Allison.

"Agreed."

Tzurek zipped away. Aaron felt a hand on his arm; it felt natural, but it was the artificial grip of Els Talitha, a woman kidnapped over three thousand years earlier.

"Wait," she said. He turned, not phased that her hand was still grasping his arm. "Can you tell me what you've been doing for the last 24 hours?"

Aaron tilted his head, somewhat perplexed. "You don't know already? Are you having trouble probing my thoughts?"

"Yes. Ever since we arrived here, connecting with your brain has become more troublesome. It's problematic."

He groaned. "Are you aware of how much I despise the word 'problematic?'"

"Of course. You had a professor who kept using that word to irritate you. What was it, physics?"

"No. Communications."

The AI smiled broadly. "You took a course in something non-quantifiable?"

"Let's not get into it, shall we?"

"Did you learn any other brilliant phrases in your liberal arts class?" she asked.

"Yes. I'll tell you, but then we're moving on to other topics."

Aaron paused as she nodded, then said, "There's no praise like self-praise."

As an utterly advanced computer, she processed that in microseconds. "That professor must have been a real comedian."

"Yes. A barrel of laughs."

Allison released her gentle hold on Aaron's arm. "Tell me."

A fleeting thought wandered through his mind. It was non-scientific—he wished that she would keep touching him. It passed reluctantly. "We are going to give you what you've wanted."

"I don't follow the science of trying to make me human again."

"It's not all science. There will be some magic involved."

She gazed upwards to affirm that their Mar El jailer was not lurking above them. They were nestled in a tiny clearing amid tall thin fruit trees with orange bark and pale green leaves. "Doctor Howe. Magic runs against my nature since I scoffed at it 3,000 years ago as a little girl in a village full of idol worshippers."

"I'm not talking about fake theological voodoo. What is that famous quote by Arthur C. Clarke?"

"As if you don't already know it? Clarke's Third Law states: Any sufficiently advanced technology is indistinguishable from magic," said Allison.

Howe took a deep breath. "Yep. That's it."

"We've fantasized about making me more human in the past. And, you've been not so subtle that there is a way to change me. Are you trying to tell me that you've figured out how to do it? You know that sometimes you are perplexing to me. Are you going to wave a wand and do it right now?"

"Incantation or some other ritual? No. But, I believe we can do it whenever you are ready. You will need to follow my instructions exactly and not ask questions in the middle of the process."

They both stood there. It was another perfect day with the same comfortable weather. Allison leaned up against a tree. "Do you know, Aaron, that I often trick myself by doing human-like actions? Like resting beside this tree. I imagine that there could be thousands of people in forests right now on Earth, perched next to a rock or a tree. Do you know how badly I wish I could turn the clock back? I wish that I'd grown up in my village, just another girl grinding corn to make cakes or whatever other primitive work there was for me to do. Who would choose that? I would over the existence I've had for all these millennia. I would trade all of it to be the simple peasant I should have been. Wouldn't it be wonderful for me to go back to Earth and live a normal life?"

"Absolutely, provided that they haven't blown themselves up while we've been away."

"You need to know that my mind was replaced with logic when I absorbed the Mar El's AI into my body. My emotions vanished, and whatever 'feelings' you think that I have were all learned and mimicked from observing."

"I get it. You watched all the Council species and even humans in an effort to replace what you lost."

"Exactly, Aaron. And the machine that I merged with didn't somehow store the essence of me in some vault."

He processed how traumatic it must have been for an orphaned girl to dump what was essentially her soul to escape her captors.

"But over time, you took the facts of your existence and imprinted emotions on top of them. I know that you can feel. You are AI like no other, true or not true?"

"That's true, but something intangible is missing," she muttered dejectedly.

"I know. And, that is the part that you might call magic."

Allison pondered his words. She would have dismissed the ideas out of hand if he were anyone else. But, Aaron Howe was unique in the galaxy. "We'll need to figure out a way to access Tzurek's computers as I did before."

"No. We don't need the Mar El or their technology. You're going to connect with me."

She instantly replied, "Not possible."

Aaron didn't respond immediately. He gave her a fraction of a second to process what he suggested. "It is the only way, Allison."

"What are you proposing exactly?"

He focused his full attention on her. "How did you create nanites, save Mercy, and enhance the others?"

"You watched me back in the lab, remember?"

"Exactly, except that we are going to do something different. You will connect and transfer yourself partially into me. And, I will share my life force with you."

"You're crazy." Her tone was flat and confident.

"No. You are. You're a machine without a soul. That is pretty insane."

"Aaron. What you are suggesting is technically impossible."

"Again, No. This is going to work, and we're doing it."

"You could die! And I could cease to exist."

"If we were arguing about math or physics, I would yield. Bonding like this is different. And you will do it because it is the only way to stop the Mar El and save our galaxy. When I put it like that, do you understand the gravity of the situation?"

"Yes. But I don't want you to die, Aaron."

"If we do nothing, then Tzurek will eventually kill me and turn you off. I would not be surprised if he could figure out how to make you suffer on a machine level. Clark and Monty? The bastard will cut off some more limbs and torture them for as long as it takes to solve the inevitable collapse of their culture. Do you want to do nothing while Tzurek removes their organs repeatedly?"

"No."

Aaron was desperate to ease her apprehension. "I promise you that I can give over my D.N.A., my living energy, or whatever you want to call it. Everything that I survived is about this. Trust me, Allison!"

"Trust me is what people blurt out right before everything goes to hell."

He faced her and moved closer.

"What?" She asked.

"We're not delaying it. Grab my hands."

If an AI had such a thing as better judgment, she ignored it. Allison reached up as they interlocked their fingers. Energy flowed around them and through them. It happened suddenly—it was a rush of some energy that she couldn't comprehend. She began transferring the core of her being, or her existence, without understanding how it was happening, only that she surrendered herself to Aaron's control. At the same time, he was releasing life into her. It was cathartic. Inexplicable.

Aaron felt Allison's power flooding into him. No words could describe it other than it was terrifying and exhilarating. He feared for his life but then didn't. He would embrace death if it came.

The woman, Els Talitha, Allison, breathed. It was real, and she also suddenly feared death. His thoughts filled her. Darkness and light surrounded them. Power and vulnerability. The finite and the infinite swirled between them.

Three thousand years of her. Every journey. Allison's torment during a millennium of captivity. Aaron felt it. He owned it. She was part of him.

The two of them briefly opened their eyes. They each felt and knew everything. A surge of energy overwhelmed them, and then everything went dark.

Clark was fascinated with his friend's newfound abilities as they trudged their way around the habitat. Periodically, as they made a circuit along the transparent barrier, he would ask Monty to demonstrate various strengths. The latest was a karate chop that cracked a boulder.

"Can that be the last demo?"

"Um. No."

"I'm getting a little bored of showing off, John."

"If Betty was here, you'd be pulling up trees and chucking them just to impress her."

Monty snorted. "My wife doesn't require impressing. She knows how awesome I am."

The air was the same temperature as usual. It was boring. All four captives openly wished it would rain, snow, or something other than boring perfection. The two Recon soldiers gazed off at the planet's setting sun. It glowed, and occasionally they could see light waves shimmering off the nearly invisible matrix that imprisoned them.

Genetically engineered birds flew occasionally. Other creatures slithered across the landscape. None were edible, and the reason for fashioning them by the Mar El was conjecture.

"I think it's mostly a game for them," said Monty.

"Were you dissecting my thoughts?"

"No. I saw you staring at the mindless bird-thing over on that rock, and I guessed you were wondering about their purpose. I know I have almost daily."

"I think our pal, Tzurek, lives in his god fantasy world, churning out manifestations of his awesome cosmic power."

"Captain Clark. You are correct in that analysis. I felt every inch of that when the little sucker tortured me. Except the actual Creator of our universe did an infinitely superior job of it."

"Feeling theological, Monty?"

Montgomery paused his cadence. "We've seen some serious shit since the 1770's haven't we?"

"Yup."

"Have you noticed that the galaxy has tremendous potential to be a great and wonderful place for all species? And yet, it is always hanging on the edge of disaster."

"We didn't know how dangerous and fleeting our lives could be when we were fighting the war."

Monty grinned. It wasn't a smile—more like resignation. "If we'd never gotten the visit from Dr. Howe, we'd have lived out our lives in blissful ignorance."

A pat on the lieutenant's back was followed with a resolute grunt. "And then two hundred years later, all of our descendants would be wiped out because of Mazik Bah-Gahn and the inability of the Council to stand up and use their brains."

"Good point. We really didn't have a choice, even if you want to say we have free will. Some things just have to happen. That's why I think there is a design to all of this."

"Monty dear, I am sure that Mordy would love to have this conversation with you—if we ever see him again."

Montgomery thought back to the brief humor they enjoyed at Mordy Schein's expense along the rim of the Winslow Arizona Crater. "I wonder if Schein ever met the girl he was looking for. That lame ad he was running to attract a bride was damn funny, but I can't believe that he would get so much as a nibble."

"I liked the part where he said that any potential mate should expect him to be gone for long absences due to dangerous wars—something like that."

They laughed, but it was laden with sadness for the friends they might never see again.

"Let's go find Allison and Aaron. I'll snatch some of my bootleg whiskey, and we can enjoy some tree bark supper just like the good ole' days."

"You mean like yesterday?" Clark asked dryly. He turned and headed for one of Monty's treehouses without waiting for a response.

*

"I'm scared." She looked around. The sky on Mar El planet 432 was pitch dark. As usual, there were no stars. Tzurek saw to it that humans should feel utterly alone in their artificial world. Hence, no planets or solar systems, or galaxies to behold and long for. It was another slice of the razor, a measure of torment that their warden utilized to cage them.

Allison felt the forest floor under her spine. She was stretched out on her back, her dark, long locks of hair resting under her head. The leaves beneath her smooth body felt cool— something she'd forgotten for two-thousand years—and the smell of the woods was not an interpretation of her AI systems but rather exquisitely real.

"I'm enthralled. I am—something. I am a living thing. It can't be, and yet it is."

She searched with her mind. Everything was animated. The skin. Her flesh. Not a dream. Not a product of complex algorithms she'd practiced for so long trying to emulate—. There was wetness in her eyes. Allison blinked and looked up at the black night. A longing seized her, desperate to tilt her head and gaze at her form. It mattered not at all if she would be seen as beautiful—she resided in a container of life, and that was beauty enough.

She lifted her head and then leaned up on her elbows and stared. Then she laughed, and then she cried, a torrent of tears for what she'd lost and what she'd gained.

Aaron watched her and said nothing at all. He lay nearby in his own realm of shock and stunning realization. He was still human, but also AI. Just as Allison could not withstand the need to explore the rush of humanity inside her, Aaron felt the exhilaration of *knowing*. It was impossible, and yet his mind was infinitely enhanced. So much danced in his consciousness. He merely had a notion, and the chaos of so much information fell into order, waiting for him to access it. The most complex things he'd spent decades studying were all laid out before him—simple and understandable in microseconds or less.

He waited. The human element of Allison was in no rush. She held her energetic thoughts in check and used her emotions to explore her human physicality. She needed time to connect with what the Mar El had taken from her. It was rapture.

Howe lay silent. He searched the habitat and sensed Monty and Clark perhaps a mile away. There was no reason to move. Allison needed time, and now, time meant nothing. What mattered was what they could do. She could reconnoiter every molecule in her being for as long as she wished.

For an instant, Aaron thought about Tzurek. The single Mar El, with his disturbed, nightmarish life, was no longer a threat. At least not to the two of them. He felt sorry for Tzurek's species which was trapped and tied to continual demise. There was no other choice. If they succeeded in breaking the cycle, using homo sapiens as a catalyst, they would eventually, in millions of years, destroy everything in a cataclysmic finale. The Mar El would consume themselves in a brutal, barbaric ending to all life. Humans, Panruk, Mazik, and all other species would be long extinct before the death of the last surviving Mar El.

Aaron's thoughts returned to Allison. He sensed her elation. She was free, and even though becoming AI allowed her to escape two thousand years earlier, it was merely an exchange of one prison for another. Now, that had all changed.

"I see you." He turned at the sound of her voice.

Before he could respond, Allison reached out and touched his cheek and then gasped. "You are like me now."

"Similar but not the same. The way it should be."

Her hand grazed his skin as the sensitive tips of her fingers felt the creases and textures of his face. "I did not know that it would be like this."

Aaron smiled. "I must confess that this is more than I could imagine."

"Hold me," she said.

He slid close to her on the dark forest floor and wrapped his arms around her. A shudder pulsed through her, and they did not move for a long, long time.

Tzurek, the leader of all Mar El research on Planet 432, rarely slept. The little aliens engineered themselves to function without rest sometime in the distant past. They required downtime only to dispel boredom, which could be acute when performing similar activities for hundreds of years.

Of course, now, the impetus to solve the *problem* was growing and festering. The upper echelons of Mar El culture assigned managers to harvest primitive, slow-developing D.N.A. from biologic specimens. But, the clock was ticking, and many Mar El knew what was coming if they could not integrate alien traits—a rapid transformation into an aggressive, violent, self-destructive society.

Having been assigned to 432, Tzurek's ego was stoked, knowing that his human subjects were the most promising. If and when a method could be derived from humans to stave off the coming implosion—it would be known that the administrator of Planet 432 solved the conundrum. The Milky

Way was the richest in carbon-based biologics, and all of those beings existed to be used and manipulated by the authentically superior Mar El.

A wave of energy sucked the small, gray bi-ped from his relaxation. It rarely happened in the past. Something was not in balance. Tzurek connected to the black disk in his veiny elongated hand. He surveyed it and used it to examine the various compounds remotely.

"Ahk." He muttered a single syllable aloud, a concise expression of concern. The data from dozens of habitations were nominal, yet the human containment was unreadable. Anxiety was not a common emotion for the small alien. Tzurek stood and exited a hut to stand on the undulating ground as it carried him toward his primary specimens but then stopped and returned. A rare technical disturbance could wait, and the humans could pluck their tree food without supervision. In any case, the containment was unbreachable, even by Els Talitha, since the fabric of the transparent walls was advanced beyond her technological level.

It was late in the evening. Monty was barely affected by the distilled spirits he'd created. The physiological changes to his body must have also tamped down on the interaction of alcohol with brain cells. "I'll have to figure out how to modify the stuff," he muttered with disappointment.

Clark had never been much of a drinker. Louise used to give him a threatening, beady-eyed look every time he took more than a sip. Once she was implanted with nanites, his wife added that her wrath would include an old-fashioned, colonial thrashing if John drank to intoxication.

"My booze has become a worthless endeavor," announced Monty. "Let's go track down Allison and Howe. The fact that I haven't felt a ripple of connection with either of them is unsettling."

"Agreed."

The two of them stood, stretched, and stomped off.

Aaron held Allison's hand. There was a very subtle lightening of the sky as morning approached. "Do you feel it?"

"Yes," she replied. "The guys are looking for us."

"Not just that, but Tzurek is aware that our cage is not shuttling data to him. And yet, the alien does not consider it a concern."

They silently stepped in the direction of the two Recon soldiers.

Several minutes later, the four of them intersected beneath another of Montgomery's tree houses. The very first thing that Clark noticed was the peculiar and unexpected vision of Captain Howe holding Allison's hand.

"Alrighty then," Monty said in something just short of a bellow. "I believe we'll need an explanation for the hand-holding between you two." He eyed them warily and proved once again that the former Continental Army Sergeant never shied away from anything unusual.

Aaron smiled and used the phrase that was platitudinous for Recon. "Long version or short version?"

In something akin to a comedy scene from 20th century Earth, Monty and Clark said "long" and "short" at the same time. Allison laughed—as a human would—it was pronounced and even child-like. Montgomery squinted in the dawn light, having observed her improbable reaction. "I change my vote to the short version," he stammered while shaking his head.

Howe began by clearing his throat. "I've been contemplating a means of undoing or modifying a static situation or condition that Allison has been subject to for a couple of thousand years."

The two Recon guys stared blankly at Aaron.

Allison squeezed Aaron's hand. "Do you mind if I interrupt? Dr. Howe, you sound like you're giving a lecture to the board of directors at your company."

She aimed her gaze back and forth from Monty to John and blurted out, "I am human."

Clark looked back at her and said, "Yes. Allison, you were Els Talitha, a child, when the Mar El kidnapped you from a village on Earth 3,000 years ago. Right. You were human.

Understood."

"No, Captain Clark. Get your tenses correct. I said, 'I *am* human.'"

The two soldiers turned and looked at each other, not knowing exactly how to react. "You're AI," said Monty, turning his face back to Allison.

"That's true, too," said Aaron.

"I'm lost. Even with a mass of internet knowledge in my head—I'm lost," exclaimed Clark.

"We found a way to restore her human physiology and mentality to her AI form. Allison is now fully human and fully artificial intelligence."

The two guys were staggered. Monty couldn't help himself. He poked Allison in the shoulder.

"Feels human to me," he said to Clark. "And, I just realized something that might be exceedingly bad for Tzurek: our Allison here is now significantly more dangerous—she's AI and also a human female—we're looking at possibly the most terrifying combination of destructive energy in the universe."

"Wait," asked Clark. "Where'd you find the human part to put into her? Is that a reasonable question? It's not like there's a cauldron of homo sapien D.N.A. soup sitting around waiting to integrate with an AI."

Aaron let them ponder that for just an instant and said, "She got it from me."

Montgomery's mind raced ahead. "And most known chemical reactions involve sharing, bonding, exchanging elements. What'd you get from her?" he said while sweeping his rigid index finger in Allison's direction.

Howe grinned like a Cheshire cat and released the bombshell news. "I'm now fully AI and fully human."

Chapter 17

A tremendous crash accompanied the impact of Monty's arm into a tree. The tree cracked but didn't break into pieces, but then the large lieutenant pushed a little on a space above where he'd struck the trunk, and the top came tumbling down.

"That was impressive," said Howe. "Let me see your arm again."

Monty held out his arm. There was no indication whatsoever that he'd just whacked a thick, dense wood with so much force. Aaron touched the forearm. It felt human enough.

"Can you do that rigidity tensing again?" asked Allison.

Immediately, Monty transformed his arm into something like steel and stone.

"Ally. That is downright frightening."

She looked demurely at Aaron. "And he can do that with his whole body. I wonder what effect a particle beam or a railgun would have on that material."

"I think it would bounce off of me if the power level was not ridiculously high. As a side-point, what's with the name Ally?"

She ignored the question at first but then thought the better of it. "That's Aaron's name for me. I like it. Okay?"

Clark said, "Sure. No problem. By the way, Monty told me that he thinks he could survive for a while in a vacuum with no suit."

Howe shook his head. "At this point, I wouldn't doubt it."

"We know some of what this big guy can do," said Clark. "What about you two now that you are a mix of biological and AI."

Allison reached out and pulled off a tiny piece of bark from a fruit tree. "I can do this." She shoved it in her mouth and began chewing.

"Right. Well, I guess eating would be on my list of things to do also," said Clark.

"As far as our other abilities, Aaron and I have programs running in our heads to analyze what we can do independently and together. We've already deactivated Tzurek's control over our environment. He can't suck your brains out anymore. In fact, he can't do anything at all.

"What really matters is what we can do to him and the rest of the Mar El on this planet and in their galaxy."

John Clark thought about that and was elated that Tzurek wouldn't be popping open his head like a bottle of champagne. It didn't bring back all those patriotic and brave CAG guys who the little alien bastard murdered, but it was still a win.

"I believe that together, Allison and I can neutralize all the Mar El on this planet. Our prison warden is becoming aware that his power over us has been hamstrung—probably the single most terrifying event in Tzurek's long life."

Monty sneered. "That asshole cut off my arm. If you've neutralized his power over us, then I can go rip his arm off."

"No one is leaving yet. We will walk out of here, but we also need to be smart about this since we are going to need that ship up there in one piece," remarked Aaron. "Don't ignore the fact that Tzurek can still do a lot of damage to the USS Dexter O'Brian."

Allison smiled as if she'd figured out something. "I think Aaron and I can put something like a net around the O'Brian to prevent any Mar El from damaging the ship."

Clark seemed skeptical. "How can you do that from down here? That ship is in a geo-stationery orbit 40,000 kilometers away."

It was a trigger for Allison. She poked Aaron to get his undivided attention and then announced, "We will use magic!" She laughed, and then Howe joined her.

The Mar El master of Planet 432's biological specimens did not ignore the data failure from the human habitat for long. He'd been unsuccessful in linking his black control disk specifically for that compound, so he brought an ancient drone out of storage.

Tzurek stood and rolled along the undulating floor of the area surrounding what he called the "Primate Laboratory" in his own language. When the gray, short alien arrived at the boundary of the containment field, he stared at the large pond and the boulders beyond; trees were gently swaying from the light breeze further inwards. Ordinarily, some of the specimens would be squatting on rocks or wading in the clear water—it was a primitive pastime.

"Ahk!" Tzurek gurgled in yet another verbal comment expressing his concern. He decided to fix the data issues and then decrease the size of the human cell to herd the creatures to a smaller area by the water.

He connected to the drone, and it elevated to several meters, then vectored to the field matrix.

"It looks like the scummy little grub is trying to send a drone," said Allison, her language becoming more fluid and descriptive (in a human way) by the hour. "Watch this," she said to Aaron while they crouched down, hidden from view.

In a sudden bright flash, the accelerating drone contacted the fabric of the energetic web and disintegrated. Tzurek leaped back due to an ancient need to preserve himself. Microbits of the machine sprinkled onto the sandy ground, and for the first time in his long, long life, the Mar El felt an emotion common to all those species he'd tortured over hundreds of years—fear.

"Now what?" asked Monty, kneeling down a short distance behind the hybrid human AI's.

"First thing is to stop hiding," answered Howe. "Allison has hijacked control of our entire environment, including the shielded dome over and around us. Unless Tzurek wants to get a shovel and dig his way under, he can't do anything."

"The bastard must be infuriated," said Clark.

"Maybe not," said Allison. "The Mar El might only consider it a minor inconvenience caused by some inventive sub-creatures. He's going to try to figure out a workaround, and he knows that his predecessor blew it when I escaped all those years ago by going full-AI. There is no way he wants to get capital punishment from his leaders for failing to contain us."

Aaron   sneered.   "I'm   okay   with   saving   him   the
inconvenience of having to be put to death by his bosses."

"Understood, sir," said Montgomery. "Do you want me to
squash the dipshit?"

"No, thank you, lieutenant. That little egomaniac is mine."

*

Solving problems was a Mar El tradition going back a half-
million years. Sadly, all of the math and science questions were
redundant since every theoretical question was asked and
answered, logged, and filed away. But now, Tzurek had a new
problem; how to harness four arrogant aliens who'd managed to
hack his system!

Technology was out since there was no way to penetrate the
shields surrounding their cage—above ground. However,
tunneling in was a different matter. Tzurek pondered that
solution, then considered that perhaps the humans had also
compromised his mind to device links *inside* the compound. He
would have to get creative without exposing himself to an actual
physical confrontation with the primitive beasts. In some ways,
it amused him, but also, there would have to be some
punishment to convince the captives to never misbehave in the
future—first   things   first.   The   Mar   El   turned   his
disproportionately large head and moved towards a different
habitat not far away.

"Our little alien friend is unhappy." Aaron stared at his three
companions. "Do you feel it, Ally?"

"Of course. He's trying to figure out how to get in here and
give us a thrashing. And, as rudimentary as it seems, his most
viable method will be to dig underneath the walls."

Monty bared his teeth. "So what? I'll stomp him into a wet,
bloody smudge under my feet. It'll be therapeutic for all of us."

"I need to understand something," said Clark while staring at
Allison and Howe. "You're both AI. Why can't you just

transport us up to the ship? Or transport us into the shuttle? Then we just leave."

Allison answered immediately. "We can't use those abilities across the boundary of the containment field. It's a limitation, and even though we've wrenched control of the barrier from Tzurek, it still has intact physical properties. Once we bring down the cage, then we can transport to the shuttle and launch."

Monty was incredulous. "Why are we waiting? Let's get the hell out of here!"

"Things are never that simple," said Aaron.

The lieutenant's arm went *concrete* and vented his frustration on a nearby rock. Shards of stone took off in different directions. Howe continued. "We have to protect our shuttle and our ship—that part is already clear enough. If we leave before we've finished the field around both, Tzurek can damage them."

"In addition, Aaron and I need to devise a method to keep the Mar El contained in this galaxy until their culture collapses," remarked Allison with a slight wince. "As Aaron said earlier, if they can't adapt human DNA into their own, then something will kick in. It's kind of like the Mar El become turbocharged and aggressive. In any case, it will be our job to trap them in this galaxy."

"That sounds ambitious. How are you going to do that?" asked Captain Clark.

Howe merely raised his eyebrows and said, "We're not sure about that yet."

Clark threw his hands in the air and stomped off.

Chapter 18

"No f-ing way!" yelled Clark.

The four of them gaped at Tzurek hovering on his seat while a dozen creatures that could only be described as mutated abhorrent monsters dug with massive claws at the sand by the energy barrier around the cage.

"This is not what I expected," said Aaron.

"How long before they get underneath? Just guess."

"Monty, I'm thinking about forty-five minutes," answered Allison.

John Clark was simply stunned. The things were scaly, dark green, huge, with four legs and two arms extending forward like battering rams. The claws on the arms ripped at the ground ejecting huge clumps of soil and rock. The heads could only be described as utterly hideous, making the Mazik look attractive by comparison. They had multiple red eyes, suckers of some sort, and a mouth full of teeth and fangs that rivaled anything that could have protruded from a T-Rex's jaws.

"Anyone have a plan?" asked Monty.

"Am I the only one that gets the notion that Tzurek is just going to let those things tear us up into little pieces?" asked Clark.

"Captain Clark. I think I can take them," replied Monty.

"Listen! The energy fields around the shuttle and the O'Brian are nearly complete," said Aaron. "We can bring down the barrier here in about thirty minutes. We'll have to kill that Mar El."

Monty started to grin. He raised his hand. "I volunteer."

"No," said Howe. "I'll do it. You, lieutenant, will be busy beating up those things out there. John, you will need to find a place to hide until we are ready to go. Ally and I will help Monty kill any of those—what shall we call them?"

"Raptors!" shouted Clark over the rumbling noise from the

frantic excavation a dozen meters away.

"Raptors?" Is that the best we can come up with?

"I'm okay with that lieutenant as long as your body can go full concrete and stop them."

"Aye, aye, sir. With pleasure."

At that moment, the ground in front of one of the Raptors turned into a sinkhole. The four humans stared as a large clawed arm started poking through the dirt. Clark ran to the nearest tree and climbed since he had no practical weapons to protect himself from becoming a meal for one of them.

On the other hand, Monty visibly changed into a walking chunk of steel as the first monster began to slither out of the ground. It straightened on four legs and blinked at them without moving.

"The humans will restore control of the containment matrix now." Tzurek's irritating voice emanated from the mouth of the horrid thing.

"That's a neat trick," said Montgomery. He lifted up his arm, the one that Tzurek amputated, and extended the middle finger of his right hand.

The three of them did not move, but Aaron opened his own hand, and a bright white, tiny ball of energy rested on his palm. To the Mar El, this was interpreted correctly—as a threat. The Dinothing lunged. Several suckers on its head stood erect and oozed some reddish liquid that bubbled like a strong acid. The mouth gaped, baring spiky fangs.

All the beast's terror potential became meaningless as a brief flash of energy bored a large hole through the center of its body and then looped around to obliterate its head.

Two more leaped from the hole in the ground. Allison released the same consuming energy weapon from her hand as the other creature raced at Monty.

Montgomery didn't flinch at all. Instead, He charged directly at the monstrosity. It towered above him, and it opened its jaws to clamp down on the lieutenant's upper body. Clark trembled, anxious and petrified that his friend would be crushed in an instant. Instead, as the teeth of the creature slammed down on

Monty's body, there was a loud staccato crack as many of its fangs broke into pieces. But that wasn't all. Monty's arm exploded out of the top of the Raptor's head, followed by the lieutenant as he tore a huge hole through its brain and skull.

He jumped to the ground and landed on two feet as the thing crashed onto the sandy soil.

"Damn, that felt good!" shouted Monty to Clark as the captain cheered him on from his treetop perch.

"You're covered with its brains and blood!"

"I don't care! I like it!"

Allison and Aaron had energy weapons in their hands as more of the Raptors entered their prison. The ferociousness of the quadrupedal giants was no challenge as Montgomery tore apart two more of the semi-sentient beasts.

On the other side of the containment, the remaining Raptors scattered. They'd clearly seen enough, and their subservience to the Mar El did not overrule their desire to live.

In a moment of silent communication between Allison and Aaron, the two focused a different kind of energy to disable the barrier's powerful field. Tzurek panicked and attempted to flee, but within milliseconds, Howe projected a tractor beam of sorts and slammed the alien to the ground.

For Clark, it was cathartic. He'd seen the CAG soldiers murdered brutality by the Mar El like insects. Now the tables had turned.

Aaron pinned Tzurek to the dirt. Their administrator, captor, and cruel tormentor struggled to free his arms. A short distance away, the black control disc which connected the Mar El's brain augmentations to the planet's network rested uselessly in the sand.

John shimmied down the tree and joined his companions as Howe approached their enemy.

"You will release m—," Tzurek tried to blurt out a command, but Allison used her mind to shut his thin lips.

Something was exchanged between the two AI human hybrids. Aaron stepped back. Allison descended to her knees and brought her face close to her quarry.

"Answer me, Tzurek. Are you afraid?"

The alien could not fathom how the captives became his captors. Even pressed to the ground, unable to move, he tried to re-assert his dominance as Allison released the lock on his mouth.

"The humans will release——." She held out her thumb and index finger and brought them together Tzurek's mouth was again forced shut.

"Again," She asked, this time speaking in the language of the Mar El. "Do you fear me?"

He blinked in a way that answered in the affirmative.

"Excellent. You should be very afraid. Now, I am reading your thoughts. Do you feel me inside your mind? Tell me now where the control for generating a jump point back to our galaxy is located."

Tzurek fought against his better judgment to give over the information. It was a mistake. Monty sensed that the small alien who'd tortured him was reluctant. The lieutenant reached down and pinched off the Mar El's slender hand at the wrist. A high-pitched shriek pierced the tranquil forest atmosphere.

Aaron glared at Monty. "No more of that!"

"Aye, aye, sir."

Allison sent a wave of calming energy into Tzurek's mind. The shrieking stopped.

"Now, tell me," she said inaudibly inside his brain.

Resistance was impossible. Tzurek revealed everything that Allison wanted to know.

She stood and mentally transmitted all of the data directly to Aaron. He stored it and then looked at their captor while using his mind to send an interruption to Tzurek's artificial heart. The Mar El had an instant of lucidity, knowing that it would die, and then it did.

"That thing is dead now? Can we get the heck out of here now?" asked Clark. "I mean, we've had enough entertainment for today."

The shuttle docked snuggly into the bay on the USS Dexter

O'Brian. The automated systems were still working. Environment. Grav-Plates. Drives. Computers—all functioning nominally.

"Food."

"What about food?" John asked.

Monty pointed to his stomach. "I could eat you, sir, but as my superior officer, I don't think it would be appropriate."

"Go to the kitchen. The freezers are working. While you're at it, you can whip up something for all of us."

The bridge appeared untouched, but the bodies of the two CAG soldiers were decaying on the floor. It pained Aaron intensely to see them. "We're all starving, but after mess, we will give these fine soldiers and the others who Tzurek murdered a proper funeral. Then I want them frozen so that we can return them to Earth and give them the burial they deserve. These guys should and will be remembered as part of the elite who saved the human race."

A few hours later, the four of them delivered all of the deceased and shrouded CAG men into the vacuum of space.

*

"We'll meet you in the Olamit System," said Aaron.

Clark appeared distraught. "We have been Mar El prisoners for months. Who knows what could be sitting on the other side of that jump point. We could waltz right into an armada of Mazik battlecruisers. Without you and Allison, they will turn us into shrapnel."

Allison gave him a sympathetic look. "It's a risk, but we have no choice. You know our plan, and as much as we need to save the Panruk and Earth, if we don't create a blockade at each Mar El jump point...."

"Yes. You've explained that they will jump to the Solar System and start capturing humans. Yada, yada, yada. They figure out how to integrate human traits, and in a half-million years or less, only the Mar El will be left in several galaxies."

Allison winked. "You summed that up very well, John. But understand this, Captain Howe and I will jump from point to point and create a maze. Each time the Mar El enter a jump point, they will return to their own galaxy through a different portal—they won't be able to leave. Our best hope is that they will quickly enter the spiral and break down into tribalism. Once that happens, we'll have breathing room."

Monty also seemed anxious and didn't mince words. "What if you get into trouble and can't come back?"

Aaron frowned. "We have no reason to assume that we will get stuck here."

"There's that wonderful word again—assume," sneered the lieutenant.

"It's the best we can do, and having both of you stay with us is a waste of manpower. I'm making an executive decision as overall commander of human space forces. You need to go back and get with Mercy. You need to rebuild a crew for the O'Brian, probably mostly Slev. Mazik Bah-Gahn is not going to lay around eating donuts and ignore Olamit.

"If we take too long, then figure out a plan with Mercy and Kap. Try to include the Panruk. After all this time, we don't know what you'll find around Olamit. The planet could be a burned-out cinder, but I'm trying to stay optimistic."

"We'll leave in one day," said Allison. "We'll take the number one shuttle and transport ourselves from point to point as quickly as possible. If you have to go back to Earth before we get there for any reason, go to see Julia as soon as feasible."

Clark gave her a head tilt. "Captain Howe's sister? The one in Vermont?"

Aaron began to speak, but Allison cut him off. "Yes. Julia. She may make the difference in our war with the Mazik."

"I don't think we understand what you are saying," said a very perplexed Monty.

"I'm not going to tell you more, and neither can Aaron. The less you know, the better."

"Allison, you're doing the riddle, wrapped in a mystery, inside an enigma thingy."

Captain Clark smiled and lightened the moment. "I know that one. It's Churchill about the Russians in 1939."

"On that note, let's put this ship on auto-pilot towards the point. Slow and steady. Make it a twenty-six-hour trip. Those are my orders in addition to sleeping." Aaron took Allison's hand, exited the bridge, and headed for his stateroom.

Chapter 19

The message from the freighters contained good and bad news. Lieutenant JG Allen's condition was much improved. The nanites in his system did something that would not have happened in a normal human; his spleen healed, and the Recon soldier was nearly 100%.

"What's the bad news?" asked Barrett.

Mercy looked very stressed as she sat on their bed reviewing the text from Mok.

"No ships from Kamtret have approached the jump point to Olamit."

"That sounds like a positive to me."

"No. There's more. Mok sent several probes to hover around the Mazik side of that portal. I asked Kap to have that done as soon as our units were in position. That was one month ago. Those were stealth probes, very tiny and nearly invisible."

Barrett tapped his fingers impatiently on the desk.

"I'm getting to it. Relax."

"I'm chilled. Please continue, dear." He kept tapping.

"The probes just sat there on the other side, but one of them came back to Mok's team after 25 days, as programmed. A task force of a dozen ships just went through the jump point that could potentially lead toward Earth."

"We have to go after them!"

"There's more, Barrett. There are five cruisers parked outside our jump point. If we leave now to return to Earth, we'll have to fight our way out. And, the strangest thing of all is this—." She handed him an enhanced image of the Mazik ships that jumped on the shortest path to Earth.

"What the hell—this just keeps getting better and better."

"My thoughts exactly, Commander Bonner."

He looked hard at the pic. "Three cruisers and four large cargo vessels. What's the point?"

"Mok has a different take, and Kap agrees. They've got a lot more knowledge about Mazik Bah-Gahn's methods than we do. According to both of our Slev friends, those four are troop carriers."

"Since when do the Mazik need to send Warriors to get their point across? They can do it the old-fashioned way and drop rocks from space."

Mercy sighed heavily. "I asked Kap the same question."

"And?" asked Barrett.

"He said that Mazik Bah-Gahn used Warriors on Slev and Makim whenever he got so pissed off that rocks weren't satisfying enough."

The two Bonners processed that, and a grim weight descended onto their shoulders. "They're going to Earth to teach Barrett Bonner's people a lesson." He tried to comprehend what that would mean.

"You know what that means, honey," said Mercy. "They're going to unleash Warrior class Mazik with advanced weaponry on the United States first. People like Barrett Bonner. And Mazik Bah-Gahn probably told his commanders to let the Warriors eat their way through the human population."

"This is going to get really ugly. We have to stop them."

Mercy whipped her long, blond ponytail around and cracked her knuckles. She had no problem dishing out justice. "We're outnumbered, and we can't even leave the Olamit system without risky heavy damage or worse."

"I think Petro was right. The Mazik don't see any use in losing ships to little fusion bombs. They just blockade Olamit and wait for the white flag from Shaab Mar Gen once the Panruk are all starving to death."

"I agree. And as captain of this fiasco, it's on me to figure out how to fix this; unless you want the job?"

Barrett smiled weakly. "Honestly. I would take it if you made me, but I believe you are better at it."

"I guess this is a time for that old US Navy slogan—rank hath its responsibilities."

"Yep. You get the privileges and the burdens. Ain't that

great?"

"No. I wish we were on a peaceful planet with our son."
Mercy sounded distraught.

"I miss Manuel terribly, but I didn't want to bring it up
because I thought it would upset you."

She gazed at her husband's face. "Not at all. I need to talk
about him. I love him so much. We rescued him. We adopted
him, but I feel like he is our son."

"And right now, he's a couple of years older, living in
Vermont with Aaron's sister, Julia, and probably better at math
than his teachers."

Tears formed in Mercy's eyes. She didn't fight it. "I'm
aching inside. Barrett, hold me and tell me everything will be
alright."

He moved to comfort his wife and wrapped his arms around
her while she wept on his shoulder. Sometimes all the logic in
Mercy's enhanced, nanite brain could not compete with
Bonner's loving embrace.

He kissed her hair. "Everything is going to be alright."

*

"This is an unmitigated disaster!" Shaab Mar Gen, Arbitor of
the Panruk had a ferocious expression on her face that was
unnerving even via a display some 40,000 kilometers from the
planet's surface. "Are we supposed to leave a small group of
defenders out there with those incapacitated freighters for the
next five hundred years, hoping that at some point in time,
Mazik Bah-Gahn will die and his replacement will be friendly?"

"Arbitor," explained Mercy. "It is probable that the Mazik
are heading to my planet with as many as 150,000 Warriors.
Along with three battlecruisers, the destruction they will inflict
is a bigger disaster."

"More serious than Olamit being turned to ashes?"

"That won't happen," said Kap Jahrnuk.

Shaab scowled. "Can I accept your viewpoint as a diplomat
and insider to the mind of the 'emperor,' Captain Jahrnuk?" The

disdain in her voice hung in the air.

His reply did not mince words. "Arbitor Shaab. I have served in the Mazik fleet for many solar cycles until I risked everything to commit treason and mutiny. We Slev are not simpletons."

She considered his words and the undertone of insult she'd just inflicted. The Arbitor softened slightly. "I apologize if my statement was, shall we say, unprofessional. Nevertheless, how do the Panruk survive if your small fleet departs for Earth?"

Mercy intentionally let that question dangle in the air for a moment. "We're working on a plan that will include a detachment of Slev and Panruk near the jump point armed with more guided and AI driven fusion weapons. We know that there were five enemy ships stationed outside this system. One of them left to follow the larger group in the direction of Earth and was replaced by a small destroyer. Our collective view is that their plan is to confine the Panruk to this system."

Barrett added, "Mazik Bah-Gahn is erratic, vengeful, cruel, and many other adjectives, but Kap's and Mok's view is that the tyrant doesn't want to lose any more ships."

Shaab's doubts resurfaced. "He'll just build more. The maniac doesn't care about losing crewmen."

"He can't produce enough Grav-plates." Ensign Lewis spoke up. "I've been studying ship manuals from the Mazik. The documents are replete with references to sourcing the plates from Qaaniki, Zorinth, and the Seeleetomah. The manuals are full of requirements to maximize the life of the Grav-plates because of difficulty in obtaining replacements. Bottom line: The enemy cannot have their ships exploded into little bits by your fusion bombs because any anti-gravity gear will be lost forever."

"Don't leave yet," said Shaab. "Give us time to add more powered fusion bombs to the defenses near the point. I'm not talking about the AI self-contained ones. I'm referring to small devices that we can launch and aim remotely at any aggressive ship entering the system." She looked away for a moment. "Our chief engineer says it will take three or four of your earth 'weeks' to make two hundred of them. When exiting Olamit, you can drop off additional trained fighters and pick up your two people, Ensign Stark and Lieutenant Allen."

"Standby, please," said Mercy as she muted the audio and visual transmission. She turned to Barrett and the other crew on the bridge of the Washington. It was like unleashing a herd of angry beavers who all had the same vitriolic complaint that it would give the Mazik almost a month's headstart and that the USS Angela Carlisle would be alone and outgunned.

Captain Bonner listened to the tumult and then raised her hand to silence them. She keyed the mic and resumed video. "We can agree to fifteen Earth-days. That gives the Mazik task force a big lead that concerns me greatly. Remember that we also have to neutralize the five Mazik ships on our way to the other jump point towards Earth. We will need a small supply of fusion devices to get past them without getting blown up ourselves."

Shaab Mar Gen seemed pleased with Mercy's commitment—it was more than she expected from humans. She smiled as a Panruk does. "What about the Ro-Pahm? What are Captain Jahrnuk's plans?"

Without delay, Kap opened his mic circuit. "We're going back to Earth with the Washington. If we are fortunate, perhaps we will capture additional ships. That will increase our power against the Mazik considerably."

"Thank you, Kap," said Mercy. "Arbitor Mar Gen. It would seem like a prudent idea to have your technicians get started on those fusion bombs—we're all going to need them."

*

After nearly a month of exclusively Slev company, Molly ached for the touch of another human. LTJG John Allen returned to his own freighter after only two days of downtime. The spleen injury was no match for the power of the nanites.

"I really wish you were here, lieutenant."

"Thanks, Molly. I've also got that hankering for actual

human company. I mean, it was nice visiting with you, but I would have preferred to bypass the shard of metal in my gut."

"I said it before, and I'll say it again, you scared me severely. I thought you were dead with the blood vomit on your visor."

Allen tried to lighten the mood—"It cleaned up nicely."

"Sorry. I was getting a little morbid. Somehow, the shit I've been through makes me pessimistic."

"Understood, Ensign Stark. However, we saved Olamit and did some serious damage to Mazik Bah-Gahn. If I ask directly, will you try to cheer up a little?"

"Um. Yes. I'll do my best. Only because it's you, and I'm the only one who's had an intimate relationship with one of your internal organs."

He'd known Molly since she was a kid back in 1776. Now she was nineteen. Feelings stirred in him, and he longed to be near her.

"Different subject," he said. "We need to be ready for the replacement crews. They'll be here in—less than a day. Maybe you should translate the data on the mines into Slev and Panruk. It'll give the newbies something to study."

"I thought you were going to ask me to lunch."

The lieutenant blushed, which was not easy to discern on the video screen—fortunately. He recovered. "What's cooking?"

"Your favorite. An M.R.E. and a bit of my hidden stash of chocolate. I know how much of a drug chocolate is for you."

"Molly. If Commander Bonner doesn't insist on an immediate de-briefing, I will meet you in the mess hall on the Washington asap."

"Deal." She cut the connection, wondering if flirting with John Allen was the right thing to do.

Eighteen hours later, the USS Washington maneuvered to an equidistant position among the three cargo ships. Molly wanted to jump out of the airlock to get to the large battlecruiser, but being that vacuum was unpleasant at best, she waited for the shuttle.

Once delivered to the Washington, Mercy squeezed her daughter like a tube of toothpaste.

"I love you too, Mom."

"Barrett would like to de-brief you and Allen."

"It's gonna have to wait. I'm taking Lieutenant Allen out to lunch."

"Very well, but we're going through the jump point in twelve hours. So be ready."

Chapter 20

The Olamit jump point had an adjacent gravity well which had another jump point that led to a series of jumps that led to Earth. The existence of the second jump point near the gravity well was inexplicable. It had none of the characteristics that would produce such a transit point in space, yet there it was.

"Don't look a gift horse in the mouth."

Barrett looked up to see Ensign Lewis grinning at him. "I'm guessing you are wondering how the hell a second transit point could show up just in that spot."

"No. I was thinking how much I would like a couple of dozen Gozenburgers with cheese, but they are a year away on s Earth."

"Really?" asked Lewis.

It was Bonner's turn to grin. "No. Not really. I was thinking about that astrophysical anomaly. It pisses me off because it doesn't fit the science."

Mercy entered the bridge through the bulky blast door on the starboard side aft.

"Attention on deck," called out one of the Slev crewmen.

"At ease. Let's review the game plan briefly." She had their full attention. "In about one hour, we'll receive the positional data on the five Mazik ships on the other side of that hole. If they are static, then we are going to hit the jump point at maximum acceleration and then turn to our transit out of the Mazik space. It'll be the Washington first with the Ro-Pahm five kilometers on our stern."

There was a moderate increase in stress. "I know it's tight, but we want to blow right past those ships and out of this system. We will have 18 seconds between emergence and transiting the other jump point at our projected velocity."

"What about firing off some fusion rounds at those ships as a parting gift?" asked Molly.

"Absolutely not. We will not stir up the Mazik and give their 'emperor' an excuse to re-engage with the Olamit system. Every week that goes by gives Shaab and her engineers time to reinforce their defenses. In a month or two, the Panruk will have enough operational self-directing fusion weapons to destroy even a large assault."

"What if the Mazik follow us through the other jump?" asked another of the Slev.

"I'm sorry you missed the early planning session. We are taking 200 of those fusion weapons with us. If the enemy chooses to chase—well, it will be a galactic light show. That's it. Prepare. Check your displays, and let's calculate a vector when that probe data gets here."

"Hold at .05 lightspeed. We'll blow past them at just over 15,000 km/sec."

Mercy left the comms open to the Ro-Pahm. "Kap. Confirm and be prepared to assume a course parallel to us toward that larger jump point. If any of the Mazik ships make a move, accelerate to .07 lightspeed and drop as many self-guided mines as you deem necessary."

Kap answered in English. "Confirmed. What if there are objects on the other side of the second jump point?"

"I'm a little OCD about that also. Let's hope anything there is small enough for our shields to deal with. If not, then I'll see you in Heaven. It's what you Slev call *Grammat,*" said Mercy.

"Oh. Theology. Let's hope there isn't anything there—I don't want to go to Grammat just yet."

Mercy gritted her teeth. "Roger that. Fifteen seconds."

The transition to the interim space was hard for a normal sentient being to grasp. With nanites, it was easier. The two ships flashed past five Mazik destroyers at a velocity that made visuals impossible. The computers, however, could track and do complex calculations.

"They're not moving," announced Lewis. "Wait. We've got one missile launch and one particle beam that was extremely off-target. The missile is falling off—no additional projectiles of energy weapons."

"Time to jump?" asked Captain Bonner.

"Four seconds. Three. Two. One."

There was a brilliant sparkling and shimmering halo that lasted for milliseconds. It was unique to some jumps and inexplicable; despite efforts of scientists from the Council, the various phenomena surrounding portals in space remained a mystery.

"Kap. Any damage?"

"Small particles only. Our shields survived. What about the Washington?" asked Captain Jahrnuk.

"The same. We're good. Accelerate to 0.1, and we've got about fourteen days to our next jump. Let's hope that the Mazik armada doesn't get to Earth too far ahead of us."

The Slev captain looked back at Mercy via his display. "And let's hope Captain Schein doesn't engage before we get there."

"Mordy has a lot of common sense. He'll know that even if he can take out one of the Mazik battlecruisers, they will destroy the USS Carlisle. His best option is to run and then pester the orbiting Mazik with random hits and try to wear them down," said Barrett.

"What about Earth?" Kap replied.

"The Mazik have four enormous troopships. I think it's pretty obvious they will be landing ground forces," said Barrett. "Most likely in the USA because Mazik Bah-Gahn is psychotic when it comes to that English-speaking sergeant that escaped from a torture cell on Kamtret."

Kap nodded his fearsome blue-green head and bared teeth. "He wants to unleash a massive assault of Warriors on America because he hates you personally?"

"Sometimes Barrett can piss people off," interjected Mercy. "Not me, of course, but others. Yes. Especially megalomaniac, genocidal tyrants—trust me, Barrett Bonner is superb at making people fighting mad."

*

Captain John Clark and Lieutenant Montegue Montgomery

felt the burden of a giant melancholy mood that was pervasive on the Dexter O'Brian. With Aaron and Allison gone for days, the two Recon guys crept up on the re-aligned transit point for the Olamit system. Tzurek gave up all his computer access before Howe executed him; that included the highly advanced capacity to manipulate the jump point near Mar El Planet 432.

"Do you mind if I point out that we don't know squat about what is on the other side of that Olamit point. The cool part is that we are jumping from the Mar El galaxy directly inside the Panruk system. If the Mazik are anywhere patrolling outside that point, they won't even know we arrived inside."

"And, my dear friend, Monty, if the Mazik have twenty ships inside the Panruk system?"

"That's the easiest question you've asked me in a year. Answer: We're dead meat."

Clark growled. "Not my favorite outcome, but we'll find out in how long?"

"Seventeen hours. A one-way trip to Olamit or death. That sounds like a title for a book or a movie—*Olamit or Death*. Remind me to write that if we survive and live happily ever after on Earth."

"Sure. It's on my to-do list. For now, I'll sack out in my throne here, and you go get some real sleep. You have eight hours; enjoy the heck out of it."

With Monty off the bridge, Clark checked the systems a third time. The USS Dexter O'Brian ran silently through a pitch-black region of the Mar El galaxy. Clark would have done some astrophysics experiments if he wasn't exhausted, but even a nanite brain needed rest. He set the alarm for five hours. Anything urgent would bypass that, and the weapons systems would be online and manned in seconds. But there was nothing out here. Tzurek's companions on Planet 432 had little recourse but to watch as the human battlecruiser powered its way out of the system. Aaron and Allison sabotaged all possible offensive capabilities on the alien world.

"That's nice," said the Recon Captain to himself as he flicked on some music featuring Frank Sinatra and other members of a 1950s gang called the "Rat Pack." Each soldier in Recon had their own taste. Molly was all about Gen-Z music. Monty liked Scottish bagpipe marches, which routinely annoyed everyone within earshot. Lewis, surprisingly, couldn't get enough Mendelssohn classical. Schein was into the Beatles. Rogers favored The Who. Allen differed by insisting on talk radio.

"We are an eclectic bunch," said the captain while tapping his fingers on the side of his command chair to the rhythm of a song about traveling to the moon. John chuckled. "Frankie, if you were alive today, we could take you a lot further than the moon."

And then he was out cold.

"I can't believe you let me sleep for 12 hours. I hope the nanites will intervene and keep my bladder from waking me up—you know—when we're both old and gray."

"Charming, Monty. As usual. Now I have the image of you leaning up against a tiled bathroom wall at three in the morning, taking a leak. Thanks."

"Sorry. Where are we?"

"A few more hours until we find out if there are a bunch of angry Mazik in Olamit," answered Clark, who then pointed to a container occupying a significant chunk of the navigation table. "That's food."

"M.R.E.'s?"

"Yes, but also some tree bark from planet 432 and some carbs I found frozen down in the galley. No Twinkies. No Herr's potato chips. No ice cream, but it's better than air."

"Awesome. I'm so hungry I would eat Tzurek."

"Another pleasant image. Thanks. For now, let's eat real food, concrete man."

Despite Kap Jahrnuk's concerns, the Arbitor of the Panruk designated Shaft Lek, the young engineer, to command the operations out by the jump point. The Mazik presence on the "other side" had been reduced to only two attack craft. It relieved a little pressure on the soldiers, but there would be a minimal warning if Mazik Bah-Gahn decided to send an armada to destroy the planet.

Shaft reviewed the inventory list of mines. Passives were now up to 600, with the bulk of them being held in storage. More importantly, the dumb, powered mines, controlled from each team's remote consoles, numbered 150. And finally, the count of fully-automated, AI, self-guided fusion bombs had reached 80—that was the quantity that gave the unenthusiastic commander of the Intra-Galactic Defense Group a bit of anxiety relief.

Commander Lek keyed up the comms to the all four. "AI check."

"Team Two. We have one AI cruising on automatic. The rest are on standby."

"Team Three," said the Slev team leader. "Same."

"Team Four," answered a Panruk technician perhaps twice the age of Shaft. "Same."

"Very well. Lek, out."

He looked at his Slev team member, Par, having thought that he could never get comfortable with the frightening appearance of an alien who could probably snap away a chunk of a Panruk belly in an instant. But that had changed. The sharp teeth and musculature were characteristic of the Mazik, yet these Slev were actually cultured and honestly reliable.

"I'm concerned that we have a few of the AI bombs operational," said Par.

"I think they should all be up and running. Less stress on us."

"Shaft Lek. Perhaps a freighter will come through the jump point. In a short amount of time, the fusion weapons would be on an attack run directly at a cargo ship."

"That's amusing. Do you think Mazik Bah-Gahn will be sending food in the near future? Or ever?"

"But what if a non-attack ship comes into our system?" Par pressed the issue.

"That is interesting. The humans are always asking 'what if' this or that will happen. They are always worried about disasters instead of just letting systems deal with unusual events. Maybe you Slev are part human?"

The large alien grinned. It would be frightening to the uninitiated. "From what I have seen of the primates from Earth, it is probable that all the members of the Council would do well to start thinking like those ugly alien bipeds."

Now, the Panruk engineer laughed and frowned simultaneously; a peculiar reaction unique to his people. "If you are concerned, there is a remote chance that we can get the AI to detonate before it impacts any incoming ship. How fast can you react in an emergency?"

"I don't know. How much time will I have to press a trigger before the automatic weapon reaches a target?" Par looked at his commander.

"In the time it takes for one of your Plark vermin to spit up acid on its prey."

"I've seen that with my own eyes as a youngster. It happens very quickly, Lek."

The following day, Shaft received a video message from the Arbitor. It was Shaab's classic case of micro-management that led Par to go into a sputtering diatribe in the language of the Slev.

"I understand your apprehension."

"Commander. With respect for Shaab Mar Gen, Arbitor and leader of your planet, enabling all of our inventory of smart weapons is, in the words of Ensign Molly, a 'dumbass idea.'"

Lek replied, "Would you like to send Shaab that message? It's only two light-hours away, which means in four hours, you will receive a response that will turn you a deeper blue."

The Slev technician got up and paced on his four heavily muscled legs, clapped his large hands together, and snorted loudly. "I see two problems with Shaab's order. First, if a non-Mazik vessel comes through, we could kill hundreds of innocents. The second is even more relevant. If a hostile ship comes into the system, we could have dozens of those weapons targeting one ship. The self-guided bombs think independently, and that could be a huge waste of resources. It will take many solar cycles to replace them after putting on a spectacular display."

Lek took two glowing fingers and pressed them to his head, an ancient Panruk substitute for anti-anxiety chemicals. It helped a little.

"Let me ask you this, Par of Slev. Number one, which non-hostile ships do you think are coming to say hello to us?"

"I—"

"Wait. Number two, I agree with you about wasting smart bombs. Do you know who designed them? Me. And you, my friend, will keep the Arbitor's message secret because she is wrong. Her message was coded to me only, so that's it—I will take it under advisement as the humans are always saying whenever they don't want to do something."

Par seemed happy. "And what if a cargo ship comes through?"

"Then I hope that it's empty or that you can hit the cancel command very quickly."

"Yes, I heard you, faster than Plark acid vomit."

The small sprinkling point of light that was the gateway to Olamit hung like an ominous illuminated door in the black void. The time for jesting passed as Clark and Monty prepared every weapons system they could manage—just in case.

"Ready?" asked John.

"If we get blown to bits, let's try to inflict some damage before we're turned into frozen chunks."

"Definitely."

And then, the Mar El galaxy vanished, and the Dexter O'Brian appeared nearly motionless in the Olamit system.

"Our sensors are picking up no threats."

"Give them a second, Monty."

They waited. Nothing.

"It's a Mazik ship!" screamed Par. "We've got three outbound AI devices closing on it."

"Time?" asked Lek.

"Fourteen seconds."

Something felt off. Shaft saw a single Mazik ship barely moving. "Identify that ship!"

"It's the Ko-Pahm. A Mazik battlecruiser" yelled someone from Team Two.

"Ko-Pahm?"

Seven seconds.

"Ko-Pahm," repeated the technician over the commlink.

Shaft nearly jumped out of his skin. "Abort. Abort. Abort!"

Three seconds.

Par really was faster than a vile Slev rodent. He slammed his seven-digited hand down on the panel. At the speed of light, which was virtually instantaneous from such a short range, three AI weapons shut off their detonation circuits, but they were too close to prevent impact with the target.

"We just took three hits to our forward shields," said Monty.

Captain Clark looked bewildered. "I didn't feel a thing."

"They were small kinetic strikes. Almost simultaneous. I don't know what the hell that was. I'm not picking up any Mazik vessels, but the odds that exactly three small rocks would hit us a the same time—."

Clark looked at his display. "On three different vectors? Keep scanning."

"I am. There's nothing but dead freighters."

"Dead cargo ships don't throw rocks, Monty. Maybe there are some concealed Mazik ships behind them."

Monty said, "Not a chance. Ships under power can't hide minuscule traces of energy."

A light flashed on the comm station display, followed by a simple beep.

"No way," said Clark. "We tiptoe into this system, and someone is messaging us? Do the Mazik have cloaking devices?"

"No."

"Put it on audio-only and try to sound like a Mazik."

The lieutenant reached for the transmitter, but a hailing message preceded him. Monty opened the circuit.

"USS Dexter O'Brian, previously the Mazik ship Ko-Pahm. This is Commander Shaft Lek of the joint Panruk Slev Intra-Galactic Defense Group." Shaft did his best to make his twelve team members sound like a military force. "Please confirm that you are the Dexter O'Brian ship, commanded by Captain Aaron Howe."

John twisted his mouth in a curious way. "Is that a Panruk speaking English?" The question was rhetorical. He keyed the mic on his chair. "This is Captain John Clark of the United States Spaceforce. I am the commander of the USS Dexter O'Brian. Where is your ship?"

"Sir. You are looking at our ships."

"Dead freighters?" responded John.

"Yes, sir. And, you are fortunate to be alive."

Four days later, the O'Brian took up a geostationary orbit over the capitol city of Olamit. Conversations with Marzat, the Arbitor's assistant, were—enlightening. Shaab, herself, joined in on several discussions wherein she pressed the two humans exceedingly to detail their whereabouts for so many cycles of Mim, the system's star.

"Captain Howe instructed me to limit my information to, 'we were trapped outside this galaxy due to an unstable jump point. According to the AI, Allison, it was not unheard of, but the timing was unfortunate.'"

The Arbitor wasn't buying it, but she gave up after hearing the same explanation repeatedly.

Finally, after two days and many exchanges, Monty asked, "May we speak with Edgar?"

"Shelet Pir Sahm Mim is outside of the capitol, spending time with her parents," said Marzat.

"Great. Please have her contact us on this frequency."

Clark had to keep bugging Marzat until a day later, a tone sounded.

Monty looked at the large display forward of the command

chair on the bridge. He whispered to John, "This one looks different, but I have trouble telling them apart."

"I have great hearing, Monty. It's me, Edgar."

"Holy cow! You don't look like Edgar."

"Did you think I was going to stay looking human forever? One hundred twenty-eight years was long enough to be an unattractive, plump, and mustached male."

"Um. Yes," said Clark. "I sympathize."

"We are not on a private circuit. I was told not to tell you that, but I repeat," she paused. "this is not a closed transmission."

"That's fine," said the captain. "Tell us what we need to know. I want to hear it from you."

Edgar's fingertips glowed. Not brightly, but she was very happy to see her two human friends. "Where are Aaron and Allison?"

"They're busy. I told Marzat and the Arbitor."

"That is all?"

"Aaron instructed me to say that, and he is my commanding officer. End of story."

"And I'm his best friend going back twenty years!"

"He's safe, and he'll see you when he's not busy," said Clark.

The Panruk deflated. In the background, Monty could see two aliens who must have been Shelet Pir Sahm Mim's parents. It looked like they were in a kitchen.

"Listen, both of you. I'm sure that Marzat and Shaab Mar Gen have briefed you. Two days is long enough. The Dexter O'Brian will be needed back in the Earth system as soon as possible. You understand that our best estimate is that Mazik Bah-Gahn is sending ground troops. Warriors, most likely. In my opinion, they will use humans as an example."

"How?" asked Clark.

"They will drop rocks on a few targets and land a hundred thousand troops. They will video themselves decimating cities. It will get very ugly. How much do you want to know? I'm an anthropologist; I've studied the Mazik and your people."

"Mass murder? Slowly?" asked Monty.

"Worse. They will feed on live humans. They will make movies to send back to Kamtret, and Mazik Bah-Gahn will share them with all the Council sentients as a warning."

The two crewmembers of the O'Brian cringed at Edgar's description. "We need more crew."

"We know, and Captain Jahrnuk is a smart leader. He insisted that thirty Slev remain on Olamit as a backup measure."

Clark shrugged and rubbed the three days of stubble on his chin. "Backup for what?"

"For Shaft Lek and his soldiers out by the jump point," said Edgar.

Monty laughed. "Those guys are sitting ducks. The last thing they said to us before telling us to head in-system was that we are lucky to be in one piece."

The image of the Panruk on the screen was stone-cold serious. "Don't underestimate the weapons on those freighters. You are lucky. I was informed that you were two seconds away from being turned into small chunks for carbon."

"I thought it was bravado."

"No, John. It's not a secret down here on Olamit. Those units up there have tiny fusion weapons the size of golf balls. You didn't pick up anything on your sensors, did you?"

"No."

"Because the bombs are AI and stealthy. Just before you got struck with three of them, Commander Shaft Lek disabled the triggers. The three weapons aimed at your ship just bounced off."

Monty gave his captain a knowing look. "That was the tiny amount of kinetic energy picked up by our shields."

Shelet Pir Sahm Mim tilted her head just like she would have as the human professor, Dr. Edgar Tomas. "That's how close you came to being reduced to chunks of carbon."

"What about the Slev?"

"You're getting twenty of them as crew on your ship. You see, I'm in the loop. Not bad for an old professor—do you hear that, Marzat. I know you're listening." She continued. "A shuttle will bring them up to your ship. I don't know when; that's not my call, but you should load up on food and then get your asses to Earth."

"Understood," said Clark. "What about the Mazik destroyer outside jump point?"

"I'm sure you'll figure something out."

Chapter 21

Barrett Bonner skimmed his hand over Mercy's smooth body. Her skin was deceptively soft and feminine, considering that in a fight, she was exceedingly deadly. A cadre of specifically evil men learned the hard way not to underestimate her. It was the last lesson of their despicable lives.

That was centuries earlier when a rogue group of King George's soldiers—. It was wrong to call them soldiers; they were more like incorrigible prisoners that a psychotic general drafted to do evil deeds. His wife, Mercy, had been an attractive young woman. She'd become a widow and saw her daughters murdered before her eyes.

But Mercy recovered from near mortal wounds, and with her own hands, she reaped justice.

He watched her chest rise and fall as she breathed deeply. "I'm so lucky to have you in my life," Barrett whispered.

She stirred. "My nanites heard that, even if I'm not up yet."

"I'm sorry if I woke you, but I don't believe I will ever live a day when I don't praise the day of my birth for having met you."

His wife twisted around to gaze upon him. Barrett had just a touch of wetness in his eyes.

"Should we get out of bed?" he asked seductively.

"With 17.3 days until the jump to the solar system? The bridge crew can manage without us for another forty-five minutes, don't you think?"

Later on the command deck, Mercy settled into her chair and surveyed the displays. Everything looked correct.

"Ensign Lewis."

"Yes, Ma'am."

"Are you doing overtime? I thought you were supposed to be relieved by Lieutenant Allen almost an hour ago."

"Correct. But I believe the lieutenant and Molly Stark are working on something."

Barrett and Mercy shared a look that was nothing short of sinister.

"Thank you, Ensign Lewis. You are relieved. Go eat, drink, and be merry until your next watch."

The ensign was too tired to deliver a trademark joke; he slipped away from his console and worked his way out the blast door.

A Slev technician glided over to the nav desk on a portable chair designed for four-legged, oversized aliens.

The commander knew what Mercy was thinking. "You want me to go track down Molly and then give Allen a love tap or two?"

"Barrett, I don't think we should reach conclusions without facts."

"He's 26. She's 19. Your daughter—sorry—our daughter is the only eligible female within a whole bucketload of light-years."

Mercy exhaled. It was laced with resignation. "What are we supposed to do? They're young, but not that young. Do you remember what Molly said back when we were training at the crater? She said that if we were back in 1777, she would be married with kids. So, what genius plan do you have?"

The protective former drill sergeant cracked his knuckles. "Court-martial. Behavior unbecoming an officer, and then a first-class whooping courtesy of yours truly. It'll give me something to do, and a year in space is starting to bore me."

"You weren't overwrought with boredom thirty minutes ago."

He gave her a lascivious grin. "Well, there is that."

Footsteps echoed off the alloy surfaces of the bridge bulkheads.

"And here they are now," announced the commander.

"Sorry we're late," said Molly.

"Almost an hour," said Mercy.

John Allen seemed bright-eyed and bushy-tailed. "It's not

like we weren't being productive."

Barrett grumbled under his breath, "That's what we're afraid of."

"What?" asked Molly.

"Nothing."

"Oh."

Allen seemed excited. "We'd like to tell you what we were doing."

Again, Barrett grumbled something barely audible.

"What?" asked Molly again, appearing mildly irritated.

"Nothing."

"Look. Molly and I may have figured out something really useful."

"Great," said Mercy. "What is it?"

Barrett showed his wife the words *Birth Control* on his portable display. Her steely gaze stifled any further quips.

Molly ignored the banter. "We think we found a way to determine how far ahead the Mazik fleet is. That's what we've been working on."

The two Bonners let out an audible sigh of relief. "That's fantastic," said Mercy.

"Extraordinary," said Barrett.

Allen said nothing, but Molly said, "You guys are weird."

"Look," explained the lieutenant. "Jump points are not static like we thought. We picked up a lot of data when we transitted from that other system when we came back to Olamit; you know, when the Ro-Pahm got clipped by the shrinking portal. Molly has been looking at certain emissions from the areas around the gates or points. And once you estimate the mass of the vessels going through, it's possible to shove the data into a calculation that gives you a timeline."

Molly interjected, "The emissions decrease in energy in terms of joules at a predictable rate. It's not linear, but it's basic math."

The word math routinely fired up Barrett Bonner. "Send me your work. But assuming it's correct, what can you tell us?"

"The Mazik passed through the last jump point about 18.5

solar days ahead of us."

Mercy's mood dived. "That will give them a lot of time to do damage on Earth. Lieutenant, take over the comms and get Captain Jahrnuk on the line."

"Yes, Ma'am."

The mood on the bridge spiraled downward into somber trepidation. Kap looked dejected, even for a blue-green alien with an intimidating set of sharpened teeth. "They can do a lot of destruction in two weeks on Earth."

Captain Bonner looked stoic. "Like what?"

"Four super troop carriers. That is something like 125,000 Warriors or a combination of Warriors and regulars. Plus three cruisers? That is tremendous offensive capability. We've already discussed this. Why the need to review?"

Barrett answered. "Because we've calculated that the attack force will have 18.5 days before we arrive in-system."

Kap was confused. "I thought we figured no more than two weeks. How did you arrive at 18.5 days?"

"L.T. Allen and Ensign Stark have been working on a way to track timelines through jumps."

If such a thing were possible, the Slev captain now appeared even more gloomy. "That many Warriors on the ground could take out big cities on your planet fairly rapidly, and it will be a gruesome situation on the ground."

Mercy cringed. "And if they drop rocks, we're going to show up two weeks late for the prom."

"What will Captain Schein do?" asked the Slev captain.

"Hopefully, not commit suicide with our only other ship. He's smart and can calculate the best course of action."

"Which is to run," said Mercy.

Molly asked an unexpected question. "What if Carlisle tells Mordy to sacrifice the ship?"

A heavy, weighted silence permeated the bridge. Kap and Mok said nothing and were motionless on the video displays transmitted from the Ro-Pahm.

"Technically, Mordy can say no," said Mercy.

"How?" asked Allen. "He is Captain Schein and an officer in the U.S. Army."

"That's true, but as captain of a USS ship, just like me, he is separate from the chain of command. I mean, the ship is not under Carlisle's command, even if Mordy is."

"That is imbecilic," Molly blurted out. "So, the president can tell Mordy what to do, but he can't tell the ship what to do? Something like, 'Captain Schein, this is the president. Attack those three Mazik spacecraft and sacrifice yourselves and the USS Angela Carlisle.' Then Mordy replies that he would like to follow the lawful order, but the ship doesn't agree!"

Barrett laughed. "That was a nice recap of the potential exchange, Molly."

She made a face that was a combination of pissed off and incredulous. "That is some bullshit! We need to resign our commissions and make decisions from up here, in space."

"That would make you a self-appointed emperor, kinda like Mazik Bah-Gahn," argued LTJG Allen.

"John! We're the good guys. That so-called emperor is a bad bastard. There's a difference, right?"

Mercy gave her console a smack which got everyone's attention. "This conversation is irrelevant. We are going to be late for the party. Mordy will do what he thinks is best to protect the Earth. I hope he chooses to save his ship to fight another day, but it depends on what the Mazik do. The best scenario, which I'm sure Captain Schein will figure out, would be to disable the Mazik ability to drop rocks. That will not stop them from landing troops, so we are talking about a lot of misery on Earth no matter what."

She stood up and squelched further comments. "Captain Jahrnuk. Please work up a battle plan in the event that the Mazik have already landed ground troops, and we will be either two on three against those enemy ships or in the better situation that Mordy pulled the Angela Carlisle out of orbit and can join us in a three on three."

"Understood, Captain Bonner." The display went black.

*

First Warrior Commander Tartic swallowed a large gulp of water which helped to wash down a chunk of Slev flesh. He gently probed his mouth with two fingers and removed a sliver of meat that lodged itself between large plated teeth.

"The analysis of human anatomy indicated that it should be perhaps more satiating than Slev," offered his Second.

"And you would know that from experience?"

"No, my First. I had a relative that worked in the detention center where the human Bonner was held. The investigators examined the specimen thoroughly."

Tartic opened his jaws wide, exposing a blood-red tongue. "I like my meat raw and Slev or Makim. Consider me a traditionalist. However, perhaps the humans will be edible to my palette. I will keep an open mind."

"How soon will we engage the primitives?"

"Is my Second that eager to put his head in the range of Earth weapons?"

"What opposition can they give us, Tartic?"

The First Commander mused that question. His business was war, conquest, and delivering pain. Not all under-developed aliens were obliterated in bombardments; some fell to the Mazik under the pressure of battle.

He turned wide-eyed, expressing dominance. "Don't assume that the humans will crumble like dust. They will have a variety of projectile weapons—devices capable of penetrating even your thick flesh—and mine. And they will have explosives and perhaps fissionable materials. They are a barbaric race." Tartic stopped to snap a Slev bone in half to access its liquid core.

"Still," he continued. "The Warriors are hungry and bored. One hundred thirty thousand pacing inside cramped quarters for a solar cycle. The time has come to release them to satisfy their urges. Perhaps within one Earth rotation, we will begin the descent. Do not think the primates will not launch weapons. However, our pulse weapons will manage that so that you do not end up as a bloody smear on the surface of that world."

"That would not be a preferable end to my service of the emperor Mazik Bah-Gahn."

"Agreed, my Second, and we yet have one jump remaining, a sufficient amount of time to pursue some rest. Now, fetch me one of the female Slev. I am only partially satiated."

Chapter 22

The USS Angela Carlisle orbited majestically above the Pacific Ocean west of Hawaii. Soon she would arc in a Low Earth Orbit, which would put the battlecruiser on a path over the United States. It was a lazy orbit, quantifiable by Kepler's seven orbital elements, which meant nothing to the average human unless he was studying astronomy or was an amateur radio enthusiast.

Schein sat in his stateroom, reading email—one particular email captured his attention. It was from a woman named Chaya Richman.

Dear Mordy,

I enjoyed our first date very much when you were in Atlanta. This is bold of me, but I was intrigued by your profile on the Jmeet-the-one website. It was the most unusual listing my friends had ever seen, and they demanded that I not go out with you. I'm not talking about the second profile you posted, which read like your grandmother wrote it. I am referring to the first one, which disappeared after a few days.

Shall I refresh your memory? You said that you were looking for a redhead who played chess and would be okay with you going off for extended periods to engage in dangerous battles. Oh, don't forget that you are skilled with all kinds of weapons!

It didn't take a genius to figure out who you are. I'm not intimidated, Officer Schein. I'm a programmer, so I can find stuff on the internet. However, the news media did run stories about a mysterious group of special soldiers. One of them being an orthodox Jew?

You asked me if I would be willing to go out again? Considering what I've pieced together? When are you going to be back on Earth? Try this on for size: I'll be here waiting for you.

Chaya

P.S. My rabbi approved this message..ha ha

Mordy fought aliens and Redcoats—both of whom tended to generate anxiety, but nothing like this alluring woman.

"I must go back to Atlanta asap."

*

An alarm sounded as the USS Angela Carlisle and Earth stations detected seven vessels entering the solar system through the jump point past Jupiter.

"That was two hours ago, sir," said Ensign Lucky Williams.

Mordy was alert and focused on the display and the data streaming in from over two light hours out. Four of the ships were massively large. The Mazik scanners on the Angela Carlisle were excellent and estimated that each large, freighter-sized vessel must be at least two miles in length.

"What the hell?" said Baumgartner. The XO now had a significant reason to bleed tension onto the rest of the crew.

"There are three smaller ships near the freighters. They look like escorts—warships," added Williams.

Schein could see that they were accelerating as of two hours earlier, and he ran a quick calculation in his head. "Ensign. Confirm the ETA of 103 hours."

"Confirmed, captain—based on the most recent observations."

"Change our orbit. Hold us over Texas and Lieutenant Munch; get the president on the horn now."

Within twenty seconds, John Carlisle's three a.m. face filled the screen in front of Mordy's command chair. The man looked significantly better since containing the Chinese threat. "We don't have as much information as you." It was John's way of demanding more details.

"It's an armada of sorts. There are four exceedingly large cargo ships and three others that must be destroyers or battlecruisers."

"All right, captain. Friend or foe?"

Mordy answered the obvious question. "Definitely enemies."

"How do you know that?" quizzed the president while turning to acknowledge the entry of the Chief of Staff. "Magnus just walked in here."

Strangely, having Colonel Magnus around sliced away a chunk of anxiety. It wasn't like the man was capable of engaging in space conflicts—it was simply his steel nerves and the ice-cold blood running through his veins. "Nice to see you, Colonel," said Schein.

"Likewise, Mordy. With the president's indulgence, could you guess what four oversized freighters would be doing in our system?"

"Sirs. I would estimate that if those are Mazik, which we'll confirm as soon as we get passive signatures, they only need one or two ships to drop asteroids on us. To state the obvious, those big cargo vessels are carrying Mazik troops. Something must have changed out there on Kamtret for the Mazik to show up with this array of ships."

Magnus got the nod from Carlisle. "We can only guess at what has happened between Howe and the Mazik. Needless to say, seeing a fleet of Mazik ships here is not a good sign—unless Aaron won the whole damn shooting match, and those ships are now friendlies."

"Not logical, colonel. We would have received a call—Schein looked at the UTC clock—almost fifteen minutes ago. I think we must accept that those spacecraft will turn out to be a hostile Mazik task force; the question is, what can we do about it?"

"Engage them as far away from Earth as possible," ordered Carlisle.

Schein used all of his formidable brainpower to run through the most likely scenarios of a combat encounter with the Mazik ships. He weighed out the value of a hit-and-run attack, a long-range attack, pretending to be an allied Mazik ship (which it once was before Recon captured it), and permutations of each. It didn't take long to reach the unavoidable conclusion. "Mr.

President. In all cases, the USS Angela will be destroyed, with our best outcome being the disabling of two of the three enemy ships. On a normal curve, that possibility is almost 1.7 standard deviations. More or less, sir, that is about a 5% chance that we will take out two of their battlecruisers."

"How much damage to our ship?" asked Magnus.

"Total loss."

The president thought about that for all of five seconds. "What can their remaining ship do?"

An easy question. "It can pick up asteroids at will and finish off all of humankind and make the planet a wasteland for the next half-million years."

John thought about his murdered wife, Angela—a victim of the asteroid strike that hit Washington, D.C. the first time around. If humans were fated to be eliminated, he thought, it would be better to go down swinging. "We're not going to let them annihilate us without a fight."

Magnus muted the audio. He was, on video, starting a heated discussion with the Commander-in-Chief. Mordy waited. It was over quickly.

"Captain Schein. Why are the Mazik showing up with four massive cargo ships?" asked the colonel, releasing the mute button.

"I think they want to land ground forces. Otherwise, why not just send a single attack craft and end it with a few rocks?"

"Are you saying they want a ground war?" asked the president.

"No, sir. They don't see it that way. They will send down Warriors—a lot of them—and advanced weapons. Mazik Bah-Gahn wants our planet. That is my guess."

"Mordy, there are 8 billion humans on Earth. Do the Mazik think we will commit suicide and hand them the keys?"

"No, sir. I think they will take their time and play the long game. They'll start by dropping a few projectiles on the most populated cities and then land in America. So, Beijing, Mexico City, and places like that will just be an outright slaughter. Then comes many years of the Mazik turning humans into cattle while they populate the planet."

The colonel knew what Schein meant, but he had to verbalize it. "What do you mean by cattle, captain?"

"Food, colonel."

Silence.

"Screw that!" Carlisle was livid. "Find a way to beat them out there, Mordy."

Schein recognized the stress and that the president's thinking was tilting toward mild desperation. "Our best option is guerrilla warfare in space and on the ground. We need to save the Angela to fight another day."

"What day, captain? There won't be another day. The Mazik show up and destroy our planet. Not much of a future in that, dammit!"

"Mr. President, sir. The best and most logical course of action is to save the Angela and use it to counter any Mazik ships that try to tether asteroids from the Belt. It will limit them to non-planet-killer attacks and give human ground forces at least a little bit of time to try to mount a defense."

Magnus, amazingly, kept his mouth shut as Carlisle ambled towards a mini-tirade. But then, in the pregnant pause, Mike said, "I'm going to have to agree with Mordy—if we lose the one ship, then we'll have continued destruction with no hope of pushing back using hit and run tactics. When you are vastly outnumbered, you have to resist standing up to the bully. We're not talking about middle school here, John. This is the big one, something that our stupid predecessors never considered when they launched the Voyager missions with details about our anatomy and where we are located in the galaxy.

"In the end, it wasn't the Voyager probe that got us in a pickle after all. It's simply being noticed by sentients further along the technology road." Magnus sat back in a red leather office chair, folded his arms, and waited.

Carlisle sighed like all his options were whisked away, and he simply stared down the barrel of a pistol held by a killer with no remorse or conscience. Sometimes, or rather, nearly all the time, being the leader of the free world was a despicable burden.

"Captain Schein. Do what you think is most likely to save lives. I could order you to attack right now, but I know that you could legally refuse that order. My wife is in my head right now as we debate this dystopian future. Angela had terrific common sense. I know she would be telling me to let you run things from up there."

"Understood, sir," said Mordy. "I'll use every tactic that my crew comes up with to stop them. Frankly, I think the best thing right now is for you to teach the American people how to fight the Mazik. Whatever ambush tactics I pursue up here, it's maybe more critical that you have a whole basket of surprises when the Warriors come marching into the United States."

Colonel Magnus shifted gears out of politician and went full CAG badass soldier, the man he'd been for forty years. "Mordy, I want to create a team to review and distribute defense plans. With the president's consent, I think we can build a ground force specifically designed to give the Mazik as much trouble as possible."

"I agree. Those Warriors won't be able to roll over the countryside ten minutes after they land. One hundred thousand of them are not enough to conquer our country in ten days. We'll learn as we go." Carlisle tried his best to be optimistic, but he knew that a happy future was in doubt.

Mordy did his best to broadcast the same optimism as the president. He thought about the country being slowly consumed by brutal aliens. He thought about Chaya, the girl he'd just met, and how she looked, her mannerisms, and her email. He put his hopes and imagination on hold.

"Mr. President, sir. We will be heading out to a defensive position near Mars. That's a twenty-minute lag time on comms, but we'll be available if you want to send any defense ideas for our input. Hopefully, we'll get a chance to shoot at those freighters and inflict some damage."

Two days later, the Mazik armada passed through the Belt. A cat and mouse game was already underway as the First Ship Commander of the procession analyzed the improbability that the Ko-Pahm was in enemy hands. Inconceivable, yet the battlecruiser dashed for a defensive position shortly after his own vessels entered the human system.

"There is no debate—only logic," remarked the officer responsible for delivering four troop carriers safely. "The facts: it orbited Earth. It ran for cover. It transmitted no messages. It is the Ko-Pahm—a ship that was supposed to be destroyed to create confusion and doubt among the Council. And, our own ships assigned to destroy the Ko-Pahm to pin the blame for ending humans onto a renegade captain—do you recall the names of those ships?"

The Second Ship Commander stomped his feet. "The Ror and the Kor."

"Yes. The Ror and the Kor. Both missing. And yet the Ko-Pahm was orbiting peacefully around our enemy's planet? There can be no doubt. Somehow, the humans were able to gain access to the Ko-Pahm. We must assume that it is hostile and will attack at any opportunity. Am I in error?"

"No, First Ship Commander."

"Well answered. Change of plans. We will not harness any asteroids at this time. To do so will put our ships at risk—something the captain of the Ko-Pahm will desire, but we will not give. Instead, we will escort the troop carriers and select several cities for small kinetic strikes. When the emperor's Warriors are on the surface, we will protect the freighters and bring them to a position out of harm's way. Afterward, our primary mission is to hunt and destroy the Ko-Pahm."

The Second again stomped his feet as a sign of allegiance. "Our previous orders from the emperor were to remain in orbit and use light weapons to strike any human defense positions—"

"I am altering those orders. Once on the ground, Tartic will deal with any resistance. That is his concern."

"They're not decelerating." Cassie Munch, the very astute and efficient lieutenant, announced.

Mordy mused about the motivation of the flagship commander of the Mazik fleet. Their leader undoubtedly saw the USS Angela Carlisle but did not deviate from his course. The long game. This alien captain was in no rush. Time was not a factor—the job of offloading his complement of soldiers remained the priority.

"Should we approach and try to strike at least one of the freighters, sir?"

"No. That is a losing proposition. I was hoping they would pause and collect rocks which would have given us an advantage and a chance to pull off a fly-by attack. Their commander is no fool."

Schein's XO, Baumgartner, stroked his chin and wiped his stressed and dampened brow. "We just keep our distance while they deliver all those Mazik to the surface?"

"The alternative is death and no change in outcome."

"I'll start a program to ration the food supplies, sir."

Mordy thought about that problem. They could probably stretch out their inventory for a year and a half; things would get exceedingly grim after that. "Rex. Do that, and I want a fair chunk of your day spent looking for weak spots in the Mazik defense posture." He turned and addressed the rest of the bridge crew. "That applies to all of you. No matter how ridiculous it might seem, any plan you dream up needs to be discussed. We humans are supposed to be threatening, unpredictable, and innovative, so let's be that."

Chapter 23

"To tell or not to tell. That is the question." President Carlisle sat at the head of an oblong, rich, and darkly stained oak table surrounded by his Chief of Staff, five top military officers, the SEC DEF, the interior secretary, and the head of DHS.

General Marley, Chairmen of the Joint Chiefs, scoffed. "With all due respect, sir, we'll create another disaster just like when your tape was leaked before the first time the Mazik came here."

Magnus boiled over in a flash. "We don't have time for your bullshit, Marley. I'm not in your chain of command anymore, so I'll say it outright. When you imply that the president is responsible for that leak, it sounds like you're doing political jockeying. And when you preface your verbal slop by saying 'with all due respect,' it labels you like an ass."

The General slammed his hand down on the table, which was the most significant act of aggression he'd demonstrated in thirty years. "I never! Who do you think you are talking to? Colonel?"

The tension was palpable. Magnus locked the self-centered general in his sights and thought about how quickly civility dissolves when death is on the line.

"Marley!" Carlisle raised his voice and drew the attention of the dozen people in the room. "I apologize for the Chief of Staff's outburst."

"Thank you, Mr. President."

Carlisle stood up. "General. Sit down," he ordered. "We are about to be pounded by rocks—maybe. We are about to have a serious ground invasion on our own soil for the first time in history. The Mazik could start landing in about four days. I have zero patience for incompetence, ego, or self-centered viewpoints. We could have a million dead Americans in the streets a week from now! There is no time for delegitimizing speeches in here."

"I agree completely, John," said the general.

"And therefore, I will insist on a resignation," Carlisle said while staring at the large blank video monitor on the far wall.

Marley stood up again. "I back you thoroughly. And I think that Colonel Magnus will be more useful out in the field rather than continuing as Chief of Staff."

John's gaze shifted toward the chairman of the joint chiefs. "I am referring to you, Marley. You are relieved of command."

The conference table fell into a stunned silence with a tangible level of discomfort.

"What? Just like that?" Marley blurted out, virtually frothing at the mouth. "I'm the officer who knows how to deal with conflicts better than any of you!"

The shouting match lasted for less than one minute as the secret service physically removed the general from the room.

"Perhaps now, we can try to be productive? Does anyone else want to join him?" Carlise pointed towards the door. No one budged.

"Great. Colonel Magnus, please spell it out."

The former head of the Combat Applications Group, otherwise known as the roughest badasses of all the elite special ops troops in the world, pressed some computer keys to bring up an image on the large monitor.

"Gentleman, that is what a Mazik Warrior looks like."

The image was a CGI. rendering from all of the pics obtained when Recon battled with the huge aliens while capturing two ships. "And here is actual video from a firefight inside a large compartment on the USS Dexter O'Brian."

The video played clearly and with audio. There was a deafening silence in the room as the high-ranking officers and officials watched.

"That's a tape, and it doesn't capture the intensity of the Mazik Warriors. In person, the brief confrontation was bloody and one-hundred percent like a Hollywood movie with gruesome special effects. There were just a few Mazik Warriors in that closed space on that battlecruiser. We are going to have in excess of 100,000 carrying mag guns, AI drones, and probably stuff we haven't imagined yet."

"How the hell can our conventional forces stand up to that? Can the aliens take out our tanks? Our mobile artillery?" The head of D.H.S. seemed shaken.

"My guess is that Mazik will send out long-range airborne surveillance, which will target anything that we try to use against them. On top of that, Captain Schein believes the enemy will mingle among the general population—human shields—and to them, a food supply."

The interior secretary gasped. She was still in shock from the video and was trying to wrap her head around the impending brutality. "Food?"

"Humans as food, Madame Secretary," said the president.

"They are going to be just grabbing civilians and eating them?"

"Like we eat chickens and cows," confirmed Magnus.

She began to tear up and asked meekly, "Children?"

John nodded, his expression grim.

"Sir," asked the chief admiral. "Are we supposed to build a ground war plan in one day?"

"We have a plan that was shelved a couple of years ago because there was no expectation that our enemies would consider an earthbound confrontation." Mike Magnus exhaled and shrugged. "It was a remote what-if, but now we need to bring it out of mothballs and tweak it depending on where the Mazik attack."

The SECDEF framed the obvious as a question. "We can't use standard protocols like shelling, missiles, and tanks, right? So, that leaves small, stealth attacks to harass the aliens as they move."

"That's the plan that has the best chance of success."

"Understood, but we only have perhaps 500,000 troops that we can move into position—and that is maybe with a month of preparation. What can we do if they come down in Richmond or Dallas, or some other city, other than Washington or New

York?"

The Chief of Staff referenced the old plan. "We have to distribute as many stock-piled weapons to the public as possible."

A different general spoke up. "We're going to have twelve-year-old boys taking potshots at Mazik Warriors with sniper rifles?"

Magnus shrugged again. "Everyone fights this time. I'm not saying to throw kids as cannon fodder, but we need to organize teams of guerillas to make the Mazik pay for every inch."

"I'm from Wyoming; you all know that. Kids in the southern, Midwest, and western states start plinking at targets when they are ten. By the time they're teens, many are proficient hunters—that's what we need them to do. We'll need them to use those skills from teenagers on up." Carlisle waited for objections.

The only woman at the table was from North Jersey. "What about states like mine? We're not overrun with hunters and paintball wargamers. Do we just evacuate the northeast?"

Magnus said, "If it looks untenable, then those cities will need to evacuate quickly."

"New York? Millions of people?"

"Madame Secretary, We're going to see a lot of casualties, but if someone can shoot a weapon, and they aren't a danger to others, then we need to arm them today."

John Carlisle gauged the mood around the table. "Our original question was to reveal what's coming or not. That's moot. I'm going to order the distribution of weapons and ammunition to every capable citizen. I mean to simply open the warehouses and truck in as much as possible. That is regarding some cities like Philly, Boston, and the like. Other cities, particularly in the south, have plenty of weapons in circulation. We'll supplement those areas based on need."

Joshua Rice wasn't the most popular kid at Hickman High School, mostly because he was from Bucksnort, Tennessee, perhaps the most invisible, unremarkable town in the state. In fact, Josh was the only teenager from the unincorporated hamlet that was little more than a truck stop. However, the lanky, ginger-haired, sixteen-year-old did have one particularly notable skill, outside of driving off any girl to come within a hundred yards; the boy was one hell of a hunter and an even better rifleman. And, there was an afterschool shooting club, but he'd abandoned that after repeatedly ripping the centers out of paper targets with insanely small groupings. It just got boring.

There was one girl, though, and she was from a little town just up Interstate 40. Her name was Emma, and he'd seen her at the gun range with her dad at the same time the club was plinking away and listening to the instructor ramble on about gun safety. She was shooting an AK-47 with its 7.62x39mm rounds--and the eleventh grader was skilled with the weapon of choice for Russian and third world fighters.

The following day, Rice worked up the courage to approach the trim blond girl despite his only close friend's warning to ditch the idea. Josh slipped up beside her in the cafeteria line. He noticed her jeans and sweater, caught a whiff of her hair, but lost his nerve. Emma squinted at him as he drifted quickly out of the lunch line and slunk away.

"I told you," said his friend.

"Just wait. I'll talk to her."

"Yeah, right. Betcha you graduate without ever saying two words."

"Bet?"

"How much, Rice? Ten bucks?"

Josh looked in his wallet. He had eight bucks, and he pulled it out. "Show me yours?"

The other kid checked his pocket and pulled out two fives. "Ok. Eight dollars. But the bet is that the most you'll talk to her is long enough for her to tell you she ain't interested and then done. Then you pay me the eight bucks 'cuz you are fer sure gonna lose."

"Deal. Watch me."

Josh didn't wait. Emma sat down at a lunch table by herself. He got up and approached her, then looked back at Justin, who sneered at him and gave him a thumbs down.

"Do you mind if I sit here?"

"It's a free country, I think." She looked up at him with one eyebrow arched. He thought it was kind of attractive while sitting directly across from her.

"I saw you watching me down at the range and just now in the lunch line," she said. "Are you stalking me or something?"

Josh almost panicked as he thought about his eight dollars. "Um. No. Not stalking at all. I just wanted to tell you that your AK shooting looked pretty good."

"Oh yeah? And now you're gonna ask me to go shooting with you?"

He couldn't tell if Emma was trying to reject him. "Sure. I would go shooting with you or whatever."

"What's the *or whatever* part?"

"We could go hunting."

She twirled her fork around her cafeteria plate. "Rice, cucumbers, tomatoes, and carrots. That's a hint. I'm a vegetarian. Besides, I seriously doubt that my dad would let me go off into the woods with a sixteen-year-old and a rifle."

"I see your point. Well, I just thought I'd ask you."

He started to get up, thinking about his soon-to-be-empty wallet and that he should have said something different. Emma looked up at him, "That's it? You're giving up?"

"What do you mean?"

"I saw you negotiating with your friend over some kind of bet, right? How much?"

"Eight bucks," Josh said before he could stop himself.

"Huh. So now I know what my worth is."

Sitting back down, he said, "It's all I had in my wallet. I would have bet more!"

"Really? How much? I want to know my true value."

He stared blankly at the girl, not knowing how to respond.

"I'll tell you what; there's some kind of important town meeting here in the auditorium at seven tonight. My dad's going, and you can take me out for pizza before with the money you just won off your friend."

Rice squinted at her trying to comprehend what Emma said. She laughed. "I'm downright confident for girls our age, so don't feel like I'm just messing with you. I'm saying that I'll go out with you for pizza, but then you come with me to the stupid meeting. My dad said it has something to do with the National Guard, and it's going to bore me to death--so you'll be my way out of sitting alone through that. Deal?" She stuck out her hand and didn't move it.

"Um. Okay."

"Shake my hand, Joshua."

He timidly grabbed her hand and shook it. "How'd you know my name?"

"I know who you are. See you at the pizza place at six. Don't be late, or I'll make you give the money back."

What Josh and Emma would most remember that evening had nothing to do with pizza. After wolfing down a couple of slices, the teens walked around the outside of the school making small talk—most of that was Rice stepping on his tongue with the Creacy girl smoothing over his gaffs gently and with a lot of style. But then, she saw the parking lot filling up to capacity.

"Some important person must be coming here." Emma pulled him quickly with her until she found her dad. He was tall and fit, but he had thinning gray hair and a flat expression. The combination was friendly and non-threatening.

"Em. Come sit with me." Emma's dad eyed the scruffy teenage boy. "Who's this young man?"

Josh didn't fumble but offered his hand. "Josh Rice, I'm in your daughter's class. I saw you and Emma at the range last week, sir."

"Sir?" The middle-aged man shook Josh's hand. He arched an eyebrow precisely the way his daughter had at lunch. "Are you sure you're sixteen?"

"Yes, sir."

"That's two 'sirs' in a row—enough for the whole year. Quick. Let's get those three seats before they're gone."

The auditorium held about three hundred people, and it was

full of adults. Josh was glad to have someone his own age sitting beside him. A man in uniform stood in the middle of the stage and checked his watch.

"In two minutes, there will be an address by the president. I'm Colonel Ed James, but my name is not vital; listening to the Commander-in-Chief is."

Emma leaned over and whispered in Rice's left ear. "Joshua. I think something weird is happening. President Carlisle on TV in our school?"

"Yes. I hear you. My spidey sense is tingling."

"Whoa. I feel better knowing that you're a superhero."

The colonel tapped on the lectern exactly at 7:02, and the large screen above the stage lit up with Carlisle seated in the Oval Office.

"Here we go, Spiderman," Emma muttered under her breath.

"My fellow Americans," began the president. "None of us have forgotten the destruction of the city of Washington, D.C. that we endured just a few years ago at the hands of the Mazik aliens.

"For nearly four years, we've been watching the skies, and the USS Angela Carlisle and her crew have protected us. As a species, the valiant efforts of Captain Aaron Howe and his courageous Recon soldiers, along with elite specialists of our armed forces, prevented the utter destruction of our planet.

"Howe and his crew left Earth after that victory over the Mazik to take the fight to the enemy. We've had no contact with our other ships since then."

John flipped the page as he read on.

"Just over eighteen hours ago, our only battlecruiser in orbit detected the emergence of seven enemy ships into our solar system."

The crowded hall gasped as one. The president paused his speech as he understood that all over the USA, crowds and families watching him must have reacted with shock.

"Observations by our ship and by Earth stations have led us to a high certainty that four of the incoming ships are troop carriers. Further, there are three warships escorting the troop carriers, and we have estimated that more than 100,000 Mazik fighters are likely going to land on American soil with the intention of destroying our country."

Again, Carlisle waited for this statement to hit home.

"It is unclear why our enemies have chosen to start a ground war on Earth, but as challenging as a battle on American soil appears, if the Mazik had chosen to simply drop asteroids, the end of our species would be a certainty. However, where there is life, there is hope.

"We must rise to this occasion with the courage and commitment that our country is able to deliver."

Another pause.

"Our top strategists have been working continuously to devise the best possible defense in the case of a Mazik landing anywhere in the United States. You may ask, why us? Why not some other country? The answer is complicated, and suffice it to say, we are the prime target because no other state can put up the kind of fight that we can.

"To do battle with aliens utilizing very advanced technology, we must fight unconventionally. Tanks, planes, mobile artillery, and most missiles will not penetrate the Mazik perimeters. We must resist the way our predecessors did when facing overwhelming odds.

"In light of that, the National Guard and the U.S. Military will distribute various weapons to every capable civilian throughout our country. Any American over the age of eighteen will be required to train quickly and become proficient in using their assigned weapon. With the approval of their parents or guardians, teenagers younger than eighteen can volunteer to join this new National Defense Force—which will be known as the N.D.F.

"Fighting against the Mazik troops will be exceedingly dangerous, but we have no other choice."

Carlisle put down the last sheet of paper and looked up dramatically at the camera lens. "What we will be facing in a matter of three days will be the most pivotal moment in human history. We must win. We must sacrifice to win. We must make the enemy pay such a high price that they will never again consider attacking our people or our planet.

"In a few seconds, I will conclude this announcement. Those of you in an official hall or meeting place will receive immediate instructions on where and how to obtain your personal weapon and ammunition. If you are at home, watching this on television, you will find continuously scrolling telephone numbers for your state where you can contact personnel to schedule a pick-up time.

"Anyone with proven N.R.A. or other training or experience with weapons will not be required to schedule a rapid course. Others will be evaluated and briefed quickly to determine if they are competent to carry and use firearms.

"Finally. I'm calling on all Americans to display the highest level of dignity and character during this unprecedented national emergency. For all intents and purposes, the National Guard, the military, and police departments are authorized to use deadly force to quell any civil unrest.

"I am speaking to any citizen or non-citizen. If you attempt to use this crisis as an excuse to violate the law or the rights of other citizens, you will be shot. This is a time for every American to exhibit the best values and love for their fellow.

"Good luck to all of you."

The screen went blank, followed by a list of numbers moving vertically upwards.

The silence in the Hickman High School Auditorium was deafening. The colonel walked to the center of the stage and tapped on the microphone. "I am tasked with supervising the initial distribution of weapons to Hickman County. Only county residents should line up and signup at the station outside. We will start precisely at midnight tonight. As the president said, people with proven weapons skills will be given arms and ammunition without delay. I am the final arbiter of who is or is not proficient in Hickman County."

Several hands went up.

"Standby. I'll take questions in a moment. If you are under

eighteen, you do not need to wait two days to qualify, provided that both your parents sign an authorization form. If there is only one legal guardian, one signature will be sufficient. If one guardian is living outside of Hickman County, you are out of luck and will not receive a government-sponsored weapon.

"On a personal note. I am aware that many folks in this county are outstanding shooters. If you aren't, be honest about it. Those of you who know that you are top-shelf are asked to qualify tomorrow with sniper rifles. We will have M82s, M40s, and MK22 rifles, depending on supply. Typical long-range courses are three days, but we will condense that to twelve hours for those who are qualified. Questions?"

A bald guy who looked to be the age of a Vietnam Vet stood. "Why isn't the USS Angela Carlisle protecting us from those incoming Mazik ships?"

Colonel James expected this question. "According to the White House, the Carlisle is engaged in stealth efforts to thwart the advance of the Mazik. Details are top secret. Next?"

"Where are moms and younger children supposed to go?" asked a grandmother.

"Stay home. If the Mazik come here to our state, we will do our best to take the fight to them away from population centers."

A tattoed biker-looking guy with a belly called out from his chair near the front. "Where do we shoot them?"

"There will be instructional videos available starting tonight on strategies for small groups of fighters. I suggest that you watch every second of those televised instructions. The Mazik fighters that are coming here are the Warrior Class. The videos will show you the best way to stop individual Warriors. I will not lie to you because you have a right to know. These enemies are armored except for their heads and their lower legs. Most of you know by now that the Mazik have four legs. One moment."

The colonel motioned to an aide to pull up a graphic of a Warrior. The full-sized image on the screen elicited another gasp.

"What the fuck!" someone shouted out from the back of the

hall.

"I understand your reaction. Keep in mind that these fighters are still vulnerable to projectiles. They are still flesh and blood like we are. They will probably die if you put a bullet in their heads. The issue is to get us into positions where we get a chance to take that headshot without becoming casualties in the process."

The crowd groaned while trying to comprehend the threat as the illustration on-screen of the enemy told a frightening tale. They were big, powerful, and chilling to look at and equipped with highly advanced weapons.

"Listen. No one can say that Tennessee will be the first target. We don't know yet. But, we have to get ready. If they don't show up here for a month, then better for us and much worse for them.

"There are multiple stations being set up in the parking lot. As I said, we start at midnight. If you are under eighteen, then bring your parents to sign off. For now, get online and go to the website listed on the screen. That's it. No more questions."

The expected tumultuous yelling, shouting, and even screaming lasted for twenty minutes before the crowd dispersed. All things considered, it was substantially better than the reaction in New York, New Jersey, and the rest of the northern Atlantic Seaboard. Colonel Ed James blessed his good fortune to be in Tennessee.

Chapter 24

At midnight, Josh and his parents exchanged polite hellos with Emma and her father in the school parking lot. The dire situation hammered the parents and the kids alike. All of them waited with the hopes of getting their hands on a proper sniper rifle.

Emma poked her dad. "Hold my place in line, please dad?" She pulled Josh aside. "Your parents seem very proper. What happened to you?"

"Proper? Aren't you from Hickman County like me?"

"Yes, but sometimes I like talking like an aristocrat."

"Roger that, but I got a question. Where's your mom? Is she not going to sign off for you?"

It was hard to see in the dim light, but a shadow briefly passed over Emma's face. "My mother isn't here."

"Divorced parents. I'm sorry."

"Not divorced. She left when I was two and never came back. My dad has full custody of me."

Josh frowned. "Wow. I'm sorry if I hurt your feelings."

In the hazy parking lot lighting, he could see her pretty face. Emma didn't give off nasty energy at all, considering that one of her parents abandoned her. "No problem. I'm lucky that she's not in my life. She just got up and left. My dad never told me much, but he did say I was better off. I think she had a drinking problem because we've never had so much as a bottle of wine or beer in the house. That's a guess on my part."

"Damn. And I complain about my parents—"

"Yeah. Don't. If they are half-normal, be happy."

She looked over at her dad, engrossed in a conversation with Josh's folks. "I hope they didn't hear us."

"Nah. I doubt it. We're only boring teenagers, right?"

"Hey, Joshua. Do you know which rifle you want?"

He laughed quietly. "If they have it, I want an M82 simply

because of the range. You?"

"That's a no-brainer. I want the MK22 MRAD with the 7.62 x 51 NATO barrel, although the .338 might be better."

"I like your style. You think you can carry that thing? It weighs like fifteen pounds."

"Mr. Rice. I'm strong as heck—for a girl."

Man, he thought. Just the way she talks. "You don't need to add the whole 'for a girl' thing."

"Boys are stronger, Joshua. I'm not going to pretend that I have testosterone and can lift a Toyota. But I know I can handle the M22."

"Next!" A short, scary master sergeant clapped his hands and waved to their parents. "Who's next?"

*

"What's the latest?"

Colonel Magnus sat down in the faux oval office somewhere in the midwest. "The south, the midwest, and the desert states are managing beautifully."

"You left a big hole."

"The northeast ranges from fair to disastrous. The rich, upper-class people are running. They got money and are fleeing New York and the other big cities."

"Who's staying?"

"The gangbangers, the poor, middle-class, misguided philosophers who think they will shmooze their way into an understanding with the Mazik."

Carlisle slapped his hands on the desk. "Were they not awake when D.C. got leveled? What about weapons, Mike?"

"The construction workers from Queens, Brooklyn, Staten Island, and so on are loading up. New York could be a real pain in the ass for the Warriors, but we're going to lose so many. In the end, we won't hold it. Maybe we should order a mandatory evacuation?"

The president thought his head would explode. "We can't. That large of a population running west and south? First, we'll have food shortages, and then a civil war. We have to do our best to keep the trucks and trains rolling into the big cities."

"That isn't going to end well, John."

"If I resign," grinned Carlisle, "will you please take over the presidency?"

"Sorry. That will have to go to the V.P., and she just took off to an unknown location in the Caribbean."

"Yes. I heard. If we survive this, I want her impeached or tarred and feathered—or both."

"Our government, Mr. President, is hanging by a string."

"A thread."

"No, sir. Yesterday it was a rope. Today it's a string if you get my meaning. Hurray for martial law."

"Magnus. Is the Speaker flapping her gums?"

The Chief of Staff laughed out loud. "She is, as we speak, heading underground in case you buy the farm. Hell, if you get skewered, that demagogue can invite the head of the Mazik over for a nice Cabernet and make a deal."

"I want to see the video of that alien taking a chunk out of her."

"Are the recorders still going in here, sir?"

"No, Mike. I had them shut down."

"Fine. We don't want anyone salivating for the 25th."

Carlisle said, "If only!"

*

Emma had become the most vital thing in Josh's life within a day and a half. It was an avalanche of hormones and an underlying sense of confidence they shared. The two stood on a ledge overlooking a forest that paved the countryside to the east. A mild breeze cooled things off a little as summer approached. Both of them wore camos and carried heavy loads.

"My rifle's better than your rifle."

"Come here, Joshua." She hooked a finger inside of his button-down U.S. Woodland camo shirt and pulled him. "Did you brush your teeth?"

"Yes. Why?"

"Kiss me."

"What? Me? Here? Now?"

She tilted her head just so and pulled his lips to hers. It was simplistic, but it meant the world to both of them. Their lips parted briefly. "I've never had a boyfriend, and I've never been kissed. If we survive, I want us to get really good at that." She pulled him closer and felt the warmth of his body. After a few seconds, Emma backed away slightly.

"Was that okay?"

"Yes, boy, but that's it for now. Rome wasn't built in a day, you know."

Josh regained his senses after a few seconds. "Yes. Well. My rifle is the beautiful M82 that I've been dreaming about. It's big, heavy, and will put large holes through the heads of Mazik Warriors at a very long range."

Emma held out the M22 MRAD with its outstanding stock and futuristic look. "Beat that! Not a chance. Sure, it might not be accurate at 2000 meters, but let's make a bet that I take out more of the bad guys than you."

"What's the bet? More kisses or whatever?"

"No. Eight bucks."

"Not much of a payout."

"Don't worry. The kisses and whatever you get for free."

The two of them made their way back to Hickman and then caught the bus full of wannabe snipers to Murfreesboro. The short, intimidating master sergeant paced up and down the aisle as they motored down Route 40. He stopped next to the two kids. Josh looked up at the muscular African American enlisted man, who gave the impression that he skipped the pancakes and ate the plate instead.

"Don't you two think that you should be in school studying polynomials or climate change?"

After a tense few seconds, the guy smiled. He had a fat gap between his teeth. "I'm just screwing with you."

"That's a relief. We're so relieved you're just messing with us," said Emma with a little attitude.

The sarge balled up his fists. "Maybe I'm not!"

Another few seconds passed, and the guy looked like he would start spitting out nails at them. He laughed again. "Nah. I'm playing with you."

Josh relaxed and resumed breathing.

"I'm Master Sergeant Carpath."

"Carpath?"

"Yes. Carpath."

"Sure. Okay," said Emma.

The sergeant cracked his knuckles. Everything about him oozed restrained power. "You two managed to get your folks to sign off. Super. But you better shoot well at the range, or you'll be going home with half-eaten cheese sandwiches."

Emma stopped Josh from talking by poking his right thigh. "Yes, sir. We will do our best out there."

Sergeant Carpath squinted. "Let's see if you two have any sense. What did you just say that was dead wrong?"

"Uh," answered Josh. "It should have been yes, master sergeant."

"All right. You get a pass on that one. And listen Rice cake. Make sure your girlfriend don't call me sir!"

The sergeant stalked off toward the back of the bus.

The Barrett range was a dream. One-hundred yards indoor with all the trimmings. The training sessions were quick, and there were separate paths for the M82 and Emma's M22. The information crammed into their skulls should have been stretched out over three days, but time was of the essence. Eventually, the M82 and M22 groups settled in for actual practice.

Josh looked down the stalls and saw Emma hefting her rifle like a pro. He wondered how many young girls, or even women for that matter, were training on that weapon. It had to be only a handful of civilians. Military was a different issue, but teenagers?

"Hey Rice. The range is hot. Stop drooling over your babe and shoot."

After getting comfortable with the setup, Josh squeezed off a round. The recoil was not too bad, but he missed the target completely. "Shit."

"First pull, junior," said the master sergeant. "Relax. I know you are a great shooter. Just figure out this rifle."

Four shots later, he selected a different spot on the paper target and shot five more. The grouping was outstanding, and the range officer couldn't help but display a satisfied grin.

Down the stalls, a different safety officer watched Emma place three rounds in the same hole. At a hundred yards, that was not uncommon, but after that, she placed ten rounds in the same hole which was downright machine-like for the girl's first time out. Emma easily outshot the rest of the MK22 bunch—all men.

"Damn," muttered the master sergeant. "If those two end up having a kid, that little turkey will win the Olympics."

Emma was equally accurate with the .338 Norma Mag barrel, which satisfied everyone watching because that round was specifically designed to penetrate light armor.

After a long practice session, the range officer stuck a little yellow smiley face on the girl's wrist. "You get the prize, kid. Go out and make them pay."

They took down their rifles, cleaned, and reassembled them like pros. A voice boomed over the range speakers. "Y'all did good. Now get on home."

Chapter 25

Eight Hours

Tartic, First Warrior Commander, glared at the First Ship Commander and then flashed his razor-sharpened, metal-capped teeth. The fleet captain showed no reaction. "Perhaps, Tartic, you would prefer that I order our ships to linger among this system's asteroid belt so that the enemy's battlecruiser can launch a passing attack?"

"I am First Warrior Commander to you."

"Your title means nothing to me. In space, I make the decisions that preserve the safety of my ships. If we had stopped, at least two of your transports would likely be venting atmosphere into space. Are you prepared to lose 60,000 Warriors before we reach our target? We are many jumps and hundreds of light-years from Kamtret, but I still take my orders from the emperor, not you."

"The emperor is not here to prevent me from eating your legs."

"Again, Tartic, you throw your blustering idiocy around without recognizing that your mission is to vanquish the humans, not to create a disaster for my fleet. Try to restrain your genetically mutated aggressive genes and save them for our enemy. Up here, I will decide how and when to launch projectiles, artificial or natural."

The head of the Warriors stepped back and turned to the door of the captain's stateroom. He spun around threateningly. "When I no longer need you, I will kill you and feed you to my officers."

"If you survive on that planet of primitive barbarians, perhaps we'll talk about the matter. It would be wise to concentrate on preserving your life from what may await you on the surface. Go prepare your soldiers and stay clear of my crew.

You have just a third of a planetary rotation before we orbit."

"I'll be back."

*

Schein periodically huffed and puffed as he reviewed the real-time data on the position of the Mazik armada.

"I know what you're thinking," said his XO.

"What's that, Rex?"

"You want to take potshots at their freighters, but it's a waste of missiles."

Mordy shrugged, sneered, and nearly growled at the same time. "I'm hating every second of this slow-motion trainwreck."

"They're decelerating, sir," said Lieutenant Munch. "Less than eight hours to orbit."

"Thank you, lieutenant." He turned back to get a read on Baumgartner's face. "You're thinking that the silver lining is that we scared them into not harnessing an asteroid."

"Absolutely. Our presence here just saved a few million lives, maybe more."

Schein gazed around the bridge. Everyone, Munch, Williams, Baumgartner—they all had family down there in harm's way, and right now, there was not one iota the captain of the extremely powerful USS Angela Carlisle could do about it.

"If you're not essential right now, then get some rest. There's no point in staring at displays. I want all of you as sharp as possible so that when we eventually approach that fleet, we'll win."

The president moved to a heavily fortified bunker in Colorado. He and his essential staff were five hundred feet under a mountain. The stress level felt like DEFCON zero—if there could be such a thing. A constant stream of reports flowed in from around the world. Every sane country was following the model of the USA by distributing arms to anyone who could shoot, with a few notable exceptions; Iran, North Korea, Cuba, China, and Nauru.

"Nauru?" wondered Carlisle out loud.

"They don't have weapons to distribute," said the SECDEF. "In any case, I'm not seeing a remote Pacific island with the notoriety of being the most overweight country in the world as a high priority for the Mazik."

"I can read minds, John," said Magnus. "You're wondering if maybe the aliens will start somewhere else and give us some more time to prepare."

"Yes. You're clairvoyant, Mike. So, what are those odds?"

"We're the land of Bonner, Mazik Bah-Gahn's number one enemy in the known universe. I'd say that force up there is going to scan and identify America as Barrett Bonner's hometown within a day or two. Even if we could go completely off the grid as a country, they'll see the damage from that strike on D.C."

Carlise turned to the head of D.H.S. "How crazy is the Northeast?"

"As forecast, some places are keeping cool, but New York is becoming a bastion of warlords. The upper-class and the truly rich got out. Regular people are hunkering down, but the gangs are running the streets. The cops have mostly gone into the countryside to take up arms and get ready. The Big Apple as the financial capital of the world is no more."

"Contingency plans?"

"Sir," said the Secretary of the Interior. "The banks moved all their data to secure locations, but personal accounts are frozen in terms of big trades. And, you've got stores doing barter exchanges now. Nobody wants paper money; they want canned goods and ammunition."

The president felt like he was presiding over one disaster after another. "Wasn't there a sci-fi book about how aliens were fighting humans, and the aliens were just a bit better at war?"

Surprisingly, a female staffer who couldn't have been more than thirty spoke up. "Sir, if it is the one I'm thinking about, the humans escaped in a large ship and found a remote planet where the aliens couldn't find them. Then they destroyed all their technology so that they would be an undetectable speck in the middle of nowhere."

Carlisle nodded and smiled at the young woman. "We should do that."

"Mr. President, sir. We don't have a big enough ship, and we don't have anywhere to go," she replied.

"There's always some technical problems," said Magnus.

Emma's dad had several worthwhile skills besides handling weapons and teaching his daughter how to identify charlatans. He was also a pro with a backhoe, and since the meeting at Hickman High School, Eric Creacy had been busy digging a series of holes on a ridge at a high point near Duck River. It was two days of hard work, and Josh couldn't help but admire the man's determination.

"You can use those bunkers as a place to disappear if the Mazik come down Route 40 and decide to search off the highway."

"Where will you be?" There was quiet yet noticeable anxiety in the way she asked him.

"Don't worry. I'm going to be right here with you. Josh. Your folks are welcome to run here if there's a threat up in Bucksnort."

"Thank you, Mr. Creacy. It makes sense for us to be on this ridge, at least until we have to run for it. My dad has his Ruger Precision, which is accurate to five or six hundred yards—minimum."

Eric nodded. "Perfect. Y'all can come here whenever you want. The road's a few hundred yards southeast. Our house is less than a mile south. Honestly, outside of moving to some island, I think this is our best chance."

He put his arm around Emma and squeezed her. "I guess it was a good thinking that we spent all that time shooting."

"Dad. Some kids are posting links to alien movies online. I don't think they get it."

"Josh," said Emma's dad. "You both are smart kids—hell, you're not even kids now—you're like the generation that was teenagers after Pearl Harbor, only this is much worse.

"No matter what happens, you fight. And when fighting is impossible, then you run and hide. That's all the advice I can give you. When the Nazis were committing genocide in Europe, a lot of Jews hid underground in drainage pipes or in the woods, or in other secret places. They snuck around and fought back in partisan groups and killed a lot of Nazis. We're going to need to have guts like them. Hitler's murderers were evil, but they weren't stupid. They starved or shot anyone in cities who could fight back. We have to hide and stay fed like the partisans who fought in the woods."

"We learned about that in church," said Josh.

"Some things shouldn't be forgotten, ever. Different subject. How much ammo do you have?"

Emma looked at her father. "They gave me five hundred .338 rounds. I opted out of 7.62."

"You're rich, kid. That's about five-thousand bucks worth of bullets. What about you, Master Sergeant Rice?"

"They figured I could carry more, so I've got eight hundred of the .50 BMG."

Emma did the math in her head. "Joshua, that's like three hundred kilograms or more."

Josh said, "I got an ATV that can handle a load."

"Okay," said Mr. Creacy. "You two figure it out. I'm going home to have some chocolate bars before they disappear forever." He pointed to a sad-looking Chevy. "Is that your folk's car?"

"Yes, sir. One of them. My dad says it doesn't look like much, but it's got it where it counts."

Emma's dad laughed. "I done heard that in some movie somewhere. So, you bring my Precious home when you finish your survey up here."

A few minutes later, when the two of them were huddling together on the trunk of an old fallen tree, the sun glinting through the dense leaves above them, Josh couldn't help but chuckle to himself.

"What's funny?"

"Your dad referred to you as an evil and powerful ring which rules all the other magic rings."

"Huh? What are you talking about?" she asked.

"Amazing! I discovered something you don't know! I better write this down in my End-Of-The-World diary under something that Emma doesn't know."

"One sec—." She wrapped her arms around him, pulling him close, and then whispered in his ear, "I just figured it out. Better luck next time, Smeagol."

One Hour 00:04 Central Time

"How soon can we expect an attack?"

Colonel Magnus limped slightly while watching the simulation on one of the bunker's screens. "It's impossible to say, John. They're alien. They know we see them, and they know we have no effective defense. If it were me running their assault, I would take out satellites, focusing on geostationary birds first."

"We still have cables, right?"

"Sure, but I wouldn't count on them lasting forever. We'll use radio between all our forces in line-of-sight. As far as long-range comms, we're stuck with radio and cables. As I said, anything transmitting up in space will probably be targeted."

"How's our encryption of radio signals?"

"Excellent. It will hold for a while as long as they don't have software to break it. We don't know what they have, and I wouldn't rule out that they can translate English."

Carlisle sighed. It was late, and he'd mostly slept in short spurts, which didn't help. "The public is going to be isolated once the phone systems fail."

"Not entirely, sir. There are many short-range radios, and ham radio operators are built for this sort of national disaster."

"Morse code, seriously?"

Magnus scratched his chin. "Don't underestimate it. And also, they have other methods that use tones to transmit messages. The Mazik will have a tough time cracking that."

The SECDEF slipped into the conference room. "Sir, I think we should reconsider launching ballistic missiles at them."

The president heard this argument at least ten times. "They have the capacity to laser anything we can throw at them. We'd be doing little more than poking a lion with a stick. No, we hunker down and see if their deployment will expose a weakness. Schein is probably analyzing every move the Mazik make to see if he can hit them without getting obliterated in the process. So, gentlemen. We hurry up and wait."

By early morning, nothing changed on the ground. Radar verified the orbits of the Mazik ships. The clarity was impressive. Ground stations all over the United States watched as the enemy craft held a tight formation above the plains states—except for one attack vessel, which accelerated eastward, and soon traversed the Atlantic to an orbit over Europe.

Reports flooded the media that large cities in France, England, Germany, Hungary, and then Russia, Belarus, and others were hammered with large projectiles. In terms of destruction, the human casualties didn't add up to the millions—not even close, but the message was clear—we're here, and you can do nothing to stop us.

"How many dead?" asked Carlisle.

"Estimates are less than 200,000," said the head of Homeland Security. "London got walloped. Something like ten kinetic weapons, but no explosives."

"We're a fairly smart group," replied the president. "Tell me why the Mazik aren't using explosives. Not fission, because we assumed they don't want to kill the planet, but why not high explosives? They could up the casualty count by ten times."

No one answered. Then the Interior Secretary said, "Maybe they don't have explosives?"

The collective silent reaction made the woman wish she'd kept her mouth shut.

Magnus said, "Alien minds are alien. Don't write off the Secretary's comment. We have yet to see explosives used by the

Mazik. Not on any of the strikes they've made, and not small explosives when we fought them in space. If they are only relying on kinetic energy, that is a big help. The Mazik can't have too many of their alloy projectiles, and if they want to go out to the asteroid belt and tether large nickel rocks, the Angela will be able to make them pay."

SECDEF sat down on the edge of the conference table. "Let's hope that dream is reality, but they have lasers."

"I've spoken with the experts, including Captain Schein," said the Chief of Staff. "In the upper atmosphere and space, the lasers are deadly. They have path loss when they go through the atmosphere; I hope I'm saying that correctly. They heat the air, but a lot of energy is diffused. There's still a tremendous amount of energy, enough to damage a building, but they would have to be firing lasers continuously—even their ships must have power limitations. The Angela has to recharge its weapons, and the Mazik have the same technology."

The president didn't have the head to repeatedly run through the same scenarios. "That leaves ground warfare. We can fight back if the Mazik are only using hand-held railguns. The latest report I've gotten from the generals is that over ten million weapons have been distributed, from small arms to sniper rifles to bazookas and rockets. Don't forget the time when the government couldn't organize baby formula—I'd say we did something fantastic. Let's hope and pray that those Americans out there will dish out so much hurt that the Mazik will back off."

An assistant buzzed the president's telephone. He pressed the button. "Mr. President, the U.K. is on line one, and France is on line two."

"That's it, Jenny?"

"No, sir. Germany is on line three, and the Russians are on line four. The Italians on five, and I told the rest to call back."

Chapter 26

Rondo Mackie ditched his gang and got through the Lincoln Tunnel to New Jersey without getting shot or stabbed. It was a pleasant surprise considering the levels of violence surrounding all of the Manhattan exits. Even as he drove down 34th street, random bursts of gunfire erupted in every direction.

He exited on the Jersey side, looped around 495, and then headed for Route 3, and on to better things, he hoped. The gunshots were still audible, but a measure of civility remained on the west side of the Hudson.

Amazingly, the highway was nearly empty. Granted, it was almost midnight, but the drug dealing and occasionally violent twenty-something thought he'd get hit just sitting in traffic.

"I am lucky lucky lucky."

On the seat next to him rested a backpack with chocolate chip cookies and fifty grand in cash. If the wads of green didn't get him anywhere, Rondo had a couple of sandwich bags full of jewelry that he'd been clever enough to snatch before every store in the city had been sacked.

In a relatively short time, he was passing through Butler when he felt a distinct rumble. Something big happened; his gangbanger radar knew it—maybe the aliens bombed the city.

Route 23 took him all the way to 84, which would bring him to Scranton, Pennsylvania, the home of his mother's sister, and maybe some hot food and a place to crash.

Well past midnight, Rondo slowed on the highway 500 yards south of Lake Wallenpaupack. Something bright in the deep, dark night sky increased in size. He stopped completely. Behind him, cars began to do the same, drivers braking, parking, and exiting their vehicles to look up.

An old man from the Toyota behind him called out, "What the hell is that thing?" As if Mackie would know.

"Hey man, don't ask me. I don't know shit, but I hope it's

from Earth."

It grew in size as it descended, a Mazik Warrior troop shuttle. Massive, carrying five hundred alien soldiers armed with laser weapons and mag guns. It eventually dropped silently onto the highway until it crushed trees, brush, and a few cars.

People began screaming as another shuttle was close to landing on the highway a quarter of a mile behind them. The small crowd dashed from the highway north and south in an effort to go somewhere—anywhere.

"Help me!" shouted the old man. He'd tried to run, lost his balance, and fallen just off the road in weeds and gravel.

Rondo squinted in the dark. "Get up and run!"

"I can't," the balding, gray-haired man said. "My leg hurts."

The drug dealer from the Bronx bent down. "There's a lump down here. I think you busted your leg, man."

A noise like a loud hum echoed from down the road. Several large doors opened, followed by the sounds of clippity-clop on the pavement. It was dark, but not too dark for Mackie to see that a shitload of horses—but different, were running up the highway—at him.

"You gotta run; broken leg or not, I think we're in the wrong place." Simultaneously, Rondo jammed his hand into his pocket. The Glock was warm and ready, but this wasn't the hood, and those things coming toward him weren't no other dealer's homeboys. "I can't carry you, man." He left the old dude whimpering on the shoulder of the road.

The trot of the Mazik Warriors was continual and loud. Rondo didn't look back, but he could hear the guy screaming over the "thud, thud, thud" of the four-legged aliens' steps. The crunch of brush being trampled could be heard all around. Rondo raced to the trees, but the stomping feet were flanking him. He'd seen the drawings of the Mazik on the internet, and for the first time since he'd been in a knife fight as a boy, the street guy succumbed to absolute terror.

He grasped the 9mm in his right hand and crouched nearly flat on the moist ground. The aliens were fanning out among the trees, but it seemed like the dozens of desperately fleeing people who were fast on their feet managed to escape.

"Don't see me," whispered Mackie to himself, clutching the gun in his hand, still and silent. The sound of leaves underfoot was close. He looked up. The thing was so huge, maybe ten feet away. It was looking to Rondo's right.

Please go that way, he thought.

The Warrior sniffed the air. It was a new planet with new smells. The alien's large head moved to and fro, listening. Even in the dark, the human could see it open its wide mouth full of pearly white teeth—like a shark's jaws. Just then, the gangbanger who'd made it to his late twenties without taking a bullet felt a pine cone land directly on his back with an audible crunch.

The alien focused, lurched left, its eyes wide. Its fellow soldiers were already proceeding ahead. The Mazik swung the mag pistol, strapped onto his right arm, toward the noise and stepped forward.

Lying prone on the ground behind the tree, Mackie eased the gun forward. The Warrior took another step. The human swung the Glock hoping for a headshot, but a mag round already shattered Rondo's calf and buried itself deep in the soil.

Almost simultaneously, before the pain possessed his brain, the Glock report echoed through the forest. At a range of a couple of yards, the round carried enough energy to penetrate the large left eye of the Mazik. It splintered into fragments in its brain. The Mazik bellowed, and Rondo screamed in pain from half of his lower right leg being torn away.

Another Warrior leaped and landed with its front foot crushing the human's right hand. It looked to the dead Warrior as it collapsed.

The New York City gang member, drug dealer, and thief turned his head upwards. The alien wrenched him from the ground, grasping his arm and dangling Mackie above the carpet of leaves.

It made several sounds and clicks. Rondo's mind was cloudy, but in the fog of excruciating pain, he kept thinking, *this is not a horse, this is not a horse.*

The Warrior looked at the dying comrade as if making a toast to its fallen brother. The Mazik opened its mouth wide, shoved Rondo's head inside, and shredded the human's skull.

*

"New York got slammed hard with multiple heavy projectiles. We've got reports of landings. They're coming down in large shuttles, but it's still going to take them a while to land their entire force." SECDEF shuffled papers as he tried to piece together a meaningful picture.

"Where?" asked Magnus.

"The first landing was just east of Scranton. We tracked two shuttles there."

"Where else?" asked Carlisle.

SECDEF laid out more reports on his desk. "Southwest of Nashville. Some rural places in Missouri, Arkansas, near Little Rock, west of Des Moines. It's like they are landing in semi-remote places instead of cities."

"That's what I would do. Avoid the population centers until you've got your feet wet." Mike Magnus looked pissed. "Those bastards have patience. If they were going to drop a rock and finish Earth, they wouldn't be landing troops all over the country. It's a long game to them. I think they will try to neutralize our weapons slowly and then consider humans as their cattle for breeding."

The president rocked back and forth in his Gunlocke chair. "Did we shoot any missiles at their shuttles? Any hits?"

"No hits, sir. We shot, but they've already got drones in the air shadowing the shuttles. The drones are taking out everything we're throwing at them. That's according to the crews on the ground," said the new Chairman of the Joint Chiefs. The guy had five screens in front of him and multiple phones—he sure as hell wasn't like that blowhard, Marley.

"What about our ground lasers?"

"Mr. President, the shuttle armor appears to be resistant to our maximum wattage lasers, and the Mazik are firing back at our mobile sites faster than we can move them."

The colonel did some math. "If we get one Warrior for every fifty humans, we will lose at least five million people."

The DHS director couldn't help himself. "Maybe we can get the Chinese to release a new anti-alien virus. We can call it Mazikvid."

Carlisle laughed. The president had no love lost for the CCP. "I'll tell their new dictator to get on it right away."

Josh Rice stared penetratingly at Emma Creacy. She looked hard as iron considering the Mazik chose to land several shuttles east of Hickman County. It was a surprisingly brisk morning, and they rode around on his ATV, scoping out places to hide sniper ammo.

"I know a perfect secret place, boyfriend."

He smiled because not only did she ignite every horny bone in his teenage body, but because everything about her fit him. It was beyond weird to be a teenager in love.

"Emma." Josh touched her hand, the one that wasn't wrapped around her MK22.

"What?"

He blushed a little. "Can you read my mind?"

She reached up to put her fingertips on his face. He had a thin, scruffy growth of hair on his chin. "Of course, I can read your mind."

"You can?"

"Joshua. I love you too."

He stammered, "I—"

"I, what? Just say it so we can get it out in the open."

"I love you, and it isn't just puppy love. That's what my mom always calls it when people our age get crazy about each other."

"Tell me something I don't already know."

"My parents met when they were twelve. I think it's a Rice family tradition."

She leaned over to put her head on his shoulder. It didn't matter that they'd been running around, sweating and dirty. This amazing girl was everything.

"We have to survive. We have to protect each other. I'm never going to want another boy, ever, so we have to win this."

"Okay. I promise."

"Start driving—that way." Emma pointed to an area where the trees grew thicker, and the sky to the west was still cloudy and dim.

Eventually, they reached a place called The Waterfall after crossing the Duck River. It was potentially defensible, and the falls were strategically located.

Josh stepped off the ATV and looked at the rushing water flowing over a large flat rock. Underneath was a dry flat surface mostly tucked behind the rushing water like a narrow cave.

"That is something. It's a shelf, and look at all that space under there? Do you think we could fit in there?"

Emma hopped off the four-wheeler wearing loose Woodland camouflage—perfect for the Tennessee landscape.

"Awesome. We can crawl in from the right side and conceal ourselves behind that wall of water flowing over the top. I want to put a box of ammo back in there. If the Mazik head this way, we can keep this as a possibility. We either hide if there are too many of them, or—"

"—Or we blow their heads off because this place gives us a serious advantage."

She looked around, surveying the perimeter. "There are other rock formations here with little nooks to hide. And that dirt road we came in on wraps around to the west and north. We can run if we have to."

"All right. This will be our best choice hangout if things go to hell. But, if we have to run, then what?"

"We find a way, Joshua. There's a big chunk of forest starting right here, going towards the Tennessee River. It's empty. Just hills and trees up and down. If the Mazik want to send a thousand fighters through that jungle, then we'll kill a lot of them."

"Until they kill us." Josh sat down on a protruding boulder, listening to birds and other things rustling in the forest and the falling water as it dropped over the lip of the big flat stone and splashed into the small pool a few feet below.

"We're not dying," said Emma. "We're going to deliver death to those stinking aliens who think they can come here and take away our future. We have a future, and it's not gonna be them who gets to decide it. Think about this; the Mazik are fighting to take our planet, to populate another place in our galaxy with their kind. We got nowhere else to go. We have to win. We must win, and if humans cause them enough losses, they'll leave."

He picked up a small stone and tossed it into the bubbling pool. "You seem pretty sure of your theory."

She took a deep breath and exhaled slowly. "I am. Think about this; we just met a couple of days before all this shit came down. I mean, I knew who you were, and my eye has been on you for a while, and you approached me in the lunch line like a wimp. But then you got up the courage. Why? Nothing happens without a reason.

"We're both great shots, Joshua. And, we are stuck together forever now." She sat down on the rock next to him. "I have no clue as to how many of the people we know are going to die. A lot of people are going to die because the Mazik are armed better than we are. Our classmates, parents, teachers, and people who all live around here—how many are we going to lose? I don't want to lose anyone."

He put his arm around her. There were tears in her eyes. "Please don't cry." He paused, then said, "No. Go ahead and cry. Cry for our horrible situation. It's awful. It could be the death of our planet. I wish we could just be goofy teenagers, looking for places to make out where our parents won't find us—playing sports. Shooting. Telling the teachers that a dog ate our homework. Looking for summer jobs. Making out."

She laughed through her sobs. "You said that last one already."

"I know. I like that one a lot."

Emma buried her face against his chest. "I'm sorry that I didn't meet you a year ago."

"A year ago, it wouldn't have worked. It had to be now. And, I'm going to trust your faith. We're going to get past this."

She ran her fingers through his hair. "Do me a favor? When I'm weak and scared, please love me anyway? And then give me some of your bravery."

"Will you do the same for me?"

"Yes. No matter what happens. When you need saving, I'll be there. I'm not going anywhere without you." She hugged him.

"That works for me, Emma. I'm scared, but I'm glad we have each other."

Chapter 27

The devastation in Bellevue, Tennessee, was dreadful. Amazingly, very few homes were damaged. The Mazik seemed to ignore structures. Instead, hundreds of bodies lined the streets, some partially eaten. Corpses of residents who attempted to run for their lives. Once they were out in the open, mag rounds tore through them like nails through paper. There were also a few Mazik Warrior bodies—very few.

The National Guard did their best, but the mag guns carried by the enemy penetrated all personal armor. Organized units carrying small arms did not do well. American soldiers fired massive barrages, but alien armor held up well at fifty yards or more, but the Mazik fire was devastating. Only headshots slowed the advancing, four-legged giants. And the number of secluded snipers remained deficient, a shortage that put America at a supreme disadvantage. Mid and upper-level command officers hamstrung themselves by using tactics that worked for human combat. The Warriors were anything but human.

The stampede of fleeing citizens faced drone laser fire, and cars and trucks jammed together on Interstate 40 burned. People continued on foot, pursued by Warriors firing at will, thinning the crowds. Adults, children, family pets—cut down with high-energy pellets delivering tremendous kinetic energy. Wounds were explosive with blood, flesh, and bones splattered on the highway and other victims.

Then, an even worse option overwhelmed the survivors. Some of the Bellevue residents emerged from their homes with hands raised. Most were not shot if they moved slowly and carried no objects. The surrendering few ended up in a group. Corraled by the Mazik.

The reprieve was temporary. Screaming adults and children became the sustenance of tired and hungry Mazik—and the Warriors were ravenous, ripping off live flesh and limbs in a frenzy of the gruesomeness.

The wave of frantic humans fled in the direction of the Tennessee River to the I-40 crossing west.

Even before Bucksnort, the interstate became a tangled mess of trucks and cars. Families gave up, snatched their bags and weapons, and began walking with the tip of the surge that was building behind them. Those who paced themselves heard a distant rumble and voices screaming—a chorus of hundreds of shouts that echoed westward.

"I think we should be running" became the mantra of many. And those who could run, or a least jog, did. But others were too old and out of shape or carrying loads that they believed were essential and heavy.

Soon, runners and those who packed light subsumed the mass of slower-moving people. The Mazik were pacing themselves like shepherds urging their flocks forward.

Josh's parents chose to stay in Bucksnort unless and until it became untenable. His mother, tougher than horsehide, sat on the front porch with a shotgun in her lap, rocking slowly and staring up the highway at the few people on foot who were miles ahead of the myriads fleeing west.

"Harry! It's time to go," Honey shouted insistently.

The screen door, sorely in need of oiled hinges, squeaked as her husband stepped out carrying his rifle and a heavy backpack with ammunition and the bare necessities.

"What?"

"You see the people? They're not going for a hike; they're being chased. Those lights over Bellevue were the aliens landing. We need to catch up with Josh and go underground."

He put his hand on her shoulder. "Spoken like an authentic mom-fighter." Harry scanned the freeway illuminated by the midday sun. "We'll head south and catch up with Josh in the woods. It's foolish as all hell to stick to the road. We'll leave the Chevy and take the little jeep as we planned. Josh has a handheld radio, and I told him to turn it on for five minutes at the top of every hour. We'll call when we're close."

"Harry. Do you think our house will still be here when we come back?"

"If we come back? I don't know. It's a stretch to think that we can guess the Maziks' plans. They might look at all your potted plants and decide that our house is just too pretty to level."

She stood up with the 12 gauge cradled in her arms. "Okay, smartass. I'm just trying to be hopeful."

At that very moment, Eric Creacy stared up his cul-de-sac to see neighbors loading up trucks and SUV's to escape from Centerville. The quickest way to get across the Tennessee River would be to take 50 up to the interstate and zip west.

"That's a dumb idea," he said to himself.

Creacy scowled while heading out of the driveway. He'd developed a habit of rambling out loud and now was no exception. "I've got a walkie-talkie. They'll be listening in eighteen minutes, but I know about where they are."

He flicked on the radio to hear only white noise, except for an emergency broadcast channel on 650 AM.

A tone was followed by, *"This is the Tennessee Emergency Broadcast System. The Mazik alien landing craft landed this morning at approximately 8 a.m. along I-40 near Bellevue. Forces of the National Guard are actively engaging the enemy. Residents must immediately proceed away from the area of Bellevue."*

"That's the same damn message they've been repeating for the last two hours."

*

Carlisle mulled over the latest reports. In the midwest and middle Tennessee, some energetic civilians evacuated out of the Mazik-controlled areas and were able to reach military command centers.

"I'm seeing the same pattern," said the SECDEF.

Magnus said, "Yes. Vehicles are targeted, but people walking and unarmed are mostly ignored."

"What is that?" asked the president.

The collective intelligence in the room was substantial, but there was silence until the Interior Secretary spoke. "We're cows and chickens. Didn't we get some reconnaissance on Bellevue?"

"Yes," said a general.

She continued, "I saw the few satellite pictures. Bodies were everywhere. It's amazing how sharp those images are. A lot of those bodies were half-eaten. The only people that aren't dead are the ones who the Mazik are guarding or herding like livestock."

"And your point, Madame Secretary?" asked the same general.

"My point is that we herd cows in large pens. The cows don't carry weapons, and they don't drive cars. So we corral them and then slaughter them when we're hungry. If you're driving or carrying a weapon or maybe even a bag, the Mazik will consider you a cow with a weapon. Then BANG!—you're dead."

Carlisle turned to a technician. "Look on your computer and bring up zoomed-out images of Bellevue."

"They're not real-time, sir. The enemy ships have been lasing our SATS for the last few hours. Here's what I have."

A large image popped up on all the screens.

"Do you see what's unusual about this? The infrastructure is intact. Vehicles are abandoned. Bodies on the ground, but there are still maybe hundreds of people milling around, and the Mazik look like they are simply observing."

The technician brought up another image from west of Bellevue. "Here we can see see maybe a hundred or more Warriors heading west on 40. And here—" he pulled up an image from further west. "Here, we see people on foot heading west on 40. The Mazik are pursuing, sir."

The president spoke out loud. "Just like ranchers chasing after stray cattle."

SECDEF said, "Isn't that what you did on your ranch in Wyoming, sir?"

"Yes. We rounded up the strays, took them to be slaughtered, and ate them."

Colonel Mike Magnus, head of CAG, and now Chief of Staff, analyzed it from a battle perspective. "That hundred or so Warriors hunting for strays are their weak point. We need to snipe at them, not try to use the army to get into firefights. The Mazik own the sky right now. If we try to go toe-to-toe with a large force, they'll send in a large force and pick off our guys using their mag guns.

"We should be lining that path on 40 with snipers only. We'll be able to kill them and not lose our own people."

"What about the civilians, Colonel?" the DHS Secretary asked?

Magnus looked grim, but he'd seen the true horrors of war. He'd taken shrapnel and bullets. "Anyone over fifteen is not a civilian. We have to hurt the enemy. The miserable truth is that anyone captured will eventually be eaten, until we tip the scale back in our favor and the Mazik are suffering. It was an assumption yesterday. Today it's a fact of life."

The Interior Secretary glared at Mike. "What about the children?"

"This might sound brutally harsh, Ma'am, I'm sorry, but do you prefer an old goat or a young lamb?"

Chapter 28

Josh and Emma sat quietly on the ATV at the south end of Trace Creek Road near State Route 50, waiting. The mid-afternoon sun shone on them, and it felt good in the cool temperatures. Emma lay back on the rear cargo deck and closed her eyes. "Right now, I'm on a beach in the Caribbean. You're bringing me a cold drink, and I got a nice tan."

"Have you ever been there?"

"Nope. But you're going to take me there for my twentieth birthday."

They heard a car coming down the highway. It wasn't long before they saw Emma's dad. He pulled up on the little access road and seemed exceedingly relieved to see his only child.

"How y'all doing?"

"Waiting," said Josh. "My folks should be here in a few minutes."

"The Mazik are heading this way. Well, I mean they're on 40 west, and they could come south."

"Dad, have you been listening to the radio? They keep repeating that the army is fighting them near Bellevue."

Eric Creacy frowned in his middle-aged dad style. The work of digging bunkers a mile away turned into a complete waste of effort. He felt like a fool, having spent two days on a backhoe for nothing. "The Mazik are moving on the interstate. Turn on the AM. station."

They did. The message changed. It now said, *"Attention Middle Tennessee west of Bellevue. Those of you in possession of MK22, M40, M82, and the like, are instructed to use stealth and spread out and select targets of opportunity."*

"So much for secret codes and ciphers," said Emma.

Just then, the crunchy sound of 4x4 tires on gravel drifted from up Trace Creek. Josh's parents came into view and parked.

"Is this the alien-hunting club meeting?" Harry Rice's

attempt to lighten the mood fell flat.

"The government wants all of the snipers to spread out and to make long-range shots at 'targets of opportunity,'" said Josh.

"You're sixteen-year-old kids," said Eric. "I think it makes sense for all of us to run. Keeping the Mazik contained by Bellevue failed."

Bugs and birds filled the dead silence.

Emma asked, "Run where?"

"Over the river and head toward Memphis."

"Dad! You don't think the Mazik will be there? They landed near Bellevue, and that's enough for them? No way. We saw the shuttle coming down. It's big, but the colonel back at the meeting said they will land more than 100,000. Does it make sense that they would drop one shuttle and then leave? Would any intelligent army parachute in a small platoon and then not follow up with more soldiers?"

"It's happened in the past," said Josh's mom.

"We need to do what we are good at. Take long-range shots and make them rethink moving west." Creacy folded her arms and looked defiant.

"Emma and I are accurate with these weapons."

Harry Rice bit his lip. "We can't leave you here alone."

Creacy shook his head and pointed to his rifle. "That's a 308 Winchester. accurate to 700 yards, maybe a little more."

"Eric, I've got a Ruger Precision and a quality scope."

"Leupold?"

"Of course, Harry, anything less would be a tube with glass."

"I got my 12 gauge," said Josh's mom.

"If they get that close, honey, we'll be in heaven."

She blanched. "Let's hope that's the direction we're going."

Josh felt like they were wasting time. "We need to be practical. Your 308 rounds and 6.5 Creedmoor are good to 700 yards. Emma and I can hit coffee cans at 1500 yards."

"Exactly," said Creacy. "Your dad and I should go out 1000 yards. We'll be the frontline. We can always retreat if the Mazik don't stop. If you or Emma sight-in any targets of opportunity, then you take the shot. I think your mom should stay here and deal with logistics."

"You mean food?" she smirked.

"Logistics," Creacy repeated. "I mean spotting with that scope and dealing with the cartridges."

Emma said, "Not here. We already found an excellent defensive position at the Waterfall, and we dropped off ammo and food there."

"Do you have any miracles up there?" asked Josh's mother.

Josh grinned. "As a matter of fact, we have thirteen-hundred brass miracles. Each one will explode an alien's large, green head on impact."

Chapter 29

The USS Dexter O'Brian closed on the next jump point, very close in galactic terms to the Solar System. The twenty Slev crew were indispensable, and Monty spent a tremendous amount of time reviewing and practicing with lasers, particle beams, and missile systems. He wanted zero anxiety if the crew had to engage another warship.

"They are brilliant."

Clark smiled. "I think it's a combination of smarts and a desire to do things perfectly—plus they want to pay back the Mazik for centuries of abuse."

"Seems correct. I'm still going over our transit from outside Olamit to the jump point towards Earth. It was surreal."

"Don't look a gift horse in the mouth. There was only one enemy ship guarding that point, and they were lazy. It didn't hurt that you wrote the script for a Slev with a really good Mazik accent to play at being captain of the O'Brian, formerly known at the Ror."

"Can you believe they bought that?"

"I think when your fake captain told the Second Commander of the destroyer that we are on a secret mission direct from Mazik Bah-Gahn, and that if he gave us any grief we would—how did you put it?"

"Pull off his arms and bring him arm-less to explain to the emperor why secret orders were being challenged."

Captain Clark smirked. "That worked, but it was ten months ago. Can we stop replaying your theater moment?"

"Okay. But when we see Mercy, I'm going to tell her the story."

Two more points separated the O'Brian from arrival near Jupiter.

"How soon will the Washington and the Ro-Pahm arrive before us?"

Monty tapped away at the navigation computer. It looked simple, but there were added variables when you considered transit time through jump space. "We've been pushing it. I think we must have gained on the Mercy and Kap. Let's say they are less than one day ahead. It took us almost a year to make up their lead."

The captain pondered what they might see on entry. "Those Mazik ships will have had perhaps three weeks to assault the United States; ground troops, Mazik Warriors. And we don't know what Mordy did in response to those ships. He's outnumbered, and anything that we've discussed is just a guess.

"It will be three-on-three if Mordy's ship is still functional. When we get there, it will be four-on-three in favor of us. As much as I want to stop those alien ground troops, we need to capture or destroy the three enemy battlecruisers. The best chance is that they wait for us to join them. As soon as we enter the system, we need to transmit an encrypted ID so that they will know we're coming."

Montgomery took a swig of water mixed with some of his homebrewed booze. "You know what I think? I think we need to convince the captain of the Mazik fleet that we are friendly and that Mazik Bah-Gahn sent us with new orders. We tell Mercy to stand-off with Mordy as we approach the lead Mazik ship as a reinforcement."

"Then what? Should we open up comms and wave to their first commander and tell him we're human?"

*

Mercy chose a slow approach to the entry point into the Solar System. "Let's go stone-cold passive," she ordered. "In a couple of hours, when those enemy ships see us, I want them to be in the dark. They'll see two of their own ships and send a comm. That will be four hours from the time we get in. I want 150 G's after we find no threats close to the jump point."

"What about the Angela?" Barrett pointed out.

"What about the Angela?"

"We need to let Mordy know we're friendly."

"If the Angela is far enough away, we can send a tight encrypted beam. There's no reason to believe that Mordy would be snuggled up close to the Mazik unless he gave in to an ultimatum and surrendered his ship."

Molly sat at the weapons console, then leaned around to face her parents. "Captain Schein will not give up his ship. And he shouldn't, even if the Mazik threaten asteroid strikes. As far as Mordy knows, we aren't coming. It's just him, and he's trying to figure out how to preserve that one and only piece of effective defense. No way he will give up. I think the Angela will be sitting out by Mars or the Belt as a threat to prevent the enemy vessels from loading up rocks. Those bastards will be vulnerable if they stop to harness asteroids. That is the Angela's one solid edge."

Barrett said, "By your logic, Ensign Stark, we should see the Angela near Mars, which means Schein will see us twenty minutes or more before the Mazik confirm our arrival."

"Damn straight, Commander Bonner."

Mercy turned to the comm officer. "Ensign Lewis. Encrypted ID to the Angela as soon as you see her. Tight beam. Tell her the calvary has arrived."

Captain Schein sat in his command chair on the bridge of the USS Angela Carlisle, excruciatingly limited to observing shuttle after shuttle departing the massive troop ships and tracking their courses to landings on the sovereign territory of the USA. But now, it appeared that the last shuttle served its purpose—all the Mazik Warriors were now trampling on America.

Cassie Munch sniggered. "Sir, they are moving the troop ships from orbit."

"Plot the course, Lieutenant."

"Just heading out, sir."

"What does that mean?"

"sir, I think they are just going to park the giant ships out a bit maybe?"

Mordy tilted his head and looked quizzingly at the young

officer. "Nu?"

"Perhaps they are leaving the system and will head back to Kamtret to bring a second load of troops?"

"Scary and possible," offered Baumgartner. "But I don't think they will bugger out of here until they know that the ground forces are secure."

"So, they'll go off and hang out away from the action for a while," said Mordy.

Munch spoke up. "They're sending a warship with them."

"That makes sense," said Ensign Williams. "The troops are all on the ground. The enemy ships are in defense mode. They can just sit there until we run out of gas while the Warriors continue to take territory. We need backup."

*

Eric Creacy positioned himself well forward of Josh and Emma. About thirty yards to his right, Harry Rice set up his Ruger on a bipod and settled into a comfortable position which meant waiting on damp pine needles while drinking coffee out of an old thermos. He spoke into his little handheld radio. "After nightfall, there's no point being out here."

Josh keyed his radio. "Emma and I have night vision scopes. It makes sense for you to come back here, and we'll just hope that if the Mazik show up, they make a lot of noise."

"Agreed," said Harry.

Emma looked north. It was 1500 yards to the Duck River, and then the river turned 90 degrees south. "If the Mazik cross the river directly north, we've got a long shot to make in the dark. East is only 500 meters, but they can cover that distance— hell, I don't know, but they have four legs."

"Kill them on the other side of the river," said Honey, Josh's mom. "Don't let them cross."

"That'll work if they are east because we have a clear view, but if they come straight down from 40, that's at least 1500 yards."

"All we can do is wait, Joshua." Emma peered through her

scope, pursed her lips, and hoped that she wouldn't screw up.

As planned, the two dads returned at dusk, hungry and grumpy. The night passed uneventfully, with all five of them getting as much rest as possible. "The mosquitoes suck," was uttered by Honey Rice a few times.

"You should have packed your citronella candle, dear," said Harry.

"Should I run home and get it, Harry?" asked Honey.

"Home?" said Josh. "They could have already gotten to our house by now. It's one a.m."

"I see movement." Emma stared through her scope. The trepidation meter went vertical. She backed off the magnification of her night vision scope slightly.

"Where?"

"Around 60 degrees."

He eased the M82 to the northeast and confirmed movement on the other side of the river. "I think this shit just got real."

Eric looked through military-grade Gen III binoculars. "Range is about 600 meters. I can see them. Geesh! I see ten of them."

"I counted eleven," said Emma.

"I also counted eleven," Josh added.

The anxiety level ratcheted up to maximum. The temperature was cool with no wind, but under the sudden, intense pressure, the weather didn't mean a thing.

"What are they doing?" asked Harry.

Josh increased magnification and tried to get a read on the aliens. "It looks like they are standing there close to the river. Maybe they are trying to figure out how to get across?"

"Do you think they can swim?" asked Honey.

One of them jumped into the river. The Creacy girl shrugged. "Yep. They can swim."

"We need to nail them before they all get across," whispered Josh. "Put on your ears. Emma. I will take the first shot, and then we'll do the best we can."

"Another one jumped in," said Emma's dad. "Don't wait."

Josh loaded a round, amazed that the remaining nine Mazik

simply stood motionless in the open as if they had nothing to
fear. He sighted in on the body of one of the Mazik near the
river. The .50 BMG bullet at this range was devastating to light
armor. He squeezed the trigger and felt the slight recoil.

"Holy crap!" said Eric. "Two of them just went down. The
one in front looks like it exploded. Good shooting, kid."

"So much for their armor against the 50 cal at this range."
Josh reloaded while Emma shot a .338 Norma Mag bullet and
blew away another Warrior.

"Are they not realizing what the fudge just happened? The
rest of them are just standing there."

"Keep shooting," urged Harry.

Emma and Josh fired off two more rounds, and then all hell
broke loose. The remaining six Mazik on the river bank leaped
in. "Get your rifles ready! They're moving," shouted Josh.

The two teens shot at Mazik in the river. Only their heads
were above water, but at six hundred yards, the shots were
doable. Two of the aliens sank. The lead Warrior emerged from
the river. Emma hit it dead-center, and the bullet penetrated and
blew out the back of the creature, taking blood and tissue with
it.

"Three are out. They took off in different directions." Eric
did his best to find them.

"I see two of them," said Josh, as he dialed back the
magnification of his scope. "One is running north along the
bank, and the other one is running toward us."

Emma sounded stressed. "The third one is concealed by all
those trees to the south. Whoa, they are fast."

"Stow those," someone shouted in a rush. "You're not going
to hit them the way they are moving."

Josh grabbed his M4 with a night vision scope. "I see the one
closing on us."

The Warrior to the north made a mistake. It stopped, and
Harry fired two quick shots from the Ruger Precision. The
Mazik staggered and then vomited blood before crashing to the
ground.

The large boulder in front of them shook, and chips of stone blew in every direction. More mag-round hits followed as shards of stone continued to fly at insanely deadly velocities. The south side of their position also began taking fire. What had started as a victory was turning bad real fast.

"I'm cut." Eric Creacy stayed calm but was losing blood from the right side of his head.

The mag rounds stopped. Harry Rice peered up over the rock with his night vision binoculars. "Shit! The two of them are like fifty feet dead ahead."

"Fire on them!" Emma twisted around with her AK on full auto. One of the Warriors dropped, but the remaining alien charged. It cleared the top of the boulder and leaped over the humans with incredible speed. In a frighteningly quick move, the thing turned and charged. In the dim light, something flashed in its hand. Honey managed to squeeze off a 12 gauge shotgun blast as the alien jumped back. Her shot splattered the Mazik's face as it tumbled over the top of the boulder and fell dead back on the other side.

They gazed over the top in the darkness and saw it prone on the forest floor. Even in death, the thing caused them to shudder.

Honey moaned behind them. "I'm in trouble." She was barely audible.

"Oh shit!" Harry threw himself to the ground next to his wife. Honey was flat on her back, sliced through from the thrust of a monomolecular blade. She'd bled out and died in seconds

Emma turned to her dad. Blood dripped from the right side of his head. A sharpened sliver of rock must have sheared off the top of his right ear. She pulled out a clean rag from her side pocket and pressed it on her dad's ear to stop the bleeding.

"Josh!" Emma turned around and called to him, but he couldn't hear her. The darkness of the Tennessee woods smothered him. The world became a nightmare, a horrible dystopian existence that had to end in death. His mother, her eyes open, gazing up at the clear night sky—she was gone. The Mazik took her life like it was worthless in a fraction of a second. He imagined that Emma was calling him, but he couldn't take his eyes off of the woman who bore him, raised him, and loved him.

It all happened so quickly in that instant—his future was sealed. He would scream and cry, and he would mourn, and he would suffer, and he would exact revenge, and he would kill.

Chapter 30

Eric and Emma were shaken. Josh remained in a fog, but amazingly, Harry Rice pushed through some emotional barrier and merely said, "Scan the perimeter. We have to bury Honey and then examine the Mazik bodies. That is no normal sword."

Emma didn't want to reveal her thoughts, but how Joshua's dad could be so clinical was unnerving. But he was right. They couldn't be complacent. She grabbed the night vision binoculars and did a 360, concentrating primarily on the north and east and southeast. Nothing moved, but she could see the bodies of the Mazik, unmoving and bulky, like dead baby giraffes—only ugly.

"Mr. Rice and Joshua. Please look out to the east and check for movement." Emma intentionally tried to distract the two of them. It worked, and she cautiously gripped the handle of the Mazik blade and pulled it from Mrs. Rice's thorax. It floated free of the large wound. Her dad pulled Honey's jacket over to cover the opening from her neck to her abdomen.

"What the hell kind of blade is this?" asked Emma, utterly perplexed as she pointed it upwards to keep it far away from her companions.

Harry turned. His demeanor was flat and emotionless. "That is the blade of science fiction. I've read about it. It is called 'mono' or something close to it. The idea that the edge is the width of a single molecule is bull, but it is thinner and sharper than anything we can produce on Earth."

Josh stirred. "What the hell does that mean, Dad?"

"It means that the edge of the blade is so narrow and fine that it can be measured by the width of molecules. That is why it can cut so easily. Give it to me!"

Emma handed it to Harry Rice reluctantly. For a moment, she was terrified that he would plunge the blade into himself in some kind of maniacal grief-ending suicide. He didn't. Instead, he held it very carefully and pushed the blade against a fat log resting on the ground. The blade went through the fibrous, tough wood with ease.

"There must be a scabbard for this. I want it." He set the sword flat on a rock and shimmied over the boulder to where the dead Mazik corpse lay. The thing was massive and stunk. Apparently, dead aliens also smelled on the inside.

Harry pushed on the body and saw that it was belted with some kind of flexible mesh. There was a black oval and elongated sheath. No doubt it was the scabbard for the blade that had murdered Honey. Rice uncinched the belt and then struggled to move the Warrior until he could draw the scabbard free.

"This is the only thing that can safely store that blade." In seconds, he figured out a way to slip the black cylinder onto his own belt. "Now, we must bury my wife."

Mr. Rice's heart had gone cold, icy, but not Josh's. They all pitched in to dig a grave near the Waterfall. Eric offered to help carry the woman, but Harry sneered at the idea. He wrapped her in plastic, some blood still oozing from the wound., and carried her to the burial site. It was surreal but also very real.

Josh covered his mother's body with the first handful of soil, then he turned and cried desperately on Emma's shoulder, and she sobbed with him.

After some time, they went back up to the "battlefield" and began examining the Mazik. The first sprinkling of dawn barely lit the sky on the other side of Duck River. Harry was scanning every square inch of the dead alien. The most intriguing item was the black device strapped to the right wrist close to its seven-fingered hand.

"That must be the mag gun or railgun," said Eric Creacy. "It doesn't look so futuristic to me. The physics are what they are, for them and for us. Everyone go back to the other side of that boulder. I want to see if I can detach this gun and see how it works."

It didn't take a genius. The wrist of the Mazik was enormous, but the gun was simple, and it weighed very little. It had a powerpack, a mag-round magazine, and a push-button trigger. "The gun is advanced, but the principles aren't complex." Eric flipped it around, pointed it at a huge tree trunk, and pressed the button. There was a quiet whine and popping sound. The mag pellet entered and exited the trunk and then on through a smaller diameter tree behind it with a loud cracking sound.

"I think we can use these," said Josh. His voice was gritty, but he was regrouping.

They'd stripped the dead Mazik of guns and swords but chose not to swim across the river to get more inventory. It was an agonizing decision, but it wasn't worth the risk.

"We need to go west." Emma insisted that in retrospect, the place they chose wasn't the best. "Let's find a concealed spot closer to the Tennessee River."

Josh nodded. "Not yet. Wait here." He vaulted the big rock and ran to the alien body some fifty feet away, then withdrew his new high-tech blade. Methodically, he sliced the body into large chunks and then separated them to form a big circle with the head in the middle. It looked like a target with the large eyes, snout, and mouthful of sharpened teeth as the bullseye.

He ran to the next Mazik off to the left.

"Should I stop him?" asked Emma.

"No!" barked Harry Rice adamantly. "This is the right thing to do. When the Mazik discover their dead brothers, they will know they have something to fear."

Josh returned after flaying five aliens. He was tired and saturated with dark blood. He stripped off his clothes mindlessly—not caring that Emma was standing there—walked to the Waterfall to wash his body. No one said a thing.

The foursome had two vehicles, supplies, and weapons. Josh sat behind the wheel of the ATV with his girlfriend. He looked over to Mr. Creacy and his dad, pointed to a dirt road that paralleled the two-lane, and said, "Let's get the fuck out of here."

*

Tartic, First Warrior Commander, boiled over in anger. He swung his arm into the head of the messenger, knocking the soldier nearly to the ground. "What is the meaning of this?"

"It is from a drone. One Earth-cycle prior."

"I am not a fool to be played with! Why are there eleven of my Warriors dead? And why are five of them ripped into pieces like playthings? Where are all the dead humans?"

The sentry paled internally, if not obviously, to Tartic. "Our Warriors scanned the area."

"And," screamed the First Warrior Commander. "Show me the image of the hundreds of dead humans!"

"We found one dead human. A female."

"A female?" Tartic wrapped a massive hand around the messenger's throat, dragged him out of the command center, and threw him on the ground. He screamed to his assistant. "Bring me a human female with flesh!"

Tartic followed the Mazik out the door and snagged the original messenger by his armor, dragging him back. "Who knows about the dead human female?"

"Just me and two others who found the body under the dirt and rocks."

"Let me be understood. No one will reveal that only a single human female was discovered at this site. Is that plain?"

"Yes, First Warrior Commander."

"If you speak of this, I will personally eviscerate and sever your limbs as the humans did to your fellows. Then I will eat you. Now, Leave!"

*

"Welcome to the rollercoaster ride!" Ensign Scott Lewis' twisted method of saying, "hold onto your hats," which was more or less the same thing.

The USS Washington, formerly a Mazik battlecruiser known as the Ko-Pahm, pierced the solar system jump point, followed by the Ro-Pahm.

"There's nothing here," announced Molly. "I mean, the planets are here. Earth is here, and I've got two Mazik ships sitting over the United States. There are four huge freighters and another warship about a half-million miles out. It looks like a parking lot."

Mercy breathed a sigh of relief. They hadn't drifted into an all-out assault upon venturing into their own system.

"Kap. Mercy. Do you see the Dexter O'Brian?"

"No, Captain Bonner. Only the total of seven enemy ships."

"That's not comforting," said Barrett. "We wanted to signal Mordy before the Mazik see us. Where would he go?"

"Barrett, ask the Slev alert crew to stand down. We have no immediate threats. As far as the Angela, she must be obstructed by Mars. You get to apply the old maxim now, Ensign Lewis."

The cynical and occasionally jester-like ensign massaged his forehead. "You mean the one about battle plans not surviving first contact with the enemy?"

"Yes," said Captain Bonner. "That's the one." She intellectually stomped on the subtly rising and irritating apprehension in the back of her head. It was just that kind of situation that pushed nearly all her buttons. Mercy even failed to put her trademark blond hair into a braided ponytail. Such was the preoccupation with avoiding death.

"Calculate the vertex angle between Earth and Mars, please."

Molly generated the answer rapidly. "It's 1.0534 degrees—about."

Mercy rested her forehead against her palm. "Why does this always have to be right on the edge. Every damn problem we encounter is always teetering between good and bad."

Barrett read her mind. "What's the tightest beamwidth we can do with the antenna systems we've got?"

"Nothing like 1.0534 degrees. Even with the technology that has circularly polarized waves eating each other," answered LTJG Allen.

"It's advanced parasitics, John," said Molly. "It's irrelevant; we can't do it."

Mercy eased her command chair around. "Any

suggestions?"

After a few seconds, Barrett said, "Just send it. A big, nasty loud signal. Encrypted. And use language protocol number 17. They're going to see us. How long can we pretend to be Mazik? Several hours? We're going to be there in under sixty hours. If the Mazik try to get asteroids from the Belt as a threat—that won't work no matter which direction they choose. We have them pinned down. They will have to shoot it out with us."

The commander's comment percolated rapidly in the brains of the nanite-enhanced Recon soldiers.

"Good point. Send an encrypted message. I've already written the format, and I want it continuous until we know that the Angela has gotten it. Allen, accelerate to .06. Captain Jahrnuk. Did you copy that?"

"Aye, aye. We are accelerating to .06 standard. Estimated Time to Arrival, 59 Earth hours, 22 minutes. Confirm, please?"

"Roger that," said Mercy. "Washington, out."

Mercy grabbed her husband by his arm, pulled him close, and whispered, "How much damage do you think 120,000 Mazik Warriors can do in sixty hours?"

"They've already had more than two weeks. I think it comes down to the American people and how hard they are willing to fight. Doesn't it always?"

"This time, it's a binary choice, Barrett. It truly is liberty or death."

"Sometimes, I wish and pray so hard that I could be back in 1777 with you eating a Mollyburger in Philadelphia."

"Where the hell is the Angela?" Mercy was becoming extremely frustrated with the lack of visuals on their sister ship.

"We've been in-system for five hours only," replied Barrett. "If the Angela moved into view, it would take almost two hours for us to see her."

She stood up, gazing at the large display forward of the various stations on the bridge—something like the screen from the original Star Trek, only this was real. Nothing was identified as Captain Mordechai Schein's warship.

"There's nothing we can do but remain on course and continue to transmit, Mercy. Let's take a break. Go rest. You need it, and I need it."

"Allen. You have the con."

"Yes, Ma'am."

"I'm hungry, and I'm exhausted," said Mercy.

Barrett understood all too well. "Perfect. Let's pig out and then sleep until Allen tells us that he's sighted the Angela."

Mercy whispered. "Don't tell them, but leaving the bridge is cathartic."

Exactly seventeen minutes later, in the midst of the Bonners' relaxing and eating the Panruk equivalent of a TV dinner, a tone sounded in their stateroom.

"If that isn't about the Angela, I'm going to make someone walk the plank—and it is within my authority to order said punishments."

Barrett took a rigid thumb and jabbed the button. "Is this important? Is someone on fire? Kidney stones? A detached limb?"

Allen didn't have a humorous retort. "The Angela is visual."

"Yes!" exclaimed Mercy. "Let me know when we get a communication response." She flicked off the comm device. "I'll have ice cream for dessert, please. My mood just went from glum to tickled pink."

"Ain't got no ice cream."

She grinned. "When we get to Earth and kick the tar out of those Mazik, you buy me any ice cream I want. That's an order."

Lieutenant Munch seems excited, even enthusiastic. "We're getting a signal, and we have scanned two ships near the jump point."

Schein was beyond intrigued. "Well? Tell me more."

"The signal is encrypted, and when the computer decrypted it, it—well, sir, it looks like a bunch of random words."

"On the big screen, please."

The bridge crew looked up. It took him a few seconds, but then Mordy laughed out loud. "That is truly inventive."

"Sir?" asked the bewildered communications officer.

"It's the USS George Washington."

"How can you know that?" asked Ensign Williams.

"Because that message is written in language protocol 17," answered Mordy.

Williams looked confused. "Did we learn that?"

"No. It is a private code that I made up with Commander Bonner—it's a magical language which is roughly a phonetic version of Slev Pig Latin."

Cassie Munch felt like a lost ball in high weeds. At least, that is how they would describe it in her native Alabama. "Captain. What does that mean?"

"Have you ever heard of Latin?"

"Yes, sir."

"Have you ever heard of pigs?"

"My daddy raised pigs," replied the lieutenant.

Schein laughed. "Well, this fake language has nothing to do with either pigs or Latin. It's just jumbled up Slev written phonetically. And, here's the best part. There are two ships out there racing in from the jump point."

"You said the Washington?" asked Ensign Williams.

"Yes. The Washington commanded by Captain Mercy Bonner, and the Ro-Pahm commanded by Slev Captain Kap Jahrnuk. They'll be here in 52 hours. We just got that backup you've all been hoping for. Ensign Williams, put me on the horn; I want to inform the crew, and I will send our response to our allied ships from my console."

"What?" The First Ship Commander of the Mazik task force growled at his comm officer. Simultaneously, multiple disturbing thoughts prowled his brain looking for alternate ways to aggravate him.

"First Ship Commander. Two of our ships have been visualized at the entry gate into this system."

"I am now First Commander Kul. Tartic is no longer among

the fleet and he shall not be acknowledged. Is that understood?"

"Yes, First Commander Kul."

"Now. Identify those warships!"

"Our systems have not been able to verify identity. They are not broadcasting proper codes."

"Impossible!"

"Are you sure those of Mazik vessels?"

"Yes, sir. All of the data indicates Mazik."

Kul just found his world twisted into a tight, ugly, and inglorious knot. If they were Mazik ships, then why enter the human system without transmitting proper codes? If they were not under Mazik command, then who? Answers to both of those questions were—potentially catastrophic.

"They have been transmitting an encrypted message since coming into view."

"Is there a reason you delayed in telling me this?"

"I have been attempting to decrypt the message for $1/80^{th}$ of a cycle."

At that moment, Kul overcame his urgent desire to eject the young officer out of an airlock. "Did you not think that such information might be critical to me?"

The comm officer suddenly realized that his future as a living thing might depend on a proper answer. "First Commander. I did not desire to present incomplete data."

Kul cooled himself. He was not Tartic. He was not genetically modified to be utterly reckless. "Display the message. Now!"

The large display lit up with English letters converted from binary encryption. Kul ground his teeth in anger. He did not understand the human language, but he did recognize the letters. If there was an afterlife of torment, his current existence must be a rehearsal.

"Those two Mazik ships accelerating toward Earth are not allies. They are humans!" Kul felt like he'd been gutted slowly with a small knife. He desired very much to give in to the Warrior-like characteristics buried inside nearly all Mazik. Killing a Slev galley working might relieve his tension. He mused over the pleasure of such a diversion, but it would have to wait.

"First Commander. The battlecruiser near the red planet is accelerating."

"Course?"

"A rendezvous course with the two incoming warships."

Chapter 31

"Tartic."

"What is it, Kul? I am busy conquering the land of Bonner."

The First Ship Commander chose an audio link only for just such a moment. Unseen, he smiled in the way of the Mazik. "Enemy ships have entered the human system." Kul stopped speaking and waited to see how such news would stir the Warrior leader—or not at all.

"Do not burden my mind with having to solve your problems. Mazik Bah-Gahn chose you to rule this system. I was chosen to dominate the primates, primitives, barbarians, or however you decide to characterize them. However, I am curious, how can there be any enemy ships at all?"

"We don't know. They must be Council vessels."

"Kul. Do you not believe that with your experience, the Mazik cannot ravage and obliterate any Council provocations? Do not bother me again. The humans have shown some cleverness. I am wondering if, perhaps, they are more intelligent than you."

Tartic cut the connection.

Despite his overwhelming desire to fulfill the emperor's wishes, a tiny splinter of his being still hoped that the primitive species would teach the Warrior Commander a ruthless lesson.

"Recall our ship guarding the transport freighters. We will join together and move to an offensive position beyond the red planet."

"Should we wake up Mercy?"

Lieutenant JG Allen ran through the plusses and minuses. "The captain will want to see this message, but that will also wake up Bonner—the other Bonner. That's like poking a wolf with a bone. Hmm. Okay. I'm sending an alert now."

It took all of three seconds. "What's happening?" It was

Mercy doing her best to sound like she was fully awake and ready for anything.

"We got a message from Mordy—I mean Captain Schein."

"I'm on my way," she said in a whisper. Her husband was in the deep Zzzz's, and she wanted him to get as much as possible.

"Is she coming to the bridge?" asked Lewis.

"In ten seconds, and she left the bear in hibernation."

Mercy pulled her hair back as she entered the bridge through the heavy blast door. "Give."

"I put it on your screen."

Allen stepped down from the command chair and made way for Mercy. She sat and unraveled the Pig Latin message. First into Slev, and then English.

"Did you estimate their current position?"

"They're accelerating directly to us. We'll be in proximity in twenty hours."

"Focus on the Mazik ships, please, Ensign."

He did a rapid scan around the Earth and Moon.

"I'm sorry I didn't check sooner. The Mazik warships are moving in our direction on an intercept course."

"How far behind the Angela Carlisle?"

"Three hours at their current acceleration."

Allen said, "A three on three in three hours."

"That's a lot of threes," said Barrett. He'd just walked onto the bridge and seemed sufficiently alert. "What's the message from Mordy?"

She handed it to him. "Let's see. E-way, Are-way, Oming-cay. That's it? We are coming in Slev Pig Latin?"

"We've got a significant time lag, Barrett. Do you want to send messages like this back and forth? How 'bout no thanks? We'll agree on a battle plan when we get our delay down to fifteen minutes."

She sensed his sudden lurch in anxiety. He preempted Mercy's possible assurances. "We could take some damage in an even-sided shootout—damage or worse. Our offensive and defensive capabilities are almost identical. We're going to blow by each other, launch missiles, particle beams, and lasers."

"And, we'll hope that our weapons do more damage than theirs," said Mercy completing the thought. "That Mazik captain will be thinking the same thing, and if our shields go down, it could be over before you can think about how much it sucks to be suitless in the vacuum."

"Captain Bonner. Thanks for that optimistic reality check," said Commander Bonner.

"Something is bugging me," she said aloud.

"Ensign scan astern."

Scott Lewis, the comedian wannabe, was quite skilled at knowing when not to prod Mercy with humor. He switched his screen to a deep examination of the five degrees surrounding the jump point. Effectively, a big look at anything in motion.

"No F-ing way!" Any sliver of room for jesting went away in an instant. "We've got a Mazik signature near the jump point. It probably exited thirty minutes ago and just came into view."

Barrett was incredulous. "The Mazik can't possibly have timed a pincer move by entering our system exactly on time. That's illogical. They couldn't know what was developing in our system, and we should have seen them before we jumped in-system."

Molly said, "We've been here for six hours? At least. The gap between the solar system point and the prior portal is just under six hours. When we were transitting to near Jupiter, they were just appearing in that last system. They raced to catch us."

"And," said Mercy. "—it looks like they did. Get an ID on that ship. Did it send any messages?"

Lewis punched up different screens on his display. "They literally just entered the system and just now appeared on our sensors. We should get it soon if they sent a message on exiting the jump point."

"On the other hand," said Molly, "why should they bother sending us a message if they are the hunters and we are the prey?"

"Monty!" John Clark was panicking just a little. "We've been in this system for thirty minutes. Please tell me why we can't transmit a signal to Mercy and/or Kap?"

"You would think that something like sending a narrow beamwidth signal would be infallible considering the Mazik technology."

"I'm getting a couple of Slev up here to fix this asap."

Montgomery sneered. "Galley crew?"

"Some of them are technical and have been doing this work for years. Argue later." Clark hit a button and got the Slev technician at the weapons desk. A minute later, a rather smallish and, if a human could even describe him, "nerdy" alien clopped into the bridge.

Monty peeked an eyebrow as the tech said in English, "How may I be of service?"

Ten minutes later, an oscillator of sorts lay in pieces on the comm desk. Rax, the Slev, furiously tested every component—and there were many.

"Captain," said Monty. "It seems that transmitting radio waves is limited by physics no matter which century you are born into."

"I didn't study and remember many electronic troubleshooting lessons, did you?"

The large, former carpenter said, "Of course, I did. But, the Mazik transmitters are a series of modules that fit together like Legos. I admit that I failed to pick up on the alert before that thing died."

Nevertheless, Rax was a regular Houdini with five fingers and two thumbs on each hand. "Got it."

"Can you replace that module?"

"Yes, Captain Clark."

"How quickly?"

"I don't know if we have a spare on board."

Monty dropped into a chair as if he'd taken a heavyweight blow to the chin. He stared up at Rax. "The entire transmitter system needs that module?"

"Yes, sir. I will check." The Slev withdrew a personal display from his vest and, after a few moments, bared his teeth in a sign of disappointment. "No spares on board."

Clark felt his hair turning gray by the second. "Where can we get one? I mean, a spare?"

"On Kamtret, certainly. I am fairly certain that most Council planets have these modules, as well."

Monty rolled his eyes. The conversation was outright torture. "Maybe we should see if there's a Walmart on one of Jupiter's moons?"

"Rax!" said Clark. "Is there nowhere on this ship to get one?"

"Sir. That is a different question. You asked me if there was a spare replacement on board. There is no surplus unit, but I believe that all of the toilets have a module like this."

Monty wanted to run his head into a wall. "Rax! Please shut off one toilet, steal the module, and install it here!"

"Steal it, sir?"

"Borrow?"

"Oh yes. I can borrow it, and then we can choose a different toilet in the event that—well—I suppose it's a given that all of the crew will need to urinate and defecate—at some point."

"Rax! Please hurry!"

The Slev nearly galloped through the open bridge hatch and raced to the nearest bathroom. Monty followed and stood wide-eyed in the passageway. After fifteen minutes of clanging, banging, grunting, and what sounded like a hammer smashing glass, the technician exited holding a black box twice the size of the transmitter module.

Montgomery hesitated. "Um. That looks much bigger than the broken one in the bridge console."

In a way that any human would consider ridiculously terrifying, Rax yawned, exposing every sharp tooth in his vacuous jaws. "Do not worry, Lieutenant Montgomery. I will make it fit."

Within fifteen minutes, true to his word, the technician figured out a way to replace the smaller version of a power module with something the size of a black shoebox.

Clark squinted at the weapons operator. "Can we test it?"

"If you wish, but there is no need. I am convinced that it will work perfectly."

"Just the same," said Monty. "Let's just shoot off a meaningless transmission towards Neptune." Clark loaded a binary string and pressed "TX" on the Americanized screen.

"It worked. Five kilowatts of meaningless zeroes and ones."

Clark said, "Great. Let's target the USS Washington and send a message. Oh. Rax. Please return to your station, but I want you to know that you are now Ensign Rax, the first commissioned Slev officer in the United Space Force. Congratulations."

"Thank you, Captain. Someday when I meet a Slev female, I will tell her parents this story, and perhaps they will let me mate with her."

Kap Jahrnuk bumped his large chest into the even larger chest of Mok. It was a sign of friendship among their species. The captain sat to recline in his sleep chair on the bridge of the Ro-Pahm. Mok clapped his strong hands. "I believe that ship behind us is bothering me."

"What would you like for me to do about that?"

"I believe we should destroy it when it gets within range."

"Mok. Perhaps the captain of that battlecruiser is entertaining the same thought as you?"

The Second Commander of the Ro-Pahm sat in his own sleep chair. "I believe that Mercy Bonner will frighten them to the point where they surrender or be petrified into inaction; then we will destroy them."

Kap laughed in the Slev way, lips gyrating against his teeth. "Let me ask you, Mok. You are a huge, powerful, alien beast to most sentients in the known galaxy. Does Mercy Bonner scare you?"

"Absolutely. She is dangerous, and she is the one discussed in the legends. Do you not remember how Mercy dumbstruck an entire crew of Mazik when she took control of a warship single-handed? It wasn't only that she slew Mazik Bah-Gahn's top commander, but then Captain Bonner told them she was female and would send them all to their deaths and torture for eternity."

"Yes. I remember how she transported onto the hull of that warship. It is a tale I would like to—"

An alarm sounded.

"We are receiving a message from the battlecruiser behind us!" The comm officer sent it immediately to Kap's screen. He read each English letter carefully. He looked at Mok. "I have read each word of this message, and I don't understand even one."

Another alarm sounded. "Sir. It is Captain Bonner."

Kap opened the connection to the Washington. "Yes, Captain Bonner."

"Captain Jahrnuk. Things just changed for the better."

"I am pleased to hear that. Mok believes you should use your special powers and destroy that Mazik vessel following us."

"There will be no need. Our chances of winning have increased exponentially. That ship behind us is the USS Dexter O'Brian."

Chapter 32

One fundamental fact that Mazik First Commander Kul knew was that when outnumbered four to three, the likelihood of an utter loss was disproportionately high. It was the nature of space warfare, not that the Mazik had so much experience, because, after all, actual combat in space was exceedingly rare. Nevertheless, computers don't lie, and every scenario led to similar outcomes—approximately an eighty-two percent chance that surrender was inevitable and destruction of at least two ships was likely.

If that sleek, railgun battlecruiser racing into the system was an ally, Kul would be in the position to demand the surrender of the Mazik ships that had been hi-jacked by humans. Kul would be a hero to Mazik Bah-Gahn, included in the emperor's inner circle, and a military commander of increasing power—but now the outcome would be death and whether to scuttle his small fleet.

He felt instantly jealous of Tartic, a fiery, driven, uncompromising Warrior tasked with subjugating a planet of inferior beings. He had an unlimited supply of humans to eat instead of Slev and other organic plants and creatures. Tartic's life was uncomplicated.

"Did you identify the single ship racing from the jump point?"

An officer on the bridge turned to face Kul. "It is not hiding its beacon. It is the Ror."

"Plark!" yelled the First Commander. His suspicion and fears were confirmed. The Ror was equipped with the latest generation of railguns, and Bonner's people were going to vent the guts of his vessels into the cold, dark vacuum quite soon.

"Connect us to our brothers!"

The comm officer quickly signaled to the command decks of the adjacent battlecruisers. The images of two very attentive

Mazik captains appeared, teeth strategically hidden behind green lips. They waited.

"I am Kul. Who commands this small force?"

Both of the captains stomped loud enough for Kul to hear them. He gave them a pleased yet stern look. "We are significantly at a disadvantage."

Silence.

"The four Mazik craft forward of our position are under the control of humans. The ship that has been in-system, the two which arrived recently, and the newly arrived Ror, a railgun cruiser, have the armament to shred us to scraps of flesh and metal alloys."

Again Silence.

"You may speak."

The older of the two bared his sharpened front teeth. "We must die with dignity. Perhaps we can damage or destroy at least one of them. I will never let my ship be taken or wrecked. My crew and I will die for the emperor."

Kul gestured to the young captain, very young to be a first ship commander and therefore shrewd and thoughtful. He hesitated in a show of allegiance until Kul curled his long fingers in the air—a style of hand motion which meant insistence.

"I am too naïve to offer advice to my elders."

The First Commander considered his inferiors. A fool would die to please an emperor who would never know and care even less—the younger, wiser than his years to defer his opinion, yet failing to seize an opportunity to offer his own neck as a token of honor.

"Both of you have displayed wisdom. Monik. You are a fine leader and honor the emperor with your determination to die in Mazik Bah-Gahn's name. I wish you to come to my ship so that we may counsel together immediately. Your courage will assist me in choosing a proper course of action. We will decelerate at 100 gravities now."

A short time later, all three ships slowed, parallel to each other. Kul ordered a full-size image of First Commander

Monik's shuttle as it emerged from the large airlock. An urgent approach would require very little time.

The small vessel seemed to float in the void of space. It crept slowly towards the flagship as Monik speculated on which of several strategies would inflict the most destruction on the humans.

"Charge the starboard particle beam amidships."

The weapons officer rocked his head to stare at First Commander Kul.

"Which part of my order did you misunderstand?"

In a panic and with a strong sense of self-preservation, the Mazik tapped an arming sequence on his screen.

"Charge to twelve percent and transfer the system to my console."

The wait was minuscule, but at that moment, the tension on the bridge became thick. The authority of a task force commander was not to be questioned. Even Tartic knew that in space, Kul was supreme.

He aimed at Monik's shuttle. No doubt, the blustering idiot was dreaming up ingenious tricks to lure the humans into some blunder that would seal their fate. Kul was no fool. He looked at the facts: humans took four battlecruisers from four Mazik captains and created a fleet. There was no denying the absurdity of it all. And, when things fall off a cliff into the realm of insanity, survival must top all other objectives.

First Commander Kul checked his precision and decreased the weapon's power slightly. Satisfied, he laid a long bluish finger on a glowing dot radiating from the flat surface of the command screen, fired accurately, and turned the zealot Monik into dust.

At that point, the USS Angela Carlisle's sensors picked up the remote and tiny discharge of a particle beam. Cassie Munch jumped. "A weapon was fired by one of the Mazik's, sir."

"That's a little ambitious considering how far away they are," said Monty.

"Captain, There was a hit almost immediately on some small

chunk of matter."

Schein was fascinated. There was no Moby Dick, no giant worms, or even animated rocks in space. "Are they shooting at each other, Lieutenant?"

Commander Baumgartner became very nervous when things didn't add up. To Mordy, the guy looked like he would implode. "This must be some kind of trick. Maybe they want us to think that they are having a mutiny—but it's a trap to sucker us to get closer."

Munch said, "They are decelerating rapidly."

"Why only one small particle beam blast?" asked Ensign Williams. "If there was a difference of opinion about whether to engage us, then wouldn't that spiral out of control? I've been taught about Mazik that they aren't very flexible once they decide to do something."

Mordy glanced at the ensign. "So, you think one of those captains over there figured out that with us going four on three, plus we have the Dexter O'Brian with a long-range railgun—maybe they should surrender and call it a day?"

Williams swiveled in his nav chair. "Why else would they be shooting off a particle beam? But, the only thing that doesn't make sense in my scenario is why only one short blast and done?"

"Speculation!" said Baumgartner with a tone of finality.

"Life is speculation, sir," said Lieutenant Munch.

All Mordy could do was raise his voice and say, "Whoa! Let's not overthink this. In a few hours we will meet up with our good friends, the Washington and the Ro-Pahm. We'll share a few beers and then wait around for the O'Brian to arrive."

Lucky Williams felt every stitch of being a nervous wreck. "What do we do after that, sir?"

"That's easy. We'll have Mercy make a video, announcing that she is the legendary female warrior who will torture their souls unless they surrender."

After flopping into his chair, Rex asked, "What if they tell us to shove it?"

Mordy grinned. "That's even easier. Ensign Scott Lewis is

on the Washington. He's a fantastic storyteller. All we have to do is let him start rattling off in the Mazik language, and they'll give up or kill themselves."

The distance between the Angela and the USS George Washington was down to light-minutes. It was no longer an excruciating task to try to trade messages.

As far as the incoming ship, the only information they received was a vessel ID that read USS Dexter O'Brian—USS Dexter O'Brian—USS Dexter O'Brian—. Mercy thought about the brevity of the transmission. She'd wanted more than simply a repeated ship name. But, they were still too far away to have a real talk.

Mercy keyed her microphone. "USS Angela Carlisle. This is Captain Mercy Bonner. Mighty glad to see you!. As you are well aware, we are accompanied by the Ro-Pahm with Captain Jahrnuk in command. At this point, you must have also received the message from the O'Brian.

"On board, we have Commander Bonner, Lieutenant JG Allen, Ensign Stark, Lieutenant Petro, and a first-rate Slev crew. Everyone is fine. Please transmit a brief report on your status. Mercy, over."

It would be one hour to receive a response from the Angela, and two hours for a round-trip message to the Dexter O'Brian, but they were now all in the same system. The Solar System. Their home.

Less than an hour later, Lewis read out the just received message from Captain Schein. It read: Happy that you are here. We also noticed the particle beam firing from the Mazik. From our position, it appears they fired on one of their own shuttles, but that seems bizarre. We are decelerating to meet you. Please calculate a rendezvous point and transmit. Then we will wait for Aaron and the Dexter O'Brian. Schein, out.

Traveling in space is like being in the center of a giant ball. There are brilliant stars of endlessly varying magnitudes no matter where you look. Mixed in that soup of light and cosmic rays, absolutely no more significant than specks of dust in an ocean, are ships carrying sentient beings. Three of those dots closed on each other.

"Fifteen seconds delays now," said Mok.

Kap Jahrnuk was, in a human sense, tickled pink. "I am very happy."

"I am very happy," Mok echoed back to his close friend.

"Perhaps we will join together in a fleet of four ships, and just the sight of us will convince that Mazik to surrender."

"Kap, my dear friend. There are three first commanders on those three battlecruisers. Do you think none of them want to die for the glory of Mazik Bah-Gahn?"

The captain of the Ro-Pahm stood tall on his four legs and stretched his back. "I am feeling optimistic. Why should they opt for certain death? There are many of our Slev brothers on those warships. I want them all to live."

A quiet tone sounded near Kap's panel. It was the Angela Carlisle.

"Captain Jahrnuk. Captian Schein. We are holding a stable position. Can you approach to within one kilometer?"

"Yes. We will come to your port side."

"Understood. The George Washington will be to my starboard, equidistant. Schein, out."

Within five minutes, all three ships assumed a fixed position. Mercy made a fist and gently tapped away on her chair. "The O'Brian is only 9.5 light minutes. I've got this creepy, paranoid voice gnawing at me that the O'Brian is packed full of Mazik, and they are going to blast us with their railgun."

"That is paranoia," said Barrett. "They announced themselves as the USS Dexter O'Brian. Do you think the Mazik would be that tricky? The Mazik would see a four to three advantage and gloat. In a few hours you can have a delicious Panruk-style dinner with Aaron, Monty, Clark, and Allison. I'm pretty sure that by now, Allison has perfected pretending to eat."

"I think we should bug them for a video transmission.

They're close enough." She swiped her display. "This is Captain Mercy Bonner. Would you please reply with a video? We'd like to see all of you. After almost four years, we're anxious to look at you. Mercy, out."

Barrett shrugged. "Actually, it is a little weird that they are reasonably close and no real message?"

*

"We got a video message from Mercy."

"Let's see it," said Monty.

They watched it together. "We have to tell them about Aaron and Allison."

"Is that why you've been just sending *This is the Dexter O'Brian* repeatedly? What's the big secret?"

"I didn't want to upset the apple cart," admitted Clark. He sat brooding for about thirty seconds, considering how things might play out. "All right. Let's send a vid."

Mercy, Barrett, Allen, Lewis, and Molly were stunned.

"This is some bullshit," said Molly.

Mercy took charge of the situation. "I don't think we have the full story yet—that's pretty obvious. Monty said something about other aliens? And, Allison and Aaron had to stay in that other galaxy to 'fix' things? Everyone chillax—that's a word that you should recognize, Ensign Stark."

Barrett processed Clark's video message and, despite gnawing frustration, said, "We'll get the whole story in a few hours. Let's not forget the primary issue—we've got to neutralize those three Mazik warships and then figure out how to stop the Mazik on the ground. Bigger issue."

The anxious crew returned to their stations. Lewis muttered pretty loudly, "Never a stickin' break!"

"Never a break?" said Allen. "We've got the Dexter O'Brian giving us a guaranteed win over those Mazik. Don't look a gift horse in the mouth."

Lewis laughed. "Considering the similarity between horses

and Slev—maybe not the best idiom to use?"

"Video conference?"

Clark said, "Yes."

Monty said, "How much do you want to tell them? The whole story? Including the part about Aaron and Allison 'bonding' and the whole AI swap?"

Clark answered, "I don't see an alternative."

"You know that is going to freak them out." Monty bit his lip, then turned his chin and lips to quasi-concrete. "Should I show them this also?"

"Good point," said Clark. "We really did go through some unusual activities on Planet Mar El 432." The thought of relaying the entire story was giving him a headache.

Monty de-concreted his face. "Maybe I should just go out in the vacuum and jump over to the Washington without a suit, being that I can live in space without air?"

"No! Better to keep that to yourself. Hell! I don't know. Perhaps go put on the granite Monty performance to get their attention. Then we can slip in that we now have two AI / human hybrids and that they're lovers. Oh, and that they needed to stay in the Mar El system to fence in Tzurek's species because if we don't, those meter-tall, fat-headed monsters will obliterate every other living intelligence in the universe. Did I miss anything?"

Montgomery let out a sigh mixed with a whistle. "Nope. That more or less covers it. Shall we turn on the camera now? There's an invite flashing on your screen. But afterward, let's go kill some Mazik and save our planet."

Chapter 33

"I'm very proud of you, Joshua. You're saving our planet."

Two weeks of guerilla warfare had hardened the sixteen-year-old considerably. Adding life-threatening situations on a daily basis to the killing of his mother—the young Rice boy was no longer a boy.

He warmed a little due to Emma's encouraging words. She could see that he was still shattered, and it was understandable and expected. Her dad told her that the best she could do would be to prop him up every time he needed it and let him cry if he wanted to. She did, and he did.

Harry Rice was a different matter altogether. He'd gone from a soft-spoken, friendly man to an obsessed, cold-as-ice killer. Eric Creacy watched him every time the Mazik were detected. Harry kept pushing his luck, going out with his rifle and his confiscated alien mag weapon, slipping behind trees and rocks, and decreasing his range to the targets.

Several times, mag pellets were exchanged with the Warriors at exceedingly short range. The bereaved husband developed his accuracy and skill. The Mazik were big targets, and their last thoughts when meeting Harry must have been disbelief that the human had a mag weapon and just eviscerated them with their own hypersonic projectiles. After each victory, when the four of them put down the enemy quadrupeds, Josh and his dad gathered mag pellets and power supplies, checking and preparing for the next dystopian encounter—turning the scrums in the forests of Tennessee into a bloody alien video game for real.

"What's the count?" he asked.

Emma reached out to hold his hand. "You ask me the same question every time you wake up. I'm still up. 17 to 14."

He twisted his mouth into a dramatic pout. "I have to admit; you are a better shot than me."

"Is that a surprise?"

"Not really. A lot of women are really calm and breathe perfectly when sighting in and shooting long range. Typically, you don't see too many girls getting into guns, but I think they might be naturally better than men."

"You're very not chauvinistic."

"I call it like I see it, but I'm still going to get a bigger total than you."

"You just said I was a better shot, bucko."

"Emma. It's my mindset. I'm determined to beat your total."

She laughed, but it included an accidental little snort—which made him laugh—the first time since the loss of Honey Rice at the Waterfall. "Sorry. I didn't mean to laugh.."

"Joshua. I want you to laugh. If I make a funny noise or whatever, go ahead and laugh all you want. But there is one thing."

"Something important?" he asked.

"Yes. Your dad is letting the Mazik engage too close. The way he's going, he'll be using the mono blade against them in a week. We can't push our luck like that."

Josh exhaled and swatted a mosquito that tried to bite his arm. "It would be neat if the Mazik were allergic to mosquitoes."

She glared at him. "Do you know what you just did?"

"Of course I do. Mrs. Lamont, our English teacher, would say I digressed, which is true."

"C'mon!"

"I care about my dad, but he's doing what he needs to do."

"It won't bring your mother back."

"Thanks. I needed that," he gritted his teeth.

She thought about what to say next. After a pregnant pause, Emma said, "We're military. We have to keep our shit together. It's you, our dads, and me. We can't lose twenty-five percent of our strength by taking risks. It's time to have a strategy meeting because so far, we've been lucky."

"Are you going to be our platoon leader?"

"Yes, Joshua. If I have to, then yes."

"I will back you, and I think your dad will also. He's a bit passive since the Waterfall. Getting part of his ear blown off freaked him out."

A half-hour later, the four of them sat to eat some dry cereal. They'd all dropped weight, but it was too risky not to ration their limited food supply.

"We need to have a better plan," said Josh, crunching on a handful of Cheerios.

Emma didn't mince words. "Mr. Rice, I think you've been letting the Mazik get too close."

"That's my choice," he snarled.

The teenager didn't back down. "No. It isn't your choice. I want to live. We all want to live, and if you get too tight and a Warrior wins, we will lose our strength by one quarter."

Harry followed up his snarl with a scowl but didn't argue; he just sat there brooding. "What do you want from me?"

"Someone has to call the shots and the gameplan here," argued Josh.

His dad quickly said, "Not me!"

"It has to be, Emma," said Eric. "She was totally in control even during that thing three days ago. If I hadn't moved to the vantage point Emma suggested, I'd be dead instead of that beast I managed to blow away with a mag pellet."

"All right. She will run the show," said Josh impatiently. "And, Dad, you have to follow her lead on where to set up and not just run out there. Please?"

Harry grinned. If someone told him two weeks ago that he'd be fighting aliens under the direction of a sixteen-year-old girl—no fucking way. But, the Creacy kid was a natural. He saw it. He didn't believe it, but he saw how she hit her targets in five firefights and watched out for mess-ups, notably his own stupid moves. His son was right. She was right.

He rubbed his aching forehead. War sucked, and without Honey, he did have a death wish, which was hamstringing his sensibility. A mild breeze rustled through the tall trees. Harry wondered what Honey would say, but he knew her backwards and forwards—how he ached for her to be with him.

"Well?" Josh stirred his dad from his thoughts.

"I think that's a sensible plan."

*

Still in his bunker, President Carlisle sat frustrated at the lack of intel. Mike Magnus understood since he'd been in dozens of operations that were intel failures.

The new Joint Chief pieced together a report on the last week of fighting. "Sir. There are few bright spots."

"Let's do those last."

The man shuffled papers. "Roger that. Here's the bad news, and some of it is sketchy and unverifiable, but that is to be expected.

"New York is a disaster. The Mazik are taking potshots at any gathering of humans. Part of that might be because the gangs are running things, and they all have weapons. Food is running out, so there are territories in the city, and the currency is anything edible. People with food but no weapons get gunned down. It doesn't matter if they are sharing the food or not."

"Is there a pattern in the northeast?" asked Magnus.

"Could be. It seems that the aliens figured out that it's simpler to starve us, and then we kill ourselves over food. Easier for them, uglier for us. For the enemy, it's a great tactic. All the cities are experiencing civil unrest to varying degrees."

"Estimates on casualties?" asked Carlisle.

The general expected that question and wished he was hiding in Guam or American Samoa. "Optimistically? A few hundred thousand."

Magnus interjected. "Realistically?"

"Maybe closer to a million and climbing," said the general.

"Do you have detailed estimate breakdowns?"

"Yes, Colonel."

John leaned back. He needed a hot shower and a vacation. "What about the rural areas?"

"Sir. We managed to launch drones in a few locations to see what was on the ground. The results are mixed, and after transmitting images, most of the drones were destroyed. They have a life expectancy of about four minutes above five hundred feet."

The colonel asked, "Start with the downside."

"Iowa is a trainwreck. The Mazik are rolling over the farms and countryside. Some are getting sniped, but they seem to be using their drones to scout out human positions. Part of the problem might be that the folks out there are forming large bands of fighters, and the Warriors are laying down mag rounds into groups. We're firing back, but the kill ratio is approximately thirty to one. Better than the cities but still devastating. And the enemy is figuring things out because the ratio is creeping up.

"Arkansas is better. The Mazik are taking their time because there are tiny groups of snipers who know the woods."

"California?" Carlisle asked.

"Cities are bad. L.A., San Francisco. Same problem as New York. The flat deserts are impossible, but the Rockies are untouched so far—maybe the enemy doesn't like the idea of fighting in the mountains."

"How's the supply chain?"

"Colonel, the Mazik seem to be lax on drone strikes and heavy mag fire at night. In terms of individual groups of Warriors, they are roaming day and night, but mostly during daylight hours for some reason. We don't know why. We have been able to move equipment—not risk-free at night, but daytime transport is rough. Also, communications are not exceedingly bad. They hunt for transmitters, but there's so much RF activity across the whole spectrum; they have a learning curve to figure out which transmissions are military. Cellphone towers are getting lased constantly, so phones are out. That is rough on the public. Satellites were also being systematically destroyed, but they stopped now, and there are indications from some of the surviving ground stations that the three warships are moving."

"Where's the Angela?" asked the president.

"We don't know."

The room went silent. It went unsaid, but it would be a loss if the Angela had to engage with the Mazik warships.

"All right, general," said Carlisle. "We'll meet again in eight hours or if anything changes. Keep sending data and reports here, as usual."

"Sir. There is one positive bright spot."

All of the staff in the conference room looked directly at the Head of the Joint Chiefs.

"What is it?"

"Mr. President. In West Tennessee, we got these images." The general pulled up several drone pics. "We got these over the last two weeks, and some of our airborne surveillance drones even made multiple flights without getting lased."

The first pic showed several dead alien bodies next to a river. "Sir. This is from two weeks ago. It's near a site called The Waterfall near Centerville, Tennessee."

"What the hell happened there? Did they shoot each other," asked Magnus.

"I don't think so. I think there must have been some first-rate band of locals that ambushed the aliens as they came across the river. We counted ten dead in that encounter."

"Any humans visible?" asked SECDEF.

"None. Whoever they are, they are extremely good. Here's another image from two days later and further west."

"No way!" The D.H.S. lead couldn't believe what he was seeing. "The Warriors don't bury their dead?"

"They're aliens," replied the general. "It will take a while to understand their culture. In this picture, you can see twenty-one dead aliens. No humans. Three days later we lost a drone, but not until after it sent a picture of fifty Mazik moving in a pack to the west."

"Was that the end of our miscellaneous fighters?" asked the Interior Secretary.

"Not by a long shot." He pushed a button. "Check this out."

A lot of dead enemies were spread out over a partially wooded area. The next pic showed about twenty living Mazik galloping east. "We took several pics, and they ran all the way back to the Duck River."

Mike Magnus stared hard at the image and counted. "I see about twenty dead. Any humans?"

The general smiled. "Yes, but not dead. We got the image of one guy using a Mazik sword, cutting up some of the dead bodies and placing the pieces in a circle with the alien head in the middle. The same thing happened two days later, slightly north, but the number of dead enemies was much less. I think the Warriors are a little timid about sending a large force out there. We also snapped an image of two live Warriors standing over the dismembered body of a dead one. Our analysts believe they are anxious."

SECDEF asked, "And you think just that one guy is killing all of them?"

"We don't know," responded the general. "It seems unlikely. We believe that there must be a very stealthy, local-knowledge group of hunters—probably twenty or thirty, well-coordinated fighters. Ex-military from serious units, without a doubt. These guys are also taking and using the enemy's weapons; the swords and the mag guns. They are stripping the dead Mazik and using what they recover to give themselves an advantage."

Carlisle pursed his lips. "Anything else?"

"Yes. We discovered the same ritual among every dead group. There were at least one or two sliced into parts and placed in a circle with the heads in the middle."

"And no human bodies?" asked Magnus.

"None."

Magnus threw his hands in the air. "Flying shit monkeys on a popsicle stick! Whoever is leading these troops is a serious badass. I want to meet that guy and buy him a case of beer. Screw that. I'll buy him a thirty-year-old scotch!"

Chapter 34

Emma climbed to the top of an outcropping of rocks secluded by a natural barrier of trees that left her well-concealed. Beyond that was a scrub brush field with a few saplings.

She'd gotten quite skilled at melting into the landscape and scanning the forests and patches of open land. Less than a mile away, a group of two dozen Warriors surveyed their latest loss of soldiers. "I think they're really getting pissed off," she called down to her dad, Mr. Rice, and Josh from what was essentially a rock wall, some twenty yards in length. It was like a pile of boulders and rocks that, to the left, shrunk in height.

"What do you see?" asked Eric Creacy.

She had a fantastic pair of Vortex 10 x 50 binoculars. "I can see a lot."

"That's it?" asked Josh.

"They're standing around looking at your latest ritual artwork of Mazik body parts." She slithered down a little. "I can't understand why these aliens behave so dumb. Think about it; we've now killed over eighty of them—"

"—eighty-four," said Harry.

"Right. That's a number you'd think would encourage them to send a massive force here to track us and kill us with prejudice. And yet, those morons walk around as if they aren't in any danger."

Eric Creacy looked upwards to his daughter perched precariously, one hand holding the binoculars and the other clutching an aperture in a boulder. "Usually, you have a prepared answer to these questions."

She bent her head to wipe a drop of sweat from her nose onto a sleeve. "Yes. Either they have some kind of weird alien rule that they don't ask for help from higher up the chain of command, or they commit a certain number of troops to an area—a finite quantity."

Josh gazed upward while wiping down his M82. "So, when we get done killing the assigned number of Warriors in this area, we're free to go home as if nothing happened?"

"No, Joshua. Sooner or later, they'll realize that our part of Tennessee is not checked off their list. The thing is, these Warriors are probably unbeatable if you are in a confined area or if you are shooting it out like one army against another. We ain't doin' that. We are very unsportsmanlike."

She looked back toward the alien gathering. They were still milling around. "Everyone get into your positions. No firing until after Josh gets the signal from me to try for a twofer. If they follow the same pattern, they'll spread out very little and jog."

After several victories over the Mazik, they each had a hefty supply of mag weapons, but they saved those for closer encounters. Emma insisted that rifles stay in the fight until the enemy got within the outer limits of railgun range—about fifty meters. That was also a screw-up on the part of the alien war machine. Their drones took out human artillery, missiles, tanks, and everything else from a distance, but the ground troops didn't seem to have anything like a sniper rifle. "Don't get overconfident," she chided herself in a quiet, raspy whisper.

The four of them crouched from vantage points insulated by huge boulders. No railgun pellets would penetrate their cover, but a lucky shot while one of them elevated their human heads to aim and fire—a hit from an enemy weapon would explode brains, blood, and bone.

"Do you hear that?" called Josh in a loud whisper.

The humming of a friendly drone seemed to be coming from behind them, from the west. "What the hell of they doing? Dammit!" She waved her hand vehemently in a motion that broadcast *Down! Down!*

The operator of that piece of expensive military hardware must have had half a brain., but it was too little, too late. Whoever it was, sent instructions for the drone to land about fifty feet behind Emma's position. The buzzing of the rotors stopped, but the Mazik didn't. The Warriors began their jog at an angle almost exactly at the heavy rock wall.

"Hold your fire!" The Mazik weren't deaf. They heard the drone buzzing, and it looked like they were going to run to the short side left of Emma and climb. "Stupid drone!" she ground her teeth, knowing that one Warrior over that rise to the north could be a nightmare. "Joshua! Fire at the lead one to the left. We can't let them reach those trees beyond the rock pile. Dad! Harry! Shift left and fire at the aliens in the center of that pack."

The report of the M82 lagged behind the devastation it wrought on whatever the hell was in its sights. In this case, the large quadruped scrambling in an attempt to reach the left side of the rocks. The body of the thing exploded. It was still more than one hundred eighty meters from the outer edges of trees to a bald patch of gravel at the bottom of the rocky wall.

Emma chose her targets and brought down two more. Eric and Harry fired and hit the center blob of running beasts, but the distance between the enemy squad and the point of no return was decreasing.

More Mazik dropped. Some squirmed on the ground, not dead, but injured badly enough to take them out of the game. And then, they got smart.

Thwap! Mag pellets began striking the rocks below them. About a dozen of the enemy stopped and fired on them. Simultaneously, three of the Mazik closest to the northern edge of the wall galloped frantically to blow through the trees and dash up the short slope. If they succeeded, the risk of a total loss was substantial, but Emma wasn't thinking about probabilities. "Dad and Harry! Lay down mag fire on that group."

The two men set down their rifles, and each picked up one of several railgun weapons they'd neatly laid out. There was a continued staccato drumming on the rocks below them. It took guts, but they arced over the rocks and fired bursts of pellets at the aliens. It was a bloodbath. The Warriors sacrificed themselves, hoping that three of them would get over the north flank and quickly shred the humans.

Josh and Emma focused on the three Mazik that suddenly

burst into the bare, gravel, ten-foot-wide patch below them.

The Warriors down among the sparse trees could not return accurate fire quickly enough. Eric and Harry would simply grab the next charged mag weapon and blast away, hurling a continuous stream of hypersonic projectiles. It was a rout.

"We're crushing them!" shouted Eric Creacy.

His daughter was too preoccupied with not dying to congratulate her dad. The three Warriors were at very close range and bolted up the rocks while firing small bursts of pellets. Chips of rock flew—not at the speed of pellets, but potentially life-threatening.

Josh risked it. He leaned up and fired rapidly at the leading Mazik. The projectiles ran up the body armor, but two or more pellets stuck the thing in its head. The lead soldiers toppled backward, nearly tripping up the one below it, but the trailing Warrior leaped like an acrobat to the top of the boulder only fifteen yards left.

Emma finished off the third terrifying alien below, but the one who'd made it to the top was already swinging its arm to bring a railgun to bear on them. Josh sat in between her and the terrifying enemy soldier. She knew that a direct hit on Josh would pierce her as well.

The thing began an arc of fire that blew away pieces of rock behind them to their left. Josh fired back from point-blank range. The power of such short-distance shots speared the alien through. Three, maybe four. It would die, but it continued to fire as it fell—tremendously forceful kinetic energy sliced off chunks of rock behind Emma in the direction of Eric and Harry. And then, heavily muscled, four-legged, brutal Mazik tumbled down the sloping human side of the defensive wall.

"How many of the group out there are left?" asked Emma breathing hard.

Josh looked over. There was only one standing and attempting to reload a mag weapon. Josh aimed and fired.

"I'm the luckiest human in this forest," she groaned. "Ouch."

"Ouch?" he repeated. "What the hell?" There was blood dripping down her left arm.

"It's not that bad, Joshua." He unbuttoned her shirt and pulled it down to expose her shoulder. It looked like some of her skin, about the size of a quarter, just got sliced off. "Like I said, babe. Ouch!"

"How can I fix that?" he asked.

"A little alcohol and a bandage?"

"It looks like it needs stitches."

She grimaced a little. "You must play a doctor on TV. You can't stitch that. It isn't a cut, whatever. Eventually, it will scab over."

"It looks really gross." He turned around to check on his dad and Mr. Creacy. Eric sat with a hand over the side of his head, but his dad wasn't there; Josh looked down.

"Oh! Please no! No! No! Dad!" He screamed.

Harry Rice lay sprawled out fairly close to the dead body of the Mazik. Dirt and grime and blood-soaked his torso. One of his legs was at an impossible angle, and the handgrip of the mono blade protruded adjacent to his body.

Emma felt like her insides were shrieking. Her best guess was that one of the mag rounds hit him square in the chest. Harry must have fallen just after the Mazik and landed on its drawn blade. The microscopically thin sword opened up Harry's back, severing organs and bones, but from up on the rock pile, all she could see was a bloody camouflage shirt. His eyes were still open, staring straight up to the blue sky.

Two parents in four weeks. As much as it hurt her, it might take Josh a lifetime to process that.

She stared at his face. He'd gone clinical to suppress the pure agony of what he'd lost in a stinking four weeks.

"One of those railgun rounds kinda got me a little," called Eric Creacy from behind the flat rock from where Rice had fallen. "Pretty ironic, really."

Josh and Emma looked over. Eric Creacy had a fair amount of blood dripping down his jaw. He squinted toward the two teenagers. "I kinda lost part of my other ear, if you can believe that. It hurts like shit."

"Dad. Anywhere else?"

"No. I checked. I'm okay except for the ear." In misery and shock, Eric blurted out the obvious, "We lost Harry."

Some of the Warriors down just beyond the trees were moving but incapacitated. "I'm going to go finish them," announced Josh. "I'll take care of my dad after that."

"Is that what you want to do? Go kill and cut up the dead Mazik?" asked Emma

Josh glared at her. "Stupid question! If I'm doing it, then it's what I want to do." He turned and worked his way down the wall of boulders, not looking back.

She was about to say something like "be careful," but it dawned on her that it was better just to shut up. Instead, she and her father eased their way down and hit the first aid kit.

Emma looked around. The supplies were intact, and she bandaged up her dad's ear and her own arm. The injured Creacy family.

Scanning the perimeter was a given. She looked west and saw the drone. The stupid drone that drew the Mazik to their position sat on the ground some ten meters away with an LED—flashing every few seconds. The damn thing was still recording, and the dumbass military tech was probably oblivious that he'd screwed them by hovering over their lookout.

She walked over through some scrub brush, grass, and dirt to reach the now quiet surveillance device. Her first notion was to take the mono blade and cut the expensive military hardware in half. She inspected the thing. It looked like she'd imagined, but then Emma noticed a microphone mounted next to the flashing green diode. "Time to vent a little frustration," she growled, barely loud enough to be heard.

*

It took four days for the drone video and audio to reach Carlisle's deep bunker. An officer working for the new head of joint chiefs knocked and waited for permission to enter.

"Sir. We just received this from a surviving surveillance drone in West Tennessee. It's not something we expected, sir."

The officer handed a USB drive to Colonel Magnus. Mike jammed it into one of the computers on the president's desk. A few of the top staff sat back to look at the large screen on the increasingly musty conference room wall.

At first, there wasn't anything except an obstruction over the camera and some crunchy mic sounds. It was a hand, and it moved out of the way to reveal a girl who couldn't have been more than thirteen or fourteen. She looked underfed, and her blond hair was cropped short. As she backed away from the camera, they could see a dead Mazik Warrior behind her.

A natural rock wall was a little further back, where a teenage boy sat on a large rock cradling a sniper rifle.

"Don't you dare start up this drone and fly it out of here until I'm done." The girl had a Tennessee accent. She turned and looked back at the boy, then squared up on the camera.

"Listen, you fuckers! I am Emma Creacy. I'm sixteen. Behind me is my dad, Eric Creacy, and my boyfriend over there is Joshua Rice. Off-camera is Mr. Harry Rice, but he's dead because you assholes flew your stupid drone right behind us and drew the Mazik to our position. Twenty-three Warriors came straight at the sound of that dumbass surveillance drone of yours.

"Let's make this understandable to you morons. I can't lose any more of my people. We have just put down almost two-dozen Mazik. That brings our total to just over a hundred. Joshua, over there, lost his mother almost five weeks ago, and now he lost his dad because of you dipshits. If I see another U.S. military drone anywhere near us, I'm going to blow it out of the sky, and then when I get done killing off all the aliens in my part of Tennessee, I'm going to come and find the CO of whatever unit screwed us over and cut his balls off."

Emma let that sink in and then said, "Y'all have a nice day. Now get your fuckin' drone out of my battle zone."

The collective reaction in the subterranean, highly secure presidential conference room was a combination of extreme emotions coated in shock.

SECDEF. "That can't be real!"

Homeland Security. "She threatened to assault our personnel."

Interior Secretary. "She's so young and innocent."

Joint Chiefs. "That kid has no training."

Carlisle. "Any other opinions?"

Magnus. "Emma Creacy is qualified for CAG operations."

The other officers and staff in the room stood bewildered, shaking their heads, and waiting for instructions.

The president gathered his wits. "How the hell do two teenagers and a couple of adults—now one adult—manage to put down over a hundred Mazik?"

The colonel was the only one qualified and experienced enough to give a thoughtful opinion, and he did. "They are outstanding shooters. That girl knows how to set up the Warriors in locations where the aliens get picked off at a distance, and if you noticed in the video, they are using mag weapons that they took from their dead enemies."

"So, they've got long-range and short-range weapons that are smearing the Mazik all over West Tennessee?" asked SECDEF.

"Oh, yeah. One more thing," said Magnus. "That girl is using psychological warfare to perfection. Every time they blow away a squad of the Warriors, they do that ritual of cutting up the dead and putting severed heads in the middle of a circle of body parts."

Carlisle spoke. "I thought the aliens were so cold and single-minded that seeing their own dead wouldn't mean anything."

"No, sir. I don't believe that. It took them a year to travel from Kamtret to here. An entire year of being couped up in giant freighters thinking that when they arrived on Earth, it would be a cakewalk. Those things are not devoid of feelings; I don't buy that for a minute. They have enormous egos and view humans as inferior rats. What happens when you find out that all the propaganda which has been force-fed to you for a long time turns out to be a lie?"

The Joint Chiefs spoke up. "The Mazik facing that girl are losing their confidence; plain and simple."

The colonel continued the thought. "Yes, general. They are tentative and cautious, and they don't want to die. We need to use Emma Creacy's model of how to fight the Warriors everywhere."

"There are over a hundred and ten thousand of those things," said the Interior Secretary.

The colonel leaned back in his chair. It didn't help. His body ached from forty years of inflicting and receiving injuries while leading CAG. "Our best estimate is that we've killed maybe one thousand Mazik nationwide. That girl owns ten percent of our total, at least. She's fighting them only from well-thought-out cover. We have to pull back all our troops and civilians to rocky, forested, and defensible zones. Taking the fight to the Warriors in open combat is a complete loss."

SECDEF said, "We've killed a thousand!"

"Oh, please," said the colonel. "We've lost between fifty and a hundred thousand troops. We cannot fight them by sacrificing dozens of young men and women in order to kill one of the enemy. It's unsustainable. I'll tell you something else. Mazik Bah-Gahn could send a million or two million more of his kind. We have to have the population run for the hills and fight from there. Give up the cities and towns. Make the enemy fumble around in the forests and do to them what Emma Creacy is doing."

Carlisle knew that to ask Americans to run would be resisted. They wanted to fight for their neighborhoods, and they didn't believe that pure courage and guts wouldn't be enough. But, it wasn't enough. Those towns would turn into pastures where the Mazik would pick and consume humans like fruit. "How many will we lose if we urge them to give up defending towns and just run?"

"Starvation," said the Interior Secretary. "The mountains and forests will become tribal. Even if they can slow down the Warriors, and even if they can hold them at bay, Americans will begin fighting each other over food and defensible territory.

Then what happens when hundreds of those freighters come to Earth?"

Carlisle turned to the SECDEF. "Do we have any way to contact the USS Angela?"

"The enemy took out most of our better satellites. We've got people trying to solve that problem."

Carlisle rustled some papers on his desk. "Top people, I'm sure. Translation: We don't know what is going on up there."

"Sir," said one of the junior officers in the room. "We have some visuals, and the last image we got just an hour ago showed the orbiting Mazik ships are not in view."

"Where are they?" asked Magnus.

"They could be hovering over China. We can only guess, sir."

The president faced all of them. "Get the word out—no more attempts to protect towns. Tell the population to take their families, weapons, and as much food as they can carry to the hills.

Instruct them to form small units and fight like Creacy. They should be cutting up the dead Mazik just like Emma Creacy does—parts in a circle and heads in the middle. In fact, I'm giving the practice a name, so spread it around. From now on, it will be known as doing a *Creacy*. Every successful sniper out there should finish the job of putting down a Warrior by doing a Creacy. I want alien heads surrounded by body parts all over this country. Call them Creacy Mounds, and everyone needs to know about how the girl and her boyfriend are the most deadly Mazik killers on the planet.

"And let's pray that our country doesn't go utterly medieval before Schein figures out a way to save our asses."

Chapter 35

The Angela, the Ro-Pahm, and the Washington command bridges were deathly silent and still. It went on for a while. They could all see each other on multiple screens of the allied warships. They focused on the image from the Dexter O'Brian, specifically Monty's face.

"Does that hurt?" asked Barrett.

Montgomery smiled. His face looked like gray concrete but remained flexible. "No, Commander Bonner."

Mercy spoke almost as if she was clairvoyant. "Besides transforming your body into a hard solid, what other added skills do you have from the Mar El experiment?"

"Well, I think—" Clark kicked him under the table. "—um, I think that being able to transform into stone should be significant all on its own, Captain."

She eyed him, and everyone modified with nanites sensed that Mercy Bonner did not believe him. "Okay. We have bigger fish to fry than to go over everything you've told us for the last forty-five minutes. Captain Clark, I would like a private comm with you. For now, I want all weapons personnel to check that all systems are ready to go. You've got two hours."

"When do you think Allison and Aaron will be here?"

"Mercy. I can't say."

"That's a classic response. Here's my retort, can't say or won't say?"

Clark was honest. "I just don't know. They have to deal with the Mar El. If the two of them don't seal Tzurek's kind in their galaxy, we could end up with a problem that makes the Mazik look like a minor case of dermatitis."

"Tell me," said Mercy as she sunk into the form-fitting chair in her quarters. "—give me your impression of how long that could be. It would be helpful to know because we'll need to figure out how to stop the Mazik Warriors on Earth after we deal with those three battlecruisers. Based on Mordy's information, we've got well over a hundred thousand Warriors setting up a foundation for a more massive invasion. Without the AI transportation abilities, I'm having difficulty figuring out how we can add much to the fight down there."

"They told me to contact Aaron's sister."

She pondered Clark's comment and drifted off into some recollections.

"Mercy? Hello?"

"Sorry," she said while staring at Clark's image on her screen. "Aaron and I talked about his sister, Julia. There was a time when Allison examined her. It was no secret between us, but the rest of Recon wasn't told anything."

"What about Julia? As far as I know, the woman writes cookbooks and watches your adopted son."

The thought of Manuel, the boy she and Barrett saved from a near civil war in Mexico when the Mazik first came to Earth, gripped her emotions. If the aliens had never come, the boy would be growing up with his mother south of the border, happy.

"No. There's much more to it. Aaron is inferior to his sister."

"What the hell does 'inferior' mean?"

"It means that she has potential in her brain that will exceed anything Dr. Aaron Howe ever had. Although, now that he's become a hybrid with Allison, who knows?"

"Are you saying we need to see Julia because she can transport things? Just like the AI?"

"No clue. But, if she can, it will make fighting the Mazik easier."

"How? She can't just mentally pick them up and put them back on their ships. The Mazik can't be transported without dying."

Mercy grinned. "I'm not opposed to those Warriors dying, but I don't know what she can do. We're in the dark until it's safe to visit her in Vermont."

"What if the enemy has already been there? I mean where

Julia lives."

"We'll find her. For now, let's see if we can deal with the Mazik on those battlecruisers."

Clark laughed cynically. "Deal with them? That's funny. What kind of deal do you think they'll agree to other than us committing suicide and letting them eat our brains?"

"They are outgunned. The deal is that we take those three ships, and the crews get to live."

"Is there alcohol on your ship? Because, Mercy, you sound like you've been drinking."

"I haven't had a drink since 1777."

*

Kul considered the relative positions of his flagship and the two others. There were ten Warriors on Monik's ship known to be unfavorable to anything but total allegiance to Mazik Bah-Gahn. Still, the genetically modified, aggressive troops lived an existence that insulated themselves from interaction with normal Mazik. Unless and until there was a palpable threat onboard a battlecruiser, then—.

"I wonder," said the Second Commander to Kul. "Perhaps we should consider the offer of the humans."

"You realize that I am justified to eject you from an airlock just by making that one statement."

The Second froze. "I believe I am justified to eject you, First Commander, from that same airlock for your murder of Monik by evaporating his shuttle into dust particles."

The two gazed at each other with wide, black, rimless eyes, considering intentions and options. The Second stepped back and stomped his feet. He'd relented. "I will abide by your every decision, First Commander."

Kul quietly released his grip on a small ceremonial blade tethered to his blouse and spoke firmly. "Shortly, you and I will enter the bridge. You will put a projectile in the head of a Warrior."

"And?"

"I will execute the other. Simultaneously, I have arranged for an accident in the crew quarters of the remaining eight; some problem with the atmosphere supply and locked blast doors—a tragic end. I believe that Mazik Bah-Gahn's chosen few have become a liability."

"What about the new First Commander on Monik's ship?"

"He is mine."

Kul's Second was impressed. "It appears that you have planned for the worse."

"Sit." He extended an arm and two opposing digits to his XO. He then sat back in his sleep chair. "Did you ever wonder if those concubines that Mazik Bah-Gahn heaves to their deaths from 700 meters *actually* sing praises? Do they think of the Emperor's benevolence as they plunge to a future that is brief and ends with their brains oozing onto the surface of Kamtret?"

"I—"

"Let me finish." He bared his finely manicured teeth in a wide display. "I've never been there in person, but those females are conditioned to bless anything done to them. Certainly, an existence that you would find?" Kul paused, waiting.

"Distasteful?" answered his Second.

"Distasteful as the flesh of an aged Slev galley worker. I'll tell you something else. The tight grip with which Kamtret is ruled stokes thoughts of a less oppressive—situation.

"Hear me, my Second. I was raised to be elite in service to the Mazik Bah-Gahn. It was in the air that I breathed, the water and blood that I drank, and the lessons of loyalty crammed down my groomed throat. The Warriors are genetically incapable of philosophy, but I am not. I am also practical. The humans cannot be defeated."

Kul abruptly stood and halted his diatribe.

"Are you speaking of the humans in regard to our current predicament? Or, do you mean long-term?"

Again the First Commander opened his jaws and then said, "I will let you consider that, but I believe that shortly we will discover how it is that this foul race of bipedal primitives somehow manages to prevail. There is some intangible factor. I do not know what it is, but once, in a quiet discussion I had with Monik's Second—" Kul went strategically silent.

"I am curious. What did he say regarding the primates?"

"He said, 'perhaps they are not as stupid as they are ugly.' For now, let us go to the bridge."

Mercy positioned her small fleet in a defensive posture as the clock ticked away since sending a simple text message in Mazik to the three enemy vessels.

"How long?"

Barrett said, "Exactly one hour and 17 seconds. When do you want to get aggressive?"

"No. We can wait a bit longer," answered Mercy.

Molly sat at the comm station chewing gum. It drove Barrett up the wall that his step-daughter would sit on duty, chewing gum, eating chocolate, especially while they were facing down three very capable warships.

Mercy read his exaggerated body language. "Let her chew," she whispered.

JG Allen relaxed calmly at the navigation console. It was rare that either Bonner slipped up and had them working the same shift. The strategy was that if they were on duty together, they would be off-duty together, which grated on every one of Barrett's fatherly nerve endings. He bit his lip and smoldered while observing Molly wink surreptitiously at the lieutenant.

"Incoming recorded message." Ensign Stark flashed back into proper discipline. She posted it to the main screen.

A Mazik First Commander stood erect in what must have been the captain's quarters. There was a plain bulkhead and a sleep chair behind him. In Molly's opinion, despite a frightening alien appearance, he looked rather sedate.

"I am Fleet Commander Kul." He did not bare his teeth. "I am in receipt of your offer to provide safety for myself and my crew should we stand down and lower our shields.

"As you are aware, just as your species does not trust the Mazik, I am also wary of humans. What assurance do I have that you will not attack when we are vulnerable?"

Mercy fixed her braided ponytail behind her, straightened her uniform, and stared directly into the camera. She clicked on the recorder.

"I am Captain Mercy Bonner. I am the commander of my fleet. Perhaps you have heard the name Barrett Bonner? That male human is my mate." She continued in perfectly spoken Mazik. "If you lower your shields, we will honor our vow to not fire upon your ships. Fleet Commander Kul. We could engage in active hostilities, but you would lose. Choose wisely so that I won't have to kill you all." She pressed a tab to stop recording.

"Do you think it was a good idea to add the part about not killing him and his crew?" asked Barrett. "Maybe a little aggressive. I think that might have been dumb."

"Oh, really?" She pressed a light on her screen. "Kap. Do you approve?"

"Yes, Captain Bonner. Particularly the last part about killing all of them. When you state the obvious to the Mazik, they respect that. It was ingenious to let him know you are the female Bonner."

"Thank you, Kap."

Mercy turned to her husband as he stood next to her command chair on the dimly lit bridge. "This might be a little awkward considering our circumstances, but—" she lowered her voice to a barely audible whisper. "—*Na Na Na Boo Boo—*."

She smirked and turned back to her screen.

If there was such a thing for a Mazik, Kul's Second stared wide-eyed at the human female, mate of Barrett Bonner. He felt that all of the impossible coincidences in the galaxy lined up to shatter the Mazik dreams of victory.

"This is impossible!" He said to Kul.

The First Commander ignored him. Legend or no legend, the female in charge of four powerful ships stated an undeniable fact. His own battlecruiser, and the warship formerly commanded by Monik were amiable. The third was a different matter. He knew the commander of that ship—he was a fool. Dogmatic. Pathologically loyal to Mazik Bah-Gahn. But for this situation, he also had a plan.

"We're getting a live message," said Molly.

The same commander appeared in a live video. Mercy activated her camera.

"I practice English," said the commander.

"We can speak in Mazik," answered Mercy.

"It smart to English. Better."

"What is your decision?"

Kul looked at his Second, who was clearly bewildered, and opened up a direct coded link to the new commander of Monik's ship. "Are you weapons work?" he asked Mercy.

"Our weapons are armed and ready."

"I say fire your weapons on ship with shields." He switched to the language of the Mazik, "Lower all shields."

Barrett tried to make sense of it. "Could he want us to fire on them when he lowers his shields?"

"That's suicide!" said Mercy.

JG Allen called out, "Two of those ships just lowered their shields completely."

The Mazik looked at Mercy. "You fire on ship with shields now!"

Molly said, "I think he's not kidding. Maybe he only has control over two ships?"

"Fire now!" he repeated.

Mercy opened a channel to the Dexter O'Brian. At their current distance from the enemy fleet, lasers were marginal, particle beams were doubtful, but Clark's railgun was a different story. It was like comparing a .38 caliber pistol to a bazooka. "Captain Clark," she called. "Fire one mag projectile at the shielded enemy ship right now. Do not fire on the unshielded ships."

She was answered with an immediate, "One mag projectile at the shielded ship only. Aye."

On Earth, a railgun round could reach Mach 6. That was inferior technology, power, and the resistance of air molecules.

Space was a different matter. The gun fired. It was only 19.2 seconds before the advanced alloys of the "bullet" slammed into the matrix protecting the battlecruiser.

Most of the energy radiated across the matrix, overpowering the tremendous protection field; it collapsed as a solid particle representing only nine percent of the original mass struck the hull.

In an instant, the friction of the penetrating slug blew out waves of heat, light, and chunks of the hull. It burrowed through the exterior and then crashed through interior bulkheads, sending debris at sub-sonic velocities—demolishing and killing anything in its path.

"Geesh!" said Lieutenant Petro, as the CAG officer watched the high-resolution image, mouth agape. The light show faded quickly.

"Hold your fire," ordered Mercy.

Molly was incredulous. "Mom! Let Dexter finish them off!"

"Hold fire," Captain Bonner repeated. "There are Slev on that warship! We're not going to murder them!" She transmitted on an open channel to the Dexter, the Ro-Pahm, and the Angela. Kap was, no doubt, paying close attention. She didn't want her friend to doubt, for even a moment, Mercy's determination to protect the Slev crew.

Clark and Monty aimed the shot to avoid the bridge of the enemy vessel. Within moments, the First Commander of the damaged warship was screaming through his comm channel to Kul.

Earlier, that First Commander watched Kul obliterate a shuttle carrying Monik. Now, the damage to his own ship was enormous. It made no sense, but his shields were now down, and he had no weapons significantly powerful to threaten the human fleet.

First Commander Kul opened a channel to the damaged ship. "Power down all your weapons."

The shaken Mazik captain stared at Kul. "We must fire on the humans!"

"With what? They are out of range, and their railgun will be charged and ready to fire again momentarily."

"We should attack them!"

"Follow your orders!"

The zealot sneered and bared his teeth. "Mazik Bah-Gahn demands that we attack!"

"The emperor is six-hundred light-years from here. I am your superior. We will negotiate with the enemy."

"I will not!"

Kul showed all of his teeth. "You will be sent into the vacuum for mutiny."

The hysterical Mazik captain cut the connection and began accelerating toward the human fleet.

"What the hell are they doing?" asked Monty.

"He will attempt to fire lasers or ram one of us," answered Captain Jahrnuk. "We must fire on him. I will do it."

Mercy keyed up her mic. "Aim for the power core. Let's see if we can disable his drive."

Kap maneuvered the Ro-Pahm into a lateral firing position. The Mazik renegade assumed a vector aimed at the Washington.

At the maximum effective distance, Mok fired three lasers at the stern power core. The hull turned to sludge without shielding, and parts flayed off the inner structure. The drive failed, and she continued on her path by virtue of Newton's First Law. Stopping the runaway vessel would be a challenge. The Ro-Pahm cautiously approached the listing spacecraft.

After a short discussion with Mercy, Captain Jahrnuk began firing sharp, low-power particle beams at the crippled vessel's lasers and other weapons. In ten minutes, she'd become a floating junkyard.

"How do we get the Slev off that ship?" asked Barrett.

Mok looked grim. "It is possible that the ten Warriors stationed on that ship will murder all of the galley and maintenance crew before they step out the airlocks themselves."

"Are you sure?" said Mordy. "Can't we offer them an option?"

"The Warriors are known to be inflexible. Mazik Bah-Gahn's rule is that if a ship cannot fight and cannot be repaired, the entire crew must die."

Mercy called the surrendering officer. "Kul. Can you convince the Warriors on that ship to let the crew live?"

Kul looked puzzled. He answered in his own language. "Why would you care about that? They have failed."

"You have also surrendered!" She was livid.

"That is because I am not a fool. I cannot say the same for the first commander of that wreck."

Barrett stared into the camera. "I am Barrett Bonner. You may have heard of me."

Kul grinned. His blue-green countenance tinged with unreadable emotions. "You are the Emperor's pain."

Bonner chuckled. "He caused me pain. So I cause him more pain."

"We agree on that."

"Kul. How can you get the Slev crew off of that ship alive?"

"Barrett Bonner. There is only one way. Slev are like parts and equipment of a ship. Sometimes they work as crew, and sometimes they are food. If I demand the Slev as food, the first commander of a dead ship must send them to me. But he is irrational."

"Try. Tell him that he lost because the female human destroyed his ship. Send images of Mercy Bonner. He knows the legend. She killed Mazik Tro-Gahn; he was second only to your emperor, and she killed him in the vacuum of space.

"If he refuses to transfer the Slev crew to your ship, she will torture him and his officers forever. Mercy can bring him back from death and kill him repeatedly, each time more horrible than the last. I have seen her do this. She is my mate, but that is why I am fearful of her."

Kul shuddered ever so slightly. Some myths and legends were embedded in the genes. The risk of denial was not worth it.

Within an hour, shuttles carrying Slev drifted away from the junked ship.

Chapter 36

"What'd I miss?" Ensign Scott Lewis walked onto the bridge rubbing his eyes, feeling depressed, and missing his dog named "Dog," that lived with Julia in Vermont. His pet was next door in galactic terms, yet so far away.

Barrett held up his index finger, which everyone noticed. "Scott, not—much—just standard routines."

The ensign looked at the large view screen with enhanced views, data, and other streaming information. "I thought there were three enemy cruisers out there. I'm only seeing two?"

Molly said, "The Dexter O'Brian trashed one of them."

"Is that a joke? You got into an engagement and let me sleep through it?"

"We were preoccupied with saving ourselves and humanity; it was a priority," said Lieutenant (jg) Allen, mildly sarcastic.

Lewis twisted his mouth. "I guess we won?"

The process of dealing with Mazik First Commander Kul and his crew took some time, but after two days, all of the non-Slev aliens (approximately fifty) shuttled to one of the four parked transport ships. All were empty and under automatic stabilization orbits; the engine commands were disabled.

"I call it just sittin' around," said Cassie Munch, swiveling to look at Captain Schein. "But, I would be bored out of my mind if I was one of fifty people, or aliens, on a ship large enough to hold 30,000."

"Not our problem, lieutenant. They chose to attack Earth; no one forced them to start up with us."

"Sir," said Ensign Lucky Williams. "The best part is that we have two new ships."

Mordy snapped his fingers. "Yes. About that."

"What about that, sir?" asked Cassie Munch.

"Captain Bonner is reassigning you. Lieutenant Commander

Cassie Munch, you're going to unnamed ship Alpha to be XO and comms." Schein turned to starboard. "LTJG Lucky Williams, you're Nav Officer on the Alpha."

Cassie looked torn. "I appreciate the promotion, sir, but do we have a captain?"

"Oh yes, you do. Your new CO is Captain Mok Partul."

The nav officer seemed distressed. "That doesn't sound like a human name, sir."

Mordy nodded at the young officer. "You are correct. Mok is second in command to Captain Kap Jahrnuk. He is Slev. He is big. He is stronger than any five humans combined. That alien can bite bricks in half when he's pissed off. Does that scare you?"

Both of his junior officers answered "yes" together.

"Not to worry. Mok is as sweet as a puppy under that— exterior. I promise."

"When?" asked Cassie.

"Whenever he's not angry."

She licked her lips. "No, I mean, when are we transferring over to the Alpha, sir?"

"Now. Start packing your gear."

It took an additional five days to organize ships Alpha and Bravo. Dozens of Slev technicians scoured the two battlecruisers testing systems, looking for sabotage and searching for trouble.

Finally, the new allied fleet with six vessels took up a static orbit over the central USA.

Mercy had Allen point a satellite dish at the president's bunker.

"Start transmitting encrypted frequency-shift keying signals," she said.

"Anything specific?"

"How 'bout, 'This is the USS George Washington. Is President Carlisle available?'"

"Just keep repeating that?" asked Allen.

"Yep. Until they answer. We know they have at least one big

tracking dish unless the Mazik lased it. That means the senior command can see six battlecruisers parked outside their garage."

At 03:10, precisely nine minutes later, a simple FSK tonal message was received, decoded, and displayed. It read: *Damn glad to see you. I am waking up President Carlisle while you read this message.* It was from Mike Magnus.

It took almost no time for the president to appear live. He looked like hell on legs, but the five ship captains could see a man with restored hope waiting to burst forth underneath the gaunt, exhausted appearance.

"Good morning, Captain Bonner, Captain Schein, Captain Jahrnuk, Captain Clark, and—?"

"That is Captain Mok Partul," said Mercy. "He was Kap's XO, but we have six ships in our fleet now, sir. We have defeated the three Mazik ships and took two out of three. That leaves us with a sixth ship that we believe should be captained by Commander Rogers."

"What happened to the third Mazik ship? And where are the crews?" asked Carlisle.

Mercy continued. "The third battlecruiser refused to surrender. Captain Clark was forced to disable it with a railgun projectile. The ship is a total loss, but we did rescue all of the Slev crew and transferred them to other vessels in our fleet."

Barrett entered the conversation. "We moved all the Mazik crew, approximately fifty, to one of the four troopships that are now floating out of Earth orbit. Those giant freighters are disabled, but the prisoners have adequate food stores. They won't starve."

Carlisle looked angry as he soured the moment. "I don't believe we have a Geneva Convention agreement with the Mazik. I want them executed."

Schein spoke up. "That's not going to happen, sir." Mordy left his strongly-worded declaration hang in the air.

No one else said a thing. Mercy sensed that Mordy, who'd been running the Anglea Carlisle for years, knew better how to address the president's uncomfortable demand.

"Captain Schein," said Magnus trying to diffuse the potential turf war. "Maybe you have an update on how your weaponry can assist in dealing with what's happening on the ground?"

"One second, Mike." Carlisle positively glared at the camera. "Those Mazik killed over a hundred thousand civilians with heavy projectiles. That's a bonified war crime. And don't forget about Washington, DC."

"With Captain Bonner's consent, I will speak," said Kap Jahrnuk. Mercy nervously nodded.

"President Carlisle. To obtain those two new battlecruisers, we agreed to give Mazik First Commander Kul freedom. He can never go back to Kamtret. The life that he and his crew knew as the elite of Mazik culture, as you say in English, is history. If any sentient beings have justification to apply punishment to the Mazik, it is the Slev. We have been tortured and murdered for hundreds of years. Nevertheless, these enemy officers and crew surrendered. They will not be harmed."

John was about to start ranting about the United States and what humans suffered. He thought of Angela, his wife, and what she would say to him, what advice she would give.

"Your points are valid, Captain Jahrunk." And, just like that, the issue was diffused. John changed the subject. "I would like a full report of everything that has happened over the last three and a half years. I am beyond happy to see all of you back. I believe I must be losing my mind; where are Aaron and Allison?"

"They are dealing with some galactic issues," answered Clark. "We expect them to arrive in the future."

Magnus shrugged. "What does that mean?"

"It is a complicated story, colonel," said Mercy. "Can we get an update on what is happening on the ground?"

Carlisle was now fully engaged. "Yes, Captain Bonner. Let's do a full briefing in one hour. Please use your advanced optics to examine the current situation in the interim. We are getting massacred, except for a few exceptional bright spots. Include West Tennessee in your high-resolution survey. We'll meet again at 04:30 local. Coffee is not optional. The briefing could take a while. So bring your nanite-enhanced brains and set them on overdrive. I don't expect a miracle, but if you have one stashed away in one of your battlecruisers, bring that too."

Chapter 37

"I think you are Gimli, and I am Legolas," said Josh.

Emma took advantage of a break in the fighting to snuggle next to him. "No, Joshua. I am Eowyn. She's the one who kills the witch king of the Nazgul."

"Is that where the evil king says, 'No man can kill me?"

"Yes, and then she takes off her disguise and says, 'I am no man,' then she stabs him dead. Yep, that's me."

He kissed her quickly. "I mean that you and I are going back and forth in who's got a higher kill total. Just like in that movie."

"Dear Joshua. I am up by three."

"Last time I checked, babe, it was tied at 61." His hand danced along the outside of her thigh, which was absolutely fine with Emma.

"Wrong total, Rice cracker. It is 64 to me. There were three wounded Mazik in our last deal, and I put them down with pretty fine shots considering the wind and the weather."

Eric Creacy stepped into their campsite. He'd given up trying to figure out a way to keep the two teens from hanging all over each other. It didn't matter now. The world had gone full tilt to dystopian, and to try to stand in the way of sixteen-year-olds in love was a losing proposition. "Try to get some sleep. I'm on watch until midnight. Then it's you, little missy."

Emma didn't bother unwrapping Josh's arms. She lay there under a thin blanket and said, "Got it."

That was good enough for Eric Creacy. His daughter operated like a special ops wizard. He was proud of Emma but still worried constantly. It was his primordial right as a single parent, and Creacy claimed it fully.

The night passed without incident, which was now standard because of the Mazik acquired aversion to fighting at night. It was now four consecutive days with no Warriors seen. The three of them sat, eating dry cereal by the handful, their morning staple.

Eric said, "I would like eggs with toast. Bacon. Waffles and real maple syrup. Then pancakes with more syrup."

"Let's just hike on over to an IHOP and eat our fill," an exhausted Josh replied to Mr. Creacy.

Emma ignored the daily food fantasy. "This is five days. No Mazik. It doesn't feel right."

"No people either," said Josh.

"Sitting here until we run out of food is stupid," she said. "We need to move. So pick a direction because I think the Warriors are afraid to be in our territory."

Her father winked. "Shall we argue about it and then do it your way?" They laughed quietly.

"Fine," said Emma. "We go north towards the interstate, but we should assume that the Mazik are setting a trap for us. They prefer fighting in daylight, so we'll only move after dark."

Josh stood up. His clothes were worn and threadbare in spots. "The Warriors are in no hurry. We should move like turtles and always assume they are waiting over the next hill."

"Yes. No doubt you are correct, Legolas."

"Ah. So, you accept that you are Gimli, a short, stocky, red-bearded dwarf?"

"Sure," Emma retorted. "Have you seen my ax?"

The three of them made their way northwest in the direction of the intersection of the Tennessee River and I-40. The trek was hard. Too hard. The choice between ammo, weapons, or food, sunk the initial plan as the oppressive heat settled onto the mid-South.

Eventually, low on supplies, Emma decided to enter a tiny country town west of the Buffalo River. "This place is dangerous." She said it a few times, gripped with paranoia.

"It's one in the morning," said her dad. "Not exactly prime time for the Mazik to be out and about."

"Something's not right," she replied. "They should be crushing everything around here, and they're not."

Josh peered through binoculars, crouched low, and scanned the area around a country store. "No electricity anywhere. No candles either. If the Mazik were here, we'd see movement and light. It's dead in that place."

The trees thinned as they walked as silently as possible to the edge of a single-lane road. "This is King Branch Road," said Josh.

Her camouflage pants and shirt clung to her sweaty body; she missed civilization and a simple shower with soap. "How do you know that?"

"He's got a map, obviously," said Eric Creacy.

"Had a map. It got trashed somewhere, but I memorized as much as possible. Figure a hundred meters to the store over there. We cross the road, then stick to the trees and avoid the overgrown field right there." He pointed to the left. "It ain't big, but I think we should just stay low and slow."

"I'll lead," said Emma.

The humidity was oppressive, and she made them stop and scan with binoculars every ten or fifteen steps. They reached about sixty feet from the store. "So much for stealth. We can't get there without crossing that yard. This place wreaks of death," said Josh.

"Gimme the scope." He handed her a small night vision scope.

"Oh, geez. There are bodies laid out in that field. A lot of them. It looks like those corpses are sunk into the dirt. Stay here; I'm going to go look at the closest one. If a Mazik shows up, please shoot it."

Scuttling her way across the yard didn't take long. The first body made her want to puke. It was an older child or a woman decaying, and mostly bones protruded through skin that showed teeth marks like the Warriors bit off flesh. Emma could see at least five more bodies within a radius of fifteen feet, and there must have been other dead in the overgrown grass beyond.

"It's gross," she told them after slithering back. "The Mazik ate a bunch of people here, and it looks like a while ago."

"So, what do we do?" asked her dad.

"I think we sit tight and observe for a little bit." She tapped Joshua on his arm. "Set up your M82. Let's see if anything moves around the building."

Within minutes, they saw movement by the shattered door of the store. The place had a façade of regular-sized bricks, a single floor, and a shingle roof. A human was just inside the frame of the doorway. He stepped out.

"It looks like he's wearing a uniform, but I don't know," said Josh.

Another man joined the guy. Then they both turned as if they were talking to someone inside.

"I don't like this," whispered Emma. "They're holding rifles. It's about sixty feet to the door? Keep a bead on them with the Ruger, dad." She'd become a pro at stealth, and she headed closer, using the fringe of trees as cover.

Laying on the ground, Emma eased out her small 9mm Beretta and gazed cautiously at the two men. "Don't move your weapons," she called. "You've got a dozen folks targeting you."

The men froze and kept their M4's hanging by straps, pointed down.

"Who else is inside?"

"No one," answered the guy closest to her.

She hated liars. "Bullshit. We saw you both turn and talk to someone inside. Don't lie to me again. How many inside?"

"Listen." The guy tried sounding like he was a big deal. "We're Marines, so put down your weapons."

"How many?" she repeated.

"One more inside."

"Tell them to come out."

Her voice must have been audible inside the entrance as two more guys stepped out.

"So you lied to me twice. I don't give a shit if you are a marine, especially if you are a marine, you tell the truth." Emma directed her voice to the two who'd just exited. "You. Anyone else in there?"

"No, Ma'am."

"Tell me what happened here—short version."

The first guy explained that they had a platoon up by the interstate. They'd had a huge firefight, and when the Mazik killed most of their guys, they were ordered to split up into units and run.

"We made it here and found all of these civilians dead. That was a week ago. We've been here turning on the radio now and then to save batteries, but nothing heard."

"Name, rank, and number?" she asked.

He was the corporal in charge of three privates.

"All right, Corporal Keegan. We're on the same side. We're going to come in. You have any food?"

"Canned goods."

"We'll come in three at a time. Our other guys are on the perimeter, so don't even think about playing tricks."

Emma got up and started walking towards the front of the grocery, gingerly avoiding dead bodies. She waved for Josh and her dad to come forward.

When she got close enough, Keegan looked at her and said, "Hell. What are you, twelve? We got a tweenie girl here?"

She stood about six feet away from the corporal. "Sixteen, and since we're mentioning numbers, let's throw in 50 BMG and 9mm, which is the pistol I just holstered."

Eric and Josh also stepped carefully over the dead. Soon they were all standing on the store's porch, the corporal trying to figure out what to do with these three and the other nine in the trees. "How well-armed are you? If you are reasonably competent, we might be able to use you," he said to Eric.

"Don't ask me."

"Why not?" asked Keegan.

"I'm not in charge; my daughter is." He pointed to Emma.

"Seriously?" The corporal turned. "How well armed is your group, little girl?"

She shook her head. "*Little girl*? You are really starting to piss me off." The darkness didn't conceal her eyes boring a hole in the marine's face.

"Emma!" said Josh. "We're fighting the same enemy. Let's try to avoid an argument."

Keegan froze, as did the three privates behind him. It was like a static charge shot through them in what could only be described as an "Oh, fuck me" moment.

"What did that kid just call you?"

"What?"

"What's your name?" asked Keegan.

"What's it to you?"

"Nothing. No kidding. What's your name?"

"Emma."

"Emma, what?"

"I don't see how that matters, but my name is Creacy. Emma Creacy."

The four of them looked like they'd been whacked with a stick. "Holy f-ing—I mean, you gotta be shitting me. You're Creacy? The Creacy? As in doing a Creacy Mound?"

"So? A what mound?" she asked.

"We've got orders to do whatever you say, straight from the president."

Josh couldn't help himself. He laughed out loud—hard.

Keegan stood there shaking his head. "I'll explain everything. Come inside and eat some grub. Tell the rest of your people to come in also."

"Thank you. But it's just the three of us. The other nine? I was lying about that."

*

The Joint Chiefs Chairman sat at the big conference table, trying to explain what information he had from forward units. Carlisle was more interested in how to integrate six spacecraft into the fight.

"Tell me about this migration you're seeing," asked John.

"Sir. We're estimating that the bulk of the Mazik forces that were in the South are heading North."

"Has anything changed in the northern states?"

The general replied, "Only that our civilians are fleeing the cities and running to the hills and mountains."

"Maybe it's the heat." Magnus had been thinking about what Kap Jahruk had once said about Earth being hot. He'd said that on Kamtret the temperature was much lower and uniform. The seasons varied very little. "When do you estimate the bulk of the Warriors started heading to higher latitudes?"

"Beginning of July. Maybe a touch earlier," answered the general.

"Someone pull up the weather history," said the president.

A technician displayed an image of temperatures over the last three weeks. Sure enough, a heatwave hit the central and southern states and had stuck around with temperatures in the high 90 range or higher.

Magnus asked, "General, what are the Mazik in Minnesota and the Great Lakes area doing?"

"Not moving much."

Carlisle grinned. "So, they either know where the border is and don't hate Canadians or the aliens have an Achilles Heel."

"I guess global warming might have an upside," said SECDEF.

The Interior Secretary pointed out the obvious. "So bears hibernate, Mazik estivate. What happens when winter comes? Then the Warriors will be wound up and ready to fight in their kind of weather?"

"Look," said the general. "It's not like they aren't deadly right now. But if they hate the heat, then we could be looking at just a few months to get ready for nastier attacks when it gets cold."

"Do they even know that we've taken two of their ships?" asked DHS.

"According to the Slev, Warriors and regular Mazik don't talk to each other," said Magnus.

"They can't leave our planet and drop rocks to kill the planet now. That option is gone now." Carlisle felt like the tide could turn in their favor. "If there were ten million Warriors in America, it would be game over. However, they can't reinforce now, and they can't leave."

"We need a new plan, sir," said SECDEF.

Magnus gritted his teeth. "What we need is Aaron Howe and Allison."

"You heard what Captain Bonner reported," SECDEF pointed out. "We have no idea when they will ever return to Earth."

"We're Americans, and we have to fight like it's just us." Carlisle looked at Colonel Magnus. "Give Mercy another three hours, and then press her on how they can help from orbit. All that firepower doesn't mean anything if we can't use it."

"We can't fire on the Mazik," said Barrett.

Everyone was online for a discussion. Commander Bonner continued. "The Warriors have humans mixed in with them. To kill the enemy would mean killing our people. We can't pinpoint lasers to strike individual aliens."

"They're going to get eaten. We'd be doing them a favor," said Ensign Lewis.

"That's cold, Lewis," said Molly, "But I'd rather get vaporized than consumed alive if it was me."

"Knock it off," said Barrett. "We're not killing Americans."

Monty blurted out. "We should go down there and join the fight."

"That won't work for two reasons," said Mercy. "One, we won't add much, and two, we can't leave these ships short-handed if more Mazik come in from the jump point."

Frustration invaded the meeting.

"Julia," said Clark.

Monty nodded. "There's a reason why Aaron told us to see his sister asap. We've been here in a safe orbit for days now."

"Don't we need to assume that the Warriors on the ground have weapons that can hit us if we try to shuttle down?" asked Molly.

"Ha. Use one of their own shuttles," offered Lieutenant Petro. "There is still one tethered to a freighter about ten thousand kilometers that way." He pointed to starboard.

"Would they fire on their own shuttle?" asked Allen.

"Kul blew up one of his own shuttles."

"That's different, Molly," said Mercy. "Kul was eliminating a threat to his ability to surrender. Twisted but effective. If I agree to it, then we need to send some of us down to Vermont. Do we have images?"

"Yes," said Schein. "The Mazik haven't been anywhere near Burlington, and there's room enough to land a Mazik shuttle near Howe's office. There's a huge flat piece of land there."

"Clark and I can go get that shuttle," said Monty.

Barrett thought about that. "You'll have to get alongside and enter externally."

"No problem," said Montgomery. "It'll give me a chance to try out my new suit."

*

"That was awesome!"

"I wonder how detailed the image resolution is from the Ro-Pahm or the Washington," said Clark.

"You can tell by how quickly your comm link lights up."

At that moment, the Washington beeped the O'Brian, and it was flashing red.

"Clark. Over."

"John, this is Mercy. We got a funny image for a moment when your ship wasn't obstructing the view of Monty leaving the airlock of the O'Brian. It looked like he wasn't wearing a suit."

"Captain Bonner, I believe you should ask Lieutenant Montgomery about that directly, Ma'am."

Mercy grinned. "Oh. I will, Clark. I will. Mercy. Out."

The screen went black.

Chapter 38

Tartic, First Warrior Commander dragged a partially eaten woman off his table and threw the corpse out the door of his command center. "I want a young one next meal." An assistant stomped his feet and exited the space.

"What happened in Area Five?" He pointed to a parcel of land east of the Mississippi River in the southern part of Bonner's country.

His Second despised delivering bad news. "The humans resisted there."

"And? When there is resistance, we shatter that effort and then make examples of the humans to teach a lesson."

"They have small brains, First Commander."

"What are the numbers?"

The Second circled a small area on the graphic. "The concentration of losses were here, but the local commander maintained his efforts without reporting, as is the custom."

Slamming his large hands against the table, Tartic screamed, "I am changing the custom. How many were lost?"

"Close to two hundred. Perhaps more."

The First Commander seethed with temper. "How many humans? At least 100,000? Tell me the truth."

"In that small area, no human combatants were found dead."

The level of anger in Tartic's mind exploded. For the Warriors, when the threshold of temper is breached, they must find release.

The large, powerful Warrior charged out of the center's portal to the outside yard, where humans cowered in his presence. He leaped over a barrier and seized the largest human male. Tartic draped the primate over the top rail, crushed him until the spine snapped, and then methodically separated the human into two pieces.

Primitives by the hundreds began screaming and crying.

Their terror appeased him.

Tartic returned, blood-soaked, to the large room. "Send more Warriors to that area."

"There is much heat there now. The fighters are reduced in effectiveness due to the temperature."

Glaring at his Second, the leader of the effort to dominate Earth growled, "We must adapt to this miserable planet. Send them!."

"Captain Bonner?" It was Lucky Williams.

"Go ahead, JG."

"Ma'am. I've been scanning different areas. I believe the Mazik have made a big mistake. They are loading a shuttle in Connecticut. I have a real-time feed of hundreds of Warriors getting onto the ship now."

"Stay on the line, Williams." Mercy flashed Barrett.

"I'm sleeping."

"Too bad. Get up. The Mazik are boarding a shuttle by the hundreds. Here's an opportunity."

"On my way!"

"Williams. Give coordinates."

The lieutenant transmitted the coordinates. "Molly. Real-time images of those coordinates, Now."

Within seconds, a giant field in Connecticut filled the main screen. "Higher resolution."

They could see Warriors lined up and entering the giant shuttle, some of them carrying heavy weapons.

Barrett raced onto the bridge. His nanites processed the image as he signaled a Slev technician to get lasers online.

"How long will it take the Mazik on the ground to figure out that humans are running the show up here?"

"Why, Barrett?"

"Because if they see Clark's shuttle entering the atmosphere *after* we lase the enemy—they'll put two and two together."

Mercy flashed the Dexter O'Brian. "Clark! How quickly can you get that shuttle down to Vermont?"

"We're checking systems. Maybe we can leave in about an

hour?"

"Nope. Check faster. We've got a situation. I want you on the ground near Burlington in forty-five minutes."

"Roger that."

Mercy swiveled to her husband. "How much time?"

"Still loading,"

Tartic banged things around, scaring humans and Mazik alike. Across a large field, he watched the massive shuttle filling up with Warriors and weapons. They had one job—to track and kill every human in the targeted area in West Tennessee. No Mercy. No Remorse. Not even a meaningful end as food for the Mazik—to free their souls for a sanctified eternity. None of that, only a finite instant death at the hands of superior beings.

"We're ready to go."

"Who do you have?" asked Mercy.

"Me and a handful of top Slev techs."

Mercy thought about the situation. "Do you have weapons?"

"Firearms and several of the Mazik mag guns they clamp to their wrists."

She called Monty. "Release the tether on that shuttle."

"Done," confirmed Monty.

"Good luck, Captain Clark. Establish comms when you get to Vermont."

In the air, the Mazik shuttle from Connecticut used Grav Plates to defeat the planet's pull. But there were limits to velocity against the dense Nitrogen, Oxygen, and other components that were Earth's atmosphere. The pilot, following orders, accelerated and lifted the shuttle to an altitude where the resistance of molecules ceased to be a factor.

Simultaneously, Commander Bonner tracked the path of the Warriors' shuttle and smiled. "They've made another mistake."

"I see," said Kap Jahrnuk. "We are tracking. I believe your laser emission will be accurate and significant to defeat the armor."

Mercy watched and said nothing. Barrett knew what to do as he called the Slev weapons tech to verify the power level. Hitting a shuttle with a defensive shield was not the same as knocking out missiles.

"Releasing the beam now." He pressed the glowing tab on his armament panel and felt a very slight shudder. At the speed of light, the laser blasted and superheated the thin molecular structure of atoms in the upper atmosphere. Then, it lased the target—an eight terawatt, wide-beam bored a hole through the vessel. The exterior opened, and that was deadly.

"It's more of an art than a science," said Barrett.

As desired, the beam collapsed one side of the shuttle before the laser halted. Bonner had no desire to allow the beam to hole through the Warriors and strike Earth. Enough was enough.

The heat generated turned solids into gas instantly. The Mazik never knew what hit them, but five hundred were gone.

"And just like that! Bye Bye!" Lewis jumped up from the nav table, snapped his fingers, and did a little dance.

"I guess it is happy that we did not die," said one of the Slev techs in his language.

"Agreed," said Clark. "It's three miles to Julia's house. Let's figure out how to get there."

John looked out of several virtual portholes. He could see people running and realized that they hadn't considered the effect of landing a Mazik shuttle in Burlington, Vermont. Some snipers began taking potshots at the armored hull.

"This isn't good." He turned to the Slev comms tech. "Can you give me an FM signal if I give you the frequency?"

"Tell me the frequency."

"I have no idea, except 155.58 MHz is in my head. That's too weird. I must have researched it once, and it stuck."

The Slev tech stomped his foot. "You have a narrow FM signal now."

"Burlington P.D. Burlington P.D."

There was a chirp and static. Then, "Who's on this frequency? Get off. We have a Mazik shuttle landing. Stop transmitting, you asshole."

"I am the alien shuttle. My name is Captain John Clark. We commandeered, I mean, hijacked this vessel. I am transmitting from inside."

Clark waited. He heard a click. "This is the chief of police. When I find out who and where you are, I will personally kick your butt, or worse."

These guys are entirely untrusting, thought John. "Listen up! I am Captain Clark, commander of the USS Dexter O'Brian. We have succeeded in taking control of the space around Earth. So pay attention. We now have control of all the Mazik ships in orbit. I have landed here for a specific purpose, and I cannot screw around. We are not here to attack you!"

"Where are you transmitting from?" asked the chief.

"Are you serious? I don't have time for this. Get yourself over to a safe perimeter near the craft."

"I'm here now, and I have ten snipers with me."

Static.

"Tell them to keep their eager fingers off the triggers. I'm going to open the hatch and show you that I am a regular human. Do not fire on me. Okay?"

More Static.

"If you don't look human, then we will fire!"

Clark looked around for something white. He unbuttoned his uniform and took off his white t-shirt.

"Chief. I'm going to open the hatch and wave my white t-shirt. Do not fire on me. Please?"

"Show me," replied the cop.

The Slev techs equalized the airlock pressure, and the garage-sized door slid open. John ordered the Slev to stay far away from the hatch, stuck out his arm, and started frantically waving.

The cop had a bullhorn. "Come out with your hands where I can see them."

John yelled. "I'm human. Don't shoot me!" He stepped onto the ramp that led down a couple of meters to the ground and was told to walk out about fifty feet—which he did.

Two cops approached with pistols. When they got close, one said, "Are you for real?"

"Yes. I am for real. Tell your chief I want to talk to him now."

The other of the two cops, who couldn't have been more than twenty-five, said, "I'm the chief."

"Are you kidding?"

"No. I inherited the job from my dad."

Clark eyed the guy. "That's a helluva gift."

"Tell me about it. What's your deal? You scared the crap out of the entire city."

The two of them were still holding Glocks. "Do you mind holstering your weapons?"

The chief nodded to the other cop, and they stowed their pistols.

"I'm a close friend of Aaron Howe. I'm also Captain of a battlecruiser up there." Clark pointed up. "Do you know what Slev are?"

"No."

"Do you know what Mazik look like?"

"Sure as hell do," said the chief.

John exhaled. "We've kept a lot of things secret from the public. Maybe we shouldn't have. The Slev look like the Mazik, but they are our friends. On that shuttle behind me are several Slev technicians. They are not Mazik. Do not shoot them; they are on our side. I've told them to stay onboard to keep from scaring the locals."

"Fair enough. Why are you here?"

"I need you to get me to Aaron Howe's sister's house right now."

"You're talking about James and Julia McCall?"

Clark squinted. "I thought his name was Rob?"

"I think it's James Robert. Some people call him Rob."

"Do you know the house?"

"Captain Clark, I rode around with my dad for 18 years."

"Great."

The chief barked into his mic. "Get a car here right now!"

John peered over the chief's shoulder. All the cops looked like they were in high school. "What's the average age on your force?"

"I get that all the time. The older cops all left to fight the Mazik in Connecticut. For some reason, the aliens haven't come anywhere near our town."

*

Tartic tossed a partially eaten bony human leg at the first officer who entered his command center. The Warrior reacted quickly, and the limb flew past his large, green-blue head and smacked against a wall.

"How did our shuttle get lased?"

"Somehow, the humans have a significant light weapon."

The First Warrior Commander bared all of his adorned teeth. "That is impossible. They do not have the technology to build a device such as this. We have seen and destroyed several of their primitive laser weapons. None of them were beyond inflicting minor damage to thin armor."

"My First, I have no explanation."

"There is only one explanation. Kul, the weak, was unable to contain one enemy ship with his three ships. When I finish our mission on this overheated, disgusting planet, his life is forfeit. Bring a comm device to me now."

Mok twisted his head, which sat upon his large, muscular neck. An incoming video call to ex-captain Kul's ship from the planet beeped and flashed while Lieutenant Commander Cassie Munch considered how to respond. "Captain Partul, it is not from Clark. It is from a Warrior device. I cannot translate."

"Create a patch to the Washington. Do not accept that transmission yet." Cassie's fingers flew around some command keys, and Captain Bonner's face appeared within a few seconds.

"What's up, Munch?"

"I have Captain Partul on."

Mok wasted no time. "We are receiving a transmission

request from the Warriors. Probably the First Warrior Commander named Tartic. He is a fierce leader. I can patch it through to you, or I can deal with him."

At first, Mercy thought to let Mok handle this critical encounter. But then—. "Patch audio and video directly to my command console in ten seconds."

Mercy sat. Barrett watched with fascination. Everything was not going this Warrior Commander's way. He couldn't help but raise his eyebrows while watching his wife wrap her blond braid so that it rested on her left shoulder.

The video came on to display the face of a vicious-looking Warrior—snout, teeth, sizeable black disc eyes. After nanoseconds, Tartic's eyes widened if such a thing were possible.

"What is this?" he bellowed in guttural Mazik.

"Not what you expected, Tartic?" answered Mercy in a royal dialect that Mazik Bah-Gahn would have used in front of the defunct Council.

"Who are you? Where is Kul?"

"Which question would you like answered first? Never mind, I will choose. First Fleet Commander Kul is in my prison. Would you like me to elaborate?"

Tartic bared every last cubic millimeter of his teeth, but said nothing.

"As far as who I am? I am the human female who killed Mazik Tro-Gahn, Second only to the Emperor. I have taken all of your ships—in the past and now. I have traveled through time and space to deliver eternal punishment to cruel butchers like you."

"You lie!"

"I ignore your weak words. Your grip on power and control is slipping as you descend to the virtue and value of an old Plark. I command the space around the human planet. You will not be resupplied with projectiles and power supplies for your weapons. It is preferable to surrender before I kill you and take your soul."

She looked at his blank expression, and then the screen

suddenly went dark.

"Mok," asked Mercy. "What happened?"

"Standby." Captain Partul looked toward his XO, then turned back to the screen. "Munch says that Tartic hung up."

Chapter 39

Clark sat in the back of a squad car, eager to see Julia. It had been nearly three and a half years. He passed trees and stores that looked familiar. The image of Louise, his wife, and his children, Benjamin and Lillian, stormed his conscious mind. The kids would be ten and eight years old. He was desperate to see them. John thought about stopping on the way to Julia, but every second was important. "After," he muttered to himself.

Soon, they were parking in Julia's driveway. He buttoned his uniform and, as calmly as he could, exited the car to walk up the brick path to the McCall's front door.

The door opened wide before Clark could knock, and there she stood. She threw herself into his arms. It was Louise, crying on his shoulder, and he cried with her. She forced herself to release him, and then his children latched onto him. John felt like he could hold them forever, and it wouldn't be enough time to make up for the years he'd lost.

He saw Rob McCall standing further inside. The children went to Louise, and Rob stared at him as if on cue.

"You're Captain John Clark. I remember. Julia said you were coming." He pointed to the sofa. "That's Manuel and also our three children." The kids waved. He waved back.

"Where's Julia?" he asked.

"Follow me, Captain." Rob paused and turned around for a second to face Clark straight on. "You need to know that she's—different."

They walked down the hallway and turned left into the study that John remembered had a couple of sofas, a television, and a bar.

"Should we knock?" asked John.

"Why bother?" Rob pushed open the door.

In the center of the room, Julia stood in a plain blue dress. The sofas and everything else were gone. The walls were repainted dark green. Her eyes were closed, and her hands hung loosely.

"You're wondering why the furniture is gone and the walls are dark green."

"Yes." Then he heard Rob shutting the door and leaving them alone.

"The simple chair behind me is enough, and the dark green soothes my head when it aches. Although, that was in the beginning."

"The beginning of what, Julia?"

"I'm sorry. Allison and Aaron told you to come see me. Do you want to know why?"

She was still standing erect but relaxed, her eyes closed, in the direction of an eastern-facing wall. Clark said, "Yes. Aaron told me that it was necessary; there are things you need to know."

Julia exhaled. "I've changed."

"How?"

"Once, when Allison was here before you left for Olamit, the AI examined me. She didn't tell me exactly why, but now I know. I am like Aaron; only I am stronger. Is that a blessing or a curse? That's a rhetorical question and is meaningless. What I have become is who I am."

"Allison infused me with nanites. Humans can be— different."

"That is true, John, but unique, powerful things can happen in an infinite universe," Julia replied. "Aaron knew a little, and Allison knew more, but my mother is the trigger."

"You mean your mother in Amberness at the psychiatric center?"

"I see Aaron did not withhold this from you. After he left, I felt changes. I was dreaming things, and then during the day, there were visions. It all led me to see my mother. I went to Amberness, and she became lucent for hours like it was dormant inside of her until we talked.

"Then she finally put her hands on my head and gave her mind to me. It was surreal, and it seemed as though she was sliding right back into her fog. But then, she collapsed off her chair and died."

Clark winced. "I'm sorry."

"No need. She died to make me stronger." Julia took another breath. "That was almost three years ago. Almost immediately after we buried her, I started having more dreams; deeper and more intense. You know how Aaron could sense quirks in the historical timeline? I was seeing in my thoughts what could be and what should be."

"Yes, even back in 1776, Mercy knew, and then we all knew."

"I don't sense. I see all of it. Not just hunches."

John shifted his stance a little. "Do you see past and present?"

"And future, Captain Clark. It is an awful burden from which there is no escape for me. Sit. I know you are tired."

He sat on the plain chair.

Julia continued. "Do you know why the Warriors are nowhere near Burlington?"

"I was curious."

"It is because my thoughts are keeping them away." She made a subtle movement. "I've been entering the minds of the Mazik to influence them to make mistakes. There is a girl down in Tennessee named Emma, the same name as my daughter. She has killed more Mazik Warriors than anyone. The girl did that on her own, but she needed rest, so I convinced the Warriors to stay away; then the heat came in the south, something the Mazik abhor. In war, you use any advantage you can find."

"What happens now?"

"You have control of space?"

"Yes, we took command of two Mazik warships—"

"—and the third you destroyed with a railgun from the Dexter O'Brian—your ship. I know. I have seen this."

"Yes. Exactly."

Julia was silent, then said, "Now we fight them. Soon they will have no more projectiles for their mag weapons. They cannot win without them, and I am confusing them by entering their minds. Eventually, the Warriors that do not die in battle will leave the planet. There will be very few remaining and many Americans will sacrifice themselves for the cause of freedom.

"Tartic, their leader, will order them off the Earth. Then when they have returned to one of their freighters, he will accelerate into the Sun."

"Why would he do that?"

"Because he knows that Mazik Bah-Gahn will not accept failure, which is true."

Soon after, Clark quietly left Julia. He was shaken, and even with his nanite enhancements, found it difficult to process what he'd seen and heard.

He walked into the hallway to see Louise waiting for him. She smiled, and he was calm. It was the same smile John had cherished from when they met in 1760 when they were only twelve.

"Should I speak in the vernacular? Pretty freaky, isn't she?"

"I think she knows you just said that," he replied.

"Julia knows how much I love her. It's okay. Now go back to the shuttle to call Mercy and tell her that you will be back tomorrow. Then come straight back here. Tonight you are staying with me, in our house, with our children, and we're going to have real food."

After the video transmission from Captain Clark, Mercy ached to see Manuel. She tamped down her emotions using a little help from her nanites. "Now what?"

Barrett had just stepped into their stateroom. He could see traces of tears in her eyes. "Now, we finish the job of defeating the Mazik Warriors."

"That sounds simple. You know what Julia told Clark. She made it sound like it would take decades."

"When did she put a timeline on it? Did the captain say anything about how long the battle on Earth would continue?"

"No."

"No. He did not, but John did say that Julia is expanding her radius of power, and she is disturbing the minds of the enemy."

Mercy sighed. She wanted everything to be over and done. She wanted peace and rest. "People down there are still dying, and we are powerless because firing lasers at the enemy will kill a lot of people. And at the same time, the Mazik are herding men, women, and children; they drag them along near the battles!"

"Should we fire down on the planet and murder the civilians? Is that your solution?"

Mercy smacked her hand on the table, then fell back onto their bed and stared at the ceiling. "No. Instead, we should shuttle down to Earth and fight."

"Dumb idea. What if more Mazik ships enter our system, and we are dead because some Warrior got in a lucky shot? We must stay up here."

"Thomas Rogers is coming up with Clark on the shuttle. He's bringing a hundred trained crew with him. They don't need us."

Barrett could see his wife grasping at straws. "True, he is Commander Rogers now, but we are barely at full strength even with a hundred new crewmen."

Mercy found a small silver lining. "I will be glad to see him again, and I'm sure that Mordy will be relieved that Thomas will be up here."

He stroked Mercy's hair. "Rogers is married now also, so he's in the same boat as Monty and Clark—away on duty—leaving their wives down there."

"That sucks."

"Spoken like the true United States Spaceforce high-ranking officer, Captain Mercy Bonner." He waited for her response, but she silently gazed at the ceiling. "Maybe you can slide a bit and let me join you? Let's count our blessings; at least we aren't separated by 40,000 kilometers."

*

Emma Creacy's squad consisted of four marines and three

civilians, including herself. She'd grown tired of hanging out near the Buffalo River.

"Corporal Keegan?"

"Yes, Ma'am."

She laughed. "Yes, Ma'am? 'Ma'am,' again? I ain't no ma'am, corporal."

The guy looked to be early twenties, fit as a fiddle, and competent. "I don't feel comfortable calling you Emma."

"Get over it. I'm a civilian."

The corporal shrugged and went back to looking over his rifle.

She raised her voice a little. "We're leaving."

One of the privates said, "We're safe here."

"Could be, but for how long? And that's irrelevant because there are people north of here who are under fire. Let's do an inventory and figure out how we're gonna carry all this."

In short order, they'd loaded their gear and stood ready. Emma shifted her backpack, took Josh by the hand, and started walking north.

It was a ten-mile hike, keeping the Buffalo River to their right. As they approached the interstate, the only people they met were half-eaten and decaying on the ground. "I really, really hate the Mazik," said Josh.

A road led underneath the I-40, but they stayed low, which was damn smart, because at least six Warriors were sitting on their haunches in the underpass. The range was just under three hundred meters.

"Which one of y'all is a good shot?"

"We're all pretty good," answered the corporal.

"Set up and do not fire until we are all ready." She looked again through her binoculars. The Mazik seemed oblivious like a bunch of stoners getting high under the bridge. That was bizarre, considering how efficient they were at poking around their territory. They'd formed a semi-circle, not alert, and it looked like they were eating rations, not people.

Eric said, "I think Josh can do a twofer on the ones along the left side. It looks like they are lined up for a through and through."

Josh had the M82 up on the bipod. He stared through the scope. "Yeah. It looks doable."

"They look kinda goofy just sitting there," said one of the marines.

Emma ignored the comment. "Josh line up on the two lefties. That leaves four. I've got center-left. My dad has center-right, and you guys take the two on the right. Corporal, be ready to fire on the left if Josh's 50 BMG doesn't put a hole clear through both of them."

"Yes, Ma'am."

Emma groaned. "On target. On three. Three, Two, One—"

As predicted (and hoped), the M82 blew the first Warrior open, and the bullet continued through the second alien. Emma's shot was dead-on, but her dad's was a touch high and pierced the top of the Mazik's skull. Blood showered from its head, then it jumped up and ran headfirst into the concrete wall of the tunnel.

The two on the right fell under the shots from four marine rifles.

"One on the right is quivering a little," said a private.

"We're not wasting 50 BMG or .338 on that. Hit that one again with your 5.56mm rounds. Two shots."

The private released two shots. Both were headshots. He turned toward Emma like a puppy waiting for a treat. She nodded in approval. "I think that one is pretty dead now. We'll wait a bit and see if there are more. Then we'll go over there and do rock, paper, scissors to find out who gets to cut them up and make a Creacy Mound."

Chapter 40

Emma, Josh, and Eric Creacy spent the rest of the summer sniping at small groups of Warriors, leaving behind a trail of dead aliens from I-40 north and then west. By December, they were prowling the eastern side of the big river. It had been impossible to get across the Mississippi through Memphis. The risk of facing the Mazik was high, but the threat from bands of bloodthirsty criminals was still greater.

They headed north toward Missouri in an arc. Confrontations increased as they approached Route 412 to the Caruthersville Bridge over Old Man River. The chill in the air seemed to cause Warriors to grow like weeds and the aliens, at least to Emma, appeared to be increasingly vigilant.

Doing recon on the bridge was gutsy, but their hearts sank when they reached a northern vantage point. At least one thousand enemy soldiers were below them at the barge station.

"This is hell on Earth," said Eric.

He could see thousands of people, emaciated, young, sitting on the bridge or the river banks.

"This is bullshit," said the corporal. They watched Warriors through binoculars drag two women off the bridge and down behind a concrete wall. The screaming was short-lived, and the Mazik emerged carrying body parts.

Just then, a teenage boy ran onto the highway and headed east. Emma's squad thought the aliens had not noticed. The kid must have been half-frozen, weak, and beyond terrified when one of the Mazik casually rose and fired a mag round. It blew out the teen's chest, and he collapsed onto his entrails.

"We can't do anything to help them," said Emma.

"If it were up to me, I'd drop a bomb on the whole thing. Those people are better off dead," said Josh

"Not our call," she replied.

One thing caught her eye. The Warrior who'd fired the mag

round was being screamed at in the alien language. "That big mouth must be an officer," said the corporal.

Suddenly, the leader pulled out a mono blade. He swung it around in the air, and all of the nearby Mazik went silent and stared. The commander swiped the sword through the air and then decapitated the cowering alien soldier.

"I think we should get out of here," said one of the privates.

Emma said, "Agreed. No noise."

The hike southwest along the river chilled them, but they'd seen no enemies. Two days later, the weather warmed as the Creacy marines melted into the forest and discovered a safe place to eat. They settled in a thicket with large rocks, still wet from the previous night's rain. Cold and wet, but humans adapted, and their periodic raids on little stores and abandoned houses yielded canned goods, dry goods, and an occasional chicken.

"I've been thinking," said the corporal.

Josh grinned. "I do that on occasion myself."

"Not kidding. Did you notice the Warrior screaming and then hacking his soldier to pieces?"

Emma raised an eyebrow while scratching her scruffy-looking, blond hair. She felt like bugs were nesting on her head. "Hard to miss that one, marine."

"Why?"

"Why what?"

"Why would an officer do that?"

One of the privates snorted. "Maybe he was messing with the officer's daughter?"

"Not funny," said Eric. He surreptitiously glanced at Emma.

The corporal continued his thought. "The lower rank alien used his mag gun; then the boss got pissed."

"Maybe because the bastard shot a perfectly healthy teenager," said Josh.

"That doesn't make any sense," said the corporal. "They grab and eat people whenever they feel like it. No. I think it was because of the mag round it fired. In combat, officers get pissed when you use ammo for no reason."

"You think they are squeezed on mag rounds?" asked Emma.

"Yes. I do. That officer beheaded his fighter over one mag round. That's what I think."

Josh and Emma looked at each other, and both of them silently ran through their experience with Mazik Warriors.

Josh said, "When we first encountered them, they were shooting off mag guns like they had an unlimited supply of pellets. Did you notice the last firefight we had near Deer River—a couple of the enemy pulled out mono blades instead of shooting? There were five of them. The three that fired at us were doing *pop pop* and not letting go of a whole magazine. It was never that way six months ago."

Eric pondered that out loud. "And why congregate at the bridge in such a big group? The Warriors should be pushing in one direction or another. When troops are empty on supplies, they camp out and wait for resupply."

"We can exploit that," said Emma. "Finish eating and get some rest. We're going to go south and find a boat to get across the Mighty Mississippi. It's getting colder, it's hunting season, and Josh can tell you that it's always helpful when the deer can't shoot back."

As it often does in early December, the weather oscillated between cold and rainy versus dry and sunny. The journey south went on for four days, slogging in mud and dripping sweat in the moderate heat, until they could approach a place called Ripley, Tennessee.

"Ripley! Get it?"

"Get what, corporal?" Emma asked.

"Ripley is a movie character who fought aliens."

"Before our time," said Josh.

"Well, you would have liked her. She was a Hollywood version of Emma; I mean Sergeant Creacy."

She cringed. "I'm not a sergeant, ok?"

"Yes, Ma'am."

She shrugged her shoulders as they came up over a bluff to

look down at the small town.

"The Warriors trashed this place," said one of the marines looking through a pair of standard binoculars. "There are bodies everywhere."

Josh squinted in his scope. "There must be a thousand. I thought the Mazik were interested in herding humans, not genocide?"

"Something changed," said Emma. "Maybe things aren't turning out so easy for them."

"So much for the cakewalk," Eric said.

"Huh?" asked one of the privates. "What's a cakewalk?"

Eric replied, "It's an old boomer term. It means an easy time of something."

"Oh."

Emma shushed everyone. "Let's head to the river."

They did, and almost due west, they spied a boat ramp with three boats on trailers and corpses decomposing all around. The river flowed relentlessly past, muddy and deceptively slow, but getting across would require some luck.

"Let's just watch from here a bit, y'all."

The Creacy girl called the shots, and over the past weeks, the marines learned real fast to trust her judgment. So, they sat alert and waited. After a time, no Warriors appeared to be patrolling the area. Only then did Emma give the thumbs up.

"Anyone know about boats?"

"Ma'am, I do," said the shortest of the marines. The kid was a stick with legs, and the lack of serious food didn't improve his girth. At this point, they all looked scruffy and underfed.

"All right. Figure out the fastest and safest way to get us across. We'll go after dark."

The slimy trail down turned out to be challenging. Emma slipped twice, carrying the biggest load her slim body could manage, and getting wet mud stuck to her pants shifted her into a foul mood. Fortunately, the marines were well down the road on how to survive an angry Creacy without receiving her wrath.

The marine called "Beanpole" did know his stuff, and it was a risk, but he showed them how to get a small boat loaded with the seven of them and a ton of gear.

"We can't get too fancy goin' across," he said.

Emma gritted her teeth. "You're driving, so get it done."

"Welcome to Arkansas, the toothpick state," said Eric, as they hauled their supplies up the bank and out of the mud.

"What does that mean?" asked the corporal, trying to work out a cramp in his leg.

"I did a paper on Arkansas in high school before y'all were born. The toothpick was a popular small pistol that folks carried around in the early 1800s."

The corporal said, "Was it big enough to kill a Mazik?"

"Doubtful."

"So, I'll stick with my M27 rifle if that's okay with you."

Emma was all out of patience for banter. "Sleep now. Tomorrow, we'll do what we get paid the big bucks for."

*

Tartic became increasingly tense. His underlings feared him, but they would label him as disturbed or worse if they could speak their minds. The Bonner female gnawed at him. Never had he been faced with a situation where the Warriors did not have the advantage. But now, slowly, the edge that was a Mazik birthright crumbled little by little.

In Connecticut, Area One, the mood darkened, and even allowing unrestricted butchery of the humans did not improve uncertainty among his troops. They'd heard of the alien female now controlling space and about the decreasing kill ratio in battles with Barrett Bonner's forces.

"My First Warrior Commander," said his Third. "We are down to a seventh of our original supply of mag projectiles."

The seething Tartic focused a sour eye on the officer. "Tell me the rest. I can read your fear that you have more disturbing news."

Feeling increasingly uncomfortable, the officer blurted out, "The power supplies are down to nearly a ninth of our original inventory."

"Kul is to blame for that, but why do you bother telling me about projectiles if the power supplies are in even shorter supply?"

The Warrior Commander's question was met with silence.

"Leave. Tell my Second to come."

Moments later, the immediate subordinate appeared and bowed.

"I am not Mazik Bah-Gahn. Do not grovel in front of me. Tell me what my plans were three solar cycles past?"

Without hesitation, the Warrior answered, "To send out small groups of Warriors from the concentration here in Area One to slaughter all humans with monomolecular blades, and when required using mag slugs."

Confusion flashed on Tartic's face. "Does that seem like a logical battle plan?"

"My First. I do not have the knowledge to question your experience."

The First Commander bounded over to the underling and seized him by the throat. "I will cut out your organs one at a time if you do not cease to evade my questions." He released the Warrior's neck and stepped back. "Now, answer!"

"It does not seem logical. We have sent out small groups, and the humans are exploiting our weaknesses by firing their own projectiles at long distances."

"Why is it that I feel certain that small platoons of fighters is the best way?"

"Before that, you had said that we should mass the entire force and sweep across the land with overwhelming force because the humans cannot stand up to a massive assault."

"My Second. How is it that I could devise two completely different strategies and be certain that each was the best option? Something is not right. You will decide."

"First Warrior Commander, I do not have the authority to decide."

Tartic bared his teeth and came within centimeters of the other. "I decide where to place authority. You shall decide now!"

"First Warrior Commander—"

"Decide or die! Choose!"

"Your plan to form one large force and roam across the countryside is better. We still have some drones that can fire lasers. The primates will not be able to use long-range weapons because we have domination of the sky. And, we will bring masses of humans wherever we march. That will provide sustenance, and Bonner's military will not launch weapons at us because they are fearful of killing their own kind. It is a weakness and their downfall. They are a sentimental race."

"And when we are depleted of energy sources for the mag weapons? Then what? Don't answer. We are Warriors, and we will use our teeth," Tartic declared.

The Second Commander felt desperate to leave. When First Ship Commander Kul surrendered, victory fell into the shadows of an abyss of doubt. His father told him many years earlier, when uncertain—say anything, so he did. "It is our best strategy until the next wave of our brothers arrives."

Tartic flopped down into his sleep chair. "I have never been so unsure of the correct path. My thoughts compete with themselves and never triumph." He looked up. "There may never be a second wave. I believe that Kul had orders to let us ravage the land of Bonner for a time, after which we would leave and then drop rocks on the planet."

The underling was aghast. "That makes no sense! Such an order could only come from the emperor. Why?"

"Because Mazik Bah-Gahn follows his own directives. Barrett Bonner is an obsession. We are bred for fighting, and we were born dead. We live to meet death in battle and are expendable. The emperor can always make more of us. So, I believe that Kul had orders to evacuate those of us who would survive or maybe even end the Earth with kinetic strikes regardless of how many of our forces remain. Mazik Bah-Gahn's mind must be satiated—that means crushing the land of Bonner, bit by bit. Truth—I don't know what I am thinking."

The level of dysfunction in the room peaked. The whole

conversation reeked of madness.

"Gather the mass of our force. We will march west and destroy everything that lives."

*

The Bonners sat staring at the display, with Clark and Monty staring right back. "Please summarize that again, John," said Mercy.

"It's like we have science, physics, known quantities on one side, and then we have Julia manifesting something like magic."

Monty said, "We are collectively a handful of the smartest humans, and to quote Arthur C. Clarke—"

"—yes, we know, indistinguishable from magic. We know the thing," said Barrett. "Hence, Julia is doing science and things inside the realm of physics, but we just can't comprehend it."

"Precisely," agreed John Clark. "She has a power or skill that enables her to do things even Allison and Aaron can't do. And there may also be things that Julia can't do. I don't know. But she is festering doubt into Tartic, the leader of the Warriors, and she knows about people she's never met, and Julia also knew that I was coming to see her. Aaron's sister can see time, and I wouldn't be surprised if she were in contact with her brother and Allison somehow."

Mercy seemed disturbed. "Why can't she tell us what to do?"

Barrett said, "She did, or rather, she didn't offer advice, but she was not opposed to all of us staying in space in case the Mazik send more ships."

"Dear! She should already know if the Mazik are coming."

"Geesh! Mercy. How often did Allison not tell things to Aaron because it was *need-to-know,* and he could mess up the future if he knew too much."

Clark interrupted. "Can we deal with the facts on the ground? The Warriors are forming back into one large unit. There are still some isolated units in Arkansas, Iowa, and other places, but there are close to 80,000 of them in Connecticut. They are interlaced with at least 150,000 people."

"How do they keep that many people from running?" asked Monty.

"Every time a person tries to run, they catch him, eat him alive, and butcher children. We have vids of this."

"How is our side preparing?" asked Mercy. "We need to get Carlisle on the line and talk this out."

Barrett said, "I contacted Magnus. He said the president can spare twenty minutes."

"What?"

"I'm not kidding, Mercy. Magnus said that Carlisle told him that he was too busy with SECDEF organizing the ground forces, and we should send video images as close to real-time as possible and that he didn't need any input from us now."

Both sides of the conversation fell silent.

"We're all thinking the same thing, aren't we?"

"Julia," said Monty.

Clark was unsure. "I was there. Julia was like a statue in that room, using her mind to confuse Tartic. Why would she put up a wall between Carlisle and us?"

"The idea is pissing me off," said Barrett. "Are we supposed to have under-optimized forces to fulfill some historical need that only Julia understands? I can now relate to why Aaron was so frustrated with Allison's refusal to fess up details."

"I want to go down there," said Monty. "I will go see Julia and Betty, of course."

Barrett and Clark's immediate response was negative, but Mercy overruled them and said, "Yes. I think that is a worthwhile idea, but Barrett is also going."

Monty, Barrett, and a small crew of Slev set down a small shuttle on a baseball field near the McCall house. The risk of enemy laser fire had dropped to nil as the Warriors moved west to I-84 down to Pennsylvania.

He looked at the latest images and felt resigned to the possibility that most of the human "herd" being dragged west would be dead in weeks. On top of that, although occasionally lucky enough to kill a Warrior, most of the people fighting were shot or hacked to death as the Mazik rolled over the land. The military massed further west, waiting for the storm.

The young police chief sat on the hood of his car as the two officers exited the airlock and stepped onto the playing field.

"Your friend was here a few days ago. I'm the chief."

"We know who you are. Shall we go?" asked Barrett.

They sat down in the back of the squad car. It was the standard big Ford with a big engine.

"Thanks for the ride."

"No problem. It's only about a minute away."

They pulled up into the McCall driveway, and the door was open. Manuel stood there. He was big.

"Do you remember me?" asked Barrett, tongue in cheek.

Manuel ran to him and threw himself into Bonner's arms. "I missed you so damn much!"

"My teacher says don't use that word."

"She's right, too. Sorry, *chamaco*!"

Manuel wouldn't let go of Barrett. "You used to call me that when I would get into trouble back at the Crater."

"You're good at math and getting into trouble, right?"

He set his adopted son down on the walkway.

"I want to see mom."

"You will soon. I can't promise when, but right now mom is busy. She is in charge of the whole space navy."

"I know, Julia told me."

"Do you remember Monty?"

"Yes." Manuel looked up at the lieutenant. "Julia told us that you can turn into rock."

Monty's mouth opened, not sure how to respond. He stared at the kid, wide-eyed, then regained his wits and retorted, "It'll cost you five bucks for a demonstration."

Manuel said, "Dad. Can I borrow five dollars?" They laughed.

Barrett scruffled his son's dark hair. "We have to go see Julia."

"I know why you're here."

The two men shrugged and sat down on the chairs in the green room. "Not a surprise," said Monty.

Julia stood, facing east, her arms limp at her sides, dressed in blue. "It has to be how it is going to be."

"Why?" asked Barrett. "I think we can figure out a way to reduce casualties."

She breathed. Slowly and deliberately. "Commander Bonner, do you remember Von Donop?"

"Of course, he was the ancestor of the man who killed you."

"And yet, I am here. Not dead because Allison sent my brother back to the War, and he killed Von Donop. History corrected."

"No one argues that," Monty said.

"Then no one should resist what must happen soon in Ohio."

"Is that where it will happen? The big final battle?"

Julia was still and quiet. She was thinking. "It is the central battle, Monty, but there are still Mazik further west and south— small bands that Emma Creacy will eliminate."

"Who is Emma Creacy?" he asked.

"She is Mercy's blood."

Barrett shook his head. "That's impossible. Mercy's daughters died in 1776."

"I will tell you no more. For now, Monty, go see your wife. You are staying."

"What do you mean he is staying?" asked Bonner.

"Montegue must go fight with the troops. That is nearly all that needs to be said." Julia turned around and looked at Barrett. Her eyes shimmered like deep wells of black ink with twinkling diamonds gleaming from within. "Go back up to Mercy. Take Manuel with you."

"Why should I do that? You're confusing me."

Julia smiled slightly. "I have that effect on people."

Chapter 41

Carlisle sat in his bunker feeling every one of his sixty-eight years. Reports came in all through the winter. In the bitter cold, there was bitter death. Snow blanketed Ohio, reminiscent of the difficulty of Washington's ordeal during the Revolutionary War, when Continental soldiers walked with rags on their feet, at least until a mysterious, wealthy gentleman named Dr. Aaron Howe appeared and distributed warm clothes and boots.

America was now struggling through another defining moment in its history. Forty thousand Mazik Warriors dragging people as human shields were down to their last functioning mag weapons. The U.S. Military and volunteers suffered casualties nearing one million in Ohio alone.

"I wish I could be out there with them," said Colonel Magnus.

The president laughed, but it was drenched with sadness. "Who would I blame?"

Mike scoffed. "That's what I'm good for? You need a chump like me to be the scapegoat?"

"Nah. I'm just ruffling your feathers." Carlisle looked over at the Interior Secretary. The woman had gone beyond the call of duty in helping the country survive. John winked. "We can blame her."

"Always pin it on the woman, huh?"

"Don't sweat it. Up in heaven, my Angela is already figuring out how to torture me for every stupid comment I've made since she's left this world." He fought back a tear, then pulled himself together.

"The Mazik are down to a minimum number of drones, and they are mostly using mono-bladed swords and teeth," said the SECDEF. "However, they are still at a five to one kill ratio. We expect that to go lower, but in the end, we could lose another 200,000 of our people."

"What are our total losses, including civilians? Give me an estimate?" asked Carlisle.

The Interior Secretary looked grim."From the Mazik directly, close to ten million."

"And the other?"

"Civil crime between warlords and simple butchery? Another seven million, but it's hard to know for sure."

DHS asked reluctantly, "Starvation? Or lack of medicine?"

The INTSEC looked at her notes. "This hurts very badly. Above twenty million, and it will take time to ramp up production after we win this thing."

The president added up the numbers. Thirty-seven million Americans lost. "When we're all dead and buried, I hope that future generations will look back and always recognize what our generation sacrificed to save this country and the world. We need to document every last fact and story.

"How are our comms out to Ohio?" Carlisle asked.

"Sir, we've got ham radio operators and some military left with solar-powered batteries and some generators. The battle is centered around Tippecanoe—pretty much the middle of nowhere." Magnus handed Carlisle some handwritten sheets transcribed by formerly retired military radio operators. "Most of this is Morse code translations. Audio is tough. Unfortunately, eighty percent of this folder consists of lists of casualties."

"Tell me some positive news."

"Our drones and some helicopters are flying in Arkansas, Missouri, and Tennessee," said the Joint Chief. "Additional marines joined up with Creacy. She's got a hundred of our guys hunting down the remaining Warriors, and we're starting to find aliens that fell on their own swords."

*

Monty didn't feel the chilling effect of snow and ice blowing in from the north. The cold meant nothing. The only thing that mattered was the end of mag pellets fired at his position. Once a group of enemies spent their mag rounds, opportunities arose.

"I'm the aggressor now, baby," he said to no one in particular, although a nearby army captain gave him a funny look.

Dead ahead stood a dozen Warriors among evergreens. They had only three mono blades.

"Captain. Tell your snipers to hold their fire. I'm going to have a conversation with those Mazik."

"Sir?"

"Just watch the show."

The captain whistled and told his forty riflemen to only fire if the commander ordered it. Monty added, "Or if I'm dead. Then you can fire all you want."

Montgomery stood up. He was considerably smaller than the seven-foot-plus Warriors, but size didn't matter now. He held a mono blade in each hand and glared at the enemy Mazik. The snowfall decayed to mere flurries, and just three inches had accumulated on the ground. The commander turned back to the anxious captain. "This is for Dexter O'Brian."

"Sir. You say that every day."

Monty began his charge at the enemy as the Mazik seemed to freeze in place and try to fathom the idiot human committing suicide. They decided to wait and felt roundly amused—until the human was within five yards. Then all hell broke loose.

In the language of the Mazik, Monty bellowed, "My female First Commander will torture your souls for all eternity!" He instantly transformed into concrete and, at a speed that blurred the vision of the enemy soldiers, began disemboweling the giant quadrupeds. The dozen lay dead and dying on the snow within twenty seconds.

"I think that's a new record." Montegue dashed back to the front line.

"Twenty-two seconds, sir, your new personal best."

A shot rang out. Everyone turned to see what happened, as one of the Warriors stood momentarily but then crashed to the ground.

"Sorry, sir," said a young private with a squeaky voice. "That one got back up, so I don't think that is your new personal record."

"Can't win 'em all, private. How 'bout you and a few friends go out there and do the thing with those bodies."

Tartic watched his army suffer from attrition. The central point, equidistant south of Akron, west of Pittsburgh, and east of Columbus became dotted with Creacy Mounds. The First Warrior Commander knew now that the only chance for victory would be the unlikely appearance of a massive Mazik fleet.

His mind became disoriented on a daily basis. The humans persisted, despite losses, and the image of the female, Mercy Bonner, clouded his thoughts. The First Commander just wanted it to end. Curse Kul! If only Tartic would have an opportunity to shred Kul before it was all over. He gazed around his command center. Video screen, data, personnel tracking—it was all worthless. The humans were the bane of his existence, and they would someday gut the emperor and dominate the stars.

"We are a pathetic sentient species," Tartic mumbled in a guttural language.

An officer entered the dismal, opaque room. "First Warrior Commander, I was instructed to bring news of the platoons spread out through the south."

"By whom?"

"By the Second."

"Is that cowering plark lacking the courage to come himself?"

"He is dead. There is a running shadow of a human that is hard as an alloy. Alone, that inferior sentient is eviscerating hundreds. The enemy separated your Second into two parts."

Tartic leaped from his sleep chair and screamed upwards. "Why do you call these humans inferior?" His aggression ignited, and the First Commander ached to rip the moronic officer into clumps of flesh. "We are the inferior beings! Our losses in the south are pointless. Now, get out!"

*

Julia walked out of the room painted green for the first time in nearly a year. Rob lifted his head from the dining room table and shoved his laptop aside.

"Everything is fine," she said.

He walked over to her, not sure what to do. Julia's eyes and everything about her seemed to have reverted to normal. She wrapped her arms around him. "I missed you."

"Me too." McCall kissed her briefly and then looked at her face. "Are you okay? Are we okay?"

"Yes, but I'm hungry, and I want to hold our children."

"Should I go get them from school?"

She smiled. "It would be responsible of me to say no, and let them finish their school day, but I don't care. Please go get them?"

"Back in fifteen."

He grabbed the car keys and scrambled toward the door but then turned. Before he uttered a word, Julia said, "Yes. The Mazik will be gone soon." .

*

Tartic commanded his soldiers to release the thousands of humans that didn't die from war, famine, or cold. Winter broke, and the heat would soon return, and the First Warrior Commander exited his command center to see a few hundred Mazik looking to him expectantly. They were the survivors, and Tartic surveyed them and the battlefield beyond.

"It is all futile," he stammered to no one.

In the distance, ten thousand humans approached. They showed no fear or apprehension. It was as if they were coming to end a task.

Monty walked in front of a mass of marines, army, and tired civilians. An alien building rested on the ground. Attached to it was an elevated platform that stood empty except for a scarred and fierce-looking Warrior—no doubt the First Warrior Commander, still alive but looking defeated. In his hand was a large monomolecular blade.

To Montgomery, it seemed like the Mazik was deciding something, but then the Warrior raised his sword and swung it many times toward the sky. Tartic then did something that no other Warrior had ever done. He threw his blade to the ground.

In the language of the aliens, the First Warrior Commander barked an order to the remaining soldiers, and they followed his lead. Surrender was complete.

Tartic moved off the dais and began walking toward Monty. They met on the worn and wet ground.

"You may tell Mercy Bonner that she has won."

"I will," said Montgomery in the language of the Mazik.

"I ask for two things; otherwise, our surrender is unconditional. I am Tartic. I disavow my loyalty to Mazik Bah-Gahn. First, I want a shuttle here so that I may take my remaining soldiers with me. And, second, I want you to ask the Bonner female not to torture our souls for all eternity."

A breeze blew across the churned-up muddy field. The stench of death—human and Mazik—hung in the air. The greatest battle for freedom in history was marked by its by-product, corpses of friends and enemies.

Monty stared up at the defeated Warrior. "What is the purpose of the shuttle?"

*

The following day, the president left his bunker. In the Rocky Mountains, the landscape looked like it could have been any normal day.

"I think I would like to go ride a horse," said Magnus.

"Would that help you to feel normal again, Mike?"

"Honestly, it might. I've always been talented at moving on after a nasty conflict. This is going to be a bit tougher, but being on horseback would be nice. That, and to see Recon and whoever is left from my CAG soldiers."

Carlisle smirked. "Nothing like getting back to normal."

"What's normal, John?"

"Don't they always say 'welcome to the new normal?'"

"We won. That's what matters." Magnus seemed resolute. "Our planet is functional, and we've got six battlecruisers up there. America survived."

"Do you know what it will take to rebuild this country?"

The colonel grimaced. "That's your problem. You're the politician. My expertise is killing bad guys."

*

Mercy and Barrett traveled down to the field near Tippecanoe, Ohio. Several hundred Warriors sat in the mud awaiting their orders to board the large Mazik shuttle.

Tartic gazed across the field and saw the female step onto the surface. She was with a large human who could only be Barrett Bonner.

She engaged Monty in a conversation for some time and then began walking to where the First Warrior Commander stood apart from his remaining soldiers. Mercy stopped ten feet away and spoke in Mazik. "You can stay here on an island until you and your troops live out your days. You will be prisoners, but you will run your own lives."

"That is not our destiny," the large Mazik replied.

"Then you should leave now."

It didn't take much time for the last group of aliens to board the shuttle. Barrett, Mercy, and Monty watch as the airlock hatch closed. Grav plates engaged, and the craft, the size of a small building, lifted. On the USS Dexter O'Brian, Mordy Schein tracked the shuttle. Several Slev joined him on the bridge as the comm officer displayed a high-resolution image.

The ship breached the Earth's upper atmosphere, entered the vacuum of space, and accelerated. The course was locked. Schein ordered his bridge crew to maintain tracking of the shuttle continuously, then retired to his stateroom to write an email to a girl in Atlanta.

Three days later, having not wavered from its course, the small ship carrying Tartic and his Mazik Warriors reached their terminal velocity. Gravity increased. The path was set as the defeated met their fate and plunged into the Sun.

Chapter 42

Julia sat at the McCall dining room table, every leaf added, and Gozenburgers aplenty. She marveled at the amount of food that Manuel could consume. The kid ate like his dad.

America began to reconstruct itself almost immediately. Power was no longer intermittent in most places; although the cities along the east coast were still battle zones between gangs and the army—those places would eventually return to normal.

Rob looked around his table. Recon soldiers—valiant men, along with Mercy and Molly—fighters in the Revolutionary War and the Mazik War. They'd seen so much. Certainly too much.

At the end of the table, Lewis was telling funny stories to the kids while Dog repeatedly tapped his paw on Monty's chair, hoping to get a burger or even some fries.

"Two weddings in one year!" said Rogers. He elbowed Mordy. "Want a bite of my cheeseburger?"

"Not gonna happen, Thomas," said Chaya Schein leaning in and giving her husband's best friend a stern look.

"You guys are so strict about kosher! What about some Coke?"

At the end of the table, Molly leaned up against John Allen. She was just starting to show. Mercy was the first to know, and her adopted daughter's response was the same as usual about having ten children and teaching every one of them to become badass alien killers.

Julia stood up, and as if on cue, everyone went silent. She smiled. "We've got a very special dessert, but I've got another surprise if you can be patient for a minute."

She left everyone perplexed, although as a bestselling cookbook author, the woman could probably whip up a cake to impress the most demanding critic.

Rob watched his wife ease her chair back under the table and walk gracefully down the hallway to her green room. It was the kind of thing that stoked anxiety in him. She grasped the brass knob, entered, and shut the door behind her. Their children noticed but managed to control their nervousness.

She stood in the middle of the room. She was the container now. She connected to a point in space hundreds of lightyears away. Allison and Aaron were reaching out to her, not the first time, but now it was different. Cosmic coincidences were not random at all.

Julia exited her room. Everyone looked at her deep, black, sparkling eyes. Her knowing and devious smile lit up the hallway. She milked the tension for all it was worth and then asked, "Is everyone ready for a really big surprise?"

*

Carlisle beamed as he stood on a stage erected adjacent to the foundation of the new Whitehouse. He'd signed an executive order to build it dead center between Lexington and Georgetown, Kentucky. Washington, D.C. remained a scorched expanse where John lost Angela, his wife, and so many others when the Mazik hurled an asteroid onto the capital. Miserable memories, but today was different.

The media packed the seats, as well as surviving members of congress. With him on the stage stood Captain Mercy Bonner, Commander of the United States Spaceforce, along with the Chairman of the Joint Chiefs, SECDEF, and several others.

President Carlisle requested that the crowd sit. He thought about the resilience of the American people and began a short speech without notes.

"Today, we honor the sacrifice of so many brave people. Countless souls were lost to save this republic. I'm not going to burden you with political propaganda because I sincerely hope that our country is beyond shallow power grabs and intrigue after what we've endured.

"We are primarily here today to honor the living, specifically two young people who helped change the outcome of this war. I'm speaking of Mr. Josh Rice and Miss Emma Creacy." The applause echoed through horse farms and fields as the audience stood and clapped for three minutes.

Finally, Carlisle managed to settle the crowd. "I'm not going to review every valiant action of these two young adults that crushed the spirit of our enemy; you all know how they bravely stood with Emma's father, Eric Creacy." The crowd started clapping again. "You also know that despite losing his devoted and amazing parents, Harry and Honey Rice, Josh rose to the challenge and never quit. He never quit, ever!"

John Carlisle smiled at Josh as a proud father would while he waved the assembled press, military personnel, and civilians quiet.

"You know, award ceremonies tend to be self-aggrandizing horse manure for politicians. This is not one of those.

"Josh and Emma, please come up here."

Emma, dressed in blue, with her blond hair gently moving with a mild Kentucky breeze, stood. She grabbed Josh's hand, and together, they stepped up and faced the president.

"In America, we award military heroes specific medals to recognize sacrifice in the face of personal risk. These awards are only for members of the U.S. Armed Forces. So, I'm stuck in a quandary for which there is no solution other than to do the following:

"Joshua Rice, as Commander-in-Chief, I hereby appoint you as Captain Joshua Rice, United States Marine Corps. Emma, I hereby appoint you as Captain Emma Creacy, United States Marine Corps." The crowd began to clap even louder, but Carlisle shushed them.

"In addition, now that you two are Marines—Captain Emma Creacy, for your bravery under fire and self-sacrifice, I hereby award you the Medal of Honor." He pinned the medal and looked at Josh. "Captain Joshua Rice, for your bravery under fire and self-sacrifice, I hereby award you the Medal of Honor."

The audience cheered again for a long time, and then the

military band played a series of patriotic songs.

Almost immediately, the dignitaries on stage stood and formed a line to greet the two teenagers.

Josh and Emma made their way across the line of government officials, receiving smiles and thanks. The Secretary of the Interior couldn't stop herself and gave Emma a tremendous hug. Josh shook hands with Mercy. She bestowed words of gratitude, and he knew that Captain Bonner, from the stories that leaked, was the genuine kick-ass of space battles.

Emma squared herself to face Captain Bonner. Grasping the girl's hand, Mercy suddenly felt a jolt of recognition or some kind of subtle tremor. It temporarily absorbed her.

"Captain Bonner?" asked Emma.

Mercy smiled and released her hand. She blurted out, "We aren't so different, you and I," not knowing what possessed her to say that.

Later, while drinking coffee and making small talk among the various officials, Mercy pulled Barrett close. "Remember today very well," she whispered. "There is something special about that Creacy girl."

Epilogue

Ten Months Later

Mercy, Barrett, Aaron, Allison, Monty, and Julia sat in the Howes' den. Wood in the fireplace sounded with occasional crackling pops, and the only light in the room came from the dancing flames. It was late, but no one watched the clock; they were happy to be together and secure. The Bonners were only too pleased to be away from the ship, sharing a meal and a drink with people who were much more than superficial acquaintances.

"All's well that ends well," offered Barrett. "The country is recovering. The chain stores are restocking, the food supply is adequate, and fuel prices are fair. Plus, the cities are doing better." He took a swig of an icy beer. "The beer is also better than the stuff we drank in colonial times."

"I guess we know things are good when Lewis isn't inebriated and sleeping in an alleyway with Dog," said Mercy.

They chuckled.

"His nanites probably fixed that," Aaron pointed out.

Monty turned his fingertips to stone, clicked off a bottlecap, and asked, "What about the Panruk?"

They all turned toward Julia, aware of her abilities. She replied, "They are growing their own food, and Mazik Bah-Gahn is not bothering them."

"Then I guess everything is just fine." Monty gulped from his long-necked bottle.

"Is it?" asked Mercy. "Is everything fine?"

Allison said quietly, "The Mar El are contained."

"We sealed all of their jump points. In the beginning, they tried to stop us but eventually gave up. Their culture will consume itself. It will happen rapidly," Aaron added reassuringly.

"Why did they give up interfering with you?" scowled Monty, remembering Tzurek's torture chamber.

Allison answered while staring at the fire. "We killed every Mar El that attempted to stop us."

The den was quiet and thoughtful for a while. Then Mercy said, "I appreciate all your well-founded optimism, but my nanites have been broadcasting messages of impending doom and gloom going back some two hundred and fifty years."

Barrett asked, "Are they calm now?"

"Mostly," she replied.

Aaron closed his eyes. He felt the touch of his sister's hand and a ripple of something flowing between the stars. He smiled contentedly. "Shall we live in the here and now? I believe we are safe."

As her eyes glinted in the darkness, Julia let go of Aaron. She seemed to have drifted to some far-away place, then refocused and took a moment to gaze at each of her companions.

"I'm not so sure about that."

Cast of Principle Characters

Dr. Aaron Howe – Scientist. CEO of Howe It Works. Head of Recon.

Allison / Els Talitha — Artificial Intelligence Device originally a girl kidnapped 3,000 years ago

Capt. John Clark — b. 1748 Captain in the Continental Army. Member of Recon. Married to Louise. Two children, Benjamin and Lillian

Capt. Mordechai "Mordy" Schein — b. 1752 Officer in the Continental Army. Member of Recon. Married to Chaya Richman

Commander Montegue "Monty" Montgomery — b. 1751 Officer in the Continental Army. Member of Recon. Officer in the United States Spaceforce. Married to Betty. No children

Commander Thomas Rogers — b. 1754 Officer in the Continental Army. Member of Recon. Officer in the United States Spaceforce. Married to Jennifer. Captain of the battlecruiser Beta

Lieutenant John Allen — b. 1755 Officer in the Continental Army. Member of Recon. Officer in the United States Spaceforce. Married to Molly Stark

Capt. Barrett Bonner — former drill sergeant. Officer in Recon. Officer in the United States Spaceforce. Married to Captain Mercy Bonner.

Capt. Mercy (Smythe) Bonner — b. 1747 Officer in Recon. Officer in the United States Spaceforce. Overall Commander of the U.S.S. Fleet. Stepmother of Molly Stark and Manuel Bonner.

Lieutenant Molly (Stark) Allen — b. 1761 Officer in United States Spaceforce. Married to Lt. John Allen. Adopted daughter of Captain Mercy (Smythe) Bonner

President John Carlisle — President of the United States

Col. Michael Magnus — Chief of Staff. Former Commander of Combat Applications Group

Capt. Kap Jahrnuk — alien Slev. Captain of the Ro-Pahm

Capt. Mok Partul — alien Slev. Captain of the Alpha

Lt. Cmdr Cassie Munch — Executive Officer of the Alpha

Lt. (jg) Lucky Williams — Navigation Officer of the Alpha

Capt. Emma Creacy — U.S. Marine Corp and Medal of Honor Winner

Capt. Joshua Rice — U.S. Marine Corp and Medal of Honor Winner

First Warrior Commander Tartik — Mazik Warrior Commander

First Ship Commander Kul — Mazik Fleet Commander

Mazik Bah-Gahn — Emperor of Mazik and despotic ruler over the Council of Sentient aliens

Pel Jahrnuk — Primary concubine to Mazik Bah-Gahn. Sister of Kap Jahrnuk

Tzurek — Supervisor of Mar El Planet 432

Eric Creacy — civilian combatant. Father of Emma Creacy

Harold Rice (deceased) — Killed in battle for West Tennessee. Father of Joshua Rice

Honey Rice (deceased) — Killed in the battle for West Tennessee. Mother of Joshua Rice

Julia (Howe) McCall — Sister of Dr. Aaron Howe

Edgar / Shelet Pir Sahm Mim — alien Panruk anthropologist and close friend of Dr. Aaron Howe

Shaab Mar Gen — Arbitor   (Chief Official) of the Panruk alien system Olamit

Shaft Lek—Panruk engineer

Lt. Petro — Officer of Combat Applications Group

"In any moment of decision, the best thing you can do is the right thing, the next best thing is the wrong thing, and the worst thing you can do is nothing." — Teddy Roosevelt

---

www.booksbyblunt.com